THE LADY FROM BURMA

Also by Allison Montclair

The Right Sort of Man
A Royal Affair
A Rogue's Company
The Unkept Woman

THE LADY FROM BURMA

ALLISON MONTCLAIR

MINOTAUR BOOKS
NEW YORK

First published in the United States by Minotaur Books, an imprint of St. Martin's Publishing Group

www.minotaurbooks.com

Library of Congress Cataloging-in-Publication Data

Names: Montclair, Allison, author.
Title: The lady from Burma / Allison Montclair.
Description: First edition. | New York : Minotaur Books, 2023. |
Series: Sparks & Bainbridge mystery ; 5
Identifiers: LCCN 2023009398 | ISBN 9781250854193 (hardcover) |
ISBN 9781250854209 (ebook)
Subjects: LCSH: London (England)—History—20th century—Fiction. |
LCGFT: Detective and mystery fiction. | Historical fiction. | Novels.
Classification: LCC PS3613.O54757 L34 2023 |
DDC 813/.6—dc23/eng/20230303
LC record available at https://lccn.loc.gov/2023009398

First Edition: 2023

10 9 8 7 6 5 4 3 2 1

TO MY AUNT HILDY, WHOSE WICKEDNESS HAS PERSISTED, AND THEREFORE REMAINS ADMIRABLE

When I am dead, my dearest,
        Sing no sad songs for me;
Plant thou no roses at my head,
        Nor shady cypress tree:
Be the green grass above me
        With showers and dewdrops wet;
And if thou wilt, remember,
        And if thou wilt, forget.

FROM "SONG," BY CHRISTINA ROSSETTI

THE LADY FROM BURMA

PROLOGUE

He sat on the edge of the narrow bed, reaching for the black wool socks he had stuffed into his shoes. She watched him, still stretched out languorously on her left side.

"You surprised me," she said.

"Did I?" he replied with a slight smile.

"Several times, in fact."

"Which was the first?" he asked, pulling his socks on.

"That you chose me out of all of the girls in the pub," she said. "There were prettier ones there."

"Ah, but they were all good girls, weren't they?"

"I'm sure there were one or two who might have given even an older gent like you the time of day," she said.

"I wasn't talking about that," he said, patting her sheet-covered hip in a manner that she was starting to see as proprietary. "There are plenty of good girls who will hop into someone's bed for the fun of it, and thank God for them. But I've had my eye on you for some time now."

"Have you?" she asked suspiciously. "Why?"

He looked around the small, single room, with its single bed, tiny bureau, and freestanding wardrobe.

"You'd like to do better than this," he said.

It wasn't a question.

"It would be hard to do worse," she replied.

"How would you like to make some real money? Something that will give you what you want from the world, but only if you're bold enough to seize it."

"Doing this?" she said with a laugh. "I haven't sunk that low yet."

"Not doing this," he said. "But doing something a good girl wouldn't do."

"I'm listening."

"I have a particular scheme in mind," he said. "I think you could make it work."

"Legal?"

"My schemes are frequently illegal, generally immoral, and occasionally downright wicked," he said. "But they're lucrative."

"I don't want anyone to get hurt," she said.

"No one will get hurt—physically," he said. "Financially, of course. That's the whole point. But there is a time limit on when this can happen."

"What would I have to do?" she asked.

"Whatever I tell you to," he said. "I won't go into details yet, but I think you're the right girl for the job."

He put on his suit jacket, then pulled a wedding ring out of one pocket and slipped it onto his finger.

"So this was a test," she said, looking at it without surprise. "You wanted to see how far I'd go."

"Oh, you'll go far, my girl," he said, grinning at her wolfishly. "Are you interested?"

"All right," she said. "What happens next?"

He reached inside his pocket and pulled out a light green advert.

"How would you feel about getting married?" he asked, handing it to her.

She glanced at the top, where large letters spelled out THE RIGHT SORT MARRIAGE BUREAU.

"Sure," she said. "Why not?"

CHAPTER 1

Have you kissed him yet?"

"That's none of your business."

The questioner was a short, intense brunette in her late twenties named Iris Sparks, co-proprietor of The Right Sort Marriage Bureau. The respondent, if the refusal to provide any actual information in her response could be characterised as a response, was Mrs. Gwendolyn Bainbridge, the other co-proprietor, a tall, elegant blonde. The two of them were returning to their Mayfair office from lunch on a cold, rainy day in November, and Iris's curiosity was eating at her.

"It is very much my business," she said. "My two best friends have started dating each other, in part because of my efforts to bring them together . . ."

"You can't have two best friends," Gwen pointed out.

"Fine. My best female friend is now dating my best male friend—"

"Which of us do you like more?"

"That's not a fair question."

"Oh, and prying into my love life is."

"Aha! You said 'love'!"

"Solely as a hypothetical description."

Each of them to the casual observer, particularly to the casual male observer, was striking, but the pair of them with their sharp difference in height were doubly so. Adding to the overall picture was their animation in conversation while simultaneously taking in the world around them, Gwen almost compulsively observing details of the expressions of the people they passed by, a habit left over from her time in the sanatorium; Iris as always on the lookout for potential attackers, a habit left over from her time in military intelligence during the war. If the casual male observer were to meet those gazes, he would quickly look away from the intensity of the combined scrutiny and move on, though not without casting one regretful backward glance of admiration.

"Still, it's hypothetically more than you were willing to call it last month," continued Iris. "So, have you kissed him yet? Or, allowing for him to have taken the initiative, has he kissed you?"

"What has he told you?"

"Sally won't say a word. He is being a perfect gentleman about it."

"Then why should I be any different?"

"Because we are women," said Iris. "And women are required to discuss matters of the heart with their closest female friends."

"Who made that rule?"

"We did. The Secret Society of Women Who Are Still Dating. You must have missed that meeting."

"Was it a close vote?"

"Not at all. So spill it, sister, or I shall be forced to write you up for a violation."

They turned off Oxford Street, heading towards the office building that contained The Right Sort in two rooms on the top storey. The lot just before it contained the steel framework of another office building being constructed on what had been a pile of rubble left when a doodlebug buzzed its way through a bevy of barrage balloons to land smack in the middle of Mayfair.

When they had first opened their office, the rubble next door was still there, as it was in the lots on the other side and to the rear of their building. One crew began clearing it in mid-May, then another arrived in September to excavate a large rectangular hole. When they were done, the steel men came on the scene. They were a cheery bunch, happy to be putting up an ordinary office framework rather than building battleships or assembling barracks and hangars across the country. Now they were gone, and several enormous stacks of bricks on pallets had been brought in on lorries and forklifted onto the muddy grounds surrounding the building-to-be, awaiting the hods and trowels.

The two women stopped to examine the site, which was notable for its lack of activity.

"There is a distinct absence of bricklaying happening right now," observed Gwen. "Do they take their tea earlier than the rest of us?"

"There was a lightning strike by the bricklayers this morning," said Iris. "Someone got fired without cause, or hired without joining the union, I'm not sure which, but the shop steward sent everyone home until it's resolved. So it will be quieter on the street today for a change."

"I'm going to miss the steelworkers," said Gwen. "They had a party over at the Five Hats to celebrate the end of the job. They invited me to join them, would you believe it?"

"Oh, you should have come," said Iris. "It was great fun."

"You went?"

"I did."

"Why?"

"They asked me. They had all been paid, and who am I to turn down a free drink from some well-muscled gents?"

"Does Archie know?"

"He does not."

"Is that a good thing?" asked Gwen, sounding worried. "When

one is dating a gangster, straying from the fold could be troublesome."

"We're not exactly—" Iris started, then she hesitated.

"What?" prompted Gwen.

"Exclusive."

"You're not?"

"No."

"Does Archie know that?"

"Well, he— Wait, we were talking about your love life. How did we end up talking about mine?"

"Because you actually have one."

"But you and Sally are dating."

"Sally and I have gone out a few times since you cleverly abandoned us after that play. But I cannot commit to anyone right now, as you very well know. I cannot even commit to the word 'dating.'"

"Does Sally know that?"

"Sally knows that I can't get seriously involved until my custody situation is resolved, and that won't be resolved until my petition before the Court of Lunacy is granted."

They opened the door to their building and began their second ascent of the day.

"What about frivolous involvement?" persisted Iris.

"Has it occurred to you that even if I wished to discuss kissing Sally—"

"So you did kiss him!"

"Whether I did or not," continued Gwen, ignoring her, "that you, being someone who has kissed Sally in the past, would not be the person with whom I would choose to discuss it."

"That was in a play!" protested Iris. "That doesn't count as a real kiss."

"A play he wrote," said Gwen.

"Well, yes, but—"

"Wrote with you in mind as the leading lady."

"That is also true, but—"

"And himself as the leading man."

"Look, I see where you're going with this, but—"

"All for the express purpose of kissing you."

"Yes, Sally had a crush on me when we were at Cambridge," said Iris in exasperation. "Which I left unrequited, apart from theatrical sublimation. Possibly a mistake on my part—"

"My turn for the 'aha!'"

"There was no 'aha!' for us," said Iris. "He evolved from a suitor to a friend, and we are both the better for it."

"How was the kiss?" asked Gwen. "In the play?"

"Awkwardly staged, as you might well imagine," said Iris, grinning at the memory. "When the lovers are separated not only by dramatic circumstances but by nearly two feet in height, there is no natural angle where it could work comfortably. He had to write a stepladder into the plot, and we had to struggle to keep from laughing when the moment came up. That's another reason why you have the advantage here, you Amazon. You don't need any props with him. There, I've shared my story of kissing Sally. Your turn now."

"I refuse."

"Don't make me resort to stronger measures," said Iris with an evil glint in her eyes.

"Iris, I appreciate your trying to distract me when I have the hearing coming up so soon," said Gwen. "But it isn't necessary. Trust me. I'm fine."

She wasn't fine. She had tried to ward off panicky thoughts about the hearing while struggling through the day-to-day existence of keeping their new business from going under, while at the same time working with Dr. Milford, her psychiatrist, to learn how to manage the terrors and the bouts of depression that had sent her first to hospital, where they treated the self-inflicted wounds on her body, then to the sanatorium, where they treated the wounds the world had inflicted on her mind.

But she had been out for two years, now. She had done the work, she had progressed sufficiently for Dr. Milford to approve the appointment with Mr. Stronach, her lawyer. It was nearing the end of the Vacation Court term when she met with him, but that was over a month ago, and the Court of Lunacy was now open for business along with the rest of the courts for the Michaelmas term. Every day, her petition date drew nearer, and the tension of the wait was agonising.

The courts had opened in mid-October with the full ceremony for the first time since before the war. Gwen, at Iris's insistence, had allowed herself to be dragged out to see the procession after all the judges attended Red Mass at Westminster Cathedral and the Lord High Chancellor's breakfast at the Royal Gallery. The two women established themselves with a good viewpoint on the Strand as the group of elderly men in wigs strode by with an air of deep importance, tempered by the relief that they could do this again without fear of bombs and bullets.

They were led by the Tipstaff, a ceremonial bailiff carrying an enormous ebony staff bound with silver bands and topped with a silver crown. Two more bailiffs followed, one with the Mace of State, the other with the Purse of State, a giant, square embroidered affair with gold tassels tipped in red dangling from it.

"What's in the Purse of State?" wondered Gwen. "Are there a Lipstick and Compact of State inside?"

"Mad money for the cab ride home," suggested Iris. "Here comes Jowitt. Hooray for the Lord High Chancellor! Even a Labour Party man can wear the fancy robes, and my, he wears them well."

Baron William Jowitt, Lord High Chancellor, PC, KC, a stern man in his sixties, walked past in full regalia, maintaining his impeccable dignity under an extravagant gown of black damask laced with gold and a long, white wig that looked like it weighed more than the mace and staff that preceded it. The very important legal legs carrying this assemblage were clad in black silk stockings and terminated in a pair of silver-buckled, patent leather court shoes.

"He could stand for some rouge and powder with that outfit," said Gwen. "It completely washes him out."

"I bet he got his stockings without using any coupons," commented Iris.

"I've got the Lord Chancellor's song from *Iolanthe* stuck in my head now," said Gwen. "'When you're lying awake with a dismal headache . . .'"

"'And repose is taboo'd by anxiety,'" Iris sang. "I wonder if he's required to learn the whole thing as part of his duties. That would take an impressive legal mind."

Jowitt was accompanied by other gaudily dressed Lords Justice, followed by the Lord Chief Justice leading the judges of Chancery, the King's Bench, and the various divisions. These wore robes of scarlet and ermine with silk breeches and stockings. And full-bodied wigs, to a man.

"To think that a man who wears a wig that length and a costume two centuries out of date in public gets to be the one to decide whether I'm sane or not," said Gwen.

"I think you're sane," said Iris.

"You, being crazy, are not in a position to judge," said Gwen.

"There is some truth to that," admitted Iris. "We're all mad here."

They watched as the collected judiciary marched in coordinated solemnity to the Royal Courts of Justice.

The courts had opened, thought Gwen as they neared the fourth floor. The thing that had to happen before anything else could happen had happened, and now she was walking barefoot over the hot coals of her anxieties, knowing the courts had to declare her sane again at last, because it would be a disaster if they didn't, for her and for Ronnie, her son.

But what if they denied her petition? That was the nagging, irrational thought that made her look longingly at her dwindling supply of Veronal each night despite her determination to wean herself from it completely by the date she had to appear before the Master in Lunacy.

"I'm going to have to be away several times over the next week or so," she said as she unlocked the door to their office. "I need to meet with my barrister and my guardian."

"How long will the court appearance take?" asked Iris.

"It depends on the Master," said Gwen. "If he accepts the petition on papers, then only a day. But if he wants to conduct a hearing, who knows? I'll have to testify."

"Would you like me to come?" asked Iris. "I'd be happy to cheer you on from the gallery."

"No, we should keep things running as smoothly as we can here," said Gwen.

"I may have to do some testifying myself," said Iris. "The criminal terms have also begun. They want me for the La Salle murder trial. I'm surprised they didn't ask you for that one, given everything you did."

"Iris, I'm still a lunatic in the eyes of the law," said Gwen softly. "I can't be sworn in as a competent witness."

"Then it's a good thing we're a team," said Iris.

"Yes, it is," said Gwen. "Hang on—what's that commotion coming from Saundra's office?"

A man had his voice raised. They could hear Mrs. Billington, their secretary/receptionist, responding in tones meant to placate him but sounding increasingly desperate, and the voice of another woman interceding ineffectively.

"Right, we'll go in hard and fast," said Iris. "I'll take him down at the knees, and you—"

"Let's find out what the situation is before we resort to full-on combat," suggested Gwen.

"You're no fun," muttered Iris.

They came to Saundra's office. The door was open, revealing

a man wearing an ill-fitting grey tweed jacket missing a button at the left cuff, the other barely holding on as he pounded his fist on their beleaguered employee's desk.

"It says nine to five," he was shouting, shoving one of their adverts in her face. "It says walk-in appointments available, yet we have walked in, not just walked in, but climbed four bloody flights of steps, which were not mentioned in the advert and I can see why, but here we are and the ladies aren't around."

"Dad, please," said a young woman, tugging on his sleeve. "This is embarrassing. We can come back, I promise."

"How am I supposed to get this one out of my hair and out of my house when the ladies aren't here for the walk-ins?" he continued. "It's unprofessional is what it is."

"The ladies are back," announced Mrs. Bainbridge from the doorway. "Forgive us if we've made you wait, but even professionals have to eat lunch if they are going to work effectively."

"I get quite cranky if I miss my midday meal," added Sparks. "And you don't want me matching people when I'm cranky. How do you do? I am Miss Sparks, and this is my partner, Mrs. Bainbridge. How may we be of service to you today?"

He turned to them. His face was red from shouting, and his eyes bloodshot. He looked later forties or early fifties, thought Gwen, but could have been slightly younger. The drinking had taken its toll, no doubt.

The daughter looked to be in her early twenties, a blonde in clothes that had seen their share of use and repair. Thin, understandably nervous. Gwen wondered what she looked like when she wasn't in distress. She wondered what she looked like when she smiled.

She wondered when that last happened.

"It's five pounds, right?" asked the father, his tone still belligerent. "Five pounds, and you'll get rid of her?"

"You can't say things like that in front of people," said the woman, practically in tears.

"We don't get rid of people," said Mrs. Bainbridge. "We attempt to find them compatible, loving partners for life, for which efforts we charge an initial fee of five pounds."

"Initial fee, and then you get the big payoff when they tie the knot," he said.

"There is a final payment of twenty pounds per client if we are successful," said Mrs. Bainbridge. "But only then."

"How long does it take?" demanded the man.

"That depends on the individual," said Sparks. "We can guarantee neither results nor timing."

"Say I make it ten pounds," he said. "Would you move her to the front of the queue?"

"There is no queue," said Mrs. Bainbridge, suppressing her irritation. "We would get to work right away with any new person, but the matching process is happening more or less simultaneously with all of our clientele. It's a continuing process."

"Then you'd better get it started," he said. "Where do we go?"

"We conduct the interview in our office next door," said Mrs. Bainbridge.

"Right," he said, stepping towards them.

"And you stay here," said Sparks, holding her hand up.

"She's my daughter," he said, bristling again.

"You aren't the one signing the contract," said Sparks. "She is of age, so she will enter into this agreement voluntarily, or not at all. That will be for her to decide, not you."

The daughter, from her safe vantage behind him, shot them a look of gratitude.

The father stared back and forth at the two partners with fury and disbelief, but they returned his look with steadiness and calm. Forced steadiness and calm, but it sufficed. After a few seconds, he disengaged, taking a step back under the combined glares of the two women.

"Please come with us, Miss—ah, we have yet to learn your name, haven't we?" said Mrs. Bainbridge, beckoning to the woman.

"It's Collette," she said, stepping gingerly past her father. "Miss Collette Forsberg."

"Then please come with us, Miss Forsberg."

"It had better be Mrs. Something Else when you come back!" her father called after her.

"Sit, you!" commanded Sparks, pointing at the sofa. "Read a magazine. Do not bother Mrs. Billington. We will be back in due course."

She followed Mrs. Bainbridge and Miss Forsberg into the office next door. Miss Forsberg collapsed onto one of the guest chairs while the two partners took their accustomed seats behind their desks.

"I am so sorry for his behaviour," said Miss Forsberg. "You have no idea what it's like living with him."

"I think we've just had a taste," said Mrs. Bainbridge. "It must be difficult."

"I'm at my wit's end," said Miss Forsberg. "Those little file boxes there? Are those where you keep all the men?"

"Our secret trove of bachelors," said Sparks with a laugh, patting the small green box on her desk marked "M." "Every index card a potential groom."

"I've been imagining you opening it, and out one will pop like a genie from the lamp, top hat, tails, carnation, and all," said Miss Forsberg. "Well, that's not how a genie would dress, I suppose."

"It would depend upon your wish," said Mrs. Bainbridge.

"I'll tell you what," said Miss Forsberg. "Take those cards, toss them in the air, and I'll marry the first one that lands. I am that desperate."

"We are slightly more scientific in our methods than that," said Mrs. Bainbridge. "Did Mrs. Billington explain the process to you?"

"Yes," said Miss Forsberg, opening her purse. "Dad gave me the five pounds. And there is a contract to sign?"

"Of course," said Sparks, sliding one to the front of her desk with a pen next to it. "Press hard, there's a carbon."

Miss Forsberg leaned forward in her chair to sign, then Sparks took the five pounds, countersigned, and gave her the carbon.

"Now, let's all take a deep breath," suggested Mrs. Bainbridge. They did. "There, much better. Tell us about yourself, Miss Forsberg."

"Not much to tell, really," she said, looking down. "We live in Woolwich. You know Woolwich?"

"No," said Mrs. Bainbridge.

"Yes, but not well," said Sparks.

"You know the Dusthole?"

"Again, yes, but not well," said Sparks.

"Yeah, that's the best way to know it," she said. "We're right in the centre. Dad's had an ironmonger's shop there for years. Sells gadgets and repairs them. The repairs are what brings in the money, what there is. He's quite clever about machines and electrics and whatnot, and people out there need to keep things working rather than buy new ones."

"And your mother?" asked Gwen.

"She died when I was thirteen," said Miss Forsberg. "That's when the problems started. We live over the shop. Mum used to help him, chat up the customers while he was fiddling with toasters and such in the back, then nip up top to do the cooking and housekeeping when there was a spare moment. So that became my job when we lost her. Dad pulled me out of school, and I've been helping him ever since."

"Why is he so eager to get you married now?" asked Mrs. Bainbridge.

"He's met someone," said Miss Forsberg. "Rosie. Just a few years older than me, but she's got her hooks into him good and wants her own family. And there's not that much room over the shop. So he wants to move me out by marrying me off, but I've never had the time for boys while running the place, and the men he's tried to fob me off on are all twice my age. So here we are."

"Here we are," said Sparks. "Let's get a few more basics, then we'll get down to the serious questions. Religion?"

"C of E. We never miss a Sunday, and Dad never fails to fall asleep when the sermon starts."

"Your age?"

"Twenty-three."

"No schooling past thirteen?"

"Some correspondence courses," she said. "And I read at night once he's fed and the dishes are done."

"Do you smoke? Drink?"

"No to the first, and I'm not a teetotaler, but I'm not one for getting too tipsy," she said. "I have to stay clearheaded enough to help him get home most nights. Rosie can take over that job with my blessings."

"Right," said Sparks. She put her pen down, then looked directly at her. "What are you looking for in a man?"

"Oh, gosh," said Miss Forsberg with a dreamy sigh. "I've been cooped up for so long. The most exciting thing about coming here is seeing Mayfair for the first time since before the war. I want a man who will take me away, show me places I've never been, and have adventures. A real man, not a brute and a braggart who thinks that's manly."

"So you'd like to travel?" asked Mrs. Bainbridge.

"I would," she said, lighting up. "But would a world traveller be available for a shopgirl with no real education?"

"That would be for us to determine," said Mrs. Bainbridge. "Do you want children? Children and travel are frequently contradictory desires."

"Not right away," she said. "I've been taking care of a middle-aged child for nearly ten years. It's time for someone to take care of me for a while. And I'll return the favour when we settle down."

The partners glanced at each other. Mrs. Bainbridge raised an eyebrow slightly, and Sparks nodded in response.

"We may know a man or two who meet those needs," said Sparks. "A few more questions, and then we'll get to work."

By the time they were done, Miss Forsberg was looking hopeful for the first time since they met her.

"How long before I hear from you?" she asked as they came around their desks to shake her hand.

"Expect a call tomorrow," said Sparks.

"Tomorrow?" she exclaimed. "I'd better get my hair done."

"I know," said Sparks. "That's why I said tomorrow. Otherwise, it would be tonight."

"Well, I'd better get going," she said happily. "If nothing else, it will get Dad off my back for a few weeks, and that's worth five pounds right there. Goodbye, and thank you."

"Good day, Miss Forsberg," said Mrs. Bainbridge.

They heard her fetch her father, whose tones took on a subdued, pleased sound from what they could decipher. They waited until they heard them descend the steps, then sat at their desks and opened their respective file boxes.

"You want to have the gentleman call rather than go through our usual method of sending letters?" asked Gwen.

"That girl needs rescuing," said Iris. "The sooner, the better. She's like Rapunzel, only it's an ironmonger's shop instead of a tower."

"In that case, it's a good thing she's getting her hair done," said Gwen.

"And I don't think we need to pick three candidates," said Iris. "I think we're both thinking of the same one."

"Let's find out," said Gwen.

They riffled through the bachelor boxes, and each pulled out one candidate. Iris waved hers around in an elaborate gesture, then held it to her forehead.

"Is this your card, madam?" she asked.

Gwen held hers up and looked across at Iris.

"Gerry Macaulay," she said. "Hooray, I was hoping for him. He's been talking about going to the Rhodesias more and more lately. And he's a real man, if her phrasing means what I think it does."

"But he's a gentleman underneath it all," said Iris. "Which is the most important part. You'll miss him when he goes, won't you?"

"My martial arts training with him has been quite enjoyable despite the excruciating agonies I incur," said Gwen. "I suppose we should give him a call."

"Suppose? Why suppose?"

Gwen looked out the door for a moment.

"You know how I get when I think someone's lying to me?" she asked.

"You think Miss Forsberg was lying?"

"I do," said Gwen.

"Why would she?"

"I don't know," said Gwen. "Well, if she is, Gerry will have her running for the truth by the end of their first date. Let's call him straightaway."

Before they could do that, Mrs. Billington appeared in the doorway.

"Yes, Saundra?" said Iris, beckoning her in.

"There was a telephone call for Mrs. Bainbridge," said Mrs. Billington, handing a note to Gwen. "I would have told you when you came in, but things were chaotic. A Lord Morrison."

"Lord Morrison called me here?" asked Gwen in surprise. "Lord Thomas Morrison?"

"I'm sure I don't know His Lordship's Christian name," replied

Mrs. Billington with a sniff. "He assumed you would know who he was."

"I do," said Gwen. "How extraordinary. Did he want me to ring him straightaway?"

"He did."

"All right," said Gwen. "Thank you, Saundra."

"And could you type up a pair of cards for our newest client?" asked Iris, handing her the form.

"That poor girl," said Mrs. Billington as she took it. "Any word on the strike next door?"

"Nothing since this morning," said Iris.

"Can't have a day go by without at least two strikes happening somewhere," said Mrs. Billington with a sigh. "Hotel workers yesterday. And the cold storage workers went out, I heard. I didn't even know they had a union."

"If you need anything kept cold, swing by my flat," said Iris. "It's freezing in there."

"That's what keeps you looking so young and fresh, Miss Sparks," said Mrs. Billington with a smile.

"Oh, that would be worth a raise if we could afford one, Saundra," said Iris.

"Maybe I should unionise," said Mrs. Billington.

"There's only one of you," said Iris.

"Then hire a second secretary, and we'll band together," said Mrs. Billington. "Time for an expansion."

"You were the expansion," said Gwen. "And we're so awfully glad you joined us. If the business reaches the point where we need someone else, we'll be doing very well indeed."

"All right then," said Mrs. Billington. "I'll give you a ring when the three o'clock shows up."

She left, closing the door behind her.

"Lord Morrison is running Bainbridge, Limited, now, isn't he?" asked Iris.

"He is," replied Gwen. "He's been the acting chief exec since my father-in-law had his heart attack. I wonder why he would be calling me."

"You do own forty percent of the company," said Iris.

"Of which I control zero percent at the moment," said Gwen, reaching for the telephone. "Well, there's only one way to find out."

She dialled his number, then waited. A secretary answered.

"Mrs. Gwendolyn Bainbridge calling for Lord Morrison, please," said Gwen.

"One moment, Mrs. Bainbridge," replied the secretary.

A moment later, Lord Morrison came on the line.

"Gwendolyn, m'dear!" he rumbled. "How are you on this fine day?"

"The weather in Mayfair is dank and miserable," she replied. "Is it any different in the City?"

"Any day in which we live and breathe is a fine day," he said. "And any city that has you in it is a fine place."

"Goodness, Lord Morrison, you are in a chipper mood," she said, laughing. "To what do I owe the pleasure of this unexpected call?"

"First, you must start calling me Tom," he said. "We've known each other long enough, and no point in taking rank seriously when we're going to be working together. Your late husband called me Tom practically from the time he could walk."

"Then Tom it shall be. Thank you."

"Now, to the main purpose. A little birdie tells me that you will be reclaiming your place on the board soon."

"If all goes well, yes, although 'claiming' would be more accurate than 'reclaiming,'" she said. "I have yet to actually take my seat at the table."

"Claiming, yes, of course," he said. "Now, I haven't a clue how long it will take with the legalities, but I can't see it not going your way. The board of Bainbridge, Limited, meets once a month on the second Monday at two o'clock. That's Monday next."

"I'm afraid that my court appearance won't be until after that, Tom," she said. "I still won't be eligible. Mr. Parson—"

"Parson will be there on your behalf, naturally," he said. "But I want you to attend. You won't have any powers or authority, of course, but you should see it in operation for yourself."

"Is that permitted?" she asked. "Harold never allowed me near the place."

"When the chief executive officer is in power, he sets the rules," said Lord Morrison. "But when he's moping about in convalescence and the acting exec is running the show, then the acting exec can do as he damn well pleases, and it pleases me to have you come as my guest. Strike while the iron is hot, m'dear! I hear Harold's improving. He won't be at this one, but he might be at the next. You would benefit from some familiarity with how we do things before he comes crashing back."

"Tom, I cannot tell you how much this means to me," said Gwen. "I will be there. Anything you'd like me to look at beforehand?"

"Talk to Parson. He'll have everything. And let me reward you with dinner afterwards. Edna has granted me permission to dine with women half my age because she knows I'm too old and slow to do anything with them."

"I am sure none of that's true, but if Lady Morrison—"

"Edna, please."

"If Edna trusts you, then you are a man to be trusted. I shall be delighted."

"Until then, m'dear."

"Until then, Tom."

She replaced the handset. Iris had watched her for the entire conversation.

"You're going to sit in on a board meeting?" she asked.

"Yes," said Gwen. "That sounds rather exciting until you realise it means you'll be sitting in on a board meeting. But it's what I need to do."

"And you have been learning the ropes," said Iris. "You won't be just another pretty face. Actually, you'll probably be the only pretty face. The rest are all men, aren't they?"

"Of course," said Gwen. "I wonder why he asked me."

"Why wouldn't he? He knows the petition's coming up soon."

"Yes, but he's known about the petition for a while, yet he waited until now to ask me. I wonder what his game is."

"Explain to me how the board works again."

"Old Lord Bainbridge, Harold's father, set up the company so that each of his sons had forty percent, and the remaining twenty was divided among five other investors. That way, if the two brothers agreed on something, they could put it into effect, but if they didn't, one would have to gain the support of three other board members to have a majority."

"And your share comes from Harold's brother."

"Yes. He died childless and left it to Ronnie, and Ronnie left it to me, his wife, who promptly lost control of it when she—"

Gwen stopped, then took a deep breath.

"When she lost control," she concluded. "When I lost control."

"May I ask you something?" asked Iris, sounding unusually hesitant.

"What?"

"You've been studying Bainbridge, Limited, for months. When you finally get to be a real, live major partner, or whatever one calls it—"

"General partner."

"Right, an even higher rank than major. When you become a full-fledged general partner, what will you do with The Right Sort?"

"Do with it? What do you mean, what will I do with it? It's our business, Iris."

"Our business, which barely broke even for the first three months, and is squeaking by now thanks to an unofficial loan from She Whom We Cannot Reveal and the absurd publicity we've garnered from solving a murder, neither of which are sustainable over time."

"It's been more than one murder," said Gwen.

"Yes, but only the La Salle case made the press, and it's not as if we were getting paid to solve them."

"That would be a tawdry way of making a living," said Gwen with a shudder. "But where are you going with this?"

"Will you be dividing your time equally between here and Bainbridge, Limited, once you've claimed your prize? Or will you, like any sensible person, decide that the operation with the most profits is the one that will demand the most attention?"

"In other words, will I abandon you once I become rich and spoiled?" asked Gwen. "Wait, I forgot. I'm already both."

"All I'm asking, as a responsible co-owner, is what will happen to us? Matching couples at The Right Sort has always been a team effort. An equal partnership with equal input."

"Iris, think about to whom you are speaking," said Gwen. "Do you really think I'd rather spend my working hours worrying about plantations and munitions and copper mines when I could be playing Cupid with my best friend instead?"

Iris smiled in relief.

"I hoped you'd say something like that," she said. "Forgive me for worrying, darling. It's just that this is all I have right now. And I had better call Gerry if he's going to ask her out tomorrow. I have a good feeling about this one."

CHAPTER 2

Iris's good feeling proved to be wrong. Gwen received the bad news straight from the horse's mouth when she showed up for her weekly lesson with Gerry Macaulay.

"It started fine," he said, holding the heavy bag while she pummelled it. "Nice-looking girl, didn't look away from my scar the way some do. I took her to a decent enough Italian place, and it got her to talking about wanting to travel. Put your weight on the other foot and spin."

"Right," said Gwen as she drove her elbow into an imaginary solar plexus. "What happened?"

"So I said I was planning to be travelling. She gets enthusiastic. Then I say to the Rhodesias. You mean the ones in Africa? she asks. Don't know any others, I said. And her face drops like I had trod on her kitten."

"Sorry, Gerry," said Gwen. "That's turned out to be an obstacle more than once, hasn't it? We'll find someone, I promise."

"I hope so," he said. "Enough of this. What say I teach you a new hold to break today?"

"Sounds like fun. Which one?"

"Have you ever been placed in a 'come-along' grip?"

"I'm absolutely certain I have not."

"Well, you're in for a treat. Step over to the mat."

She called Iris at the office after her lesson.

"Gerry and Miss Forsberg didn't hit it off, I'm afraid," she said. "Some people who say they want to see the world forget what's in it."

"Ah," said Iris, making a note on Miss Forsberg's index card. "No African adventures for Rapunzel. Very well, I'll put some more thought into it. Are you returning?"

"I need to go see Mr. Parson," she said. "I'll swing by after."

"Fine. I'll see if I can find some more prospects for her by the time you get back. Good luck with Parson."

"Thanks."

The law firm to which Parson belonged was one street off the more prestigious addresses for the legal community, not far from Lincoln's Inn. The building was a modern one built between the wars, and the firm had taken the top two storeys of the six available. Parson was on the fifth, not having risen high enough to reach the aerie where the senior partners roosted.

The lift operator let her off on the fifth with a cheery "Good day, madam!" The receptionist, a pretty young woman with curly blond hair, glanced up with a smile as she entered.

"May I help you, ma'am?" she asked.

"Mrs. Gwendolyn Bainbridge to see Mr. Parson."

Something in the receptionist's face shifted momentarily when she heard the name, but the smile remained in place.

"Certainly, Mrs. Bainbridge," she said. "He's expecting you. Let me show you in."

She knows my situation, Gwen thought. She's seeing the crazy lady for the first time. And she's afraid.

Who could be afraid of me?

Other than me?

The receptionist led her through a hallway to a large central area filled with young women at desks, typing and answering telephones, while the clerks, all young men, dashed about, trying to look important. Beyond them was a row of offices closed off from the interior view by large windows covered with frosted glass, the names of the lawyers and their areas of expertise stencilled in gold leaf on the doors. The receptionist brought her to one in the middle whose lettering proclaimed OLIVER PARSON. JUNIOR PARTNER. TRUSTS, ESTATES, CUSTODY, LUNACY. She knocked, then opened it.

"Mrs. Bainbridge to see you, sir," she said.

"Send her in," came a man's voice.

Parson's office had a grubby feel to it. The case files were scattered about, half of them open with papers sliding out in apparent attempts to escape. His mess smacked of desperation, of a man too far behind in his burgeoning caseload to decide which stack on his desk to tackle first, and too proud to ask even the lowliest clerk or secretary for help. More files balanced on a small chestnut side table, next to a long, flat box and a roll of pearl-coloured wrapping paper.

The man himself was the sort that had been good-looking enough when young, but wasn't young enough to be good-looking anymore. His thinning brown hair was slicked inadequately over bald patches, and his manicure was unable to compensate for the bitten nails and jagged cuticles. He wore a dark blue wool suit with a jacket that he should have left unbuttoned, given the strain he was putting on the buttons. She suspected that there had been a third piece to the suit once, a waistcoat which had been abandoned after too many unsuccessful attempts to close it. From Simpsons of Piccadilly, she surmised, a ready-to-wear suit that had become more apprehensive than ready over time. She thought it may have been the same one he was wearing in the photograph perched precariously on one corner of the desk, showing him with a woman and two children, all forcing smiles.

Her previous encounters with Parson had been at the sanatorium, then at the Bainbridge house, gradually devolving into monthly telephone conversations. In those situations, his manner was imperious, presenting the full weight of the court poured into his person. Here, however, framed as a junior partner in a less than ideal office, he seemed pettier.

"Well?" he said abruptly. "What is it? I'm a busy man."

She realised she had been staring at him.

"I was under the impression that I was part of that business," she replied. "No doubt you will be billing me for every minute that we speak."

"Then save yourself some money and be brief," he said.

"I would like to see the most recent financial reports from Bainbridge, Limited."

"You get a report at the end of every quarter," he said. "It's only November."

"I thought that given my upcoming petition, I shouldn't wait that long to bring myself up to date."

"Your status is unchanged," he said. "Until that happy day, you will get what you are entitled to on the day it's required, no more than that and no sooner than that."

"But I thought, since the board is meeting next week—"

"As always, I shall be attending on your behalf."

"Of course," she said. "But I was planning on attending as well."

"You? At a Bainbridge board meeting?" he exclaimed, staring at her incredulously. "Don't be ridiculous. You have no legal right to be there."

"Maybe no right, but I do have an invitation," she said.

"An invitation? From whom?"

"Lord Morrison," she said.

"So, you have slithered up to an impressionable old man and inveigled him into inviting you. Pitiful."

"As it happened, he called me," she said, suppressing her rising anger. "He felt that given the likelihood of my regaining my status, I should be allowed to observe. There was no inveigling involved."

"And do you think you have the ability to fully comprehend these proceedings, Mrs. Bainbridge? Did they teach you corporate management at that Swiss finishing school? You would be eaten alive by these men. Go back to your little matchmaking shop and stay out of matters beyond your ken. I'm not about to give you anything beyond what the court requires. Besides, I only have the one report, and I require it for my own preparations, which, may I remind you again, are being done on your behalf."

"How long would it take to type up a copy?" she asked. "There are a dozen women out there who look more than efficient enough for the task. Mayfair isn't very far. I walked here in no time at all. One of those energetic young men could run it over to my office in short order. And all of this could be added to what you're billing me."

"All of that could be done," he agreed. "But it won't be. It's unnecessary."

"It's necessary to me," she snapped.

"I determine what is necessary to you, not you," he said. "Raising your voice won't change that one jot. Will that be all?"

"No," she said. "But I see the futility in asking for anything else."

"You've finally grasped the situation, then," he said, pressing a button on his intercom. "Anderson. Show Mrs. Bainbridge out."

"Yes, Mr. Parson," came a tinny voice.

"Forgive me for not walking you to the door," he said. "But I am a busy man."

"So you said," she replied, getting to her feet.

Her eyes caught the box on the side table. From Fox's of Bexley, she noticed.

"Would you like me to wrap that for you?" she asked. "I'm rather wizard at it. They did teach us gift wrapping at finishing school."

"Go now," he said wearily.

A tall, brutish man whose well-tailored suit did nothing to conceal his menacing demeanour appeared at the door.

"This way, please," he said in a voice implying dire consequences if met with noncompliance.

Some of the secretaries closer to Parson's office stared at her openly as Anderson escorted her out. Had she raised her voice that much? She couldn't remember.

Maybe she was just an object of curiosity. Or pity.

Either way, at that particular moment, she despised every single one of them, and she would have happily taken on all of them with a handful of finishing school girls at her side.

Iris looked through her index cards one by one, searching for a detail that might jump out and beg for a date with Miss Forsberg. She had hoped Gerry would be the one. He was a rescuing type, but he was travelling in the wrong direction.

She looked for men who might be heading east or west rather than south. Slowly, methodically, she plucked first one, then two more cards from the box and laid them on her blotter like a fortune-teller with tarot cards.

She heard Gwen's footsteps, and looked up quizzically when she appeared in the doorway.

"What's wrong?" she asked, seeing her partner's forlorn expression.

"I am so frustrated with being under that man's thumb," said Gwen, plopping into her chair. "When I first met him, he made me feel suicidal. Now, I'm feeling homicidal. That's progress, don't you think?"

"Not the kind that will favourably impress the court," said Iris. "Speaking of progress, I've come up with three more candidates for Miss Forsberg. Would you care to take a crack at it, then we'll compare?"

"Love to," said Gwen. "I could use a distraction from my life right now."

Mrs. Billington knocked on the door while Gwen was looking through her cards.

"We have a walk-in," she said. "A Mrs. Remagen is here, but she wouldn't let me take down the preliminaries. She didn't want to do anything until she spoke with the two of you."

"Did she explain why?" asked Gwen.

"Not at all," said Mrs. Billington.

"Very well," said Gwen. "Give us two minutes, then bring her over."

"Yes, Mrs. Bainbridge," said Mrs. Billington, shutting the door behind her as she left.

"Thoughts?" asked Gwen, turning to face Iris.

"Cautious customer," said Iris with a shrug. "She wants to examine the merchandise before deciding whether to make a purchase."

"I agree," said Gwen. "Would you like to take the lead in the interview?"

"No, you should," said Iris. "You're a more reassuring presence than I am."

"To everyone but myself."

Mrs. Billington returned and held the door for a woman who entered slowly, leaning on a cane and grimacing with each step.

"Please come in," said Mrs. Bainbridge, quickly coming out from behind her desk to help the woman to the seat in front of it.

"Thank you," said the woman, breathing hard as she lowered herself gratefully onto the chair. "Good Lord, those stairs almost did me in. If I had known you were on the top storey, I might never have come."

"Well, we're very glad you made the journey. I am Mrs.

Gwendolyn Bainbridge, and this is my partner, Miss Iris Sparks. Welcome to The Right Sort Marriage Bureau."

"I'm Mrs. Adela Remagen," said the woman, shaking Gwen's hand from her seat.

She still had on her coat, a bottle-green tweed that had seen much use and had some thin spots at the elbows. The dress underneath was a simple tan Utility outfit, belted at the waist. She wore a wide-brimmed tan fedora that matched the dress.

"Have you had a chance to read one of our flyers?" asked Mrs. Bainbridge.

"I have," said Mrs. Remagen. "It all sounds so fascinating."

Mid-forties, guessed Sparks, although the cane made her look older than she was. As did her general mien. Whatever pain forced her to walk with a cane radiated from her almost visibly. Sparks, who took ages to get rid of her limp after breaking her ankle in her first and only parachute jump, sympathised wholeheartedly.

"It is, and we hope you will find it rewarding as well," said Mrs. Bainbridge, resuming her seat behind her desk and gathering up her form and a pen. "Now, first we'll need some preliminary information about you, then we'll interview you more thoroughly about what you are looking for in a husband."

"Oh, I'm not here for me," said Mrs. Remagen with a slight laugh.

"You're not?"

"No. I would have thought the 'Mrs.' would have given that away."

"My apologies," said Mrs. Bainbridge. "We have had widows as clients before. And some divorcées, for that matter. Very well, so you have come to us to find a match for someone other than yourself?"

"Yes," said Mrs. Remagen.

"And who would that be?" asked Mrs. Bainbridge, pen at the ready.

"My husband," said Mrs. Remagen.

The two looked at Mrs. Remagen in shock and confusion. She merely sat there, smiling.

"Your husband?" repeated Mrs. Bainbridge.

"Yes," said Mrs. Remagen.

"To whom you are currently married?"

"Yes."

"Oh!" exclaimed Sparks, suddenly understanding. "Oh, no! I'm so sorry."

"Thank you," said Mrs. Remagen, her smile becoming something sadder.

"How long do you have?" asked Sparks.

"Oh, my goodness," said Mrs. Bainbridge, catching up to her partner.

"The doctors aren't certain," said Mrs. Remagen. "It could be weeks. It could be months. But it won't be years."

"And there is nothing that can be done?" asked Sparks.

"There is something," replied Mrs. Remagen. "I am doing it right now."

"Please tell us everything," said Mrs. Bainbridge. "Forgive me if I start to cry. It's a failing of mine."

And forgive me if I don't, thought Sparks. That's my failing.

"I grew up in Burma," Mrs. Remagen began. "My father owned a company that built steamships and ran them on the Irrawaddy River. We were well-to-do, and the plan was to send me to family in England for finishing, but my mother died when I was fifteen, so I had to step in to run the household in her place."

"Was this in Mandalay?" asked Sparks.

"Yes. Do you know it?"

"I know my atlas," said Sparks. "And I know my maps of the war. You got it much worse than we did."

"So I've heard," said Mrs. Remagen. "We fled in 1940. But I'm getting ahead of my story. As I said, I was the head of the house and hostess when there were events to host, which meant I wasn't able to make my way into local society as much as I could have had my mother been alive. The few suitors I had were of my father's generation, widowers looking to replace the fragile flowers they had imported from the homeland. That's cruel, I suppose, but I wanted better. Younger, certainly. And then something wonderful happened—Mandalay College started up."

"When was that?" asked Mrs. Bainbridge.

"In 1925. I was twenty-five myself, ten years into filial servitude. They had brought in scholars from Britain to instill a proper English education in the locals, and one of them was this awkward young naturalist named Potiphar Remagen."

"Potiphar?" exclaimed Sparks. "What a marvellous name!"

"He was a marvel to me," said Mrs. Remagen. "We had a group of the newly arrived professors to the house for tea. Most of them milled about, brandishing their pontifical skills, but Potiphar kept sidling over to look at the collections of insects and stuffed birds we had mouldering away in display cases dating to my grandfather's time. He corralled me, demanding information about each of them, where they could be found, what they ate, and, I blush to mention, what their breeding habits were. Needless to say, I fell in love immediately."

"And you married him," concluded Mrs. Bainbridge.

"Oh, no," said Mrs. Remagen. "Not right away. His attentions were directed at all the species below his, with little regard for his fellow members. Every free day, he was off into the local forests. Every vacation, he ranged deep into the jungles, emerging just before the new terms were about to commence, specimen jars clutched in his arms. I thought I would die an old maid—"

She stopped abruptly, clutching a handkerchief to her mouth and coughing violently.

"Sorry." She gasped. "Funny, that fear. I'd give anything to die an old maid now. An old anything. But that won't happen."

"You shouldn't tire yourself," said Mrs. Bainbridge.

"No!" said Mrs. Remagen angrily. "You need to understand him. You need to know what's right for him. Because he'll never find it again on his own, you see. He's only become more awkward and off-putting as he's got older, and I can't rest until I know there will be someone to take care of him."

That's done it, thought Sparks, glancing at her partner, whose tears were flowing freely now.

"How did you finally manage it with him?" she asked.

"He came back from one of his expeditions deathly ill," she replied. "Some parasite, he said. He wanted to describe it to me, but I refused to let him. He lived near the college, in a small cottage with a maid who had no skill in caring for a sick man. I insisted that he come recuperate in our house, and I waited on him, hand and foot, night and day. And when the fever finally broke, he looked at me with eyes clearer than I had ever seen them, and I knew. We were married the next week."

"Lovely," said Mrs. Bainbridge with a sigh.

"Did you ever go out into the jungle with him after that?" asked Sparks.

"It wasn't for me," she said. "I never liked going into the forests, but I camped on the fringes and made sure the water was boiled while he went looking for beetles. I kept him alive for each new term, and we were happy."

"Forgive me, but are there children?" asked Mrs. Bainbridge.

"No, sad to say, but we were content. We stayed in my father's house. Potiphar would bicycle off to teach every day, and our lives muddled on, through the student uprisings, the separation from India, and so on. But then came the war. The invasion. We fled. First to India, then to England. Potiphar decided to sign up. He was nearly forty. They wanted to put him behind a desk, but he told them he knew the jungles like the back of his hand, and they sent him back to Burma. There were small teams who disappeared into the jungles for months at a time. Not all of them came out again, but he did. My socially awkward, insect-loving husband went into the jungles and did terrible things, and now he speaks even less than he did before."

I know men like that, thought Sparks. Too many of them.

"And I waited for him here," said Mrs. Remagen. "I played the soldier's stoic wife for as long as I could, but I was feeling ill. Nerves, said the first doctor. Hysteria, said the second doctor. By the time the third doctor found the actual disease, it had progressed too far. I've been getting radiation treatments. I can't recommend the experience, I'm afraid."

"So you've come to us," said Sparks. "I cannot tell you how remarkable I think you are for doing this."

"I have a list of things to take care of before it's over," said Mrs. Remagen. "This was at the top. How do you propose to accomplish this?"

"Normally, we interview the prospect about his desires and dislikes," began Sparks.

"Miss Sparks, before we go any further, I would like a word with Mrs. Remagen alone," said Mrs. Bainbridge gently.

Sparks glanced over at her partner, who was gazing at their potential client with almost beatific compassion. There was no questioning her when she looked like that.

"Certainly, Mrs. Bainbridge," said Sparks, rising from her chair. "I will be with Mrs. Billington. Call when you're ready for me."

She left, closing the door behind her, then walked into the other office of The Right Sort and plopped down on the sofa they kept for potential clients while they waited for matrimonial happiness.

"Thrown you out again, I see," said Mrs. Billington from behind her desk.

"She has," said Iris.

"Having another one of her mystical insights?"

"They're not mystical," said Iris. "She has an uncanny knack for reading people, but there's nothing supernatural involved. I think."

"You should put an act together and travel with carnivals," said Mrs. Billington.

"I've had that very thought," Iris confessed. "Especially when she was wearing those turbans in August after getting her scalp stitched up."

She picked up *The Times* from the magazine rack and settled back to peruse the listings for flats.

"Is there something wrong?" asked Mrs. Remagen, looking at Mrs. Bainbridge curiously.

"I'm worried there might be," said Mrs. Bainbridge. "Before we continue, I need to know something."

"What?"

"I have no idea what it's like to be in your shoes," said Mrs. Bainbridge. "The physical pain, the humiliation of the treatments. But I am all too familiar with one aspect of your situation, and if it means what I think it does, then I cannot be a party to your plans."

Mrs. Remagen looked down at her lap in resignation.

"How did you know?" she asked.

"You're putting your affairs in order," said Mrs. Bainbridge. "That's all very well and good, but I sense a determination to bring some finality to this. You said this was the first item on your list. The last item, I'm guessing, is to end your own life. I admire your organisational skills. When I tried to kill myself, it was haphazard, flailing, and, as you can see, ineffective."

"You tried to kill yourself?" exclaimed Mrs. Remagen, looking up at her in surprise. "Why?"

"Your husband came back," said Mrs. Bainbridge. "Mine did not. Unfortunately, I lacked your strength."

"My strength," said Mrs. Remagen bitterly. "Which cannot prevail. The harder I fight, the greater the pain becomes."

"Yet you are taking rational steps in spite of it," said Mrs. Bainbridge. "And it's that very rationality which has led you to decide to take your own life. But it is my own experience with suicide that tells me I cannot help you if that is your ultimate goal."

"If this is a religious belief—"

"It is, in part," said Mrs. Bainbridge. "But there is more. Something that I, as an experienced suicide, can share with you before we go any further."

"Please don't speak to me about hope," said Mrs. Remagen, weariness creeping into her voice. "I gave up on hope months ago. Doctors have ruled out miracles in my case. Otherwise, I'd be off on a pilgrimage to Lourdes or Santiago de Compostela or somewhere. Terribly inconvenient that there are no decent miraculous healing places locally. I was going to try Saint Winefride's Well, but I heard it's dried up."

"No, I'm not speaking of hope," said Mrs. Bainbridge. "I lost hope as well, and my time in the sanatorium didn't restore it to me."

"You were in a sanatorium. I'm so sorry."

"It does beat a coffin."

Mrs. Remagen turned even paler than she had been.

"That was harsh," she said. "If you're not going to help me—"

"But that is what I am trying to do," said Mrs. Bainbridge. "I learned something in the lucid moments between the injections, when I was strapped to a bed reduced to counting the cobwebs on the ceiling. I learned that I was missing out on things. My son was growing up without me. My friends were having adventures and love affairs and learning new skills, and I was missing all of that."

"You also missed some horrors," said Mrs. Remagen. "You were lucky."

"The horrors will always be with us," said Mrs. Bainbridge. "But so will the wonders. Every moment you forego will be a wonder denied, and now that I can experience them again, I am grateful for every single one of them."

"I'm going to miss all of them soon."

"We all will someday, whether it's cancer or a mortar shell that does it. But right now, you are alive. You have climbed the four flights of stairs to our office, and I'm so sorry we are up this high without a lift in the building, but because you have done so, you've created a wonder for me and one for yourself that wouldn't have existed had you decided to end things first."

"And when I no longer have the strength to make new wonders and the pain is all that there is?"

"Then douse it with morphine and live for the lucid moments in between. The wonders will seize their opportunities. If nothing else, you can revisit the wonders of the past. Pluck down the volumes from the shelves of your memories and turn to those pages where an awkward young naturalist buttonholed you about the sex lives of insects. Listen to the birds singing outside, and marvel how they've survived the war. Wait for the next wonder, Mrs. Remagen. I promise you it will come."

"Until the day it doesn't."

"It will come," insisted Mrs. Bainbridge. "But only if you allow it. Erase suicide from your to-do list, and if you're ever tempted to restore it, put something else there instead. Will you promise me you'll do that? Because if you won't, I won't help you with the first item, and that means you'll never reach the last one."

"You are diabolical in your goodness," said Mrs. Remagen.

"Bargain with the Devil, then. We'll use ink for the contracts, though. There has been too much blood spilled in my life already."

"To help my husband, I must choose to live until I die a natural and painful death. Is that what you're proposing?"

"Yes."

Mrs. Remagen held out her hand.

"Agreed," she said.

"Good," said Mrs. Bainbridge, coming around to shake it. "Now, let me fetch Miss Sparks and we'll get to work."

She opened the door and walked over to the next office.

"Iris, we're ready," she said.

"Good," said Iris, getting up. "Are you going to tell me now, later, or not at all?"

"Not now," said Gwen. "I still have to decide between the other two choices."

They came back into their office and took up their positions behind their desks.

"I thought of something while you two were gabbling away," said Sparks. "How will this work, exactly? The practical details, I mean. I don't mean to sound morbid, but there is a final fee to be paid if we succeed and the client marries. Mr. Remagen wouldn't be bound by any contract you enter into. We couldn't collect from him, but we shouldn't receive it in advance of the completion of our services."

"What is the final fee?" asked Mrs. Remagen.

"Twenty pounds each from the bride and groom," said Sparks.

"I will have my solicitor draw up papers holding that sum in escrow for you," said Mrs. Remagen. "Payable upon completion of the contract. Will that be satisfactory?"

"I think so," said Sparks. "We're all making this up as we go. The other question is when do you wish us to start looking? There should be a suitable period of mourning. Otherwise, it wouldn't be decent."

"Oh, Lord, I don't care," said Mrs. Remagen with a sigh. "We're not Victorians. The war has made us all live faster than we ever thought we could. I don't want him to marry so quickly that people will be scandalised, but I don't want him to be alone for long. He's no good at it."

"Write him a letter detailing your plan, then give it to your solicitor to give to him at an appropriate interval," suggested Mrs. Bainbridge. "People should be told it was your wish."

"That should work," said Mrs. Remagen. "Thank you for helping me think everything through."

"Right, let me add some language to our standard contract," said Sparks, taking the forms from Mrs. Bainbridge. "'To take effect upon notification by your solicitor of final fee being placed into escrow account.' I'm putting in a termination date should Mr. Remagen decide he'd rather not use our services."

"He will," said Mrs. Remagen. "If he knows it came from me, he'll do what I tell him."

"Even from the Great Beyond," said Mrs. Bainbridge.

"Very good," said Sparks, bringing the forms over to Mrs. Remagen. "Initial here and here, sign at the bottom, pay us the five-pound fee, and we'll start the interview."

Mrs. Remagen read over the contracts, then signed both. She opened her bag and fished out a five-pound note, then held it out. Sparks took it along with the contracts, then she and her partner countersigned.

"This one is for you," said Sparks, handing one copy to her. "Right. Tell us what you think Potiphar would want in a second wife? A repeat of the first, or something different?"

"I'm not so egotistical as to think that I cannot be improved upon," said Mrs. Remagen. "Someone who shares his passion for nature, and would be willing to go back to Burma or wherever else his research takes him. Someone who will actually go into the dark woods instead of cowering on their margins."

"That narrows the field considerably," said Sparks.

"Really? I should think many women would find the prospect exciting. Didn't you ever want to marry a jungle explorer when you were growing up?"

"No," said Sparks. "I wanted to be a jungle explorer when I grew up."

"What happened?"

"I changed my mind. Many times."

"So you want someone adventurous for him," said Mrs. Bainbridge. "Or, I should say, you think he wants someone adventurous."

"I do."

"What else will he require?"

"Someone capable of looking after him without his knowing that he's being looked after," said Mrs. Remagen wistfully. "He's a messy man in every aspect of his life except for his work, in which he is obsessive. He needs a woman who will be able to fix his tie without being obtrusive about it, who will make sure the maid dusts his office without disturbing a single scrap of paper."

"He sounds like a lot of work," said Sparks.

"He is, but well worth the effort," said Mrs. Remagen. "His enthusiasms are contagious. A woman willing to open her mind to all kinds of new experience will find herself well rewarded."

"All kinds of new experience?" asked Sparks, an eyebrow raised.

"If you are expecting me to blush, Miss Sparks, you will be disappointed," said Mrs. Remagen. "I understand the implications of your question. As I said, marriage to Potiphar will be a rewarding experience to the woman who embraces it. How many of your male prospects come with such ringing endorsements from their current wives?"

"None," said Mrs. Bainbridge. "What about age preferences? Is he of your age?"

"Forty-four, two years younger than me. Goodness, I hadn't thought about that. What would be the advantages and disadvantages?"

"A younger woman would more likely want children," said Mrs. Bainbridge.

"Not always, but that is the case for most of our female clients," added Sparks.

"I've always wondered what he would be like as a father," said

Mrs. Remagen. "Before the war, I would have said he would have been an unusual but good one. He has none of the playfulness that children adore in a parent, but he is direct and honest, and would have engaged their intellects in ways that many fathers don't."

Ronnie was playful, thought Gwen. He would have been engaging with his son, given the chance. With his children, if we had had more.

I wish he had lived long enough for me to see that.

"You said he was like that before the war," said Sparks. "What about now?"

Mrs. Remagen hesitated before answering.

"I think that children for him now might be a terrible idea," she said softly.

"What changed about him since his return from the war that makes you say that?" asked Sparks.

"I don't like to say."

"Please remember, Mrs. Remagen, that we have to consider our female clients' desires," said Sparks. "We have their future happiness at stake as well."

"Is happiness guaranteed? I didn't see that in the contract."

"No, of course not," said Sparks. "But if there is a specific reason you think Mr. Remagen has become unsuited to be a parent, that would also reflect on his suitability as a match. On the other hand, we have women who share that trait as well."

"You sound quite scientific in your approach," observed Mrs. Remagen. "Potiphar would approve."

"And I will pin you down like a specimen until you answer my question," Sparks persisted. "Why would children be a terrible idea for him now?"

"As I said, when he came home from the war, he spoke less than he was accustomed to, and said almost nothing about his time in the jungles."

"*Almost* nothing," said Sparks. "But he said something."

"I asked him if he had thought about resuming his explorations. He said that he couldn't possibly abandon me while—while I was in this condition. I asked if he would continue them after I was gone."

She stopped.

"And?" Sparks urged her.

"He said, 'Once you're gone, humanity will no longer be of any interest to me. I've seen who they are and what they can do. In nature at least, there is no evil.'"

They were all silent after that. Mrs. Remagen pulled a handkerchief from her bag and wiped her eyes.

"I need you to save him," she said. "There is still a spark inside him, I'm sure of it. I won't let it disappear."

"It won't be easy," said Mrs. Bainbridge. "But it never is easy. I will promise you our best efforts."

"That's all I can ask," she said. "What else do you need to know?"

Mrs. Bainbridge glanced at her questionnaire.

"Religion?" she asked.

"He believes in nature. No organised church."

"Diet?"

So strange going through the mundane portions of the questionnaire, thought Sparks. Yet the mundane factors will be what will get us through all of this.

They finished up a few minutes later.

"Right," said Sparks. "I think we have enough to work with."

"Good," said Mrs. Remagen, forcing herself to her feet.

"Could I help you with the stairs?" offered Sparks.

"No, no," said Mrs. Remagen. "Remember me as you see me now, while I still have a shred of energy. I'll be a wreck at the bottom of the stairs by myself, if you don't mind."

They came around to each grasp her by the hand.

"I would like to pray for you, if that's all right," said Mrs. Bainbridge.

"It won't do me any good," said Mrs. Remagen.

"It might do me some," said Mrs. Bainbridge.

"Then by all means," said Mrs. Remagen. "Thank you both. This was a most fascinating experience. I feel reassured as to this one aspect of my life."

"If there is anything—" Sparks began.

"There is nothing," said Mrs. Remagen. "I don't expect we will meet again. Goodbye."

The partners remained standing in place as she left, watching her as she slowly made her way down the top flight, using both her cane and the railing. They stood motionless as she disappeared from view, and didn't sit until the last footsteps faded and the faint sound of the front door opening and closing echoed up the stairwell.

"It's so awful," said Gwen. "Her husband survived the worst kind of war while she stayed here safe in England, and now she's the one who is going to die. How did you figure that out, by the way?"

"I've seen it before," said Iris. "She was wearing a wig, did you notice? A very good one, but there was a wisp of hair that she hadn't fully tucked under, and it was very, very grey. She's become an old woman in her mid-forties."

"Poor thing. Well, should we start looking for prospects now, or wait until we get the letter from her solicitor? The second letter, I should say. The first informing us of the fee in escrow, the second—"

Gwen stopped, unable to say it.

"The second telling us to fulfill our end of the contract," said Iris. "That the designated mourning period is over. We should probably contact Mr. Remagen before we begin, just to make certain he's ready to move on."

"I'm trying to think who we currently have who might be a suitable candidate for him," said Gwen. "It's premature, I know."

"We shouldn't hold any women back for prospects," said Iris. "They all want to be matched sooner rather than at some unspecified date in the future."

"True," said Gwen. "Still, I can't help thinking that he'll be a challenge. I wonder if our Miss Forsberg would be interested. He certainly fits the bill for travel and adventure."

"If Africa made her blanch, I doubt that Burma will suit her any better."

"Doesn't Gemma Hornsby work in the Natural History Museum?"

"She does," said Iris. "But Miss Hornsby lives for mounting stuffed creatures who are safely dead in tableaux of her own creation. She is afraid of shadows. The jungle is not for her."

"Your crush at thirteen was a boy named Trevor who grew up to become a naturalist," said Gwen. "Did your love of creepy-crawlies come from that attraction, or was your attraction because you loved creepy-crawlies and he did as well?"

"The latter," said Iris. "I still go back to the museum when I can. They're reopening soon. I read that they've acquired a collection of scale insects from Professor Newstead. I'm looking forward to that."

"And may I say on behalf of the rest of England's women, yuck," said Gwen. "But if you do go, take Little Ronnie. He loves it there, and seeing it with you would be the high point of his year."

"That's a lovely idea," said Iris. "In fact, it sounds like it will be one of the better dates I've ever had. How did you get him in last summer? It wasn't open to the public yet."

"The Bainbridges are on the board, of course," said Gwen. "Carolyne arranged a private tour."

"Lucky boy," said Iris. "And we now have a series of pictures of the adventures of Sir Oswald the Narwhal as a result. Well, I'll make that a date. But you must come, too. And John, of course. A young man for each of us! That's a proper double date. Does John like natural history?"

"His bent is towards airplanes," said Gwen. "He's constantly scanning *The Times* for the latest records broken."

"Then you should be his escort," said Iris. "You know how I feel about flying."

Gwen looked at her notes from their recent interview.

"There are entries here that I'd rather not show to Saundra," she said, handing them to Iris. "Would you mind?"

"Not at all," said Iris, opening her bottom drawer and pulling out her Bar-Let. "I'll leave out those details that concern Mrs. Remagen. I doubt that we'll be forgetting them."

No, I won't forget, thought Gwen, her hand unconsciously tracing the scars below her left breast as her partner began typing up the index cards for their new client. No matter how much I wish I could.

CHAPTER 3

What to do about Miss Forsberg? thought Gwen the next morning.

She knew Iris had chosen three candidates, and it was up to Gwen to come up with three of her own. If any turned out to match, then they would trust their combined instincts and notify the lucky gentleman.

Yet her instincts about Miss Forsberg told her something wasn't right. It wasn't unusual for their clients to conceal the truth from her. One thing she and Iris had known from the beginning was that people presented themselves as how they wanted to be seen, not necessarily as who they were. It was Gwen's knack for reading in between the lines that made her essential to their business.

But how could she read between the lines when the book was closed?

Well, do your best, she thought. Travel and adventure, only not so much. Which didn't seem like adventure at all. East, but not too east. West—Canadians? Americans?

Let's try putting an ocean between her and her father, she thought.

She pulled three cards from the box, then turned to face Iris.

"Ready," she said.

Iris picked up her three.

It turned out that they both had Cyril Merriman, a Canadian sergeant from a town in Manitoba, currently stationed in London awaiting demobilisation.

"He said he already knew all the local girls there, and didn't see any of them as someone he wanted to be with for more than a minute," recalled Iris.

"Then it's time to replenish the local stock with some fresh English blood," said Gwen. "Dear God, I sound like I'm breeding cattle. All right, we'll put that in motion. Could you make the call? I have to see my lawyer this afternoon."

"Certainly," said Iris.

Rawlins Stronach, K.C., was a solo practitioner who kept his law offices on the third storey of a building on Elm Court. Mrs. Bainbridge's appointment was for two thirty. She arrived ten minutes early, her nervousness undissipated by her brisk walk from Mayfair and her near dash up the stairs.

Mrs. Merrifield, Stronach's secretary, a no-nonsense woman in her early fifties, was typing at one of the paired desks in the front office when Mrs. Bainbridge entered. The other desk belonged to a clerk whom Mrs. Bainbridge had never seen and whom she imagined dashing about the various courts with winged feet and a leather dispatch bag.

"Good afternoon, Mrs. Bainbridge," said Mrs. Merrifield, not looking up from her typewriter. "You're early. Please take a seat."

"I don't suppose he could see me a few minutes before the appointed time, could he?" asked Mrs. Bainbridge.

"He is scrupulous about his schedule," said Mrs. Merrifield. "I would no more tamper with it than I would with Big Ben. Please take a seat."

Mrs. Bainbridge sat in one of the narrow chairs jammed together across the empty desk on the other side of the office, idly watching Mrs. Merrifield type.

Ten seconds before the clock struck the half hour, Mrs. Merrifield stood, then turned to the door to the inner office. As the clock struck, she rapped on the door, then opened it.

"Mrs. Bainbridge is here to see you, sir," she said.

"Come," called Mr. Stronach.

Mrs. Bainbridge entered. Mrs. Merrifield closed the door behind her.

Stronach was a thickset man in his late forties, given to sudden bursts of energy whenever an idea seized him, which was frequently. He viewed the world over the tops of his half frames, searching for cracks in people's armour through which he could strike.

"Good afternoon, Mrs. Bainbridge," he said. "Please take a seat."

The guest chair was clear for a change, whatever files that had been piled on it having been moved and unceremoniously stacked by the radiator. Mrs. Bainbridge's file, noticeably thicker than when she had last been there, was open on the desk in front of him. She tried very hard not to read it from her seat.

"We have a time now for our appearance," he said, stabbing at a scribbled notation with his forefinger. "Ten o'clock this coming Tuesday before Brandon Cumber, one of the assistant masters."

"What's he like?"

"He favours the status quo," said Stronach. "If there is a matter that is strongly contested, he leans towards keeping the petitioner's status unchanged."

"That doesn't sound very promising," said Mrs. Bainbridge.

"As I said, that's when matters are strongly contested," said Stronach. "So far, yours hasn't been. I have submitted the reports from the two doctors assessing your mental health and finding you capable of living in the world without supervision by the Crown. I've also notified your brother, Thurmond, as your nearest relative;

your in-laws as guardians of you and your child; and Mr. Parson, your committee. I have received no letters or motions in opposition to your petition so far."

"So far. So they still could."

"In theory, yes," said Stronach. "I am prepared to face any or all of those contingencies should they arise. Have you heard anything from any of the other parties on your end?"

"No," said Mrs. Bainbridge. "Of course, I never hear from Thurmond about anything, so that's no indication of his acceptance or rejection of the petition. Still, it has no bearing on his life, so I doubt he'll stir himself enough to lift a finger against me. My father-in-law is the one who concerns me."

"He hasn't said anything?"

"No, but that would be his way. He's a cagey old lion, even in convalescence. I think he spends his entire time in bed plotting his return to power once he gets his strength back."

"Hmm," said Stronach, taking off his spectacles and cleaning them. "Perhaps you might consider bearding the lion in his den."

"Confront him?"

"Sound him out. Appeal to his vanity. See if he gives anything up."

"Won't that be an obvious tactic?"

"Make it obvious. A truly egotistical man will pride himself on seeing the tactics of his opposition, while missing their true objectives if properly concealed under the obvious."

"Did you learn that through reading law?" asked Mrs. Bainbridge.

"I learned it from living among the English," said Stronach. "They are a predictable people in their habits."

"Given all of the lunacy cases you've handled, I'm surprised you've come to that conclusion."

"The insane are also predictable," said Stronach. "Just in ways not accepted in society."

"Am I predictable?" she asked. "In either a sane or an insane way?"

"You are a rare exception, Mrs. Bainbridge," he said. "You've surprised me on a number of counts, particularly with your penchant for murder investigations."

"I wouldn't call it a penchant, exactly. I would be quite happy if none of them ever happened."

"Nevertheless, when they do happen, and they have happened with astounding frequency, you jump into them with a commitment that borders on the reckless."

"Each time, I felt I was doing what was necessary at the moment," she said. "It may be that my ability to evaluate what is necessary is dodgy."

"Perhaps that's due to your transition from one status back to another. I am not a psychiatrist, but I would venture to guess that you're still feeling your way through the world."

"Sometimes it's like I'm playing blindman's buff in a minefield," she said. "Everything is going fine until I make that one misstep. Then comes the explosion."

"Any unexploded bombs still buried? Do you feel prepared for your testimony?"

"I know all the words to say. I know all the responses to the questions I might be asked. It's like I'm playing a part in a play."

"That's litigation for you, Mrs. Bainbridge," said Stronach, glancing over to the stand which held his silks and wig. "Hence the costumes. Sometimes it's drama, sometimes it's farce. Sometimes it's both at once. Commedia dell'arte with more ridiculous outfits."

"Enter the zanies," she said with a sigh.

Iris, alone in the office while Gwen was at her appointment, went through her box of index cards for their female clients, searching for those with inclinations towards adventure and travel. This was premature, she knew. Mrs. Remagen was still very much alive, having seen them just a day before, but Iris couldn't stop thinking about her, or her husband.

The future widower whom they had never met.

The problem was intriguing. Match a man they knew only by report, and an unobjective report at that. Match him with a new woman who would be willing to leave England for the inhospitable climate of—

No, that wasn't fair. Millions of people lived in Burma. Always had. So it had to be hospitable. Just not to the English.

Find him a woman who would be willing to go hand in hand with him into the jungle, a machete in her free hand. A woman who lived for adventure, who thrilled for danger.

Dear God, I'm describing myself, she thought.

All right, so who among our female candidates is like me?

Damned few.

Amanda Courtland? She had come back from her extended tour in the Pacific Theatre buzzing with stories, having never been out of Leeds before the war. She wanted to travel, she had told them.

But this wasn't really travel, was it? It was settling down in a new place, albeit one far away with jungles in the vicinity. Would that satisfy Miss Courtland's wanderlust?

Would it satisfy Iris's own?

Did she still have any?

Her near-fatal jump during wartime parachute training had left her with a severe fear of flying. She had spent the rest of her war in London, and now channelled her adventurous spirit into running her own business. And the occasional murder investigation. And into her love life, of course. Even if she'd had enough foresight to consider her future while she was at Cambridge, she never would have imagined ending up in an office sitting behind a desk, staring at a pile of index cards containing the condensed versions of other women's dreams.

Although her dating a gangster wouldn't have surprised nineteen-year-old Iris one jot.

She was jolted out of her reverie by Mrs. Billington tapping on the doorway.

"Yes, Saundra?" she asked.

"A messenger came by," said Mrs. Billington. "There's a letter from some law firm. I thought I'd leave that to you to open."

"Good, I've been expecting something of that sort," she said, coming around the desk to take it from her. "It's for Mrs. Remagen."

"That's the lady with the cane?"

"Yes."

"Well, good for her, still trying in her condition," said Mrs. Billington. "I hope you find someone who will be kind to her."

"I'll do my best," said Iris.

It was with a pang of guilt that she watched her leave. She didn't like concealing this matter from their secretary, but this client was special.

The letter was from the firm of Turner, Woodbridge, and Farrow, from Number 78, Chancery Lane. She picked up her letter opener and slit the envelope along the top edge.

To The Right Sort Marriage Bureau, Miss Iris Sparks and Mrs. Gwendolyn Bainbridge, Proprietors, she read. *This is to confirm the deposit of twenty pounds sterling in an escrow account in your firm's name, payable upon the date of marriage of Mr. Potiphar Remagen to any other client of your firm pursuant to the terms of the contracts signed between you and Mrs. Adela Remagen. Should no such marriage take place by midnight on the fifth anniversary of the date of the death of Mrs. Adela Remagen, the account shall be terminated and the moneys therein, plus any interest accrued, shall be distributed according to the regular terms of her will. Details of the account follow on Page 2.*

It was signed by Jenkin Farrow, one of the senior partners.

Seems legal enough, she thought.

She walked over to Mrs. Billington's office.

"Everything all right?" asked Mrs. Billington.

"Everything's fine," replied Iris as she opened the filing cabinet. "There's a bit of legalese tied to this one. Lend me a paper clip, would you?"

She pulled out Mrs. Remagen's contract and attached the letter to it, then returned it to the file.

"Anne Tilsworth," she muttered.

"What?" asked Mrs. Billington.

"Thinking out loud," said Iris.

"Miss Tilsworth? For Mrs. Remagen?"

"No, of course not. I was wondering who to set her up with next. I'm going back to ponder at my desk."

"Have a good ponder, then."

Iris returned to her desk and looked at Anne Tilsworth's index card.

Mountain climber. Trekker. Horsewoman.

I wonder how she feels about tropical climates?

Mad dogs and Englishmen go out in the midday sun, so why shouldn't Englishwoman?

With that tune now stuck in her head, she made notes on both cards for future reference, then went back to matching couples who were actually available now. She came up with three and set them aside for approval by Gwen, then picked up *The Times* and pored over the ads. She was beginning to think she would have to take on a flatmate, and she loathed the idea.

She stared gloomily at the cards. Marry! she urged them. Marry in haste and pay us our bounties. Repent at leisure all you want afterwards, but I need enough money to live in solitary splendour come the New Year.

There was a buzz from the intercom.

"Yes, Mrs. Billington?"

"We have a walk-in," came the other woman's voice. "A Miss Seagrim. Are you free?"

"Of course," said Iris. "Has she filled out the forms?"

"She has."

"Bring them in," said Iris.

And please let this be a normal, desperately lonely woman with a decent life span, she thought.

Mrs. Billington came in seconds later.

"Young," she said as she handed the forms to her. "Surprised she'd be coming to us already. It gives you an idea how many lads were taken away from us."

"Twenty-two," said Iris as she glanced at them. "An Oxford graduate! Give me two minutes to suppress my competitive instincts, then bring her in."

"Will do," said Mrs. Billington. "And touch up your lipstick, dearie. You've been chewing on your lower lip."

"Have I? Blast," said Iris, pulling out her compact and lipstick. "You are invaluable, Saundra."

She made some quick repairs, smiled brightly to make sure none had got on her teeth, then kept the smile going for their new potential customer.

Mrs. Billington knocked again.

"I have Miss Effie Seagrim here to see you, Miss Sparks," she announced.

"Please show her in, Mrs. Billington," said Sparks in her best professional voice.

Miss Seagrim came in hesitantly, peering through thick round lenses in plain black frames. She was of average height, with long black hair that showed evidence of a less than competent attempt at pin curling, much of it having given up and hanging down flat. She had been more successful with her makeup, although she had a robust, rosy complexion to begin with.

"How do you do, Miss Seagrim?" said Sparks, coming around

the desk to greet her. "I'm Iris Sparks, but call me Sparks. Everyone does. Please sit."

"Hello," said Miss Seagrim as she sat in the client chair. "I—well, gosh, no one calls me just Seagrim. That's rather forward-thinking of you."

"I like to think I'm on a forward march to the future," said Sparks. "But call me Miss Sparks if you're more comfortable with that."

"Thanks," said Miss Seagrim. "Aren't there supposed to be two of you?"

"It will only be me conducting the interview this afternoon," said Sparks. "My partner, Mrs. Bainbridge, had an appointment. I hope you don't mind. We can schedule you for both of us if you like."

"No, no, this will be fine," said Miss Seagrim. "It's all rather exciting. I've never done anything like this before."

"You list an address in Perivale," said Sparks, taking her place behind her desk and picking up the form. "Where is that?"

"In the Ealing district. It's a small town. With a good running start, you could jump right over it."

"Mostly farms, I take it?"

"It was before we moved there, but it's factories, more and more. We came when Dad got the job at Hoover back in thirty-two. We live in a three-bedroom house, all very modern, on a street where you can't tell the houses apart."

"You sound like you're not fond of Perivale," observed Sparks.

"It's a nothing kind of place," she said with a grimace. "I had a nothing kind of existence there."

"Yet you qualified for Oxford."

"I was intelligent," she said. "I still am. No one really quite realised how clever I was until the headmistress at the school took notice. And Perivale did have one saving grace. Well, two, come to think of it."

"What were they?"

"We have our own stop on the New North Main Line, so London was accessible. And there's the Wood."

"The Wood?"

"Perivale Wood," she said wistfully. "It's a nature reserve. I started exploring it on my own, then I fell in with a bunch of mothing folks."

"Mothing? As in—moths? I didn't even know there was such a word."

"People who love birds go birding, and folks who fancy moths go mothing," said Miss Seagrim. "One has to be very careful describing oneself in university applications. If I had written down that I was a 'mother,' they would think I had a swarm of illegitimate children before I turned seventeen."

"How delightful!" exclaimed Sparks. "And Perivale Wood is a good—mothing location?"

"Oh, yes," said Miss Seagrim. "Go out there with a torch after sunset sometime. We've been cataloguing them. We're up to over three hundred different species."

"Three hundred? From one little patch of woods?"

"The woods, the fields, the houses and barns. They're everywhere."

"Remind me not to wear my good wool coat when I'm visiting the area. Do you have a favourite?"

"Gosh, it's hard to choose," said Miss Seagrim, her enthusiasm bubbling up. "Sometimes I long for a shuttle-shaped dart, sometimes it's the eyed hawk-moth. The cinnabar, if I'm in a party mood, or maybe the small elephant hawk-moth if it's a particularly elegant party, or the scarlet tiger if I'm going to get rip-roaring drunk and don't care what happens."

"Moth parties at Oxford must have been quite the do. I had no idea."

"If only that were true," she said ruefully. "The hardest part of being at Oxford was taking exams in the spring when I knew the migrations were taking place outside."

"I'm going to take a wild guess that you studied entomology there."

"Of course, apart from taking two years off during the war."

"You must have matriculated quite young."

"Sixteen. Thin, awkward, painfully shy except when the conversation turned to insects, which was seldom, as you can probably imagine. I didn't fit in with any group. Even the other entomology students thought I was odd for liking moths."

"Snobbery even in entomology," said Sparks in wonder.

"Well, it's all about classification, isn't it? I must say, it's refreshing to find another woman who hasn't run screaming from the room to avoid discussing anything with six legs and wings."

"I had a lengthy beetle phase in my youth," said Sparks. "Still like to sneak over to the British Museum when I can. Do you ever go to the Royal Entomological Society's lectures?"

"Joined when I was twelve," said Miss Seagrim proudly. "It was my dream to become a Fellow there someday. Only—"

She faltered.

"What?" asked Sparks.

"Well, I've reached the end of it, haven't I? Took my degree, and university is over."

"No graduate studies?"

"I'm afraid not," said Miss Seagrim. "I wanted to go on, but my parents said no. They were reasonably indulgent while I was there. They even gave me a first edition of Newman's *Illustrated Natural History of British Moths* when I graduated, but I'm back in my old bedroom and working as a secretary for a law firm in the City. Dad keeps talking about my getting a 'real' job at the Hoover factory. It's decent money—that's where I worked during the war, when they switched over to making aircraft components—but it would be more of the same for the rest of my life. If I was lucky, I'd end up in another identical three-bedroom house down the lane from my parents, married to another Hoover man."

"You don't want that."

"I don't," said Miss Seagrim vehemently. "Frankly, I'd like to get out of England entirely. It sounds ungrateful, but my happiest times were when I was in the woods, away from everyone. I was hoping to latch on to some field expedition to go off into the unknown, but it didn't happen."

"Do you have any particular deadline?" asked Sparks. "Are the Hoovers waiting to vacuum you up right away? We do have men among our candidates who are returning to other parts of the Empire. That shouldn't be the sole requirement, of course—"

"But it would be a requirement," said Miss Seagrim. "I would like to get far enough away that the gravitational pull of Perivale will have no effect. I would be willing to wait for the right—well, the right sort, as you call it here."

"Then sign here, pay the five pounds, and we will start planning your escape," said Sparks.

Miss Seagrim opened her bag and took five one-pound notes from it.

"Show me where to sign," she said as she handed them over.

Sparks handed her the contracts, which she signed with a look of determination.

Good Lord, thought Sparks as she took them back and co-signed them. I think a miracle may have happened.

All we have to do is wait for a woman to die.

CHAPTER 4

Lord Harold Bainbridge, Gwen's father-in-law, was still convalescing in his temporary quarters in the guest wing, isolated from the daily noise of the household, particularly the comings and goings, usually at reckless high speeds, of Ronnie, Gwen's son, and John, Lord Harold's son. Gwen decided to approach him after dinner, hoping that the blandness of the meal to which he was restricted didn't put him into too foul a mood.

But instead, the sound of laughter poured from his room, his joined by that of the boys, gladdening her ears. She paused in the doorway to see Lord Harold sitting cross-legged on his bed, wearing his flannel bathrobe over a pair of scarlet-and-black-striped pyjamas, engaged in conversation with Ronnie and John, who were sitting opposite him, their backs against the oaken footboard.

She didn't have to pretend she didn't overhear them. It didn't matter if she did—they were speaking Chitumbuka, the language John had learned at his mother's knee in Nyasaland, that Harold had learned among other East African languages on his many journeys there, and that Ronnie was learning now. The old man, his illegitimate son, and his legitimate grandson had become a secret club of three within the vast Kensington house, and whatever story Harold was telling them had the boys in fits of giggles.

He came to the end, his face with a droll expression, his fingers wiggling to show two people running away. The boys laughed heartily and clapped.

"That must have been a good one," murmured Agnes, their nanny, who had come up next to Gwen. "I hope it was appropriate for young children."

"We shall never know," said Gwen. "But even if it wasn't, I would not deprive them of this pleasure for the world."

"Well, it's my job to get them to bed, so I'll be the one to deprive them," said Agnes.

She knocked on the doorway, and the three males looked up, the boys with expressions too mischievous to give any hope that bedtime would be an easy task.

"Come, lads," said Agnes. "You know what time it is."

"Can't we hear one more story?" pleaded Ronnie.

"There are teeth to be brushed and faces to be washed," said Agnes sternly. "If you get them done exceptionally well, I will consider letting you have extra reading time before lights out."

"Go on, boys," said Lord Bainbridge. "Early to bed and early to rise. Shake hands first."

"Good night, Grandfather," said Ronnie, shaking it enthusiastically before jumping off the bed.

"No running!" cried Gwen and Agnes immediately, and he halted, two steps into his intended launch.

"Good night, sir," said John, shaking his father's hand more solemnly.

"Good night, John," said Lord Bainbridge, ruffling his hair affectionately.

John slid down from the bed, then turned to Gwen.

"Good night, Gwen," he said.

"Good night, dear," she said, kneeling and giving him a quick hug.

"Don't I get one?" whined Ronnie.

“Of course,” said Gwen, hugging him to her with her other arm.

She squeezed the boys together for a moment, which made them all laugh, then released them to Agnes.

“Let’s go, boys,” said the nanny.

Gwen watched fondly until they disappeared from view, the boys chattering away in Chitumbuka.

“Ronnie seems to be picking it up nicely,” she commented as she turned back to her father-in-law.

“He’s a quick study,” said Harold.

“You’re a good teacher,” she said.

“Lord knows I have little enough to do,” he said with a sigh.

“You’re looking much better,” she observed. “You always do after spending time with them.”

“They are the best therapy an invalid could possibly have,” he said. “You don’t mind? My teaching Ronnie Chitumbuka?”

“Why would I mind?”

“Because it means that someday he will go to Africa to see his inheritance,” said Lord Bainbridge. “I promised him that. I only wish I could be well enough to show him myself.”

“You will be,” said Gwen. “How many languages should he learn in the meantime?”

“Five would be adequate,” said Lord Bainbridge.

“Goodness! And they’re only teaching him Latin and Greek in school. He’ll be quite the polyglot. Well, now that I’m here, I was wondering if I could ask your advice about something.”

“Advice? From me? That’s a first.”

“It is,” said Gwen. “But it’s on a topic that you know better than anyone.”

“Ah,” he said, settling back against his pillows. “The board meeting.”

“Yes. I heard that you won’t be attending again this month.”

“Correct,” he said. “I heard that you will be.”

“Tom told you, I suppose.”

"Naturally. The acting chief exec reports to the invalided chief exec. So, what advice do you need from me?"

"What should I be doing?"

"Nothing," he said. "You have no vote. You have no powers. Watch, listen, learn."

"For what in particular should I be watching and listening?"

"Our illustrious board in action," he said with a bitter laugh. "Or in inaction. They'll discuss the monthly events, pat themselves on the back for letting a well-oiled machine run by itself, and adjourn so they can have drinks after."

"They don't actually do anything?"

"They can't. Not without me and my forty percent there."

"And my forty percent, since Mr. Parson does whatever you want."

"Yes," he said, appraising her expression closely. "I have had carte blanche ever since—"

He stopped.

"Might as well say it," said Gwen. "Ever since Ronald was killed."

"In point of fact, ever since my brother died without issue and left it to him," said Lord Bainbridge. "My son never took to learning the ins and outs of managing a company, even when he reached his majority. He usually deferred to me, gave me his proxy, and avoided the place completely. I was hoping he would come around someday, but the war took him, God rest his soul."

"God rest his soul," Gwen repeated softly. "And with luck, I will be your equal come the next meeting. I hope you'll be in attendance."

"For your coronation? Perhaps. I want to be stronger."

"How strong?"

"Strong enough to scream at everyone," said Lord Bainbridge, no longer smiling. "To let them know I'm back in business. For business, not to sit on my throne in my dotage and count my coin. I need to be stronger than all of them put together, and I'm still weak. The moment they sense that weakness, they'll be on me like sharks at a shipwreck."

"Won't they see me as weak, being a woman?" asked Gwen.

"Of course. But you're not. I used to think you were, but recent events have proved me wrong."

"I've learned to be strong," said Gwen. "I've had to."

"That isn't something you learn," said Lord Bainbridge. "You had it already."

"May I ask—without a general partner there, is there any way one of the limited partners could propose anything? Say one of them had an idea he wanted to put forth that would actually be a good thing for the company?"

"If Sandy Birch or Hilary McIntyre ever had an idea, it would be their first," he scoffed. "Townsend Phillips, on the other hand, is as full of ideas as a balloon is with hot air, and they're worth about as much."

"How on earth did they end up on the board if you think so little of them?"

"Because my father liked their fathers. We all inherited each other."

"What about Stephen Burleigh? You didn't mention him. The other member of my generation."

"Poor Stephen," said Lord Bainbridge. "Hasn't shown his face at a board meeting yet, what with his father in jail. I doubt he'll ever be a factor. Pathetic, but we've inherited him as well."

"As you've inherited me."

"Almost. Pending your readmittance to the world of the sane."

"And then?"

"And then we shall see. You can bring your own ideas to the table."

"Which, if you oppose them with at least three of the five lesser partners, will be rejected."

"Yes," said Lord Bainbridge with a sly smile. "I think it's going to be fun having you there."

"So what is your advice for Monday?"

"Ah, advice," he said. "The others don't know your strength yet. Not like I do. Don't let them. No point in showing your hand now."

"I don't have a hand to show," said Gwen.

"You will," said Lord Bainbridge.

"Thank you," said Gwen. "May I ask one last favour?"

"What?"

"I would like to be up to date on the company, but Mr. Parson is adhering strictly to his quarterly reporting schedule. I was wondering if you had anything more recent lying about."

He waved his arm at a stack of documents on a desk across from his bed.

"Be my guest," he said. "The last monthly report is in there."

"Harold, you've been remarkably helpful," she said as she collected them. "Should I be suspicious?"

"Probably," he said. "Or see this as an opportunity to work together. We both want Bainbridge, Limited, to thrive and prosper long enough for our sons to take over."

"Ronnie and John running the show together someday? Is that your hope?"

"If Bainbridge blood means anything, then it should be theirs," he said.

"Does my blood mean anything?"

"We'll talk about your blood when the madness ceases to course through it," he said. "Good night, Gwen."

"Good night, Harold," she replied.

She closed the door behind her, and immediately opened the top file, reading it as she walked to her room.

"Do you believe in miracles?" asked Sparks when she had caught her breath.

Archie rolled to his side and looked at her quizzically.

"Given what 'as just 'appened, any answer other than yes would be ungentlemanlike," he said. "What miracles are you talking about?"

"Miraculous occurrences," said Sparks. "Coincidences so unlikely as to suggest the existence of a benevolent and participatory God."

"You told me you're an atheist," he pointed out.

"I'm an open-minded atheist," said Sparks. "There are days when I hope events will prove me wrong. So, my dear Archie, do you believe in miracles?"

"Whenever the long shot comes in at Kempton Park," he said. "But then I'm usually suspicious of the fix being in."

"Especially when you were the fixer."

"Yeah, but that's not a miracle when that 'appens," said Archie. "That's planning."

"Hmm, predestination by the Gangster Gods," mused Sparks. "That would explain much of the past few years."

"What was your miracle, then?"

"A woman walked into our office this afternoon. She turned out to be the answer to a prayer."

"You don't pray, either."

"I didn't say it was my prayer," said Sparks. "We had an odd request yesterday to find a match for a man who sounded exceptionally difficult to match. A biologist who ventures into tropical forests to turn over old leaves in search of new beetles. That won't be an easy one, I thought while smiling and accepting our five-pound fee. But then this woman walked into our office."

"She likes beetles?"

"Moths, actually. But to find a female with a fancy for the phylum at all is astounding. Oxford degree, brainy, lights up when she talks about them—Good Lord, I would have married her myself if I was a man."

"Do I 'ave to start pinning bugs onto corkboards to win you over now?" asked Archie.

"No, but it's sweet of you to ask," said Sparks, nestling into him. "Still, she reminded me of someone."

"Who?"

"Me, only the me from years ago. The prewar version. When Gwen and I first learned about the Beetle Man, I said to myself, Sparks, we need to find a woman like you. And that presented a difficulty, because I've always maintained that there is no one else like me, and the actual me is unavailable."

"Because you love a spiv."

"Because of that, but also because our standard contract states that neither Gwen nor I will date any of our clients."

"Didn't know that," said Archie.

"Then this Effie shows up, and I realised that even I am not like me anymore. Or I'm not like the me I was at university, jumping at every possibility, grabbing at every adventure like an octopus wielding sponges at the end of each tentacle, absorbing whatever I could reach. I've lost that person somewhere along the way, and I miss her."

"You ever want to go back to school?" asked Archie.

"Sometimes," she admitted. "I had dreamed of graduate studies, but Herr Hitler needed to be stopped, and I wanted to do my part."

"Another adventure for the octopus."

"Many, as it turned out. Now, here I am."

"In bed with a spiv."

"I was thinking more broadly than my immediate circumstances."

"But they do include the spiv in bed with you."

"Of course, Archie," she said, kissing him where his jawline met his neck. "But I've been feeling unsettled lately, between needing to find a new flat and worrying that my business partner is going to up sticks when she gets hold of her fortune."

"As to the first problem, maybe I could 'elp you."

"Archie, we've talked about this," said Sparks. "I was a kept woman before. It was poor judgment on my part, and it didn't end well. I appreciate your wanting to help, but I don't want anyone paying my rent."

"I'm talking about moving in with me," said Archie.

"That—that sounds a little permanent," said Sparks, taken aback.

"Nothing's permanent," said Archie. "But one way to feel less unsettled is to settle."

"We said we weren't going to get married, remember?"

"We said that last month. Or maybe the month before, I forget. Doesn't mean we can't change our minds."

"Is this a proposal?"

"It's a suggestion," said Archie. "Things don't 'ave to be strictly legal. I know how you like to 'ave an escape 'atch built into everything."

"Not much about your life is strictly legal."

"Yet 'ere you are despite my wicked ways."

"Here I am," she agreed. "But soon I will return to my flat in Marylebone where all my uncertainties await me, mewling and wanting to be fed."

"You never stay the night," he said.

"Frees us both up for the morning, doesn't it? Besides, I don't have an overnight bag."

"You never showed up at the office in the same outfit twice in a row?"

"I have, but I'm trying not to anymore now that I'm an established businesswoman."

"And bug-free."

"And bug-free," she said with a sigh. "More's the pity."

They lay in bed.

"Bernie and Tish 'ave set a date for the wedding," he said, changing the subject.

"How marvellous! When?"

"The fourteenth of December," said Archie. "Are you free?"

"Free? Free for what, exactly?"

"For coming to the wedding," said Archie. "What did you think?"

"Why would they invite me?" asked Sparks. "It was The Right Sort who introduced them, of course, but usually—"

"For a Cambridge girl, you can be awfully thick sometimes," said Archie. "You would be invited because I'm invited."

"You're asking me to come to your nephew's wedding as your date?" she asked.

"The penny 'as finally dropped."

"Us going public at a family wedding—that may be an even larger commitment than moving in with you."

"The church 'as a back door, too," said Archie. "You'll still 'ave an escape 'atch if you get panicky."

"If I got panicky in a church, that would give the lie to my claims to atheism, wouldn't it?" said Sparks with a laugh. "No, it's the lady with the fear of commitment that's getting the jitters. I'm leaning towards a yes, Archie, but give me a few days, all right?"

"That's fine," said Archie. "Better than I expected, in fact."

Gwen was studying an index card when Iris came in the next morning.

"These are good," she said, holding up the proposed matches Iris had left for her. "Who is this Effie Seagrim?"

"She walked in yesterday afternoon."

"Are you thinking what I'm thinking?"

"A possible second Mrs. Potiphar Remagen."

"Amazing," said Gwen, shaking her head. "I'm almost disappointed. I was looking forward to the challenge."

"There's more good news. Bernie Alderton and Letitia Hardiman have set a December wedding date. With luck, we'll collect our bounty before the New Year."

"That would be nice," said Gwen. "A good end to a tumultuous first year in business. Did you hear directly from them, or—"

"A little birdie told me," said Iris.

"Was it perched on the pillow next to yours?" asked Gwen.

"It might have been, come to think of it. I'm glad they're tying the knot soon. I'm trying to put together a deposit on my still-mythical next flat."

"How's that going?"

"Not well," said Iris. "I'm trying to find the perfect balance between what I can afford and how far I can walk."

"You should give yourself a raise. Or at least a Christmas bonus."

"Can we manage that?"

Gwen grimaced.

"Not just yet," she said. "Two more weddings or sixteen new customers. I'm going to drop off the matches for Saundra so she can type up the first-date letters."

Iris picked up *The Times* and scanned the real estate listings, then flipped back to the upcoming weekend events, seeking free entertainment in case Archie was tied up doing something she was better off not knowing about. She ran her eyes quickly across the page, then sat bolt upright as she caught a name she knew.

"Guess who's giving a lecture at the Royal Entomological Society on Sunday?" she said the moment Gwen came back in.

"Given my complete lack of interest in the subject, there wouldn't be much point in my trying, would there?" replied Gwen. "Except—oh! Is it Professor Remagen?"

"'A Special General Meeting will be held on Sunday at two o'clock,'" read Iris. "'Lectures will include "An Examination of Palingenetic Features Among Hydrophilidae," by Sir Paul Ruddimore, and "Some Observations on Tiger Beetles Found in Kachin,"' by our own Potiphar Remagen! 'If circumstances merit, tea will be served in the Library before the meeting.' Oh, I do hope circumstances will merit! Would you like to join me?"

"A continuing no and yuck to all insect-related activities," said Gwen. "Are you seriously contemplating attending?"

"Why not? It will give me a chance to check out our future candidate. What do you say? I'm a member. I could bring you in as a guest."

"I'm busy," said Gwen.

"Ah," said Iris, nodding wisely. "You already had plans."

"Are you asking because you don't know, or because you already knew and were wondering what I would say?" asked Gwen.

"I already knew," confessed Iris.

"Another little birdie?"

"A somewhat larger one," said Iris. "Around six foot eleven, in fact."

"Did he tell you anything else about what's in store, or could I still let everything be a surprise?" asked Gwen.

"I know nothing else," said Iris. "But I look forward to hearing about it Monday morning."

They concentrated on work for the rest of the day. When they parted at the end, Iris walked a good distance before realising that she hadn't told Gwen anything about Archie's proposal.

Gwen had kissed Sally. That was the problem.

She had fended off other men since returning from the sanatorium, invoking her widowed status, her desire to straighten out her affairs vis-à-vis Ronnie and the Lunacy Court and her estate before allowing herself the frivolity—no, the luxury of dating again.

But Sally was special. Sally was their gallant, who would immediately throw his massive frame into harm's way to shield her at the drop of a hat. She also liked him immensely, which was more to the point, so when he finally got up the nerve to ask her out, having waited a decent interval after the incident with the Soviet spy so that it wouldn't feel like he was seeking recompense for his heroics, she agreed.

And at the end of a pleasant evening, which involved a pleasant meal and a pleasant chat, she let him kiss her.

It was pleasant.

Only pleasant. Nothing more.

She had been hoping she would feel more. She kept replaying the night he had intervened when she was on the verge of abduction at gunpoint, and the walk back afterwards to the Bainbridge house with him ready to charge into the shadows at the merest flicker of movement. Rerunning the reel in her mental projection room, she wanted to edit out the take where he chivalrously kissed her hand at the end and splice in one where he seized her to him and bent her back with a kiss as only a very tall man could do, given her own height. But the memory was a documentary, not a fantasy, and he only kissed her hand, then walked away, leaving her safe on her own doorstep.

Their subsequent first date was safe as houses. No intrigue, no guns.

Pleasant.

She wondered as she put the final touches on her makeup if this Sunday's date would be similar.

She heard the doorbell ring from below, followed a moment later by the squeals of the boys, never ceasing to be astonished by the appearance of the giant that was Sally.

Well, it could be worse, she thought.

She could be listening to a man lecture about beetles.

The Royal Entomological Society was at 41 Queen's Gate, a bright white, five-storey building with a balustrade on the roof that always made Sparks wonder if they were prepared to repel some rival insect-loving group that would attack in a swarm. She walked up the steps under the small portico and opened the door.

An elderly man with white side-whiskers that would not have been out of fashion during Victoria's reign sat at a small folding table in the entrance hall. He scrutinised her as if he were searching for telltale markings on her wings and thorax. Then he brightened in recognition.

"Miss Sparks, is it?" he asked, beaming at her avuncularly.

"It is indeed," she replied. "I'm surprised you remember me, Mr. Gaddis."

"There are not so many young women in the Society that I should forget any," he said. "Welcome back. It has been a while. Still at Cambridge?"

"Not since thirty-nine," she said. "Things got busy."

"Yes, they did," he said, running his fingers down a list. "There you are! Your dues are up to date, thank you very much. The lectures will take place in the meeting room, and tea is set up in the museum. Please restrict yourself to one biscuit, if you would be so kind."

"I will," she promised. "It's good to see you again, sir."

The museum was a large room to the left containing display cases of insects collected from around the world. While nowhere near the size of the collection at the Natural History Museum, it held rarities, many of startling beauty and colouration, all of which had come from locations seen by few humans and brought to England at great personal risk.

The tea was set up at one end, a large metal urn next to stacks of old and, it had to be said, frequently chipped cups with the fading emblems of the society on their sides. A short, cheerful man with a brown toupee that in no way matched the greying hair at his temples poured her a cup the moment she walked in.

"Please, take one," he said, indicating a large tray of biscuits next to the urn.

She laughed to see that they were baked in the forms of either beetles or butterflies.

"I had forgot about these," she said, looking at them in delight.

"I baked them myself," he said proudly. "Made the moulds long ago. I used to decorate them with icing and coloured sugars, but they're impossible to get right now. The butterfly is a northern brown argus, *Aricia artaxerxes*."

"Of course," said Sparks. "And the beetle is a fairy-ring longhorn, isn't it?"

"Got it in one," he said. "*Pseudovadonia livida*. It was a hurdle to get the antennae just right, especially when they have to survive the baking, but I think I did rather well with it. Which would you like, my dear?"

"One comes for the tea, but one stays for the coleoptera," she said with a smile as she plucked a beetle biscuit from the tray.

She wandered through the display cases, wondering at what stories were behind their denizens, what hazards had been braved for each. She nibbled at the biscuit, then sighed with happiness and took a larger bite, savouring the sweetness.

"Sparks?" exclaimed a man behind her. "Iris Sparks, is that you?"

She turned, her mouth still full of biscuit, her eyes widening as she saw the first person her age since she crossed the threshold of the Society. He was slender but fit, with a runner's build evident despite the brown three-piece suit covering it. He was sunburnt in a way no Londoner ever was, and held a large, weather-beaten leather case in his left hand. But most of all, he had that face, the one she had known since childhood, the alert, inquisitive eyes over the roguish smile that had carried over from boyhood and was very much present now.

She held up a finger to forestall him from saying anything else and chewed the biscuit rapidly, following it with a mouthful of tea to clear it.

"Trevor Forester," she said in astonishment. "I thought you were somewhere deep in the Amazon basin."

"I was," he said with a grin. "Came back into town for fresh supplies to find a letter waiting for me. I got the appointment! You are now looking at Professor Forester, Department of Zoology, Oxford!"

"Trevor!" she exclaimed, coming forward to shake his hand. "How utterly fantastic! When do you start?"

"Hilary term, so I have some time to move in and get settled," he said. "I'm going to be at Exeter College. I'm staying at my old digs in London until then, but I wanted to swing by here, say hello to Professor Carpenter, and show him a few oddities I caught."

He patted the leather case.

"Oh, could you give an old friend a sneak peek?" Sparks asked eagerly.

"Isn't that how we got in trouble in school?" he asked with a wink. "Your mother was ready to skin me alive. How is she doing?"

"Ready to do the same to the Conservatives," said Sparks, half laughing, half shuddering. "We don't see each other much, I'm afraid. So show me something!"

"Just for you," he said, reaching into his briefcase and pulling out a small wooden box with a glass lid.

He held it out to her, and she glanced in to see a light greenish-yellow bug with brownish wings, lying on a bed of cotton. Even in death, it looked ready to pounce, its powerful, curved forelegs reminding her of a falcon's talons.

"An assassin bug?" she guessed. "Or—no, some kind of ambush bug."

"Thought you might get it," he said. "But it's not one we've seen before. The armour at the anterior pronotal lobe is unusual in its construction. It's what made me realise it wasn't another *Phymata emarginata*. Once I present and confirm, I get to name it!"

"What fun!" said Sparks. "What are you thinking of calling it?"

"*Phymata sparksiata* has just leapt to the front of the pack," he said.

"Oh, Trevor," she said, blushing to her surprise. "That would be too much of an honour for an amateur enthusiast like me."

"On the contrary, an ambush bug would suit you very well, and vice versa," he said as he put the specimen back in his bag. "Ah, there's Carpenter coming in with Remagen, if I'm not mistaken. I should say hello. Iris, it's tremendous running into you again. We should celebrate. Would you fancy going out with an old chum before he disappears into academe forever?"

I'm dating a gangster, she thought. A gangster who wants to move the relationship to another level. This would be a very bad idea.

But it would be nice to dine with a man who could actually talk about what he did for a change.

"I'd love to," she said.

She pulled out her notepad, scribbled her number on it, then tore it off and handed it to him.

"That's my office number," she said. "Easier to reach me there than at the flat."

"Who are you working for?" he asked as he folded it carefully and put it in his waistcoat pocket. "You were more or less at sea when I ran into you last."

"I've started my own business," she said.

"Really? What sort?"

"A marriage bureau. I'll tell you all about it when we get together. Now, go hobnob with your new boss."

She watched as he went over to Professor Carpenter, the president of the society, a man in his mid-sixties with fine grey hair and black-rimmed glasses. Next to him was a man in his forties, wearing a worn tweed jacket over a green vest, his tie knotted haphazardly. He watched intently as Trevor walked up.

Assessing him, thought Sparks. Looking for weaknesses. Expecting them.

There was something cold and predatory in the man's eyes, a look that she had seen in men who had been handpicked for certain missions during the war.

Commandos. Assassins. Killers.

Carpenter greeted Trevor warmly, and a moment later the three men were peering at the specimen he had removed from his case.

"Miss Sparks!" came a woman's voice from her left. "You weren't joking about being a member."

Sparks turned to see Effie Seagrim standing there. The younger woman held up a butterfly biscuit, one of its wings already bitten off.

"These are good, aren't they?" she said. "How are you?"

"Very well, thank you," returned Sparks. "Why would you think I would joke about being a member?"

"Oh, I thought it might be some kind of sales talk," said Miss Seagrim. "Pretend you have the same interests as the new client to ingratiate yourself, that sort of thing."

"No, no," said Sparks. "I've had a passion for beetles since childhood. My membership was a birthday present from my parents when I turned nine. You must be disappointed there weren't any moth-shaped biscuits."

"They're all lepidoptera in the end," said Miss Seagrim. "Looks like the group is moving into the meeting hall. Will you sit with me?"

"I'd be delighted," said Sparks.

They passed by Remagen, who was being greeted by another man she didn't know.

"Your wife won't be coming?" she overheard him ask.

"No," said Remagen. "She's under the weather, unfortunately."

"Well, give her my best," said the man. "I'm looking forward to your presentation."

The two women sat three rows back as Professor Carpenter took his place behind the lectern.

"Welcome, members and guests, to this Special General Meeting of the Royal Entomological Society," he said in a dry voice. "The great advantage of a Special General Meeting, as opposed to an Ordinary General Meeting, is that we may dispense with the reading of the minutes from the previous meeting."

He glanced over the audience.

"However," he continued, a glint of amusement in his eyes, "I have brought the previous set of minutes in case you are so attached to them that you demand their being read anyway."

"No! No!" cried several members of the audience.

"I thought that might be the case," he said. "Our first presenter, Sir Paul Ruddimore, needs no introduction, but insisted that I give one anyway. Sir Paul came to Oxford in 1911. . . ."

Police Constable Hugh Quinton pulled up on his Triumph Speed Twin at the edge of Epping Forest, turned off the engine, and lowered the kickstand into position. He retrieved his kit from the rack behind the seat, then turned to where a man was standing by a path leading into the woods, massive old oaks and hornbeams looming on both sides. The man wore a brown wool coat and a leather cap, and was clutching a leash, the other end of which was connected to the collar of a springer spaniel, which was barking excitedly.

"Good afternoon, sir," said Quinton. "Did you call it in?"

"I did," said the man. "Quiet, Lizzy! My name is Ratchet. Is it only you?"

"County is sending a team over," said Quinton. "I'm to go in and secure the scene. I'll have to send you back out for them."

"The wife's going to be frantic," said Ratchet. "I guess there's no help for that. Come on, then."

They started onto the path, Lizzy straining at the leash.

"How far in?" asked Quinton.

"About a quarter mile," said Ratchet. "Lizzy got excited."

"She seems excitable," observed Quinton.

"Yeah, well more than usual," said Ratchet. "Wouldn't leave the spot, so I gave her the lead. That's when I found the woman."

"Was she on a path?"

"No, but not so far off. There's a bit of a climb there. Golding's Hill, overlooking the pond. People picnic there when the weather's good."

"Anyone else about?"

"No."

Lizzy began to whine.

"Here's where she pulled me off the path," said Ratchet.

"Stop a moment," said Quinton, peering at the ground.

There were boot prints coming and going, paw prints next to them.

"It rained last night," said Quinton.

"It did," agreed Ratchet.

"Would you mind stepping onto that spot there for comparison?"

Ratchet placed his feet onto a patch of bare ground, then stepped back. Quinton looked back and forth.

"Only prints I see are yours and Lizzy's," he said. "So she came from a different direction. Right, let's go in."

The footprints Ratchet had made largely disappeared as they hit the blanket of new-fallen leaves. They walked through the trees, which gradually thinned out as they ascended the hill until they came upon one lone oak overlooking the pond.

She was sitting on the ground, her back against the tree, facing the water. On the ground next to her was her bag, a half-empty bottle of wine, a paper cup, and a book lying open near her right hand.

Quinton motioned for Ratchet to remain where he was, pulled out a Leica camera from his kit, wound it, then took a photograph before he approached. Gently, he placed his fingers on her neck, then her wrist. There was no pulse. He was expecting none, as she hadn't drawn breath the entire time. Her skin was cool to the touch.

"Is this exactly how you found her, sir?" he called to Ratchet, who was keeping a tight grip on Lizzy's leash.

"It is," he said. "I checked for signs of life, of course, but she was cold."

"You didn't touch the bag or anything else?"

"I did not."

"Very good," said Quinton. "Please go back and wait by my motorcycle for the stretcher lads and the doctor."

"Yes, sir," said Ratchet.

He looked mournfully at the woman, then out at the pond, which reflected the colours of the remaining leaves in the late afternoon sun.

"Worse places to go," he said.

"There are," agreed Quinton. "Thank you for your assistance, Mr. Ratchet."

Ratchet left, tugging Lizzy after him, and Quinton turned back to the woman.

In her forties or fifties, he guessed, as he moved in closer with the camera. Dressed nicely. Tweed skirt, heavy wool jumper suitable for the weather. He wouldn't have chosen those heels for walking in the woods, but no matter. He surveyed the scene for footprints, but there were too many leaves.

Something glinted near her hand. He squatted down to see a small glass bottle lying on the ground. He photographed it, then removed a small paper bag from his kit. He inserted a pencil through the lip of the opening to pick the bottle up, read the label, then placed it in the bag.

Morphine, he jotted down in his notebook. *Prescribed for Mrs. Adela Remagen.*

"Is that you, ma'am?" he asked, looking closely at her face.

He glanced at the book and the bottle of wine, then picked up her bag and opened it. The ident carried the same name. He poked through the bag, looking for any note of explanation. There was none, but a folded-up flyer caught his eye. He pulled it out and opened it.

It was from some lonely hearts agency in London with a Mayfair address. He looked back at the late Mrs. Remagen, then down at her left hand.

She wore a wedding ring.

"That's odd," he said to himself.

CHAPTER 5

Next slide, please," said Remagen.

The screen went dark. Then came a close-up of a small, angled pile of dirt with a hole facing the camera. He walked up to it with his pointer.

"If you look closely, you'll get a glimpse of the larva, waiting for its prey," he said.

Indeed, the tips of a tiny pair of mandibles were visible poking out of the edge of the hole.

"I highly recommend, speaking from personal experience, that you not stick a finger down there," he said, drawing a knowing chuckle from the travellers in the audience. "They are hungry little beasts with a tenacious hold. What struck me, of course, was the use of the angular turret construction. I've seen those in the south of India with both *Cicindela aurofasciata* and *Cicindela goryi*—"

"You can actually tell those two apart?" someone called out.

"With practise, yes," replied Remagen. "In any case, this was the first species I had seen in this region with this type of turret at the mouths of the larval tunnels. I found it interesting that the habitats in this area were largely open grass, not all that dissimilar to the southern India regions where the other turret constructors proliferate. The other species of tiger beetle larvae I found in this part of Burma preferred ordinary holes. The advantage of the angular turret over the simple surface hole, of course, is that it conceals the tunnel from more directions as well as from predators flying overhead."

He paused for a moment, grimacing.

"This was a lesson we applied to human warfare," he continued. "The concealed foxhole provided more protection and greater potential for ambush than did the open foxhole. One needed more time to dig it, but it was well worth the effort."

"Gosh," Miss Seagrim whispered to Sparks. "It sounds like he's seen some terrible things."

"After some time, I was able to collect some adult specimens," said Remagen. "Next slide, please."

A magnification of an iridescent blue-green beetle filled the screen, prompting some quietly ecstatic "oohs" from the audience.

"I want a scarf that colour," whispered Sparks.

"My first thought was *Heptodonta arrowi,* of course," said Remagen, "but the size was wrong, and the colour tended more towards the green. It also lacked the pronounced bulges here—"

He tapped with his pointer below the creature's head.

"When I compared it with the *arrowi* in Horn's *2000 Zeichnungen von Cicindelinae,* it was clear that this was something else, something we haven't catalogued yet. Unfortunately, my correspondence to Dr. Horn was not answered before his death, and then the war prevented me from completely submitting my findings to the Society until now. I anticipate that you will agree that I have stumbled upon an undiscovered species. May I add that I consider Dr. Horn to have been a personal mentor as well as a giant in the field, and his contributions to our knowledge of tiger beetles will never be equalled. He will be missed. That concludes my lecture. Thank you."

The audience applauded enthusiastically. The lights were turned back on, and the guests began milling about.

"That was brilliant," said Miss Seagrim. "I must get him to sign my programme. Do you mind if I abandon you for that?"

"Not at all," said Sparks.

She watched as Miss Seagrim joined the group clustering around Remagen, who despite the success of his presentation looked warily at the press of humanity around him. She decided not to add to his discomfort and went instead to greet Professor Carpenter, who looked at her uncertainly.

"How do you do, Professor?" she said. "Iris Sparks, longtime member."

"Ah, that's who you are," he said. "You're not one of mine."

"No, sir. I went to the other place."

"A Cambridge lass, alas. Well, I hope they managed to give you an adequate education."

"I can read and write and identify several hundred different coleoptera, although the latter ability was largely self-taught when I was growing up. Your book on mimicry was a particular favourite."

"Very kind of you to say," he said. "Have you gone on in the field?"

"Sadly, no," she said. "Or at least, not yet, although camouflage and mimicry have been useful aspects of my life over the past several years."

"We can learn much from our six-legged friends," he said. "Thank you for joining us, Miss Sparks."

She left him and headed towards the exit, only to be intercepted by Trevor.

"When would be a good night for our date?" he asked.

"Call me at work tomorrow afternoon," she said. "We'll make a plan."

"Done," he said. "You can tell me all about how you and Moth Girl know each other."

"Of course, you both went to Oxford," said Sparks. "She was behind you, though."

"I was a lecturer and a lab assistant when she came up," he said. "I can tell you a few stories."

"I'm looking forward to them, Trevor," she said.

"Tomorrow, then."

She left, after first sneaking back into the museum to see if any biscuits remained. They had been completely devoured, leaving only a few crumbs on the trays and presumably in the mandibles of the attendees. Sighing with disappointment, she walked out the front door, wondering precisely what Trevor had meant when he said the word "date."

"What do we have here?" asked Santlofer, the medical examiner, as he squatted by the body. "A suicide?"

"You tell me," said Quinton.

"No visible marks or signs of violence. Find any instrumentalities?"

Quinton removed the morphine bottle from the paper bag and held it up for inspection.

"That would certainly do the trick," said Santlofer.

He glanced at the wine bottle and shook his head.

"I wouldn't have chosen a sauvignon blanc for my last drink," he said. "Terrible pairing for morphine. A decent claret would have been my pick."

"I'll remember that," said Quinton. "Any idea when she died?"

"Today, of course," said Santlofer. "Three to four hours ago at a first guess, but I'll give you a better estimate after I complete the examination."

This time, there was an attempt at a pleasant walk that was thwarted when the weather turned decidedly unpleasant. They ducked into the nearest restaurant, where the food was only so-so, and the volume of other people's conversations overwhelmed their own. They gave up and ate their so-so food quickly, skipping dessert and drinks.

After dinner, he drove her home, but pulled the Hornet up to the kerb a few streets short of the house. Gwen immediately knew what was coming.

"May I?" he asked, turning towards her.

"People might see," she said.

"Do you know any people living on this street?"

"No."

"Then the hell with them," he said.

For all of his massive frame, he was a gentle kisser. She tried to let it flow through her, to let her body and nerves respond in a way so that he would know.

And yet.

Don't say it, don't say it, don't say it, she prayed as he released her.

"Is anything wrong?" he asked.

He said it.

"Nothing's wrong, Sally," she said. "Or rather, nothing is wrong with you. I have the board meeting coming up tomorrow, then the court hearing on Tuesday, and I have been on edge and distractible on account of both for the past week."

"I know," he said. "It was my intent to distract you from them."

"You have, Sally," she said in what she hoped was a reassuring voice. "It's been a lovely day, and I'm grateful."

She wanted to bite her tongue off the moment she said it.

He shifted his body back and put the Hornet in gear.

"Gratitude is nice, I suppose," he said, keeping his eyes focused on the road as he drove. "It's not what I hoped for."

"Give me some time," she said. "This is all new again. I'm still figuring it out."

"So am I," he said. "Don't forget, figuring it out can be fun if you let it."

"I hope to be more fun by the end of the week," she said.

"Then let's do this again next Sunday," he said as he pulled up. "Practise, practise, practise. Yes?"

"All right," she replied. "Next Sunday."

"And may I ring you up Tuesday evening to find out how it went?"

"I would like that very much, Sally," she said. "Thank you for putting up with me."

"It's a chore, but I'm bearing up under it," he said with an exaggerated sigh.

He got out, then came around and opened the door for her.

"Say hello to the boys for me," he said as she got out.

"I will," she promised.

Then, on impulse, she stood up on her toes, placed her hands on his shoulders, and kissed him quickly.

"People might see," he said, bemused. "Especially people you know."

"The hell with them," she replied.

She walked down the driveway, then the front walk. She turned at the door before going in.

He was still standing by the passenger door, as if the touch of her lips had paralysed him. She waved. The wave he gave in return made him seem both hopeful and forlorn, she thought.

Or was she projecting her own feelings onto him?

She went inside and slipped quietly up the stairs before anyone could interrogate her about her evening.

Quinton pulled out his torch to read the house numbers as he slowly cruised down Maresfield Gardens in Hampstead, searching for the Remagens' address. The houses were all brick, turn-of-the-century constructions, three storeys high with small patches of grass or garden in front and small alleys separating them. The Remagen house had a central bay tower thrusting forward, with steps to the right of it leading up to the front door. There were lights on inside. No vehicles in front, so he pulled his Triumph into the small driveway and parked.

He dismounted, removed his helmet, and ran his fingers through his hair. He wondered for the first time if there were any children. That would make things more difficult, but there was no help for that. No help for any of it now. He sighed, then walked up the front steps and rang the bell.

He heard footsteps approaching quickly, then the door was virtually flung open. A middle-aged man stood there, blinking uncertainly when he saw Quinton. Then a look of sad and terrible resignation settled through him, his shoulders sagging under it.

"What happened?" he asked.

"Are you Mr. Potiphar Remagen?" asked Quinton.

"I am."

"I'm Police Constable Hugh Quinton of the Essex Police, Loughton Station. Do you know an Adela Remagen?"

"She's my wife," said Remagen.

"I'm afraid I have some bad news regarding Mrs. Remagen, sir," said Quinton, mustering up as much official sympathy as he could. "May I come in?"

"Certainly," said Remagen, stepping back and waving vaguely at the interior.

Quinton went past him into the entry hall as Remagen closed the door.

"We'll use the front parlour," said Remagen as he led him to the left. "Don't be afraid of my pets."

"That's all right, sir, I like animals," said Quinton.

Then he stopped short, gaping.

The front parlour had a few rudimentary pieces of furniture: a quartet of armchairs surrounded a low table in the center. The rest of the room was filled with terraria of all sizes, resting on side tables or stacked on homemade shelves reaching up to the ceiling. As Remagen turned on the light, insects, snakes, and lizards began to skitter or slither about, their circadian routines disrupted. Quinton could hear their footsteps drumming against the sides of the glass. At least, he thought he could.

When he had said he liked animals, he meant mammals. Domesticated mammals, the kinds that sat on your lap and allowed you to rub their bellies in exchange for contented sighs and adoring glances.

He was absolutely certain that he didn't want to have anything he saw in that room sit on his lap, nor was he inclined to rub any of their bellies, or thoraxes, or whatever they were called.

"Please sit," said Remagen, indicating one of the armchairs.

"That's all right, sir," said Quinton, wondering if anything lived in the chair. "I prefer to stand. But you should sit, sir."

Remagen sat in an armchair and looked at Quinton.

"Very well, Constable," he said. "Tell me."

"A woman we've preliminarily identified as Adela Remagen was found in Epping Forest this afternoon," said Quinton. "She was dead, sir."

"So that's where she had got to," said Remagen, more to himself than Quinton. "How did she die?"

"The pathologist will be making that determination, sir," said Quinton. "But I found this by her."

He pulled the bottle from the bag and held it up for Remagen, who looked at it carefully, then nodded.

"That's hers," he said.

"Could you tell me why she had it, Mr. Remagen?"

"It's Professor Remagen, if you don't mind," he replied.

"Of course, Professor. Might your field have something to do with these—pets of yours?"

"I'm a zoologist," said Remagen.

"You study animals."

"Yes," said Remagen. "Primarily insects. I am, or was at Mandalay College. That's in Burma."

"I know where Mandalay is, Professor," said Quinton. "I take it you came to England because of the war."

"We did," said Remagen. "Then I went back there with the Army. A—a special unit. Adela stayed here."

"In this house?"

"It was her grandmother's. She was still living here when we came to London, but passed away in 1941 and left it to Adela. But you were asking about the morphine, weren't you?"

"Yes, sir," said Quinton, trying not to meet the bulbous eyes of a large lizard that was looking at him speculatively.

"She had lung cancer," said Remagen. "She never told me while I was in the service. She didn't want to concern me. But she was fighting it the entire time I was fighting the Japs. And losing the battle. It must have become too much for her."

"Do you believe that she took her own life, sir?" asked Quinton gently.

"What else could it be?" asked Remagen. "I can't fault her for wanting to end the pain. I only wish—"

He stopped short.

"You wish what, sir?"

"I wish that she would have let me know first," said Remagen. "I would have helped her through it somehow."

"That would have been a crime, sir."

"I know, I know," said Remagen, leaning back in his chair and rubbing the bridge of his nose.

"When did you last see Mrs. Remagen?"

"This morning, as I was leaving for my lecture."

"Your lecture?"

"I was giving a presentation at the Royal Entomological Society," he said.

"I'm afraid I don't know what that is, Professor. Who are they?"

"Students of the insect world," said Remagen.

"I guess it takes all kinds," said Quinton. "Where was this lecture?"

"At Forty-One Queen's Gate."

"What time did you leave here?"

"Around ten this morning. I wanted to get there early to sort out my slides."

"You skipped church for that?"

"We are not churchgoing people," said Remagen, some huffiness slipping into his voice.

"And when did you return?"

"Perhaps an hour ago. I dined with the president and other senior members after the lecture. When I came home, she wasn't here."

"Was that unusual?"

Remagen hesitated.

"It was, quite frankly," he said. "We were both—I wouldn't say excited, but keen on the presentation. I thought she would be waiting to debrief me about it. It was a major event in my world. I was hoping to establish my credentials in the United Kingdom in hopes of finding a position at one of the universities here."

"You weren't going back to Burma?"

"Not with her medical treatment continuing in London."

"Of course. So when you came home and she wasn't here, did you think of telephoning the police?"

"And say what?" asked Remagen. "That I was out all day, and when I returned, my wife wasn't home? What would they have said?"

"True enough," conceded Quinton. "Any idea why she would have wanted to go to Epping Forest to—for any reason?"

"I can't imagine any. As far as I know, she's never been there. I've never been there."

"Do you know if she liked poetry?"

"Poetry?" exclaimed Remagen. "What an extraordinary question."

"She had a book of poetry with her. English Romantics. Did she read poetry?"

"There are plenty of books in the house," said Remagen. "I'm sure there are some poetry collections among them. I'm sorry, why are you asking all these questions?"

"Routine when it's a death by unnatural causes, sir," said Quinton. "The more we know, the quicker the coroner can make his findings."

"The coroner. So there will be an inquest?"

"Yes, sir. He'll be asking you the same questions, I should think. We'll need you to come make a formal identification."

He pulled out a notepad and jotted down the medical examiner's address in Chelmsford, then tore it off.

"I will see you there in the morning, Professor," he said as he handed it to him. "I'm very sorry for your loss, sir."

Remagen let him out without shaking hands. Quinton put on his helmet, climbed onto the Triumph, and turned on the ignition. He drove north for a few minutes, then braked until he was motionless, staring at a cluster of trees silhouetted against the dark sky.

"Why did you come to Epping Forest, Mrs. Remagen?" he said out loud. "Why come all the way there to bother us, when you had Hampstead Heath right in the neighbourhood? What made our forest so special?"

CHAPTER 6

The cab pulled up at the entrance to the docks. The cabbie looked down their length, which disappeared into the fog that was rolling in from the Thames, then looked back uncertainly at Gwen.

"Are you sure this is the place, ma'am?" he asked.

"I'm sure," she replied as she paid the fare.

"Do you want me to wait?"

"No."

"It doesn't look safe."

"If I wanted safe, then I wouldn't have come here," she said coolly.

She got out of the cab and stood at the entrance. She took a deep breath, the cold air coursing through her lungs, then began to walk forward.

She was wearing black. All black. Widow's weeds, the bodice of Courtauld crape that clung to her like a second skin as she walked into the cool mists, surmounted by a fine mesh that extended up to the top of her neck and spread down her arms to her wrists as if pulled there by teams of spiders, all of it interwoven with patterns of tiny black roses that set off the paleness underneath.

The first whistles came from a trawler docked to her left. Out of the corner of her eye, she saw sailors gathering on the deck to ogle her, warehousemen doing the same from the doorways to her right. The whistles became catcalls, some in English, some in other languages, but she ignored them and strode on imperiously. The men quieted as she passed by, wondering whether she was Death incarnate or merely one of her handmaidens. Behind the veil hanging from her hat, she smiled slightly, amused by the power of her appearance.

The fog grew thick around her, swirling about. Sharp, cold needles of water pierced the mesh, stinging her exposed skin in a thousand places.

There. His shop. BURTON'S CARPENTRY proclaimed a sign jutting out over the entrance. She paused, gathered her skirts with one hand, then went through the door.

The bell gave out a harsh jangle, and he looked up from where he was planing a worktable, his arms tensed under the effort. He wasn't expecting to see anyone, much less her, for his shirt was off, tossed carelessly onto a nearby counter. Sweat soaked through his undershirt.

He laid down his plane and picked up a cloth.

"Excuse me, ma'am," he said, wiping his hands. "You surprised me. I wasn't expecting anyone."

"Good," she said, raising her veil. "Then we're alone."

His eyes, those eyes which were the colour of the oceans, grew wide in recognition.

"Mrs. Bainbridge," he said.

"Gwen," she said. "Or Sophie, if you prefer. That's how you first knew me. Hello, Des."

"What are you doing here?"

"I told you I would come back."

"You said you weren't free."

She walked towards him, unpinning her hat and setting it on the counter next to the crumpled shirt.

"I'm free now," she said, putting her arms around him.

He pushed her away, but she could see the reluctance in his eyes.

"I'm engaged," he said. "Me and Fanny—"

"I've heard."

"So you and me can't—"

She put her arms around him again, this time linking her fingers together. This time, he didn't resist.

"Silly man," she whispered. "I didn't come here to marry you."

Then she kissed him, and the thousand cold places on her skin grew warm again. She reached behind her and patted the table he had been working on.

"It feels sturdy," she said, her eyes still locked on his, the oceans roiling now. "Will it hold me?"

"It will," he said.

"Will it hold us both?" she asked, her breath catching.

He put his hands on her hips and lifted her easily onto the table.

"Let's find out," he said.

She woke up suddenly, her breath coming in gasps, the clouds woven into the canopy of her four-poster gradually coming into focus. She covered her eyes with her hands, trying to summon the dream back, but she couldn't.

"Damn," she whispered to the empty room.

"I went to Potiphar Remagen's lecture," Iris said the next morning at The Right Sort.

"What was he like?" asked Gwen. "And please confine your remarks to areas neither involving the creepy nor the crawly."

"That may be difficult," said Iris. "They do seem to be his entire life. He came alive when he talked about them, but the moment the lights came up and people appeared, he wanted to scuttle for cover."

"Did you speak with him?"

"No, I felt I would be appearing under false pretences if I did that, and in any case, he was being quite beset by the attendees. He looked miserable. It's odd that a man brave enough to be an explorer and a commando could be so put off by a gaggle of harmless entomologists."

"Maybe it's his dislike of people that makes him go into places where people don't go," suggested Gwen.

"Perhaps," said Iris. "Oh, and our Miss Seagrim was in attendance."

"Was she? How did she react to him?"

"Like a teenager swooning over James Mason."

"Well, that should make it easier when the time comes."

"How was your date with Sally?" asked Iris, studiously keeping her gaze on the file cards on her desk.

"Didn't he tell you?" replied Gwen.

"I made a point after our last conversation on the topic not to discuss it with him," replied Iris. "Besides, if he wanted to cry on my shoulder, he would have to bend in half, and that would be too ridiculous a sight to arouse my sympathy. Does he need a shoulder to cry on?"

"I shouldn't think so," said Gwen.

"So the date—"

"The date was fine," said Gwen.

"Only fine?"

"This is tiresome," said Gwen with an exasperated sigh. "We strolled around the Strand, we ate at an inexpensive Italian restaurant, then he drove me home. And yes, he kissed me, so you may check that box. Satisfied?"

"Are you?" asked Iris.

"How long did it take you to load that question?"

"When one's best friend arrives at the office in an irritated mood, one tends to think that the weekend did not go well. What happened?"

"Nothing happened."

"Did you want something to happen?"

"No," said Gwen miserably. "I didn't. I really didn't. Sally is a sweet, kind, gentle man, and I want him to be happy. I don't think I'm the woman who will make him happy."

"First, he isn't gentle," said Iris. "He's trying to be gentle for your sake. You know what he did in the war."

"Not the specifics, but yes."

"If he's ever in a mood to share the specifics, be ready to have a month of nightmares after," said Iris.

"And second?" asked Gwen. "You said that was the first thing."

"The second thing is that you can make him happy quite easily," said Iris. "He's fallen for you."

"I know," said Gwen.

"So stop pretending it's about what he wants. What do you want?"

"I want—" Gwen began. Then she hesitated.

"Go on," urged Iris.

"I want to feel what I felt with Ronnie," said Gwen. "Not just love. That excitement. The rush of feelings, the racing of the heart, the loss—"

She stopped again.

"The loss of what?" asked Iris sympathetically.

"The loss of control, but in a good way," said Gwen.

"Sounds like we're speaking about sex," said Iris.

"How do you manage it?" asked Gwen. "To separate it from love the way you do?"

"I suppose I enjoy it too much to wait for love to come around," said Iris.

"You don't love Archie."

It was a statement, not a question, thought Iris.

"I'm not sure," she said.

"Yet you sleep with him."

"Yes," said Iris. "You think that's wrong of me."

"No, I don't," said Gwen. "At least, I try not to. I was raised with a very narrow and uninformed view of such things, and I came to realise that isn't how the world really is, or should be. Sex is a part of this world, even in England. And when I married Ronnie, it was wonderful beyond wonderful. Then I lost him."

"You lost him over two years ago," said Iris. "When was the last time you were actually together?"

"September of forty-two," said Gwen. "He had a brief leave. We made the most of it. Then he went over to Tunisia with the Royal Fusiliers."

"So over two years since you lost him, but over four since you—made the most of it, to borrow your euphemism."

"Yes," said Gwen.

"You were faithful to him while he was alive."

"Of course."

"And faithful to his ghost ever since."

Gwen nodded silently.

"Gwen, may I point out something?" Iris asked gently.

"Could I possibly prevent you?" returned Gwen.

"You can't duplicate anything you experienced with Ronnie," said Iris. "Hell, you can't even experience any of those same feelings even if you did find a man you wanted. You're a decade older than that teenager who fell in love, years past the young woman who married and made love to him. You're a different woman, physically and emotionally."

"But you manage to keep on with it."

"I had the most intense, the most passionate relationship I've ever had when I was in my early twenties," said Iris. "I haven't had anything remotely close to that since then. And I lost him through my own stupidity, not because the war claimed him, so I get to carry that around with me."

"That was with Mike Kinsey?" asked Gwen.

"Yes," said Iris. "And maybe I'll never match it again, but that's no reason to deny myself the pleasures involved for the rest of my life."

"You're saying that pleasure should be enough."

"No, no, absolutely not," said Iris. "But don't deprive yourself of it along the way."

"Then I should make love to Sally?"

"Does he excite you sufficiently?"

Gwen hesitated, then slowly shook her head.

"I keep hoping that he will," she said.

"Has any man you've met recently?"

Gwen blushed.

"Out with it," said Iris immediately.

"I had a dream last night," said Gwen.

"Dreams can be fun," said Iris. "Was this one of them?"

"I woke right as things were getting interesting."

"How so?"

"Let's just say I was being a much merrier widow than I am normally."

"That's good," declared Iris. "That means you still have that capability within you. May I ask without going into detail—"

"I'm saving the details for my session with Dr. Milford this Thursday, but go ahead and ask."

"Who was the object of your desire?"

"Do you remember Des Burton?" asked Gwen.

"Tillie La Salle's cousin? The carpenter with the physique of Adonis, only with more muscular forearms?"

"Stop."

"He's worth a dream or two. Do you want to chase that dream when you get your status restored?"

"No," said Gwen. "It wouldn't work in real life. You know it and I know it."

"Still, you might—"

"No," said Gwen.

"Do you mind if I dream about Des occasionally?"

"Be my guest."

"It's interesting that you had that dream after your date with Sally," Iris pointed out.

"Not necessarily."

"I see," said Iris. "Will you promise me something?"

"What?"

"When the time comes, please let him down gently, will you?"

"I will," said Gwen.

There was a knock at the door, and they looked over to see Miss Forsberg.

"I'm so sorry I didn't call ahead," she said breathlessly. "Is this a good time?"

"Please, come in," said Sparks, motioning her to a seat. "Are you here without your—"

She was on the verge of saying "keeper," but caught herself in time.

"Your father?" she asked, completing it safely.

"I am," said Miss Forsberg, beaming with pride and excitement. "I told him I was coming here, and he let me go without a peep! I'm going to sneak in some shopping before I go back. I must say signing up for your service has had some unexpected benefits."

"We're so glad we could provide you some freedom," said Sparks. "Did you have your date with Mr. Merriman?"

"Yesterday," she said, her expression changing to chagrin. "That's why I'm here. It—it didn't go very well."

"Really?" said Sparks, concealing her disappointment. "What happened?"

"Oh, he was nice enough, I suppose," she replied. "But that town in Canada where he lives, that he's going back to—it's so small. I mean, I think there're more people living within three streets of me than there are there, and there're no shops or cinemas for miles."

"Miss Forsberg, you did specify travel as being important to you," Sparks pointed out.

"I know, I know," said Miss Forsberg miserably. "I didn't think it through. I want to see wonderful places, then come back home again with lots of holiday snaps for my scrapbook. And I don't even have a camera yet. Or a scrapbook."

"Very well," said Sparks, pulling out Miss Forsberg's card and making a note on it. "More of a holiday adventurer than an explorer."

"Yes, that's it!" said Miss Forsberg enthusiastically. "I'm sorry if I wasn't clearer. I've never done this before."

"Well, it's better to find these things out earlier than later," said Sparks. "We once—"

The overhead light flickered suddenly with a slight buzz.

"Please don't be another blackout," muttered Sparks. "They've been coming at the worst times."

Miss Forsberg was staring intently at the light.

"That's not a blackout," she said decidedly. "You've got a problem with the wiring. You should talk to your building manager about that."

"You haven't met our Mr. MacPherson," said Sparks with a laugh. "He'd electrocute himself and burn the building down if we called him in."

"I could fix it in a jiff," she offered. "I could fetch my kit and come back if you like."

"No need," said Sparks. "Mr. MacPherson can bring in someone, assuming he can pry open our landlord's purse for the fee. Very well, we will rethink your candidates and get back to you."

"Thank you for stopping by," said Mrs. Bainbridge, who had been watching Miss Forsberg closely the entire time.

"Bye, then," chirped Miss Forsberg. "I'm off to the shops!"

She practically skipped out of the office.

"Interesting," commented Gwen.

"Irritating," said Sparks. "She could have saved us some time, not to mention wasting dates with two perfectly fine gentlemen. Why did you think her interesting? You were remarkably quiet this time."

"Remember when I told you I thought she was lying to us?"

"Yes?"

"Now, I'm certain of it," said Gwen. "And I know exactly what to do about it."

"What?" asked Iris.

Gwen opened her box of cards, searched through them, and pulled one out. She held it up.

"Barty Culpepper?" exclaimed Iris. "Never in a thousand years! He's not a world traveller. He hasn't even been to the seaside on holiday."

"Tuppence says I'm right," said Gwen, holding out her hand. "Bet?"

"I hate taking your money," said Iris, shaking it. "No, actually, I enjoy taking your money. Bet."

CHAPTER 7

Hilary McIntyre had given Gwen a brief tour of the offices of Bainbridge, Limited, at the end of the summer, but he hadn't shown her the boardroom.

"When you're fully invested, you'll see it," he promised her then. "For the moment, it's our secret clubroom."

She wondered now as she turned onto Threadneedle Street how he and the rest of the board members would react to her being introduced into their private sanctuary. Prematurely introduced, to boot.

The firm was located in a stolid, sturdy, stone structure on a street of similar buildings, seemingly forbidding the introduction of any colour other than grey into the surroundings. Nancy, the receptionist, smiled when she saw her enter.

"Mrs. Bainbridge, welcome back," she said. "Mrs. Stebbins will be right down."

"Thank you, Nancy," replied Gwen.

Nancy plugged a line into a jack and picked up her handset.

"I have Mrs. Bainbridge for you, Mrs. Stebbins," she said into it. "Yes, ma'am."

Carlotta Stebbins had been the office manager for as long as Gwen had been part of the Bainbridge family, and employed by the company since she was hired as an assistant bookkeeper in 1917. She was a crisp, no-nonsense woman who feared no one and tolerated no inefficiency. The sound of her heels clicking quickly towards the door behind Nancy caused a noticeable stiffening in the young woman's normally ebullient demeanour.

A moment later, Mrs. Stebbins came through the door. She was a medium-height brunette dressed in a classically cut reddish-brown cardigan suit.

"Mrs. Bainbridge, good afternoon," she said, coming forward to shake Gwen's hand. "Lord Morrison asked me to take you up. I've rung for the lift."

"We could take the stairs," offered Gwen, but Mrs. Stebbins was already tapping her foot impatiently in front of the lift doors.

They opened seconds later, and Mrs. Stebbins beckoned to Gwen to join her.

"Momentous occasion," she commented as the lift attendant closed the doors and the inner gate. "Old Lord Bainbridge would have dropped dead of a heart attack to see a woman in the boardroom."

"Fortunately, his son has already had a heart attack and still knows I'm coming," said Gwen, drawing a quick smile from the older woman.

"Lord Bainbridge has been sounding more himself on the telephone lately," said Mrs. Stebbins. "I hope he'll be back with us soon."

So does his wife, thought Gwen.

The doors opened, and Mrs. Stebbins led her into a large room filled with several young women and men at desks, some typing furiously away, some speaking on telephones. They looked up as the two women crossed through, their expressions of curiosity at Gwen's appearance immediately vanishing as Mrs. Stebbins's glare swept across them like a searchlight.

She led Gwen to a smaller room containing three desks, the largest of which had her name on a small placard. The two others were placed across from hers, each commanding a quarter of the room against her half. The two women seated behind them rose as they entered.

"I don't expect you to remember everyone's name," said Mrs. Stebbins. "Nor do I have time to reintroduce them all, but this is Miss Ginger FitzGibbons, my assistant."

"How do you do, Mrs. Bainbridge?" said a young woman who could have sprung from the same mould that had once produced Mrs. Stebbins.

"And this is Miss Melanie St. John, assistant to the head of our accounting department."

Miss St. John was a pale, nervous woman with blond hair like late summer straw. She wore a dark blue wool suit over a cream-coloured blouse.

"Mrs. Bainbridge, it's good to see you up and about," she said, stammering slightly.

"Mrs. Bainbridge has been up and about for some time, Miss St. John," said Mrs. Stebbins.

"No, no, of course, I didn't mean that," Miss St. John said hastily. "It's just that I thought, you know, there had been a recent incident of some kind, I'm sure I don't know all the details."

"A mild concussion, from which I've quite recovered," said Gwen, reassuringly. "I was still healing when I visited here last. Thank you for your concern."

"I'm sure we are all glad to see her back," said Mrs. Stebbins, giving Miss St. John a glare that made the poor woman turn even paler, something Gwen wouldn't have believed possible. "Come this way, Mrs. Bainbridge."

Despite his acting status, Lord Morrison had not taken over Lord Bainbridge's office, choosing instead a more modest one adjoining the one shared by the three women. He came immediately out from behind his desk when the two women entered and took Gwen's hand between his, smiling warmly.

"Here you are at last," he said.

"Oh, dear, am I late?" asked Gwen.

"No, not at all," he said. "I mean, here you are at last, taking your proper place at Bainbridge, and don't go on about that ridiculous court hearing getting in the way. Are you ready to see the boardroom?"

"Goodness, I feel like I'm being taken to an underground crypt with a hidden treasure room, the way you've all behaved about it," said Gwen with a laugh that she didn't truly feel. "Take me to your secret lair."

He offered his arm, which she took, and led her down a hallway to a pair of double doors at the end. He produced a set of keys, and chose one with an air of solemnity that he broke with a wink.

"When all is said and done, it's merely a large room with a large table," he said. "But you will be the first woman to enter here who was neither a secretary nor pushing a tea cart."

"You've left out the charwoman," Mrs. Stebbins pointed out. "And may I remind you, Lord Morrison, that I am no secretary and I haven't pushed a tea cart in twenty years."

"Correct as always, Mrs. Stebbins," said Morrison. "I should have said, Gwendolyn, that you will be the first woman to enter this room who is not an employee of Bainbridge, Limited. The world is turning faster, isn't it?"

"Sometimes too fast, and sometimes not fast enough," said Gwen.

"Mrs. Stebbins, would you mind waiting for the others to arrive?" asked Lord Morrison. "I would like a few moments to help Mrs. Bainbridge acclimate herself to her surroundings."

"Certainly, Lord Morrison," replied Mrs. Stebbins.

She turned on her heels and walked back down the hall. Morrison waited until she vanished around a corner, then turned the key and pushed open the double doors.

The room was thirty feet deep, with an immense mahogany

table running most of its length. There were seven high-backed chairs around it, one larger than the others at the far end. The chairs were backed with deep red leather panels attached by gleaming brass studs. At one side of the room was a chestnut sideboard, elaborately carved with figures of kudus and antelopes. Bottles of sherry and whisky stood at the ready on top.

But what primarily caught Gwen's attention were the giant portraits mounted on the walls surrounding the room. There was Harold at the far end behind the large chair, but a much younger Harold, with a full head of brown hair, dressed in some artist's fancy of explorer's garb, complete with topi. The artist had caught Harold's glare perfectly, and she wondered if he had demanded that expression as reinforcement for the older, three-dimensional version that would normally dominate the room.

To the right of that was another figure that she recognised immediately, dressed similarly to Harold, but with an amused smile, as if the idea of anyone wanting his portrait seemed ridiculous.

"That's you, isn't it?" she said, turning to Morrison. "I've never seen pictures of you in your twenties."

"I cut quite the dashing figure back then, didn't I?" Morrison chuckled.

"And still do," said Gwen, walking into the room. "I'm sure the ladies—"

Then she stopped in mid-sentence, freezing on the spot.

There, looking out at her with the mischievous glint that would always draw forth her own, was Ronnie. He was wearing battle dress, the insignia of the Royal Fusiliers evident, his flat-topped cap with the red-and-white hackle tilted rakishly.

"When was this done?" she asked, her voice shaking. "I've never seen it before."

"Before he shipped out," said Morrison. "I'm sorry, I had no idea you didn't know about it. I would have prepared you. Ronnie was supposed to have sat for it when he ascended to the board on his twenty-first birthday, but he never took his responsibilities seriously. His shares had been voted by a guardian until then."

"Who was Harold, of course. Ronnie rarely attended the board meetings when I—when I knew him."

"I'm sure he felt he had better things to do," said Morrison, glancing at her with a smile. "When Ronnie joined the Fusiliers in thirty-nine, Harold wanted to get his portrait up with the other board members before—well, in case anything happened. He had the Devil's own time convincing him to do it. Harold wanted him in full-dress uniform, of course, but Ronnie was a stubborn lad."

"Oh, yes, he was," said Gwen, smiling as a panoply of memories quickly rose, then fell. "Something he inherited from his father."

"No doubt. In any event, we will want you to sit for your portrait once you are fully invested."

"It would be an honour," she said, her eyes still transfixed.

She finally pulled herself away and looked at the others. Alexander Birch, Hilary McIntyre, and Townsend Phillips—all the rich young men who invested their inheritances wisely decades ago, whose preserved visages now looked both sage and smug in retrospect.

There was a large, blank space on the wall between the portraits of McIntyre and Phillips. Gwen walked over to it.

"Burleigh's place, I take it," she said to Morrison.

"Given recent events, we thought it would be inappropriate for him to be hanging here," he replied. "We have a few minutes before the others arrive. Sherry?"

"I think I ought to go through my first board meeting sober, don't you?"

"A little nip beforehand to ease the tensions always helped me," said Morrison, pouring himself a small one.

He turned to her, the glass held in salute.

"To your return to your proper place in the world, Gwendolyn," he said.

"Thank you, Tom," she said.

He downed it in one go, then pulled a chair from against the wall and placed it next to the one to the left of the large chair at the head of the table.

"I don't take Harold's seat out of respect," he said. "Also, he had it made with longer legs to compensate for his height, so I end up floating above the table looking ridiculous. Please sit by me."

"Where will Mr. Parson sit?" she asked.

"Across from us," said Morrison. "As the representative of the other majority holder."

He held her chair as she sat, then took his own seat. There was a leather-bound ledger in front of him. He opened it, removed a sheaf of papers from inside, and spread them out on the table.

"And now we wait," he said.

The intercom buzzed. Iris pressed the lever.

"Yes, Saundra?"

"A telephone call from a Mr. Trevor Forester," said Mrs. Billington.

"I'll take it. Thank you."

She picked up her phone, her mind filling with second thoughts.

"Hello, Trevor," she said.

"Hello, Iris," he replied. "I hope I didn't catch you at a bad time."

"No live clientele in front of me, and my partner is away from her desk, so this is perfect timing."

"Excellent. So, when are you free for our date?"

That word again, she thought. It's time to define terms.

"Trevor," she said, "when you say 'date,' what precisely are you expecting?"

"You know, the usual sort of thing. Casual conversation concealing the smouldering passions lying dormant underneath, inevitably and inexorably rousing the sleeping dragons, leading to some frenzied, primitive mating ritual that will—"

"I am seeing someone, Trevor," she interrupted. "You should know that before you launch into the casual conversation, much less any dragon rousing."

"Iris, whatever milquetoast you've been settling for while the real men were at war, you should know that he's no match for a genuine, bona fide jungle explorer," said Trevor. "The musculature of my right bicep alone from all of that machete-swinging would send him screaming for mum in short order. What sort of chap is he?"

"He's a spiv," said Iris.

There was a moment of silence at the other end.

"A spiv, you said," came his voice at last.

"A spiv," she repeated. "From the East End."

"And, just for the purpose of my own edification, roughly how high up the organisational ladder is this spiv of yours?"

"He runs the gang," said Iris. "Do you think I would settle for a mere flunky?"

"No, of course not," said Trevor. "Well. That puts a different light on the matter. So dating you under these circumstances might potentially be a life-threatening endeavour."

"Might be," agreed Iris.

"'Twas ever thus," said Trevor. "Challenge accepted. Dinner Wednesday. I'll pick you up at your office at five thirty."

This is a bad idea getting worse, she thought. Don't go sailing into the misty, uncharted waters. Turn back now!

"All right," she said. "But only conversation."

"Casual conversation," he corrected her.

"Of course," she said. "What other kind is there? Goodbye, Trevor."

"Goodbye, Iris."

She hung up, then stared at the telephone, already regretting her decision.

Here there be dragons, she thought glumly.

* * *

Alexander Birch was the first to arrive, dressed as if he had come straight from his country manor in tweeds and boots.

"Hallo, Tom, and what's this?" he exclaimed as he came through the doors. "What vision lies before me? A veritable angel descended from Heaven to bless our enterprise!"

"It's good to see you again, Sandy," said Gwen.

"Tom brought you in as a guest, I hear," said Birch.

"He did. He wants me to get used to all of this before it becomes official."

"That's the story he gave you," said Birch. "But I think he really wanted all of us to get used to the prospect of having you among us. I must say if you keep up appearances like today, the chances of our getting any work done will be slim."

"I'll try to dress more drably in the future," said Gwen.

"Don't you dare," he said. "There's plenty of drab to go around. Stay as you are, Mrs. Bainbridge, and you will rejuvenate all of us old men."

Dear God, she thought as she forced a smile. Am I doomed to monthly onslaughts of elderly flirtation?

The doors opened briefly to admit Miss FitzGibbons, who was holding a steno pad. She took a seat in a chair in the corner and virtually disappeared.

Hilary McIntyre, equally old and equally effusive, was the next board member to arrive. As Gwen came forward to receive his overenthusiastic handshake, she saw over his shoulder through the half-opened doors Oliver Parson at the far end of the hallway, stopped in earnest conversation with someone mostly concealed by the doorway in which she stood. All Gwen could see was a sliver of navy blue skirt and the tip of one matching pump.

Parson concluded his conversation and turned towards the boardroom with an expression she had never seen on his face before. A smile. Actual happiness, if she read it right. Which vanished the moment he saw her, immediately replaced by the scowl that Gwen knew all too well.

He strode towards her at a furious pace. She involuntarily backed away a few steps, pulling McIntyre, who had yet to relinquish her hand, with her.

"So you showed up," said Parson when he came through the doors.

"I showed up," said Gwen. "Good afternoon, Mr. Parson."

"She's my guest, Parson," said Morrison from his chair.

"Ridiculous and unnecessary," said Parson, brushing past her to take a seat across from Morrison.

"No need to be rude, Parson," McIntyre admonished him.

"Gentlemen, and Mrs. Bainbridge, I suggest we take our seats," said Morrison, glancing at his watch. "I expect Mr. Phillips will join us late."

"As usual," grumbled Parson.

Morrison held Gwen's chair for her, for which she gave a grateful smile. As McIntyre and Birch sat, there was a clatter of hasty footsteps from the hall, and Townsend Phillips burst through the doors.

"Sorry, sorry, everyone," he said, closing them behind him, then leaning against them, gasping for breath. "Thought I had timed it perfectly, but you know how it is. Oh, and hello, Mrs. Bainbridge! Didn't expect you this month."

"I did tell you I was inviting her," said Morrison.

"Did you?" replied Phillips, going to the sideboard and pouring himself a glass of water. "I suppose you did. In any case, there she is, hello again. I take it we haven't started yet."

"Take your seat, Townsend, and we will," said Morrison.

Phillips took the seat closest to the door, mopping his brow with a handkerchief.

Morrison looked around the table in front of him for a moment, searching through his papers.

"Forgot my gavel," he said with a brief laugh. He rapped his knuckles on the table. "It is the eleventh, the second Monday of November 1946, and the members of the board of Bainbridge, Limited, are gathered for the monthly meeting. As secretary and acting chief executive officer, I call this meeting to order. I shall now call the roll. General partners: Lord Harold Bainbridge is not present. Has anyone here been designated his proxy?"

He looked around the table. The others shook their heads.

"Lord Harold Bainbridge is absent, and no proxy shall be voting his shares at this meeting," he said as Miss FitzGibbons jotted it down. "We continue to wish him a speedy recovery. Mrs. Gwendolyn Bainbridge."

Gwen started to answer, but stopped as Morrison laid two fingers gently on her wrist.

"Oliver Parson," said Parson, looking at her with contempt. "Appointed as committee for Mrs. Gwendolyn Bainbridge by order of the Master of the Court of Lunacy, dated the twenty-fifth of March 1944. I shall continue to act on her behalf."

"Oliver Parson, present," said Morrison.

The other men at the table refused to meet her eyes, though she had the momentary fancy that the portraits of their younger selves were watching her from inside their frames.

I am the elephant in the living room, she thought.

"Limited partners," continued Morrison. "I'm here, obviously. Alexander Birch."

"Present."

"Hilary McIntyre."

"Here."

"Townsend Phillips."

"Here."

"Stephen Burleigh."

Morrison looked around the table again.

"Mr. Burleigh is absent yet again," he said with a sigh. "Has anyone been designated as his proxy? Hearing no answer, we still have sufficient voting shares to declare a quorum. Now—"

Before he could complete the sentence, a commotion was heard outside the doors. A man was arguing with a woman, the two coming rapidly closer. Then the doors burst open, and a lean, young man with messy brown hair and a moustache that needed trimming bounded into the room, almost stumbling in his haste.

Behind him, Miss St. John fluttered helplessly.

"I'm so sorry," she cried. "He pushed right past me."

"I have every right to be here!" shouted the young man. "You all know it."

"Mrs. Stebbins has called Security," said Miss St. John.

"No need, no need," said Morrison calmly. "Come take a seat, Stephen. It's good to have you with us at last. Miss FitzGibbons, please mark Stephen Burleigh as present. Miss St. John, you may resume your post at your desk. Tell Mrs. Stebbins to stand down. Please close the doors behind you."

Miss St. John looked uncertainly around the room, then shut the doors, leaving Burleigh standing unsteadily before them.

"What have I missed?" he said, glancing around the room.

Then his eyes rested on Gwen, and a sneer formed on his face.

"What is she doing here?" he asked. "I thought she was a looney."

"Just because you have a right to be here does not permit you to behave like a cloddish schoolboy," said Morrison sharply. "Take your seat, Burleigh, or get out. We've managed without you to date. I expect we can continue to do so."

Burleigh gave him a hard look, then caught sight of the sideboard.

"Don't mind if I do," he said, ambling over to it.

He poured himself a large whisky, then turned to face Gwen.

"Apparently I was being rude for saying what you are out loud," he said. "I apologise."

"You are forgiven," she said softly.

His eyes wandered to the portraits on the walls, stopping when he saw the empty space.

"What have you done with Father's painting?" he asked.

"I believe it's in a storage closet somewhere," said Morrison.

"As is Father," said Burleigh with a harsh laugh. "Gentlemen, and Mrs. Bainbridge, may I propose a toast? To Otis Burleigh, the best and the worst of men."

He was met with silence. No one moved. He looked at them with mock surprise.

"No one joining?" he asked. "He would be so disappointed." He took a long swallow from the tumbler. "Very well, I shall take my seat. Oh, good. You've had it dusted. Very optimistic of you, Lord Morrison."

"Are you drunk, Stephen?" asked Morrison.

"Should be by now," said Burleigh, holding his tumbler up to the light. "I got a head start before I came here. Needed some Dutch courage to hold down my bile at the sight of you. So did you, by the look of things."

He wagged an admonitory finger at the glass of sherry in front of Morrison.

"There is a difference," said Morrison.

"Not from what Father told me about these meetings," said Burleigh. "He used to say Bainbridge encouraged all of you to get drunk while he stayed stone-cold sober. In any case, the sun is over the foreyard, so who cares? Go on, I'll behave. Here's my pledge."

He put the tumbler down on the table with an exaggerated flourish. Miss FitzGibbons quickly got up to fetch a coaster from the sideboard and placed it underneath, then resumed her seat. Burleigh watched her do this with interest.

"Did you record everything that just happened?" he asked.

"I did," she said primly.

"I'll want a copy of those minutes as a keepsake, if you don't mind."

"You'll get them," said Morrison wearily, "just as you've got the minutes from all the meetings since you took over your father's seat. Let us resume. If there is no objection, I will dispense with the reading of last month's minutes."

There was no objection. A pall had settled over the room with Burleigh's appearance. Gwen almost felt grateful that he had taken the focus away from her.

"First report," said Morrison, picking up a sheaf of papers. "The survey work on the proposed railway link to Mpanda was completed early. I am happy to report that there was only one man killed during the course of it—"

"How?" asked McIntyre.

"Lion attack."

"Poor blighter. We made reparations to the family, of course?"

"Of course," said Morrison. "As well as to one other who died from sleeping sickness. Now, if you will all turn to page two, you will see a breakdown of the anticipated increase in profits—"

By the time the last report was read, Gwen was regretting her earlier rejection of the sherry. Not that she found the reports dull. Far from it. The worlds of mining and factories and plantations sprang to life even through the dryness of Lord Morrison's recitations, and she found herself wanting to raise questions about aspects of the company that were left out of the official summaries. Questions that she wasn't allowed to ask yet.

But it was dry in the room, or maybe it was her own nerves under the perceived scrutiny of the men in the room that parched her mouth. Parson, in particular, kept his glare fixed on her the entire time, and she had to make an effort not to return it, and more of an effort to make that effort unnoticeable. She would have loved to have made eye contact with Miss FitzGibbons, just to see if there was any sympathy in the exchange, but she was behind Gwen in the corner, the only evidence of her existence being the soft scratching of her shorthand, the occasional rustle of a page being flipped over.

Stephen Burleigh's face was the hardest for Gwen to read. There was hatred in his expression, hatred for everyone in the room, but particularly for her. Understandable, considering the role she and the Bainbridges had played in his father's predicament, ultimately sending him to prison. Yet when she looked back on their last meeting, seated together in the parlour of the Bainbridge house after a formal dinner, when there had definitely been a sympathy between them, she couldn't feel any harshness towards him. None of it had been his fault.

Nor hers, ultimately. The damage had been done by events set in motion by their elders.

It was interesting to watch the other board members in action. Despite Harold's harsh assessment, Hilary McIntyre and Sandy Birch were clearly familiar with the reports and asked sound, considered questions. As did Parson, to her grudging surprise. For all his disdain for her, he seemed to have taken his position seriously. Considering what she had heard of his toadying submission to her father-in-law's will while Harold was still in good health and command, this competence on her behalf was unexpected.

"And that's that as far as the reports go," concluded Morrison. "Any further comments? I see no hands raised. Any motions before we conclude? Very well, then I suggest— Ah, Mr. Parson, you have your hand up. The floor is yours."

"Thank you, Lord Morrison. I have a motion to put forward," said Parson as the others turned to look at him in surprise.

"Do you?" replied Morrison. "Very well. Let's hear it."

"Members of the board, what I am about to do causes me no little pain," said Parson, standing up. "However, I have a responsibility to my charge, and as the committee of a general partner, it extends to everyone present at this table. Indeed, to the entirety of Bainbridge, Limited. As you know, our chief executive officer, Lord Harold Bainbridge, suffered a heart attack in August, incapacitating him. Although he has communicated from his convalescence since then, he has refused to take an active role in managing this very complex corporation, one which not only represents a vast part of all of your fortunes, but as a supplier of raw materials and ammunition to His Majesty's Government is a vital part of the British Empire."

"Please get on with it," muttered Burleigh.

"As Lord Bainbridge has in essence abrogated his responsibilities," continued Parson, "not even deigning to designate a proxy on his behalf, I can no longer stand mute."

"You've been as far from mute as one can possibly be," said McIntyre. "What is the damn motion?"

"I am moving to have Lord Bainbridge removed as chief executive officer of Bainbridge, Limited," said Parson, looking around the room triumphantly.

"No!" cried Gwen.

CHAPTER 8

Gwen stared at Parson in disbelief. She wasn't the only one.

"How dare you!" thundered Birch. "You—you impudent bootlicker! How long have you been lying in wait for this moment?"

"I have forty percent of this company's shares to vote to your four," said Parson. "I am not anyone's lackey. Just because I have chosen not to exercise my rights—"

"Your rights?" scoffed Birch. "You mean her rights."

"Yes, which have been committed to me by the Master of the—"

"The Court of Lunacy, yes, you've made that quite clear over the past two years. You repeatedly come in, sit down, make your snivelling little declaration, then do whatever Bainbridge tells you to do. Until today."

"I will have you know that I never did anything that wasn't necessary to protect my charge," said Parson hotly, the blood rushing to his cheeks.

"Enough, the both of you," said Lord Morrison wearily. "Sit down, please, Mr. Parson. Members of the board, there is a motion on the floor. Is there a second?"

"I second," said Hilary McIntyre.

Morrison looked at him, his eyebrows rising.

"*Et tu,* Hilary?" he said. "Is this a coup?"

"Come on, Tom," said McIntyre. "We need a firm hand at the tiller, and you know it. Bainbridge is keeping warm and toasty in bed, reaping the benefits while doing none of the work. We can't just let the old firm roll down the hill because he refuses to let go of the apron strings."

How many metaphors can one man mix? thought Gwen.

"Very well, the motion is seconded," said Morrison. "I am going to speak now. Harold Bainbridge has been running this company on a daily basis for years while most of us come in once a month."

"*Had* been running," said McIntyre. "He's a general partner. He should do the lion's share of the work. He isn't."

"He is convalescing, man," said Morrison. "His heart may be damaged, but I'm beginning to think yours is completely gone. The company is on solid footing. As soon as he's well enough—"

"But will he be well enough?" asked Phillips querulously. "Do we know for certain that he's even coming back?"

"We don't know that he isn't," said Morrison.

"What has he told you, Tom?" asked Phillips. "You're on the telephone with him every day. When is he coming back?"

"I cannot say at this time—"

"You're forgetting something else," said Burleigh abruptly.

They turned to look at him as he twirled the whisky in his tumbler with his forefinger, staring into it.

"What are we forgetting, Stephen?" asked Morrison.

"The reason he had his heart attack," said Burleigh. "The reason my father is now in jail. The Mopani venture."

"That has nothing to do with this motion," said Morrison.

"It has everything to do with it," said Parson. "Our praiseworthy chief executive officer travelled to Africa at the company's expense under the guise of inspecting the company's holdings, and instead instigated a rogue mining operation, an operation meant to benefit only his own fortunes."

"And Burleigh's," said Birch.

"And Burleigh's," repeated Parson. "But not that of Bainbridge, Limited, to which he owed the highest fiduciary responsibility. It's not just a question of his physical disability, gentlemen, but of his moral unfitness. There are clauses in the partnership agreement that expressly address the removal of corporate officers for moral unfitness."

"Which, if enforced, would put every man Jack in jeopardy," said Morrison, looking around the table. "Well, perhaps we know where we stand now. The motion must carry by more than fifty percent of the shares. I am going to call—"

"Please, may I speak?" asked Gwen.

"I speak for you, Mrs. Bainbridge," said Parson. "You have no rights here."

"She has none as a shareholder," said Morrison mildly. "However, if you will review the bylaws, guests may be allowed at board meetings at the behest of the chairman, who is me. And guests may be allowed to speak with the permission of the chairman, still me, by the way. I am invoking my power to allow Mrs. Bainbridge to say her piece."

"Actually, before we do, may I ask for a, I don't know what the proper term is," said Gwen hurriedly. "A break of some kind before we begin."

"A recess," said Morrison.

"Yes, a recess."

"For what purpose?"

"I would like to speak with Mr. Burleigh," said Gwen. "In private."

"I will not allow that," said Parson immediately.

"Inside the walls of this company, she may talk to whomever she damn well pleases if I agree to it," said Morrison. "And I agree to it."

"I don't," said Burleigh.

"Stephen, hear me out for ten minutes," pleaded Gwen. "Or five, if my presence causes you that much pain."

He met her gaze for the first time since he sat at the table. She saw some internal struggle take place under his scowl. Then, abruptly, he nodded.

"Five minutes," he said. "Not a second more."

"You may use my office, Mrs. Bainbridge," said Lord Morrison. "We will adjourn until you return."

He held her chair as she stood, looking around the room reproachfully.

"I believe it is customary for a gentleman to stand when a lady leaves the table," he said.

The others got to their feet, Parson the last to rise.

"Thank you, Lord Morrison," said Gwen. "Mr. Burleigh, will you join me?"

She swept past them out the door. Burleigh looked back at Parson, she noticed, then followed her.

She didn't wait for him, walking briskly down the hall. Mrs. Stebbins and Miss St. John looked up at her with expressions of surprise as she came in, surprise that increased as they saw Burleigh behind her. Miss St. John's hand involuntarily went to her throat.

"Mrs. Bainbridge, how may I help you?" asked Mrs. Stebbins.

"Lord Morrison has lent me the use of his office for a few minutes," said Mrs. Bainbridge. "Please don't get up."

She walked into the office, then turned and beckoned to Burleigh to join her.

"Close the door," she said as he came in.

"Are you sure?" he asked, smiling sardonically. "Think of the scandal."

"If you can manage a scandal in only five minutes, then you're more of a man than you've appeared to be since you've arrived here," she replied. "Close the door, and sit, please."

She took the chair behind the desk and waited for him. He shrugged, then closed the door and sat in front of her, glancing at his watch.

"Start," he said.

"First, I want to say how sorry I am for your situation," she said. "I wanted to speak with you about it before today, but I couldn't think of any appropriate way of doing that, given the part I played in it."

"My situation," he said. "You mean being the son of a man in jail facing murder charges because you and your partner put him there."

"Your father did what he did," said Gwen. "I can't help that. Neither can you. But that doesn't mean you should bring all of this down around us."

"Why not?" he asked. "Why should I care if the house of Bainbridge falls?"

"Because this is your house, too," she said.

"Only four percent of it," he said. "I won't miss it."

"Won't you? How do you expect to be received in decent society once word gets out about your—"

"My what?" he asked.

"Your betrayal," she said. "No one holds your father's actions against you, but if you continue his legacy—"

"Everyone holds him against me," he said. "I see it in their eyes wherever I go. Oh, look, it's Stephen Burleigh, the murderer's boy, and we once thought him so grand. I am held in contempt by everyone."

"So am I, Stephen," said Gwen softly. "For myself, not for the sins of my father. And I, for one, don't hold your father against you. Maybe the rest of our overbred circle can't fathom what you've been through, but I think maybe I've had a glimpse of it."

He looked at her as if seeing her for the first time.

"What did they do to you in there?" he asked. "In the—"

He stopped.

"Were you going to say sanatorium or looney bin?" she asked. "I will accept either term."

"What did they do?" he asked.

"They did what they thought was necessary," she said. "Much of it through injections while I was strapped down. I barely knew where I was or who I was for a long time. It felt like torture."

"Torture," he repeated. "Maybe I do know a little something about that."

"I'm sure it was much worse for you," she said. "You started to tell me about it when we last met, then the events of that evening interrupted us. No, let me be honest. I interrupted us, and I am sorry for it. You were Ronnie's friend, and I wish that things were better between us despite what has happened."

"What do you want from me?" he asked.

"Time," she said. "Just a little bit. Give me a chance to come into my own before it's destroyed. Give Harold a chance to prove himself again, not have everything taken away while he's not even here to defend himself. And if he fails—you and I are the next generation of Bainbridge, Limited, Stephen. If we team up, we'll only need two of the others. We could be a force, you and I."

"Why do you think that's a better offer than what I have now?" he asked.

"Because as much as you hate all of us right now, you'll hate yourself even more if you go through with this," she said. "And it will be too late to make things right again. How am I doing on time?"

He glanced at his watch.

"You have ten seconds left."

"I think I'll save them," she said, picking up something from the desk and getting to her feet. "Never know when they'll come in handy."

She opened the door. The two women outside made no pretence that they hadn't been staring at it, trying to make out what they could from the muffled conversation. Miss St. John's hand went to her throat again.

"We're done now, Mrs. Stebbins," said Gwen. "We won't be disturbing you again."

"No bother, Mrs. Bainbridge," said Mrs. Stebbins.

Gwen walked past them. Miss St. John cast her eyes downward to avoid any scrutiny. Gwen's eyes followed the look involuntarily, but saw nothing more than her wastebasket, filled with discarded envelopes and a crumpled piece of wrapping paper.

"Gwendolyn, are you ready to return?" called Morrison, standing at the doors to the boardroom.

"Are you ready, Stephen?" she asked, turning to him.

He nodded sombrely.

"We're coming," she said.

The other men stared as they returned, trying to guess what had happened.

Morrison held her chair once again. The others remained standing until she was seated, then took their places at the table once again.

"I brought you this, Lord Morrison," said Gwen, placing the gavel she had taken from his desk in front of him.

"My thanks, Mrs. Bainbridge," he said, picking it up. "I could use some symbolic reinforcement."

He rapped it on his ledger.

"The meeting will come back to order," he said. "All parties are still present. Mrs. Bainbridge, do you wish to speak further?"

"Yes," she said. "Mr. Parson says that he is speaking for my rights. He is not speaking for my desires. I ask that you postpone this motion until Lord Bainbridge has the opportunity to respond in person."

"And if he doesn't respond?" asked McIntyre.

"One month, at least," said Gwen. "He's been on the mend. Allow him the benefit of one more medical update."

"Is that all, Mrs. Bainbridge?" asked Morrison.

"Yes. Thank you for allowing me the opportunity to say my piece."

"Very well, then," said Morrison. "I move to call the question. Second?"

"Second," said Parson coldly.

"Then we shall take a vote. Lord Bainbridge is absent. Voting for Mrs. Bainbridge is Mr. Parson. Aye or nay?"

"Aye," said Parson.

"I vote nay," said Morrison. "Alexander Birch."

"Nay."

"Hilary McIntyre."

"Aye."

"Townsend Phillips."

Phillips gulped slightly, then muttered, "Aye."

Morrison turned to look at Burleigh, who was staring into his whisky.

"The vote stands at forty-eight shares for, eight shares against," he said. "You are the deciding vote, Stephen."

Burleigh looked up, then around the room at everyone there. His gaze fell upon the empty space on the wall where his father's portrait had once hung, then settled on Gwen, who kept her expression neutral. He looked at her for a long time, then back into his drink.

"Fine," he muttered.

"Your meaning?" asked Morrison.

"Nay," said Burleigh. "No, nein, nyet, against. Clear enough?"

"That's forty-eight shares for, twelve against," said Morrison quickly. "The motion does not garner the necessary majority for passage. The motion does not carry."

Parson stood up, pointing at Gwen.

"You're a fool," he said. "You have no idea what you're up against with this lot."

"Perhaps you'll explain it to me," she replied. "I'll call for an appointment."

He turned and stared at Burleigh with open hostility.

"What are you looking at?" snapped Burleigh.

"Lipstick traces," said Parson.

Burleigh started to get to his feet, but Phillips and McIntyre immediately put their hands on his shoulders, preventing him. He sagged back into his chair.

Parson stormed out of the room.

"Let the record reflect that Mr. Parson has left," said Morrison in a tone of relief. "As we no longer have a quorum, I declare the meeting over. I am going to have another drink. Who's joining me?"

"Sorry, Tom," said McIntyre, getting to his feet. "I'm not in a celebratory mood at the moment. See you next month."

He left, Phillips joining him without saying anything.

"Those damn turncoats," said Birch. "Well, forgive me, Tom. My stomach's gone sour with all of this. Give my love to Edna. Mrs. Bainbridge, a pleasure to see you again."

"Likewise, Mr. Birch," returned Gwen.

Birch left, with Miss FitzGibbons silently gliding after him.

"Stephen, how about you?" asked Morrison.

Burleigh picked up his tumbler, contemplated it, then downed the remainder with one quick swallow. He placed it with exaggerated care in the exact center of the coaster.

"I think you should be cutting me off at this point, barkeep," he said. "After all, I'm driving the bus, ain't I?"

He smirked, then got to his feet, making no effort to conceal his unsteadiness.

"Stephen," Gwen began.

"No," he said. "You've said enough. This was fun. Can't wait to do it again. Goodbye, Gwen."

He left, leaving the doors open behind him. The two of them watched as he staggered down the hall, then vanished around the corner.

"A drink for you, m'dear?" asked Morrison.

"Please," said Gwen.

* * *

Motives, thought Quinton. Love, money, revenge, something else.

He needed to know more about Adela Remagen. He could go back and question Professor Remagen some more, but he wanted to go in better prepared. Where else could he look? He didn't know anything about the contents of her will. Or even where it might be.

He still had the book she had with her, along with her bag and its contents. He looked again at the book. A poetry anthology. Nineteenth-century Romantics.

If that wouldn't make you want to kill yourself, he didn't know what would, he thought.

He opened her bag and went through it again.

That flyer, he thought. The Right Sort Marriage Bureau. Maybe they knew something. He read it quickly, scoffing initially at the idea of the place, but then reflected on his own single status and current lack of prospects and reconsidered.

He looked at his watch. It was after five. They'd be closed for the day. He decided to head to Mayfair first thing in the morning and find out why a married woman was interested in a marriage bureau.

"You were splendid in there, m'dear," said Lord Morrison after the waiter had taken their drink orders.

"It was much more terrifying than I expected," said Gwen. "And I expected it to be terrifying."

They were at a small and exclusive restaurant that catered mainly to the financial district. Around them, men flouted the shortages with impunity, telling risqué stories fuelled by prewar vintages of wines that had been safer in their cellars than many Londoners had been in theirs.

Gwen and Lord Morrison sat at a small table in an alcove, partially shielded from the rest of the room.

He reserved this table so we wouldn't be overheard, she noted approvingly.

"Did you know this was going to happen?" she asked.

"I had an inkling," he replied. "Veiled hints, attempts to sound me out without saying why."

"From which one of them?"

"Townsend on the hints. Anyone trusting him with a secret plot might as well take out an ad announcing it in *The Times*. Hilary casually mentioned that he thought I was doing an excellent job as acting CEO, and wondered if I ever considered it on a permanent basis."

"Have you?"

"Of course," he said. "But not without Harold stepping down first. You don't stab a man in the back after prowling through the jungles with him."

"Did you tell Harold your suspicions?"

"No," said Morrison. "I wanted to see how it would play out. I didn't know how many of them were in on it. I didn't expect young Burleigh to show up, though. That was a clever move by Parson. I wonder how he persuaded him to come. It's a good thing you were there to bring him back into the fold."

"Is that why you invited me?" asked Gwen.

"In part," said Morrison.

"Why else?"

"I wanted to know if you were behind the proposal," Morrison said simply, watching her closely for her response.

Which was outrage.

"Did you think I would sabotage my own family?" she sputtered indignantly.

"Keep it down, m'dear," he said. "You don't want to attract undue attention."

"But did you?"

"I had no idea, Gwendolyn," he said. "Given how you've been treated by Harold since—well, since Ronald's death and your commitment, you would have every reason to want to bring about his downfall."

He looked down, studying his menu.

"I might even have supported you, had you done so," he said quietly.

"He's your friend, Tom," she said. "How could you say that?"

"Because I've known him for over forty years, and I know what he is capable of doing to people," said Morrison. "What he has done to you is unspeakable, he along with Parson doing his bidding. Thankfully, I am more convinced than ever that we will soon be rid of that odious guardian of yours. Whatever you said to young Burleigh in private did the trick. What did you say?"

"I let him know that I understood his pain," said Gwen. "That I shared it."

Morrison winced.

"I must reach out to him, I suppose," he said. "He's part of the board, like it or not, and it would be best for all concerned to keep him on our side. Hilary will come around if we maintain a solid front, and Townsend will go with the prevailing winds. Bainbridge, Limited, will survive. I promise you that."

"I wonder how Harold will react when he hears about this," said Gwen.

"You'll have to let me know after you tell him," said Morrison.

"Me?" exclaimed Gwen. "Aren't you going to brief him?"

"I think, under the circumstances, he should hear it from you," said Morrison. "He'll need to be reassured that you're not plotting against him. Ring me up when you're done. I'll want to hear all the details."

"Oh, dear," said Gwen.

By the time she came home, it was already bedtime for the boys. She came in to kiss each of them good night, then motioned to Agnes to join her in the hall for a moment.

"Have they been to see Lord Bainbridge tonight?" she asked in a whisper.

"Of course," said Agnes.

"And did they leave him in a good mood?"

"As they always do, Mrs. Bainbridge."

"Good," said Gwen. "Pray for me."

"I will," said Agnes. "But why?"

Gwen didn't reply. She walked down the hall to the landing that separated the guest rooms from the family rooms.

Screw your courage to the sticking place, and we'll not fail, she thought. What was that from again?

Oh, yes. Lady Macbeth.

Who failed rather spectacularly.

You need better role models, Gwen, she thought.

With that, she went to knock on Harold's door.

There was a pair of chaffinches, descendants of birds who had escaped from cages to meet and breed in London's parks, nesting on the roof of the Bainbridge house next to the central chimney. They had gone through their autumn moulting already and were in their winter feathers, their panoply of colours now tinged with brown. They had taken to this particular rooftop for safety, the absence of cats in the household being an advantage. The sun had set hours ago, there were no eggs or chicks to mind, so they were nestled comfortably into each other, dreaming of ancestral forests in the lands from which their forebears had been brought.

Then a loud, hoarse, male human shout of "HE DID WHAT?" echoed through the house under them, sending them rocketing into the night sky, sounding the alarm to their neighbours with a repeated cry of Thrup! and flapping away into the darkness without truly understanding why they did so.

CHAPTER 9

Iris made certain that she got to The Right Sort early that Tuesday morning. She was going to be without Gwen because of the court hearing, and wanted to get a head start on the day's work.

It was 8:45 when she unlocked the door to her office. Mrs. Billington hadn't arrived yet. Iris drew the curtains on the two tall windows behind their desks, opened one of the drawers where she kept some dustrags, and gave the sills and desktops a quick wipe, then settled down to the task of plucking random index cards from the box for their female clients and thinking who would be a good fit from the corresponding male box.

She was contemplating Martha Wyllie, a seamstress from West Ham who was shy about meeting people in public, wondering what to suggest to any potential match for a first date, when she heard footsteps coming up the flights below.

Mrs. Billington? she wondered.

No. She knew the sound and tread of Mrs. Billington's sensible shoes by now, and their secretary/receptionist's pace tended to slow as she reached the last flight, whether because of fatigue or a subconscious wish to hold back the workday for a few extra seconds.

These steps were heavier but regular. Made by boots. Boots worn by a man with energy and purpose.

She drifted into the Kipling poem, softly chanting, "'Boots—boots—boots—boots, movin' up and down again!'"

She had just got to "'There's no discharge in the war!'" when the boots themselves appeared in the doorway. Sturdy, well-made black boots, with the trouser legs tucked into them.

Dark blue trouser legs.

She followed them up, taking in the rest of the uniform, the boyish face, the brown hair still messy from being recently freed from the helmet which he carried tucked under one arm.

"Good morning, Constable," she said. "Welcome to The Right Sort Marriage Bureau. Are you here on your business or mine? I hope you're looking for love, because otherwise I'm in trouble."

"My business, unfortunately," he replied. "Are you Miss Sparks or Mrs. Bainbridge?"

"I'm Sparks," she said, coming around the desk to shake his hand. "Do come in and take a seat. Oh! You're not local, are you? Essex County? What brings you to London? To us, specifically? And what's your name? Answer that one first and we'll get to the rest."

"Good morning, Miss Sparks," he said, pulling one of the guest chairs in front of her desk and sitting down. "I'm Police Constable Hugh Quinton. I'm with the Loughton Station. You might want to be sitting down for this."

"This sounds like it's going to be bad news," said Sparks as she sat behind her desk.

"Do you know a woman by the name of Adela Remagen?" he asked.

He saw something shift in her eyes, a momentary sadness, before her expression became a professional mask.

"She's a client of ours," replied Sparks. "Has something happened to her?"

"I'm afraid so," said Quinton. "Her body was found in Epping Forest on Sunday."

"Poor thing," said Sparks. "Gwen will be devastated."

"Why her more than you?" asked Quinton, noting her complete absence of shock at the news.

"It's complicated. How did Mrs. Remagen die?"

"An overdose of morphine," said Quinton. "Did you know she was taking it?"

"I'm not surprised that she was," said Sparks. "Did you know that she had cancer?"

"Yes."

"What would you like to ask me, Constable? I will assist in any way I can."

"She had this with her," said Quinton, taking The Right Sort flyer from his file. "It's from here, isn't it?"

"Yes," said Sparks, glancing at it.

"I was wondering why a woman who was already married would have a flyer from a marriage bureau."

"She came to us last Tuesday to engage our services."

"Why? If it's not confidential— Is there any confidentiality in what you do?"

"No, not when it comes to police matters," said Sparks regretfully. "We learned that the hard way. Mrs. Remagen came to us because she wanted us to find someone for her husband after she had passed."

"Did she?" he exclaimed. "How would that work, exactly? How does it work here?"

"You read our flyer?"

"Yes," he said. "People pay you a fee to match them up. It doesn't say how much."

"Five pounds to become a client."

"That's steep."

"How many unsuccessful dates have you gone on, Constable?" she asked. "How much have you spent on dinners, films, clubs, taxis, and so forth?"

"I haven't done much of that since I was demobbed," he confessed. "But I see your point. What happens if a couple gets married?"

"Then there is a final fee from both parties," she said. "Twenty pounds each."

He gave a low whistle.

"Cheaper to stay single," he said.

"It is," she agreed. "Those monks have amassed huge savings."

"It seems like such a strange way to meet people. To find love through an agency."

"How did your parents meet?" she asked.

"Mine?" he said in surprise. "The way Dad always tells it, he was visiting a cousin in Tiptree. There was a dance at a local pub, and he saw this absolute vision of a girl. He goes up to her and says, 'Tell me, pretty maiden, are there any more at home like you?'"

"He didn't!"

"He did."

"And did your mum then say, 'There are a few, kind sir, but simple girls, and proper, too,' like a Floradora Girl should?"

"It wasn't my mum," said Quinton. "That was her sister, and she said, 'Yeah, we got another at home, and we've been trying to get rid of her forever. Come meet her.' And he did, and they've been man and wife for thirty-five years now."

"Well, good for them," said Sparks. "We're here for those who aren't as lucky in love."

"Or in life, in Mrs. Remagen's case. So she wanted to find the professor a new wife. How was that done?"

"She signed a standard contract with some added provisions to be executed at an appropriate interval after her death, then arranged for any potential marriage payment through her solicitor."

"You said that your partner, Mrs. Bainbridge, would be devastated by this news. Why?"

"Mrs. Bainbridge had a private talk with her. She told me after that she thought Mrs. Remagen was planning on committing suicide after settling her affairs. She elicited a promise from her that she wouldn't go through with it as a condition of our taking her on as a client. Gwen thought she had agreed to renounce the idea."

"Maybe she reneged," said Quinton.

"I guess she did."

"Do you know who her solicitor is?" he asked, trying to conceal his eagerness. "I would like to speak with him."

"Yes, of course," said Sparks, getting up from her desk. "Wait while I fetch the file—"

She stopped abruptly, looking at him with sudden suspicion.

"What is it, Miss Sparks?" he asked her.

"Why are you really here, Constable?" she asked.

"Well, anytime we find a dead person, we look into—"

"You don't think it's a suicide, do you?" she asked slowly, perching against the front of her desk.

"Actually, it's beginning to sound more like one now," he said.

"You sound disappointed about that," said Sparks, practically pouncing on him. "Why?"

"There were some aspects of the scene that seemed odd to me," he said.

"Like what?"

"Miss Sparks, I wouldn't want to burden you with the details of an unfortunate woman's demise. They're unpleasant."

"Burden away, Constable," said Sparks. "I can take it."

"I can't, Miss Sparks. It mainly comes from the crime scene, and—"

"Do you have the photos?"

"Miss Sparks, I can hardly ask you to look at photographs of a dead woman."

"It wouldn't be the first time I've done it, Constable," said Sparks. "Talk to your counterparts at Scotland Yard at Homicide and Serious Crime Command. They could tell you all about me, then would probably tell you to turn tail and run."

"You're having me on," he said.

"I'm not," said Sparks. "Look, Constable, if it was an overdose, then it will be one of the least gruesome scenes one could possibly encounter. I promise you I'll neither scream nor faint. Show me."

There were a few reactions besides screaming and fainting that worried him. Nevertheless, he hesitantly pulled out the photos from his file and held them across to her. She snatched them from his hand, studying the top one closely.

"I didn't see it right away," he said. "And I doubt that you'll—"

"Why on earth would she wear those shoes to walk in a forest?" she mused, half to herself. "And—oh! No heel marks in the leaves."

"Good Lord!" he muttered.

"I'm sorry, you were going to tell me that, weren't you?" she said, noticing his crestfallen expression. "Did I steal your thunder?"

"Well, yes, actually."

"It's obvious, though, unless— Am I the first woman to see these?"

"Yes."

"Well, there you are, then," she said. "Most women would have noticed the shoes straightaway. So if she didn't walk to where she was found, then she died somewhere else and was carried there. Is that the theory you're working on?"

"Yes."

"What about the livor mortis?"

"How on God's own earth does a woman running a marriage agency know about livor mortis?" he asked, completely taken aback.

"I mentioned the Homicide and Serious Crime Command," said Sparks. "I used to date one of the detectives. He was quite the crime scene aficionado. He'd almost burst with excitement telling me about some of them. I used to tell him it was the worst pillow talk ever, but it was strangely adorable, to be honest. I suppose hearing him talk about it rubbed off."

She had momentarily lost herself in fond reverie until she looked up to see Quinton blushing.

"Right, sharing too much again, Sparks," she remonstrated with herself. "My apologies, Constable, no need for reminiscing. So, tell me about the livor mortis and everything else you found."

"If she died in this position, with her legs resting on the downward slope, then you'd expect the blood to collect in her heels," he said.

"Of course."

"Instead, it was spread through the soles of her feet, according to the doc."

She looked down at her feet, which were dangling freely as she sat on the edge of the desk, then straightened them so the soles were parallel to the floor.

"So she died with her legs and feet like this," she said. "Sitting in a chair."

"Or in an automobile seat," he said. "Then someone carried her to the scene. I found some footprints off the path on the other side of the hill. Two sets from a man's shoes, one going up, the other going down. The ones going up were deeper."

"So they could have been made by a man with the extra weight of carrying her body up the hill," said Sparks. "That's good, Constable. That's very good indeed. The investigating detective is lucky to have you helping out."

"Erm, there isn't an investigating detective," he said. "It's just me."

"For goodness' sake, why? I know Essex County isn't London, but surely they aren't so shorthanded that—"

"I'm doing this on my own," he said bluntly. "My precinct command ruled it a suicide, so I went to Chief Peel at Chelmsford."

"You went over their heads!" said Sparks. "How did you convince your chief?"

"I reminded him that he had lectured us at the academy about learning to trust our instincts," said Quinton. "I told him I was having an instinct about this one, and how would I know if it was any good or not if I didn't put it to the test?"

"Well, good for you, Constable Quinton," she said admiringly, and Quinton found himself thinking that gaining the admiration of Miss Iris Sparks was a very nice thing indeed. He wondered if she had plucked a lucky lad from her clientele for her own. He wondered how she got that scar on her left cheek. It looked recent.

"And you are no longer alone in thinking this," she continued. "You now have me helping you."

"I can't ask you to participate in police matters, Miss Sparks."

"How many murder investigations have you done, Constable?"

"This is my first," he admitted.

"Only your first? Then I'm three up on you," she said. "No, I tell a lie. It's four murders now."

Not counting the one I committed, she thought.

"Now you're really having me on," he said.

"Look, whether you believe me or not, I have a good mind for this sort of thing, so let's take advantage of me and talk it out. You suspect the husband, naturally."

"Of course, except that she died that afternoon and he has an alibi that is ironclad, unfortunately."

"Right, the lecture at the Royal Entomological Society," she said.

He stared at her in disbelief.

"How did you know about that?" he demanded. "Are you clairvoyant now?"

"No," said Sparks. "I went to Professor Remagen's lecture on Sunday. I was curious to see what our future client was like. Besides, I'm already a member, and who doesn't like insects?"

"I most emphatically do not like them," said Quinton. "The professor's house was full of cages and cases of bugs and snakes and whatnot. Creepiest place I've ever been."

"Oh, I wish I could have seen it," said Sparks with a sigh. "It sounds utterly marvellous."

"What did you make of Remagen? Think he could kill someone?"

"I'm sure he already has," said Sparks. "He was part of a commando team in Burma. But even if his alibi is good, he still could have arranged for someone else to have done it."

"Maybe I should ring up your ex," mused Quinton. "Find out who's known for killing for hire."

"His name is Mike Kinsey," said Sparks, writing down his name and number on her pad. "Detective Sergeant Michael Kinsey, I should say. Tell him I sent you. It will amuse him. And let me get you Mrs. Remagen's solicitor's information while I'm at it."

She walked quickly into the other office. Mrs. Billington had reached the landing just below theirs when she came out and had paused to catch her breath.

"Almost made it in one go this time," she called up to her. "I see you've beaten me here. Good morning."

"Good morning to you, Saundra," replied Sparks. "We have a constable visiting in my office, so don't be alarmed."

"Which of you did what this time?" asked Mrs. Billington.

"Neither, for a change. I'll tell you about it later."

She came back inside. Quinton rose as she did, which she appreciated. She gave him a quick smile, then copied the law firm's information onto her pad below Kinsey's number.

"I thought of something else," she said as she tore off the page and handed it to him. "Remagen didn't have to look to the local underworld to track down a professional killer. He could have reached out to someone in his unit to do the job."

"Good thought," said Quinton. "I'll add them to the list. He might be more likely to try them first. I don't think there's much overlap between naturalists and the underworld, although they do have vermin in common."

Sparks, thinking about Archie and all of her friends in his gang, started to retort, then bit her tongue.

"That's one line of enquiry I could take on," she offered. "I have some useful connections in the Army. I could track down any members from his unit who live locally."

"That would be very helpful," he said. "Thank you."

"This is going to be a difficult one to prove if it's murder," she said. "Everything you have so far is speculative. A jury could still think it's suicide after a competent barrister gets through tearing it apart."

"I know," he said. "But my chief gave me forty-eight hours to make a case, so here I am."

"You've considered the possibility of assisted suicide?"

"I have," he said. "Somehow, I don't think that's it."

"Why not?"

"There was a moment—this is going to sound completely silly when I say it out loud."

"Go on," said Sparks.

"When he came to the morgue to identify her body, he stroked her face. He was gentle and sad, and it was not how I had seen him up to that point."

"Your conclusion, Constable?"

"He said that if he knew she wanted to take her own life, he would have helped her," said Quinton. "He would have wanted her to know he was there to the very end."

"Oh, my," said Sparks. "If my partner was here right now, she would be bawling uncontrollably at that. Well, if that's the case, and it wasn't an act he put on for your benefit, then he seems less likely to be a suspect."

"That's why I want to speak to her solicitor," said Quinton. "To see what's in the will. It might give me some clarity as to who benefits from her death."

"If they let you see it," said Sparks. "What was that book she had by her in the photo?"

"A poetry collection."

"Was it opened to a particular poem?"

"Hang on, I have it with me," he said, pulling it out of his file.

He opened it to the page where he had placed a scrap of paper as a bookmark.

"Byron," he said. "'So, we'll go no more a roving.'"

"'For the sword outwears its sheath,'" she quoted. "'And the soul wears out the breast.'"

"'And the heart must pause to breathe, and Love itself have rest,'" he read. "They made us recite that one in school when I was a kid. Always hated it, but you have to admit, it's a good poem for the circumstances."

"Too heavy-handed by half," she said. "It sounds like an added touch to make it look like suicide."

"What poem would you have chosen?" he asked.

"Oh, gosh, there's a terrible idea for a party game," she said with a shudder. "What poem would I leave to confound my many mourners, the bloody pages clutched in my cold, stiff hand? There are a couple by Christina Rossetti that would do. Either 'Remember' or the one that starts with, 'When I am dead, my dearest, sing no sad songs for me.' And you, Constable?"

"There's a couple of limericks I learned in the Army," he said. "If things ever got to that point in my life, they'll do the trick. Unsuitable for a lady's ears, I'm afraid."

"Even a lady who has willingly looked at crime scene photos with you?"

"There are limits, and there are limits, Miss Sparks," he said, taking the photographs back and putting them in his file. "Well, you have been very helpful. I would still like to speak with Mrs. Bainbridge when she's available. Here is the number for the Loughton Station. I'll be checking in with them regularly. I think I'll try the solicitor next, then your friends at Scotland Yard."

"Call me if you need backup, Constable," she said, shaking his hand. "Or just to pick my brain."

"As to that, I have to be careful," he said. "After all, you and Mrs. Bainbridge are suspects now."

"We are?" she exclaimed. "How so?"

"The sooner he gets married, the sooner you collect your fee," he said.

"Do you really think we'd murder someone for forty pounds?" she asked indignantly.

"Of course not," he said with a grin. "I promise you're at the bottom of my list. I don't expect to reach it."

"Well, I should hope not," said Sparks. "Why, I haven't been a suspect in a murder case since September."

"You know, I'm not sure if you're serious about that or not," he said. "Good day, Miss Sparks."

"Good hunting, Constable," she replied.

He left, and the boots began their descent down the stairs. They faded away before she could complete the Kipling poem. She had come to the line, "Oh—my—God—keep—me from goin' lunatic!" then, thinking of Gwen's current predicament, quickly shoved the rest of it out of her mind.

She was going to have to tell her, she thought. Gwen needed to hear it from her before she heard it from anyone else.

She got up from her desk, retrieved her hat and coat, then walked next door to Mrs. Billington.

"I'm going over to the Lunacy Court," she said. "If you don't hear from me by tomorrow, come fetch me in case I've been committed by accident."

* * *

Justice needs oak to function, thought Gwen as she glanced around the courtroom. Entire forests have been hewn, sawn, planed, and polished, then brought into this squatty little courtroom to surround the proceedings with their mute, wooden judgment.

A brief image of Des planing a board rose in her mind. She banished it before it could continue. Not helpful, Gwen, she thought, struggling momentarily to regain her composure. She concentrated on the back of the chair in front of her, gazing into the patterns of the grain, searching for answers in the dark, dead wood.

Forgive us, she prayed silently to the forests. Forgive us for massacring you so that we could give these barbaric rituals the imprimatur of Law.

It was not a very imposing setting. Once, in school, there had been a class trip to view a criminal trial at the Old Bailey. That was a courtroom summoned from one's imagination, designed to instill awe in all who entered. The ceilings reached towards the heavens, the judge sat on high like an Olympian god, the prisoner stood caged and isolated in the dock. She couldn't remember the charges, but there was a moment when the accused, a poorly shaven brute, turned for a moment to stare at the gaggle of solemn-eyed schoolgirls with an expression that gave them all nightmares after.

There was no dock in the well of the court here, merely a row of adjoining desks, continuing the long tradition of British schoolboys, forever linked. Were there initials of barristers past surreptitiously scratched into the undersides when the judge wasn't paying attention? The clerk and the reporter looked back across the room from desks at the same level while Brandon Cumber, Assistant Master in Lunacy, presided from behind his podium on a platform raised just high enough to remind you that he was the authority in the room, if not an actual god. An assistant god, perhaps, one delegated to do the hard work of actually running the world while the Supreme Deity sat on His throne in the clouds and saw that it was good, not realising it only appeared that way from a distance.

There was another case being heard when she entered the room with Stronach. He motioned her to the seats in the gallery, then silently took his place with the other barristers, two rows of white wigs and black silks rendering their wearers indistinguishable from ten feet away. She had no trouble finding a seat. There weren't many people in the gallery, and none would meet anyone else's eye. There was no way of discerning who was a subject for today's docket; who was a concerned third party; or who was merely an observer, come to watch out of morbid curiosity as the loonies paraded by.

We can't tell the normal from the crazy here, she thought.

She had told Stronach about the events at the board meeting. He frowned for a moment, then said, "That may not have been wise."

"I had to stop him," she said.

"I understand," he said, "but it may make things more difficult for you. We'll have to bull our way through if it does. Whatever transpires, no outbursts in court. Understood?"

"Understood," she replied.

Now, she was in the courtroom, the terror mounting within her despite her best efforts (and, it had to be said, a small dose of her Veronal that morning). Cumber was leaning forward, listening to the sotto voce murmurs of two barristers pressed against his podium, the curls of his bob wig flapping gently as he swivelled his head back and forth, following the conversation. Finally, he nodded and motioned for them to return to their desks.

"We'll adjourn the matter for another six months for a progress report," he said. "What's a good date in mid-May or thereabouts?"

The clerk flipped through a calendar book the size of a child's tombstone.

"The fourteenth, milord," he said.

"Very well. Adjourned to the fourteenth of May, gentlemen," he said with a peremptory rap of his gavel. "Call the next case."

And just like that, some poor soul has been consigned to Hell for another half year of his life, thought Gwen.

"Matter of Mrs. Gwendolyn Bainbridge, petitioner," called the clerk.

She almost bolted to her feet, but caught herself in time to get up quietly. The appearance of a tall, beautiful, blond woman in court drew an interested murmur from the seated barristers as well as the gallery, quickly quelled by a glare from Cumber.

A bailiff held open the gate to the well for her to pass through, and she took her place at the far left seat, with Stronach joining her. She looked unwaveringly ahead at the bench, trying to keep her expression calm and unafraid. Inside her chest, her heart was racing.

"Call the parties into the record," instructed Cumber.

"Mrs. Gwendolyn Bainbridge, petitioner," said the clerk.

"Present," she replied, her voice quavering.

"Counsel for the petitioner?"

"Rawlins Stronach for the petitioner," said Stronach in a firm, loud voice.

"Committee for the petitioner?"

"Oliver Parson, present," said Parson from the other side of Stronach.

She hadn't noticed him among the bewigged when she had entered the courtroom. Not surprising, given the rows of identical white perukes presenting themselves, but she had been so intent on appearing like a normal person walking into the well that she had completely failed to observe him rising to join them.

So she gave a slight start when he announced his presence, as if he had manifested himself in a puff of smoke, smelling faintly of brimstone. She resisted peeking around Stronach at him, not wanting to give him the satisfaction of being noticed.

"Good morning," said Cumber as he opened the file handed

to him by the clerk. "Be seated while I catch myself up. Hmm, hmm."

He put on a pair of reading glasses, humming to himself as he glanced over the file.

"Hmm, given temporary status under the Mental Treatment Act 1930, seventeenth of March 1944," he said.

Two years and eight months ago, she thought. Doesn't feel so temporary to me.

"Response to a suicide attempt, I see," he said, looking sharply at her over his glasses.

"The precipitating event being the death of her husband, Captain Ronald Bainbridge, at Monte Cassino, milord," said Stronach.

"We honour his service and his memory, Mrs. Bainbridge," said Cumber.

"Thank you, milord," she replied.

"But you should have done the same by carrying on in his memory," he admonished her with a stern wag of his finger. "None of this hysteria. Most unsuitable."

She said nothing, willing her hands to keep from knotting up into fists.

"And another attempt a month later," he said, shaking his head. "What was that all about? Still going on about the husband?"

"No, milord," said Stronach. "If you'll note the next paragraph, it was in response to learning that she had lost custody of her son."

"I certainly think she should have lost custody, under the circumstances," said Cumber. "Let me see, let me see. Responded after treatment and medication, good. Petition by consulting psychiatrists to have her absent on trial granted on the twenty-sixth of October 1944. Continued treatment with Dr. Milford through the present day, fine, fine. Petition by committee on the twenty-eighth of February of this year to allow her to—enter into contracts for a business? She operates a business?"

"Milord, Mrs. Bainbridge is the co-proprietor of The Right Sort Marriage Bureau, a small business based in Mayfair," said Stronach.

"Odd, very odd," said Cumber. "Co-proprietor, you said. Who is the other one?"

"Miss Iris Sparks, milord. A friend of Mrs. Bainbridge."

"Two women running a business? Was this because of the war?"

"No, milord," said Stronach. "They saw an untapped market for this service, and acted to provide it."

"And you thought that was appropriate, did you, Mr. Parson?" asked Cumber dubiously.

"I thought at the time it would provide some balm to her disordered mind, milord," said Parson smoothly. "A useful but harmless distraction. The Devil finds work for idle hands, as the saying goes."

"Still, this is most curious," said Cumber. "Let me read on. Reports and affidavits from two independent psychiatrists submitted in her favour, yes, yes. Well, although I can't say I approve of this business aspect, I suppose there is nothing to speak against my granting the petition."

Her heart leapt in exultation. Then Parson spoke.

"Excuse, milord, but I would like to be heard."

"Yes, Mr. Parson?"

"At this time, milord, I wish to withdraw my consent to the petitioner's request."

"Do you, Mr. Parson?" asked Cumber, puzzlement crossing his brow. "Rather late in the game, don't you think? This is highly irregular."

"It is, milord," agreed Parson. "Unfortunately, recent events since these filings have forced my hand. We will be serving the necessary motions and affidavits this afternoon. I'm sorry not to have them sooner, but the event that tipped the scales took place only yesterday afternoon."

"Perhaps you could give me an idea of what's contained in them before we go any further," said Cumber.

"Certainly, milord," said Parson. "As you know, milord, a principal portion of my efforts on behalf of my client have been in managing her financial holdings, which are considerable and complex."

"I am familiar with her connection to the Bainbridge family," said Cumber.

"Of course, milord. As a result of the tragic death of Captain Bainbridge, Mrs. Bainbridge inherited his seat on the board of directors of Bainbridge, Limited. I have been appearing on her behalf since my appointment as her committee, watching over her interests and voting on her behalf. I have spent a great deal of time studying the company as a result. Truly, managing her affairs has been a substantial part of my duties to her."

"You are spending a great deal of my time now," observed Cumber acidly. "Get to the point, man."

"Yes, milord. Yesterday, Mrs. Bainbridge was present at the monthly board meeting, despite the fact that I was already there appearing on her behalf."

"She was there as an invited guest of the acting CEO, milord," said Stronach.

"Is that true?" Cumber asked Parson.

"It was, milord, and I was about to inform the court of that. It would be quicker to proceed without Mr. Stronach's interruptions."

"Let him say his piece, Stronach," said Cumber.

"Of course, milord."

"Mrs. Bainbridge proceeded to disrupt the proceedings despite having neither voice nor vote. She did so specifically when I had made a motion upon her behalf that was directly for her benefit. Furthermore, she demanded that there be a recess so that she could speak privately to one of the board members without me present. When they returned, he changed his vote, defeating my motion for

Mrs. Bainbridge. I suspect she used her not inconsiderable beauty to charm the overly susceptible young man, or perhaps even some cruder form of seduction."

"How dare you!" cried Mrs. Bainbridge. "That wasn't what happened!"

"You see how she is, milord?" said Parson, pointing to her in exasperation. "Even here, in this sacrosanct Hall of Justice, she is incapable of maintaining the appropriate reticence and respect for your position."

"Mrs. Bainbridge, you will not behave like that again," said Cumber sternly. "Am I understood?"

"Yes, milord," she said. "But—"

"You have counsel to speak for you. You are to remain silent unless instructed by the court to speak. I repeat, am I understood?"

"Yes, milord," she said, her voice dropping to a whisper.

"Now, Mr. Parson, is there anything else you wish to say?"

"There is, milord, and I regret not bringing it to your attention sooner. Mrs. Bainbridge has over the past several months fallen under the delusion that she is some form of detective. The delusion is so pronounced that she has actually taken it upon herself to interfere with several investigations by Scotland Yard."

"Scotland Yard?" said Cumber. "How serious were these interferences? What were the crimes?"

"Murders, milord," said Parson, dropping his tones to the bottom of his register and drawing out the words with almost lascivious delight. "She even claimed to be acting on behalf of the Queen in one matter, yet strangely, there was no mention of that exalted personage's involvement by the press in any way, shape, or form."

"Really?" exclaimed Cumber, looking at Mrs. Bainbridge with an expression of distaste. "How often has she disrupted these investigations?"

"At least four times that I know of, milord," said Parson.

"Well, well, this puts a new light on the matter," said Cumber. "I am now more inclined to allow the petition to be withdrawn, given what you've told me."

"Milord, may I be heard?" interjected Stronach.

"Yes, go ahead, Mr. Stronach, although Mr. Parson, as her committee, is completely within his rights and powers to withdraw his consent. Indeed, it was he who approved your involvement and your fees in the first place, wasn't he?"

"It was, milord, and I was happy to render my assistance to Mrs. Bainbridge."

Was? thought Gwen with sudden panic.

"It is clear, milord, that Mr. Parson has now adopted a position adverse to that of my client," said Stronach. "I would therefore move to be allowed to continue the petition through the appearance of a next friend before the court rules upon it."

"I haven't seen that procedure used in ages," said Cumber.

"But it is still available," said Stronach. "I would therefore ask that your decision be held in abeyance so that I may have the opportunity to review Mr. Parson's papers and respond appropriately, rather than off-the-cuff here and now."

"Do you have a next friend available?"

"Not today, of course, but I have no doubt there are men of good standing who will come to Mrs. Bainbridge's aid."

"Very well," said Cumber. "I'll give you one week."

"May I request two, milord?"

"One," said Cumber firmly. "The matter is simple enough. We will see you all next Tuesday. Adjourned."

She wanted to say something. She drew in her breath, but then his gavel came down, hard enough this time to send a sharp report echoing through the room, so she exhaled without speaking.

She didn't remember walking out of the well, Stronach's hand gently guiding her. It wasn't until they were in the hallway, the final triumphant smirk on Parson's face seared into her mind before he turned and strode away, that all of it hit her and the tears, then the sobs, poured from her.

"Could someone please explain to me what just happened?" asked Iris, standing in front of them.

CHAPTER 10

What are you doing here?" asked Gwen, gasping for air. "I told you not to come."

"Who is this?" asked Stronach.

"I'm Iris Sparks," said Iris.

"Ah, the partner. Nice to meet you—now please let me have a moment with my client."

Gwen was still crying.

"Get control of yourself, Mrs. Bainbridge," said Stronach. "They can hear you inside. Bad enough that you lost control in there, but don't make it worse."

"I'm sorry, I'm sorry," she sobbed. "But what he said about me was so hateful, so despicable—"

"He did it to bait you," said Stronach, grabbing her arm and practically dragging her away. "And you leapt and swallowed the hook like every other good little fishie meant for filleting."

"I'm going to lose everything!" she wailed as Iris followed closely behind them. "I'm going to lose Ronnie, my job, my freedom! Oh, God, are they going to send me back to the sanatorium? Can he do that?"

"He can try," said Stronach grimly. "But we will stop him. Now, let's find someplace to regroup away from the court's earshot. How much did you see, Miss Sparks?"

"I came in right as that loathsome man started to speak," said Iris. "I thought he wasn't going to oppose you."

"He changed his mind," said Stronach. "Come with me. Both of you."

He led them down a series of corridors until they came to a dead end by a grimy window overlooking the alley at the rear.

"Did you know that was going to happen?" Iris asked him as she fished a handkerchief out of her bag and handed it to Gwen.

"It was always one possibility out of several," said Stronach. "I thought its chances increased after I heard about what happened at the board meeting."

"Which I only know about from what Parson said in court," said Iris to Gwen. "Is that the gist of it?"

"It was more complicated than that," said Gwen, blotting her tears.

"Give her the details later," said Stronach. "How did he know about your penchant for investigations? Especially the one involving the Queen? You told me that was all very hush-hush."

"He came in to inspect the books last month," said Gwen.

"When was this?" asked Iris in surprise.

"You were out on some errand. He oversees my finances, so the agreement was in exchange for giving me permission to run The Right Sort, he could apprise himself of how it was going."

"How often did he do that?" asked Stronach.

"It was the first time," said Gwen. "He saw the unusually large amounts that came in when we worked for the Royals, and demanded to know where they were from. I had no choice but to tell him."

"How did he react?"

"He scoffed," said Gwen. "He said he didn't believe a word of it, and I ended up telling him about our less savoury adventures. I was trying to convince him I knew what I was about."

"It sounds like you did just the opposite," commented Stronach. "You gave him ammunition for this attack, and if you testified as to the actual story, anyone listening would think you're insane. Well, nothing to be done about that now. We need to find a next friend for you."

"What is that, exactly?" asked Iris.

"Someone who will step in as a named party on behalf of Mrs. Bainbridge and petition for her."

"Simple," said Iris immediately. "Me."

"No," said Stronach. "You heard Cumber. He disapproves of your business. He disapproves of women in general, and especially women who think they know how to operate in a man's world."

"But that isn't—"

"Right, Miss Sparks?" interrupted Stronach. "Fair? Just? No, it's none of those. But we are in Assistant Master Cumber's court, which means we work by his rules and prejudices, which means no women. Who else could stand in as a next friend?"

"Sally?" suggested Iris, looking at Gwen.

"I just said no women," said Stronach irritably.

"Salvatore Danielli," said Iris. "We call him Sally."

"How do you know him?" Stronach asked Gwen.

"He's her boyfriend," said Iris.

"He isn't," said Gwen angrily.

"What exactly is the nature of your relationship with him?" asked Stronach.

"We're still working that out," said Gwen. "He thinks he's in love with me."

"Anyone romantically involved with you is out," said Stronach. "He wouldn't carry much weight with the court."

"You've obviously never met Mr. Danielli," muttered Iris.

"What about family members?" asked Stronach.

"I don't trust anyone in my family," said Gwen bitterly.

"Anyone at the board at Bainbridge? You did have other voters on your side."

"All of them were voting their own self-interests," said Gwen. "They would see this as an opportunity to shut me out permanently before my father-in-law comes back."

"Friends?"

"I've been out of touch since I was—" she began, then she stopped, her shoulders slumping. "My friends have avoided me since I was committed. I've become an outcast in my social circles."

"Well, Mrs. Bainbridge, I suggest you mend those fences quickly. We have to appear in one week with a next friend willing to sign on to the petition, or it will be withdrawn. And if that happens, my authorisation to represent you will be terminated under the terms of my contract with Parson."

"Couldn't you find someone?" asked Gwen desperately.

"It has to be someone connected to you in some way," said Stronach. "We can't just hire a friend."

"No," said Gwen. "Would that we could. Life would be so much easier."

"Get to work on that, Mrs. Bainbridge," said Stronach. "I must leave you now. I have other appearances scheduled. Call me when you've found someone. Miss Sparks, good day."

He turned and left them. Gwen turned to Iris.

"Why are you here?" she asked furiously. "I told you not to come. I didn't want anyone here. I didn't want anyone to see me like this."

"It's not important right now," said Iris. "Let's get out of here and put our heads together."

"Not until you tell me why you came," said Gwen. "You wouldn't have disregarded my request unless it was something urgent."

"I'm not here to make matters worse," said Iris.

"But there is something, isn't there?" Gwen demanded, looking at her with that sudden intensity of focus that made it impossible to hide anything, as Iris knew all too well.

"There is," Iris admitted. "It's bad news. I wanted you to hear it from me first."

"What is it?" asked Gwen.

"It's Mrs. Remagen," said Iris. "I'm afraid she's passed away."

"How?" asked Gwen, turning pale.

"An overdose of morphine. She was found Sunday afternoon in Epping Forest."

"No," whispered Gwen, starting to tremble. "She couldn't have. She promised me."

"Gwen," said Iris urgently, grabbing both of her hands, trying to steady them. "Listen to me."

"I thought she would see it through," Gwen continued, ignoring her. "I thought I had reached her. Not a suicide. Not her."

"Gwen, it may have been murder," said Iris.

"What?" cried Gwen, staring at her wildly.

"Constable Quinton, the policeman who told me about it, thinks it could have been murder," said Iris. "He's investigating it. He wants to speak to you."

"Murder," Gwen said distractedly, her eyes wandering. "You said that as if you thought it would make me feel better somehow."

"All I'm saying is that if it's murder, then you didn't fail with Mrs. Remagen," said Iris. "And if we help Quinton—"

"Help him?" said Gwen, jerking her hands away with a bleak laugh. "After what happened in that courtroom, do you really think I'm going to go through this again? I can't do it, Iris, not another investigation. They'll find out, they'll use it against me, they'll lock me up again and take Ronnie away forever."

"Gwen, I'm not saying we join the chase this time," Iris pleaded with her. "But we can help."

"Are you mad? No, wait, I forgot. I'm the mad one in this relationship," said Gwen, turning and striding down the hall. "Go back to the office, Iris. I'm not in the mood for love and marriage today. You'd better start getting used to running the place on your own. I hope you'll come visit me on weekends after they recommit me."

"Gwen!" Iris called after her.

Gwen turned towards her.

"Leave me alone," she said, her face contorted in agony.

Then she turned the corner. By the time Iris reached it, she was gone.

Kinsey was sitting at his desk at Homicide and Serious Crime Command, typing a report, when he saw Quinton standing at his door.

"Come in, Constable," he said, shaking his hand and waving him over to the chair by the other desk in the office, momentarily unoccupied. "Detective Sergeant Michael Kinsey. What brings you into the big city today?"

"Hugh Quinton, Loughton. We found one of your citizens in one of our parks. Apparent suicide, but I'm having doubts. I thought I would ask you about one aspect of the case if you have some time."

"Anyone who interrupts my paperwork is welcome," said Kinsey. "Present it to me as if you were testifying before the coroner."

Quinton cleared his throat and summarised his findings to date, handing over the photographs in response to a gesture by Kinsey, who studied them closely. When he was finished, Kinsey looked up at him.

"That's it?" he asked.

"So far," said Quinton. "I'm still investigating."

"I don't think there's much there," said Kinsey. "The scene is ambiguous at best; the husband has an alibi; you've no witnesses and no connection to the body."

"The last is why I'm here, sir," said Quinton. "I wanted to find leads on men who might do this for money. Miss Sparks thought—"

"Miss Sparks?" Kinsey interrupted him. "Iris Sparks?"

"Yes, sir. She recommended you specifically."

"How on earth did you get on to Sparks?"

"Mrs. Remagen had a flyer from The Right Sort in her bag when we found her. I followed up on it this morning, and Miss Sparks suggested that I speak to you."

"How does she keep turning up in these matters?" wondered Kinsey.

"Sir?"

"Oh, Sparks and I go back a ways," said Kinsey. "But lately, she and that partner of hers have stumbled into a few of our little messes. I'm surprised she didn't snatch the file from your hands and take over the investigation."

"She certainly has enthusiasm for it," said Quinton. "She said she learned about forensics from you when you were—seeing each other."

"Oh, she mentioned that, did she?" said Kinsey with a wince. "Well, water over the dam, thank God. What does she think about your theory?"

"She agrees with it."

"If Sparks thinks it's murder, then there's probably something to it," said Kinsey. "How did she think I could help you?"

"Given the solidity of the alibi, I thought of looking into hired killers. I thought you could point me in the direction of a few."

Kinsey looked at him for a moment, then leaned back in his chair and roared with laughter.

"Oh, you poor sod," he said, wiping his eyes. "First, if we knew who they were, would I be sitting here typing away when I could be out hauling them in? Second, assuming we had names to give you, how would you proceed? Knock on their doors and enquire politely, 'Sorry to bother you, old chap, but did you recently dump a body in Epping Forest? No? Allergies that bad in the woods? My sympathies. Good day and thank you for your time.'"

"Actually," said Quinton evenly, "I thought if I had a few photographs of men the Yard suspects of doing this kind of thing, I could show them to people on her street, or to anyone I find who saw Professor Remagen meeting with anyone beforehand. It would save me from having to go back a second time."

Kinsey went quiet, looking at the younger man for a few seconds.

"All right," he conceded finally. "Sorry, I shouldn't have ridiculed you. Let's take you to the files. Mind you, if you're looking for killers, Sparks should have referred you to her current boyfriend."

"Why is that?" asked Quinton.

"He's a gangster," said Kinsey, getting up to walk him down the hall. "Archie Spelling. Runs everything that's illegal in Wapping. He'd know anyone who kills for money, or even for sport. Not that he'd share the information."

"Miss Sparks is dating a gangster," said Quinton, stunned.

"She is," said Kinsey.

"Bloody waste," said Quinton.

"Yes," said Kinsey. "It is."

Iris sat at her desk back at The Right Sort, feeling useless.

How can I help Gwen? she thought. There's nothing I can do about the court.

But if I help prove that Adela Remagen was murdered and not a suicide, that will ease some of what's distressing her.

She looked through her address book, then dialled a number.

"Phyllis?" she asked. "It's Iris Sparks. Yes, it's been a while. Could you do me a favour? I'm vetting a candidate for a possible marriage, and I wanted to speak to men who served with him in Burma, if there are any about. His name is Remagen. Potiphar Remagen. There can't be too many of those in the British Army. Wonderful. Call me when you find out anything."

Gwen wandered aimlessly through the City of London, the swarming pedestrians around her merging in a blur through her tears.

She didn't know where to go next. She couldn't think of anyone to see. She wanted to walk up to random men in the street like a lost girl in a children's book, tugging on their coattails and crying, "Please, sir. Would you be my friend?"

There had to be someone. She considered Tom Morrison, but the way he had brought her into the board meeting as a means of testing her rankled. If he was contriving to make permanent his temporary status, then she could be putting her fate in the wrong hands.

And she liked Tom, she thought sadly. She wanted to trust him. But there was too much money at stake. Too much for both of them, she supposed. It may be that he couldn't afford to trust her, either.

She needed a friend. A male friend. Someone who was neither financially nor romantically involved with her. Someone in whom she could place her trust. Someone in whom an Assistant Master in Lunacy could put his narrow, prejudiced faith.

Someone like . . .

She stopped short in the middle of the sidewalk, drawing muttered imprecations from a pair of men who had to dodge around her.

Walter Prendergast. An investor who had had business dealings with Bainbridge, Limited. She had met him at a small gathering at the house in Kensington during which she had burst in on an informal meeting of the board members in the library. Events became chaotic in the days after that, as they so often did over the last several months, but amidst the chaos, he had sought her, knowing full well her legal status, and had asked her out.

And she had refused him.

"Mr. Prendergast, I don't know how to answer you," she'd said. *"There are other complications in my life of which you are unaware, and until they are resolved, I am afraid I cannot accept."*

"If I can help in some way—"

"You cannot. Thank you for offering, but I have to take care of them myself."

Now, it seemed, she was unable to handle those complications without help from others. Walter Prendergast checked all the boxes for a next friend. She wondered if he still wished to uncheck the one about no romantic involvement.

Desperate times call for desperate measures, she thought, reaching into her bag for her address book.

Prendergast and Company was located on Birchin Lane south of Cornhill, just past the Edinburgh Assurance Company. Birchin was a narrow street, barely wide enough to allow a single lane of traffic. It was more comfortably suited to the age of horse-drawn vehicles carrying speculators to the long-vanished coffee shops and taverns that had once fuelled the finances of the world's greatest city. There was one pub left from that era, she recalled, the George & Vulture, located on one of the even older, even narrower alleys off Birchin. She had once gone there with a friend before the war, having come across mentions of it in *The Pickwick Papers,* but it was clear that women, at least those of the higher classes, were not wanted there, and they didn't want to remain in it long enough to find out why.

Prendergast's building was built, like so many in those shadowy streets, of white stone to maximise the reflection of the narrow rays of sun that angled in for brief portions of the day. She had rung him up in advance from a telephone box to make the appointment, not wanting to take him completely off guard after so many months, but nevertheless entered the building with trepidation, feeling he could be her last hope.

The receptionist in the entrance hall, a middle-aged brunette with her hair in a blue snood, sat behind a large desk that looked sturdy enough to protect her from an enemy shell. To reach it, Gwen had to cross thirty feet of white marble floor, which allowed the receptionist to look her over thoroughly.

"You're Mrs. Bainbridge?" she asked.

Gwen nodded.

"Of Bainbridge, Limited, I assume."

"Yes," said Gwen. "I have—"

"An appointment with Mr. Prendergast, to be sure," said the woman. "Which is astonishing, given that you only telephoned twenty minutes ago. He never takes an appointment in that manner."

"I am grateful that he could see me on such short—"

"He cancelled a meeting scheduled for noon and a luncheon after that," continued the woman. "He was observed to smile when he heard your name, according to my sources, and that's a rarity as well. And we knew nothing about your relationship prior to this."

"There isn't a—that is to say, we are only—" stammered Gwen. "Honestly, I fail to see how this is any business of yours."

"I am the first line of defence at Prendergast and Company," said the woman. "Nobody gets by me, only you've already got by him, so my hands are tied."

She picked up her telephone and pressed a button.

"Mr. Prendergast's noon appointment is here," she said. She listened for a moment, then her eyes grew wide. "Yes, I will inform her."

She hung up, giving the telephone an accusatory glare, which she transferred to Gwen.

"He's coming down," she said, more to herself than to Gwen. "He's coming down himself."

"Is that unusual?" asked Gwen.

"I've never seen it," said the woman in wonderment. "They'll all want to know what happened. I won't be buying myself any drinks for a week."

"I'm so glad," said Gwen, hastily pulling out her compact, then snapping it shut as Prendergast burst through the door.

He was a strongly built man in his late thirties, with a thick brown beard and grey eyes that usually revealed little. Today, however, the eyes were bright and delighted as they saw her, not yet taking in the desolation in her expression.

"Mrs. Bainbridge," he said, practically bounding up to her. "Such an unexpected pleasure to see you again! And today of all days!"

"Why today?"

"We'll discuss that inside. Thank you, Mrs. Holliman."

"Certainly, Mr. Prendergast," replied the receptionist, watching them keenly.

"Come with me," he said, offering Gwen his arm.

She took it hesitantly, and he escorted her through the door down a corridor with offices on either side. She caught glimpses of men and women straining for glimpses of them as they passed each doorway. At the end of the corridor, he took a right and brought her past a secretary sitting in an anteroom who scrutinised Gwen as intensely as Mrs. Holliman had.

The next line of defence, thought Gwen.

"Mildred, a fresh pot of tea, please," commanded Prendergast as they passed by her and entered a corner office that was nearly the size of the conference room at Bainbridge, Limited.

"I'm surprised you don't have an office higher up, given that you own the building," she commented as he showed her to a chair by a small table near the window.

"I don't need to climb six flights of stairs to assert my authority," he said, sitting in one opposite her. "Waste of time. The five minutes I lose each trip are five minutes that could be put towards filling the company's coffers. Now, to answer your question as to the significance of the day: today is the day you become a free woman, is it not?"

"How did you—"

"How did I know it was today?" he said, tapping his hands on his thighs, a gesture she remembered from an earlier encounter. "Because, Mrs. Bainbridge, I took it upon myself to discover when your petition would be heard. I have your initials, 'GB,' marked on my calendar for today to the puzzlement of my staff. I have waited patiently, my dear Mrs. Bainbridge, for you to be at liberty so that

I could resume my efforts to determine whether or not we were suited for each other. And just when I was about to send a man to learn what had taken place, you came to me! Of all the people you could have chosen to see directly after this momentous occasion, you chose me, Mrs. Bainbridge, and I can only—"

He stopped abruptly, seeing the stricken expression on her face.

"What is it, Mrs. Bainbridge?" he asked softly. "What have I done? I have been too precipitate in my speech. What has happened, Mrs. Bainbridge?"

"I shouldn't have come," she said despondently. "You'll think I'm trying to take advantage of your kindness."

"Any kindness I can offer, I offer freely, Mrs. Bainbridge," he said. "I told you when we last spoke that any assistance I could give, I would. Did things not turn out as you expected?"

"Do you remember my committee, Oliver Parson?" she asked.

"The spineless worm who took his orders from Lord Bainbridge? I remember him as a man remembers a bout of food poisoning. Did this worm turn in court today, Mrs. Bainbridge?"

She was about to answer when there was a knock on the door. Prendergast held up his hand, then got up and opened it.

"I'll take that, Mildred," he said. "Thank you."

"But Mr. Prendergast," she protested as he took the tray from her hands. "I always serve the tea."

"And I am indebted to you for that, Mildred," he said. "But today, I will serve. Close the door, please. Thank you."

He returned and placed the tray on the table between them.

"Milk?" he asked, picking up the pitcher.

"Yes, thank you," she said.

He poured each of them a cup.

"Take a sip and allow its restorative qualities to have their effects," he said. "Then tell me what happened."

His simple act of pouring the tea, the English ritual of normality, calmed her, and the tea itself helped from the very first sip, its warmth gradually soothing the trembling that was rattling the cup and saucer.

Her account of the morning's fiasco, hesitant at first, soon spilled into a rushing torrent of words. He listened without interrupting, and when her voice, faltering again at the end, dwindled to a halt, he sat in silence for a while, so long that she became fearful she had destroyed any illusions of her he still possessed.

"You need me to be a next friend," he said finally.

"Yes. If you're willing."

He got up and began pacing the room, his hands clasped behind his back. Then he looked at her.

"You told me previously that you would not go out with me because of your situation," he said.

"I didn't say that exactly," she said. "I said that there were—"

"Complications," he said. "Yes, I remember. Entirely understandable. Your legal status, the question of your son's custody, all taking precedence over any possibility of romantic entanglement."

"Yes."

"Yet since then, I have heard that you have been seeing that giant Italian gentleman I met at your office. Danielli, I believe his name was."

"Mr. Danielli and I have gone out for dinner three times in the past few months," she said.

"So he overcame your reluctance while I was taking you at your word and maintaining a respectful distance," he said.

"I suppose it must appear that way," she said.

"How else could it appear?" he asked. "Have you—no, I will not ask that question. Why haven't you asked him to step in as your champion for this petition?"

"Because he has gone out with me," she said. "My lawyer felt that disqualified him."

"And I am qualified because I have not acted upon my desires," said Prendergast. "Being more of a gentleman than this Italian—"

"He is English," she said. "Of Italian descent, but born and raised here. Mr. Danielli is a gentleman. He has been a friend to me, and has saved me on more than one occasion."

"When you say 'saved,' are you speaking metaphorically?"

"Literally, Mr. Prendergast," she said. "I was in danger, and he came to my aid."

"I would have done the same, had I had the chance," said Prendergast.

"You have the chance now," she said.

He sat back down, his hands motionless on his lap.

"'*Dictum meum pactum*,'" he said. "That is inscribed over the London Stock Exchange. Do you know what it means, Mrs. Bainbridge?"

"'My word is my bond,'" she said.

"Precisely," he said. "I offered you my help. I will give it to you now that you require it. I neither ask nor expect anything in return, so there will be no quid pro quo that Parson may elicit from me in court."

Her tears began to flow.

"Please, Mrs. Bainbridge," he said. "The last thing I want is to make you cry."

"I can't help it sometimes," she said, pulling out her handkerchief. "You should know that about me."

"There is so much I want to know about you, Mrs. Bainbridge," he said. "But as I said, I am a patient man. Provide me with the name of your lawyer, and I will take all the necessary steps."

"Mr. Prendergast, I cannot thank you enough," she said as she pulled out her notebook and wrote down the information. "I promise, when this is over—"

"Mrs. Bainbridge, stop right there," he said. "When I said there was to be no quid pro quo, that was not only for your legal protection."

"Then what else, Mr. Prendergast?"

He looked down at his cup, stirring it idly.

"If I am ever to be loved, Mrs. Bainbridge, I wish for it to be because of who I am, not for what I own or the favours I have done. It hasn't happened yet, and the years are slipping by more quickly."

He grimaced, then finished his tea in one gulp.

"Self-pity is an unattractive trait," he said. "Enough of it. I will be your next friend, Mrs. Bainbridge. Don't concern yourself about Mr. Parson. He is now my enemy, and I shall show him no mercy."

"I hope it doesn't reach the point where mercy is necessary," said Mrs. Bainbridge. "But I am grateful for your help."

"I will walk you out," said Prendergast, getting to his feet and offering her his hand. "Smile as we walk the halls together, Mrs. Bainbridge, so that we may confound my staff once more."

She walked without direction once again, only this time flooded with happiness. No, not happiness. Relief, tempered by anxiety over what doors she may have opened by going to him. And if, by opening them, she may have shut other doors. Doors she wouldn't even have discovered had she been able to get the petition granted without interference.

Still, there was immense satisfaction in knowing she would be able to continue with it despite Parson's interference. That made twice in two days that she had thwarted his plans, and he didn't even know about the second one yet. Nobody knew yet. Her triumph was fresh and new, just beginning to stagger around on its own spindly legs. She wanted to celebrate. She wanted to tell Iris, to tell Stronach.

She wanted to tell Parson.

She wanted to tell him straight to his face, so she could watch him crumple in front of her while she stood there, haughty and proud and triumphant.

She laughed out loud at the image, drawing curious looks from passersby. She suppressed it quickly, then took a quick look at the street signs to reorient herself.

She had wandered by Lincoln's Inn. Parson's law firm was only another street away. Two minutes' walk.

No, Gwen, she cautioned herself. Don't poke the tiger in its cage.

And yet.

It was as if her legs made the decision for her, carrying her towards the building where he schemed in his little legal lair on the fifth storey, no doubt still gloating over his morning's ration of cruelty. She walked towards it, faster and faster, what was left of her good sense trailing farther and farther behind, calling to her with a voice that dissipated into the distance.

When the lift doors opened, the pretty blond receptionist looked up with her professional welcoming smile that froze before it reached its full expression as she recognised who was striding towards her.

"Mrs. Bainbridge," she said in surprise. "We weren't expecting you."

"I wish to speak to Mr. Parson," said Gwen.

"I'm sorry, Mrs. Bainbridge," she said quickly. "He won't see anyone without an appointment."

"You could make one for me, couldn't you?" asked Gwen.

"Certainly," said the receptionist, reaching for an appointments book on her desk. "When would you like to make it for?"

"Thirty seconds from now," said Gwen, walking past the desk before the other woman could react.

Gwen caught a glimpse of her pressing a button on her telephone as she went by. Doesn't matter, she thought. Won't be long.

Her appearance in the secretarial hive caused a cessation in the clattering of the typewriters followed by a low buzz of consternation, her name and the word "lunatic" bubbling to the surface as she made her way through them. Parson's door was closed, but the light was visible through the frosted glass. She reached for the handle. The door was locked.

"Open up," she called, rapping on it sharply. "Open up, you wretched excuse for a man. Open up so I can share with you the happy news that I will not be needing your services after next Tuesday. Open the door, little piggy, or I will huff and I will puff and I will blow you right through your office window. Parson! I am speaking to you!"

"That's enough, Mrs. Bainbridge," said a voice behind her. "You're wasting your breath. He isn't in there."

She turned to see Anderson, the brutish man who had escorted her out the last time she had been here.

"Where is he?" she asked.

"Elsewhere," he said. "Now, Mrs. Bainbridge, you don't want to make a scene."

"Yes. Yes, I do want to make a scene. I demand to speak to Mr. Parson. He works for me."

"No, Mrs. Bainbridge, he doesn't," said Anderson. "He works for this firm, and is assigned cases by the Court of Lunacy. He doesn't work for you because nobody works for you because you are a lunatic, which is evident, by the way. And my job is to deal with lunatics when they show up at our doorstep behaving badly."

"I take it you're not a solicitor," she said.

"No, Mrs. Bainbridge," he replied. "I am the man who deals with people without appointments. And you don't have an appointment. Let's go, shall we?"

"Very well," she said. "You may tell Mr. Parson I was here."

"Oh, he'll know," said Anderson, gesturing towards the exit.

The hive was silent, watching the two of them with horrified fascination and suppressed glee.

"You may also tell him—"

Anderson grabbed her right wrist and stepped behind her, twisting it behind her back.

"I'm also not a bleedin' secretary," he said, seizing her left shoulder with his other hand. "We are going to walk to the lift now, you and me. Quick march."

He propelled her forward through the room, the secretaries swivelling in their chairs as they passed by, their mouths agape.

"There's no need for this," said Gwen. "I will go peacefully."

"Too late for that," said Anderson.

"You're hurting me," she said through clenched teeth.

"A looney who comes in without an appointment and disrupts the workings of our firm merits some punishment," said Anderson with a smirk. "Otherwise, she won't learn not to do this again. Now, come along."

He increased the pressure as they reached the hallway and tears formed in her eyes, but for the first time that day, they were from physical pain that was reaching unbearable levels.

"The 'come-along' grip isn't easy to break," said Macaulay as he stood behind her on the mat holding her arm behind her back with his left hand on her shoulder. "But it's not impossible. First—"

She turned quickly to her left, bending her knees enough so she could duck her head under Anderson's left arm. Then she jabbed upwards with her free hand into his elbow, which had locked as she made the move. He grimaced with pain, loosening his grip.

Chin jab! Testicles! shouted Macaulay. One—

"Two!" she said, completing the sequence before she even finished the thought.

Anderson lay in a crumpled heap on the floor, clutching himself in pain.

"Next time, give me a chance to go quietly," she said as she stood over him.

She looked over at the receptionist, who stared at her fearfully.

"That will be all for today," Gwen said to her, pressing the button for the lift. "Thank you."

The doors opened. She got in. The lift operator, unable to see Anderson and unaware of what had occurred, nodded at her courteously and took her back to the ground level, from whence she escaped back into the streets of London.

CHAPTER 11

Quinton sat on a chair in an anteroom in the top storey of the firm of Turner, Woodbridge, and Farrow, watching a woman type. He was waiting to speak to Jenkin Farrow, the solicitor who had handled the late Mrs. Remagen's dealings with The Right Sort, and who presumably had handled her will as well.

Quinton's uniform had not drawn a single glance when he stepped out of the lift. He was used to causing some small nervous reaction when he appeared, some acknowledgment of his authority as a constable and sworn representative and enforcer of His Majesty's laws. But in this venerable firm, the laws were the casual meals of the employees, chewed and digested without any notice of their taste and substance; and it was clear that were any of the lawyers or clerks scuttling about to deign to notice Quinton, they would have chewed and digested him with the same indifference.

Farrow's secretary glanced at a clock on her desk, then got up and tapped softly on the door to the inner office, using just the tip of the nail on her index finger. There was a murmur from inside. She opened the door, poked her head through, and said something. There was another murmur in response, then she turned and beckoned to Quinton.

"Mr. Farrow will see you now," she announced in hushed, reverent tones.

"Thank you, miss," he said, wondering if he should bow or kneel once he was admitted to the inner sanctum.

It was merely an office, however. An exceptionally well-appointed office with a splendid view of a park, visible through a large window whose sill was covered with a row of well-maintained potted plants. The gentleman rising from the desk to greet him with a warm smile was a rosy-cheeked fellow in his early sixties, looking like someone out of an engraving in a frontispiece for something by Dickens, only with a dark grey suit that looked worth more than Quinton's annual salary.

"Constable Quinton, very good to meet you," he said, coming around to shake his hand. "I'm Jenkin Farrow. I hope you haven't been waiting long. We're busy here at Turner, Woodbridge, but never too busy to accommodate our men in blue. Please, sit, and tell me how I may assist you."

"Thank you, sir," said Quinton, waiting for Farrow to retake his seat before sitting himself. The older man beamed appreciatively at that. "I take it you know the purpose of my visit."

"You had mentioned to my secretary that you wished to discuss poor, dear Mrs. Remagen," said Farrow, sadness flashing across his face.

"You know the circumstances of her death?"

"Professor Remagen called me, of course," said Farrow. "He said she had taken her own life. Tragic, but not unexpected, unfortunately. We can only hope that her suffering has finally ended, bless her soul, and that Heaven will be merciful as to her choice. But the purpose of your visit?"

"Anytime there is a death that is, well, not from natural causes, we have to make a thorough investigation," said Quinton.

"Really?" said Farrow, his eyebrows rising in surprise. "Even in a matter this obvious?"

"It's routine," said Quinton.

"But is there any reason to believe it's anything other than suicide?" asked Farrow.

"If there was, I'm sure they would have sent a detective rather than me," said Quinton.

"I suppose they do things differently in Essex than they do here," said Farrow.

"I wouldn't know how the big boys do it at the Yard," said Quinton. "I'm fairly new to the job myself, so I suspect this was meant to be some kind of training. It's my first time with one of these."

"Well, I'm sure you'll go far, my boy," said Farrow encouragingly. "What do you need to know?"

"You handled Mrs. Remagen's legal affairs?"

"I did, ever since she came to London."

"Would you be able to tell me if she had a will?"

"Of course, she had a will," said Farrow. "We would have been quite remiss if we didn't urge our clients to be prepared for the one certainty in life, especially over the past few years. Have you made one yet, Constable?"

"Don't have much to leave," said Quinton with a laugh. "But I should get on it now that I've got a job with a real salary. Maybe I'll come back to you when I'm done with this."

"Oh, my dear boy, you couldn't afford to walk in the door here," said Farrow. "We cater to, shall we say, an exclusive class of clientele."

"Mrs. Remagen was wealthy, then? I still don't know the full extent of it. I wouldn't have thought being the wife of a university professor without a university would be a well-to-do position for a woman."

"He didn't have much before he met her," said Farrow. "But her grandmother—you saw the house in Hampstead?"

"I did. It was nice, but no mansion."

"No," said Farrow. "The mansion's out in Sussex. They leased it to the government for the duration of the war, but that's coming to an end. Her grandmother Letitia Miller left her a considerable amount, and there was an uncle in Canada who did quite well. Made his fortune in timber as I recall, then passed without issue two years ago. She was his only heir."

"So Professor Remagen will inherit all of that?" asked Quinton.

"Well, I shouldn't be discussing the precise terms of the will since it hasn't been published yet," said Farrow. "But generally speaking, yes, he gets the bulk of it."

"When was the will made?"

"The Remagens came in together before he joined up," said Farrow. "I was surprised that he went in at his age. She was distraught, but he had his mind made up. They initially came in for his will to be redrawn before he left. We had quite the flurry of estates work back then, as you can well imagine, so that wasn't unusual, but she wanted hers done as well. I remember her saying it was her way of letting him know she expected him to come back to her."

"A financial incentive to survive the war," mused Quinton. "Not the most romantic way to put it."

"She was devoted to him," said Farrow. "This was her way of showing it."

"I suppose," said Quinton. "Does anyone else in particular benefit from the will?"

"What a curious question," said Farrow, his eyes narrowing. "Why do you ask?"

"As I said, sir, I'm trying to be thorough."

"But it was a suicide," said Farrow.

"Most likely, but until the coroner makes that determination, I have to keep asking questions."

"There were some minor bequests to charities, but no other individuals."

"And if Professor Remagen doesn't get it, who would?"

"Moot point, since he survived her," said Farrow. "Unless—but that's a ridiculous idea."

"What idea is that, Mr. Farrow?" asked Quinton.

"Well, he wouldn't inherit if he—Constable, you aren't investigating this as a murder case, are you?"

"As I said, sir, that will be for the coroner to decide," said Quinton. "But it would be a normal practise to have alternative heirs in the event that the husband doesn't survive or is otherwise disqualified as the heir, wouldn't it?"

"As I said, sir, the husband has survived," said Farrow, no longer the jolly Pickwick he had first appeared to be. "The idea of this being anything other than suicide is ludicrous. You would know that had you known them as long as I have. Will that be all, Constable Quinton?"

"It sounds as if you think it is, Mr. Farrow," said Quinton.

"I do have something to ask you," said Farrow.

"What is that, sir?"

"How did you know to come to us?"

"By asking the right questions of the right people," said Quinton. "That's how it's done. Even in Essex."

"Who was the right person in this case? I doubt the professor would have mentioned us."

"I'm sorry, sir," said Quinton. "I don't reveal my sources."

"Then we are finished," said Farrow, pressing a button on his telephone.

The door opened immediately behind Quinton. The secretary stood, waiting.

"A pleasure to meet you, sir," said Quinton, as he rose from his seat. "I think I will take my legal business elsewhere once I make my fortune."

"We'll miss your patronage, Constable," said Farrow as he picked up a file from his desk and began to read it. "Good day to you."

* * *

Gwen had no idea of the hour by the time she finally reached her street in Kensington, but it was dark. She was chilled to the bone and her legs were pillars of lead, thumping along robotically to carry her home.

Percival appeared in the hallway the moment she stepped inside, his normally stolid face filled with concern.

"Mrs. Bainbridge, thank goodness," he said, rushing to take her coat. "We've all been terribly concerned."

"I took an extra-long walk and lost track of the time," she said. "I'm sorry if I upset anyone. Have I missed dinner?"

Then she stopped as Iris came out of the parlour behind him.

"What are you doing here?" asked Gwen.

"Where have you been?" asked Iris. "I've been worried sick."

"Why?"

"I called from the office this afternoon to see how you were doing. The household was quite surprised to learn you weren't with me. Given how we left things this morning, I was—"

She glanced up at Percival.

"Maybe we should take this discussion somewhere more private," she said. "Forgive me, Percival. I trust your discretion, of course, but—"

"Say no more, Miss Sparks," said Percival. "Mrs. Bainbridge, Prudence has made up a tray for you. I will have Millie bring it up."

"Thank you, Percival," said Gwen dazedly. "I don't know how much of an appetite I have."

"Did you have anything to eat after this morning?" asked Iris.

"No," said Gwen. "In fact, I don't remember eating anything this morning. I was too nervous."

"Then you must eat," said Iris firmly. "And I am going with you to make certain that you do."

"Iris, there is no need for this," protested Gwen.

"There is every need for this," said Iris. "Let's go to your room. You should stop and say good night to Ronnie and John."

"Oh, God," said Gwen, turning pale. "Do they know anything?"

"They know that you weren't at dinner, Mrs. Bainbridge," said Percival. "No more."

"Right," said Gwen. "I'll put in an appearance."

"They don't know I'm here," said Iris. "I don't want to be a distraction for them. I'll wait for you in your room."

They went upstairs. Iris slipped quietly past the boys' rooms and disappeared through Gwen's door. Gwen ducked into the lavatory. She looked at her reflection, grimaced at what she saw, then forced a bright smile before going to say good night to the boys.

They were both too sleepy to notice her tension and accepted her hugs and kisses with neither comment nor objection. She walked to her room, suppressing the absurd impulse to knock on her own door, and entered to see Iris sitting on the edge of her bed, her feet dangling a few inches from the carpet. A horn blue train case stood by the nightstand.

"What's that doing here?" asked Gwen, pointing to it.

"I'm staying the night," said Iris.

"Why?"

"Because you shouldn't be alone right now."

"That's ridiculous."

"It's not," said Iris. "You took a hard blow this morning, and you're still fragile. Anyone could see that, and I'm not just anyone."

There was a soft knock on the door, then Millie, the upstairs maid, entered with a tray of covered dishes, which she placed on the dressing table.

"Thank you, Millie," said Iris. "Will you do me a favour and wait outside for a moment?"

"Certainly, Miss Sparks," said Millie.

When the door closed, Iris slid off the bed and picked up a small bottle from the dressing table.

"What's the normal dosage?" she asked.

"That's not your concern," said Gwen.

"It is tonight," said Iris. "I am not allowing you to be in this state of mind with a bottle of Veronal handy. I am going to make sure you eat first so you can take this on a full stomach, but I am going to turn the bottle over to Millie for safekeeping. How much do you usually take?"

"A quarter teaspoon with a glass of water," said Gwen reluctantly.

"I'm going to give you half that," said Iris.

She measured it out into a glass tumbler, then capped the bottle.

"Now," she said, turning back to Gwen, "where's the rest of it?"

"I have no idea what you're talking about," said Gwen.

"Look, darling," said Iris compassionately. "I've known my share of addicts over the years, and I know you. You may have been weaning yourself from it, but you're not off it yet, and you're too clever not to have an emergency bottle stashed away somewhere. So either you fetch it for me, or I will turn this room over more thoroughly than my ex would a crime scene. Which is it going to be?"

Gwen glared at her furiously for a good ten seconds. Iris returned the look impassively. Then Gwen's shoulders slumped. She stepped past Iris and opened her walk-in closet. She removed a grey hatbox from the top shelf, opened it, and removed a small bottle from underneath the powder-blue cloche within. She replaced the hatbox, then handed the bottle to Iris.

"Satisfied?" she asked.

"I am," said Iris. "I'll be right back. Have your dinner."

She stepped out of the room, closing the door behind her. There was a muffled conversation from the other side. Gwen resisted the temptation to put her ear to the door. She idly removed the cover from one of the dishes, and the steam rising from the plate of stew with rice woke her stomach from its long hibernation. She sat down and gobbled the food up greedily.

Iris came back in and nodded approvingly, then sat on the side of the bed again.

"What happened after you ran away this morning?" she asked.

"I went searching for a next friend," said Gwen.

"Any luck?"

"Yes. Walter Prendergast agreed to be my petitioner."

"Prendergast," Iris repeated thoughtfully. "Solid member of the financial community, unimpeachable reputation, and he hasn't been involved with you romantically."

"Right," said Gwen.

"Will he be?" asked Iris.

"He said there'd be no quid pro quo," said Gwen.

"Of course, he would say that," said Iris. "But when all is settled and you're a free woman, he is going to ask you out. What will you say when that happens?"

"I suppose I will have to say yes," said Gwen. "I wish—"

She stopped.

"What do you wish?" asked Iris.

"I wish I wasn't in a position where I needed to be grateful to people," said Gwen.

She went back to her meal as Iris watched her from her perch.

"Do you like Prendergast?" she asked when Gwen had finished.

"I'm not sure," said Gwen. "I think I could like him. His forthrightness is disconcerting. I don't always want to know what someone thinks about me."

"Then you should stop reading everyone you meet," said Iris. "Let's say you start dating him. What will you do about Sally?"

"I don't know," said Gwen. "I didn't know what to do about him before. I hate this. It should get easier as we get older, not harder. We know more."

"Maybe that's why it's harder," said Iris. "Ignorance is bliss.

Well, you'll cross those bridges later. Have you told Mr. Stronach yet?"

"No, but I gave his number to Mr. Prendergast. I keep calling him that. I'll have to get used to calling him Walter."

"And so will I if you start going out with him," said Iris with a sigh. "Poor Sally. Still, it's good that you found someone for the petition so quickly. I can't wait to see the look on Parson's face when he finds out in court next week."

"Um, he already knows," said Gwen shamefacedly.

"Already?" exclaimed Iris. "But how could he? You've only—"

She stopped, staring at Gwen.

"Where did you go after seeing Prendergast?" asked Iris.

Gwen didn't answer.

"Please tell me you didn't go to see Parson," said Iris.

"I didn't see him," said Gwen.

"That's good," said Iris in relief. "For a moment, I thought—"

"But I went there," said Gwen. "He wasn't in. Or at least, he wasn't answering his door."

"But you made it as far as his doorway?"

"Yes."

"They let you get that far?"

"Not exactly."

"Tell me," said Iris. "Tell me everything right now. Do not leave out a thing. Not a word, not a gesture."

By the time Gwen was finished recounting her afternoon's adventures, Iris had her face in her hands.

"That was—" she started, then she shook her head. "That was unwise, to say the least. You gave them more evidence of your instability, you gave up the tactical advantage of knowing you now have a petitioner, and for all we know they've called the police because you assaulted one of their employees."

"He was hurting me," said Gwen. "What would you have done?"

"I would have borne the pain for the thirty seconds it would have taken to bring me to the lift and said something nasty while the doors were closing," said Iris. "Although I'm impressed that you broke the 'come-along' grip on your first try. Gerry will be so pleased. On the other hand, that security thug won't underestimate you the next time, so you've lost that advantage as well."

"I'm sorry," said Gwen. "I've been in a complete mental fog since the court appearance."

"Where did you go after that?" asked Iris.

"I don't even know," said Gwen. "I just walked for hours. I fetched up against the Thames finally, and thought, 'Either jump in, or go home.' And now I'm here."

"That choice, at least, was the right one," said Iris. "Well, what's done is done. We'll figure out the next step tomorrow. Take your Veronal, then go brush your teeth. You've had a long day, and you need your rest."

"Are you staying in the room in the guest wing?" asked Gwen.

"I am staying right here," said Iris, patting the bed. "I'm a light sleeper, so don't try to sneak away in the middle of the night. I will tackle you."

"I've had enough combat for one day," said Gwen, pouring water into the tumbler with the medication.

She stirred it, then drank it down. As she did, there was a knock on the door.

"Yes?" she answered.

"Mrs. Bainbridge," said Percival from the other side. "You have a telephone call. It's Mr. Danielli."

"That's right," said Gwen. "He said he was going to call and see how things went. Iris, I can't possibly talk to him right now."

"Do you want me to?" asked Iris.

"Could you?" pleaded Gwen. "Tell him I'm too distraught. And don't tell him about Prendergast. Not yet. I'll tell him when the time comes, but I can't tell him tonight."

"All right," said Iris. "I'll be back to tuck you in."

She followed Percival downstairs to the telephone.

"How is she?" he asked quietly.

"She's had a terrible day," said Iris. "She'll pull through, but she'll need some help."

"Then I'm very glad you're here, Miss Sparks."

"And I'm even more glad that you're here, Percival," she replied. "You and Millie. I'm going to make her take tomorrow off. You'll keep an eye on her for me, won't you?"

"Of course, Miss Sparks. Here's the telephone."

He retreated as she looked at the handset pityingly, then picked it up.

"Sally, it's me," she said.

"Sparks?" he answered in surprise. "Where's Gwen? Why are you there?"

"Gwen is indisposed, I'm afraid," she replied.

"What happened?"

"Many things. Her committee, Mr. Parson, has taken it upon himself to make her existence a living hell on earth."

"Tell me."

"I can't tell you everything because I wasn't there for everything, but here's what I know."

She summarised the board meeting, the hearing, and its aftermath, omitting the part about Prendergast. When she was done, there was a long pause at the other end of the line, although she could still hear the sounds of him angrily clomping around his flat.

"Unacceptable," he said finally.

And with that, he hung up.

She stared at the telephone in dismay, then dialled his number.

There was no answer. She let it ring for a minute and a half before hanging up.

"Sally, where are you going?" she muttered to herself.

She climbed the stairs wearily and went back to Gwen's room. Her partner was lying on her back in bed, staring up at the canopy.

"What did he say?" she asked.

"Not a lot," said Iris. "But he's very much on your side in all of this."

"Poor Sally," said Gwen.

Iris opened her train case and pulled out her pyjamas.

"Mind if I hang up my suit in your closet?" she asked.

"Be my guest," said Gwen.

Iris walked into the closet, looking at the dozens of frocks and suits hanging there. More than she had owned in her entire life. She changed into her pyjamas, hung up her suit and blouse, then came back to the bed.

"Lights on or off?" she asked.

"Off," said Gwen.

Iris circled the room, shutting off the lamps, then climbed into the bed next to Gwen. There was a half-moon out, enough to reflect some light through the window. Next to her, she could hear Gwen's breathing coming in fits and starts. She wondered how long the Veronal would take to calm her.

"Tell me something to distract me," said Gwen.

"Let's see," said Iris. "Archie asked me to go to Bernie's wedding."

"As his date? In front of the entire family?"

"In front of them, and whatever spirits haunt the parish church," said Iris.

"That's a significant step," said Gwen.

"More than sleeping with him?"

"What's done on the sly, no matter how involved, will never compare to the simple act of appearing together in public. It marks the next step down the slippery slope towards commitment."

"Whee," muttered Iris. "Do you think I should go?"

"How do you feel about it?"

"I've clawed my way back up that slippery slope more than once in my life," said Iris. "Emerged from the primordial soup to stand on my own two feet again."

"You're thinking about getting out of it before you even get into it," said Gwen.

"That sounds like you think I'm not in it now," said Iris.

"Well, what is Archie to you now?" asked Gwen. "A fling? An affair? A romance?"

"I don't like to categorise."

"Said the girl who loves beetles."

"Except for them, but that's part of the allure of beetles."

"You said you weren't exclusive with Archie," said Gwen. "But apart from a bash with our neighbouring steelworkers, you haven't mentioned anyone else. Is there someone?"

"No," said Iris. "Well, not really."

"Meaning yes, there is?"

"Meaning I'm going out to dinner with an old friend. But I don't think that amounts to a date."

"Who?"

"Remember when I told you about Trevor, my childhood crush?"

"Your fellow beetle enthusiast?"

"That's the one."

"I thought you said he was off in the Amazonian jungles somewhere."

"He was. He's back. He got a post at Oxford. He wants to grab dinner with me while passing through town."

"Is that all he wants to grab?"

"Gwendolyn Bainbridge, the words that come out of your mouth sometimes. I am positively shocked."

"Blame it on the Veronal," said Gwen, yawning suddenly. "Excuse me. So does Trevor know about Archie?"

"He does."

"And he still wants to go through with it. Brave man. Does Archie know about Trevor?"

"He does not, and what he doesn't know won't hurt him."

"What he finds out might hurt you."

"Archie would never hurt me," said Iris.

"Let's hope not. I was always concerned about that aspect of dating a spiv. Maybe going out with Trevor is a step in a positive direction."

"Tell you what," said Iris. "You wean yourself from the Veronal, I'll wean myself from Archie, and we'll both stave off commitment."

"It's a deal," said Gwen. "When is your not-a-date with Trevor?"

"Tomorrow, after work," said Iris. "Oh, hell!"

"What?"

"I didn't pack my nice frock. I'll have to run home and change over lunch."

"I can manage without you."

"You, my dear, are staying home tomorrow," said Iris. "You need to regroup. And call Mr. Stronach."

"All right," said Gwen sleepily. "Thank you for distracting me, although I'm considering reporting you to that Secret Society of Women Who— How did it go again?"

"The Secret Society of Women Who Are Still Dating?"

"That's the one," said Gwen.

Her breathing became more regular.

Starting to drift off, Iris thought. Good. Maybe—

"Iris," said Gwen.

"What?"

"Where did you say Mrs. Remagen died?"

"Epping Forest," said Iris reluctantly. "They found her sitting against a tree."

"And the police are investigating it?"

"One police constable," said Iris. "His name is Quinton. He came to The Right Sort after finding our flyer in her bag. Young, but very capable."

"Good," said Gwen, and her breathing became regular again.

At last, thought Iris. Let's both get some—

"Iris," murmured Gwen.

"What?" said Iris, beginning to regret having given her only half the dosage.

"She wouldn't have gone into a forest to die," said Gwen. "She didn't like the woods. And she was too meticulous a planner to leave our flyer in her bag where her husband could have found it. You're right, she was murdered. One constable isn't going to be enough. We need to help him."

"How did you figure all that out just now?" asked Iris, sitting up and looking at her in amazement.

But all that answered her was a soft snore rising from her partner's side of the bed.

Iris waited a few seconds for any more words of wisdom that might arise from Gwen's overactive subconscious, but it seemed to have finally settled down for the night. Iris lay back down, her own thoughts racing, but eventually exhaustion overtook her.

The rap on Gwen's door had Iris on her feet and reaching for the knife in her bag before she was fully awake and cognisant of her surroundings. Once her eyes had adjusted to the faint moonlight seeping through the shutters, she remembered where she was. Gwen was still out like a lamp.

It was unlikely that anyone in the Bainbridge house would be attacking, thought Iris. Certainly not by announcing their presence with a knock on the door first.

Still.

She quietly unfolded the weapon and held it behind her back before padding across the carpet to the door.

"Who is it?" she whispered.

"It's Percival, Miss Sparks," answered the butler.

She put away the knife, then opened the door a crack. Percival was standing there, wearing a magnificent royal blue robe.

"What is it?" she asked.

"There are two detectives at the front door," he said. "They wish to speak with Mrs. Bainbridge."

"Now? What's the hour?"

"Two thirty in the morning. Unconscionable, in my opinion, and I told them as much, but they are very insistent."

The bouncer at Parson's firm must have filed a complaint, she thought.

"Let me go down and speak to them," she said. "Maybe I can hold them off until a more reasonable hour."

"I would very much appreciate that, Miss Sparks. Some haste may be needed. Their patience was wearing thin."

"Be right with you," she said, closing the door.

No time to dress, she thought. And I didn't bring a robe.

She stepped into Gwen's closet, pulled the chain for the overhead lamp, then looked around.

There. Hanging on the door was a fuchsia silk robe. She put it on and tied the belt. It dragged behind her like a train, so she gathered it up and held it with one hand like she had gone back a century and was negotiating a grand staircase. She slipped on her shoes and stepped into the hallway, closing the door quietly.

She didn't want to know what her hair looked like, and Percival, bless the man, was too skilled a butler to react.

He led her downstairs. The two detectives were waiting in the front parlour. She recognised them immediately. And they knew her.

"Well, look what the cat dragged in," said one, a strongly built man with fine blond hair that was slicked back. "Ian, it's our favourite suspect."

"Good morning, Detective Inspector Cavendish and Detective Sergeant Myrick," said Sparks. "What brings you here?"

"Not you, for a change," said Cavendish. "We want to speak to your partner, so don't fob us off while she sneaks out the back. We're onto that dodge."

"First of all, I'm sure whatever happened was self-defence," said Sparks. "Second, she's in no shape to speak to anyone right now. She took a sleeping draught before bed and she's dead to the world."

"Not as dead as some," said Cavendish.

"What are you talking about?"

"A man named Oliver Parson was beaten to death a few hours ago," said Cavendish. "And I am very intrigued by this self-defence claim you've just mentioned."

CHAPTER 12

Parson is dead," repeated Sparks slowly while she tried to absorb and process the news. "And you've come here. Do you think Mrs. Bainbridge had something to do with it?"

"I'd like to put the question directly to her myself," said Cavendish. "So let's have her come down here for a little chat, sleeping draught or no sleeping draught. Otherwise, we might have to be a little less courteous and bring her back to the Yard."

"Surely this could wait until morning," said Sparks. "She might want to consult with her solicitor first."

"She can consult with the Lord High Chancellor for all I care," said Cavendish. "We're still going to talk to her."

"Maybe we should wait until she's awake, Nyle," said Myrick. "We could speak to Miss Sparks first. And that butler who's hovering about on the other side of the wall, thinking we don't know he's listening."

Percival stepped into the doorway.

"I am required to stay in attendance when there are visitors to the household, detectives," he said. "Do not mischaracterise my intentions."

"Aw, you've gone and hurt his feelings, Ian," said Cavendish.

"Sorry, mate," said Myrick.

"Well, Miss Sparks," continued Cavendish, "since you're already up and about at this ungodly hour, maybe you could answer a few questions."

"I've been up at this hour with you before, Detective Inspector," said Sparks. "I don't remember it being a particularly enjoyable experience."

"This time will be easier," said Cavendish. "No handcuffs. What time did Mrs. Bainbridge come home tonight?"

"Eight forty-five or thereabouts," said Sparks. "Percival, is that right?"

"Eight forty-seven, to be precise, Miss Sparks," said the butler. "I glanced at my pocket watch when I heard her come in."

"And where was she before that?" asked Cavendish.

"I don't know," said Sparks.

"Seems kind of late to be getting home from work, doesn't it?"

"She may have had plans for the evening."

"I would have thought you'd know what those plans were, being her friend and business partner. Happen to know if they included murdering Parson?"

"I doubt it," said Sparks. "She's not the murdering type."

"Unlike you."

"Be careful, Detective Inspector," said Sparks.

"Oh, I'm a careful man," he said. "Especially around dangerous women. Exactly why are you here, Miss Sparks? Something wrong with your flat? Still haven't got the bloodstains off the floorboards?"

"It took a bit of scrubbing, but they're gone," she said. "Thanks for asking. I'm only spending the night here."

"Why?"

"We're friends. Sometimes I stay over and visit the boys."

"Even when Mrs. Bainbridge isn't here?"

"No, but she's here."

"But she wasn't here when you got here, was she? Did she invite you over?"

"No," said Sparks.

"Who did?"

"Lady Bainbridge extended the invitation," said Sparks.

"Is that right?" asked Cavendish, turning to Percival.

"It is," said Percival. "As it should be, given that Lady Bainbridge is the mistress of the house."

"You ought to start calling Mrs. Myrick that," Cavendish said to Myrick.

"If I did, she'd never stop laughing," said Myrick.

"Did you happen to notice if Mrs. Bainbridge had any blood on her clothes when she returned?" asked Cavendish.

"There was none," replied Sparks.

"Then what was that self-defence comment all about?" asked Cavendish.

"She got into an altercation with a gentleman earlier," said Sparks. "I don't know all the details, but it sounded like he put his hands on her."

"And she gave him a good slap, eh, Sparks?" said Cavendish. "I remember her slapping one of our colleagues not so long ago. Ian, we may have a serial slapper on our hands."

"They're the worst kind of slappers," said Myrick.

"Was Mr. Parson the gentleman at the other end of the slap?"

"No."

"Was the gentleman connected to him in some way?"

"He works for the same law firm as Parson," said Sparks. "I assume he's the one who directed you here."

"Actually, that came from higher up," said Cavendish. "We found Parson's business card in his wallet, which led us to the firm. We woke one of the senior partners, who was none too happy about that, and he mentioned the uproar caused by Mrs. Bainbridge at the office this afternoon. Nothing about anyone getting slapped, though. She say why it happened?"

"They represent her on some legal matters," said Sparks.

"As in the deceased being her committee in the Court of Lunacy, for example," said Cavendish. "Yeah, the bigwig told us about that, too. Dangerous work, being a committee. You're dealing with lunatics and their money, and that's a bad combination. Maybe Mrs. Bainbridge was a particularly unsatisfied customer."

"She would never kill anyone," Sparks insisted.

"You start with a slap, and before you know it, someone's lying in an alley in Soho with his skull stove in," said Cavendish. "Well, this is all very enlightening, Miss Sparks, but I think we're ready for the main course. Which one of us gets to wake Sleeping Beauty?"

"I'll do it," she said. "Give us both some time to dress."

"Nothing fancy," said Cavendish. "It's just us folks here."

"Remember with whom you are dealing," said Sparks. "We are women. Even casual takes time. Percival, perhaps you could manage some coffee for the gathering? It looks like it's going to be a long night."

"Very good, Miss Sparks. Gentlemen, would you be so kind as to remain here?"

Sparks walked up the steps, pondering the news.

How do I tell her? she thought. What do I tell her?

They don't think she did it, otherwise they wouldn't be letting me go up to wake her. They're not worried about me warning her before she speaks with them.

Unless that's what they want me to do.

Timing, she thought. Gwen came home at a quarter to nine. The detectives arrived at two thirty in the morning. Sometime between the discovery of the body and now, they called one of Parson's senior partners, only the firm isn't likely to have anyone manning the switchboard at night, so it had to go through an answering service.

Still, it shouldn't take that much time to reach whoever gave them the information on Gwen. So the body most likely was discovered later rather than earlier.

Is that enough time for Percival and me to be an alibi for her?

Impossible to say. Especially because the time of the discovery of the body wasn't the time of death, and if he was killed while Gwen was wandering without witnesses through the streets of London, then she could have done it.

Only she wouldn't, thought Iris. Not even when faced with—

Actually, when faced with the loss of everything, especially Little Ronnie—

No. Gwen had Prendergast lined up. She wasn't at the point of No Hope Left. And she was too smart a woman to make matters so much worse.

Although her behaviour at Parson's firm didn't exactly give Iris confidence in Gwen's intelligence overriding her emotions.

She came to Gwen's room and went in. Her partner lay in bed asleep, blissfully unaware of what had happened, and what was about to. Iris sat on the edge of the bed, looking at the moonlit serenity of her face.

If only I could let her sleep on, she thought. I hate that I'm the one bringing her news of another death less than a day after I told her about the first one. But it has to be me.

She reached down and gently shook Gwen's shoulder.

"Gwen," she whispered. "Gwen, it's Iris. You have to wake up, darling. I'm so sorry."

There was no reaction at first, but as Iris increased both the volume of her entreaties and the speed of the shaking, Gwen's eyes gradually fluttered open. She looked at Iris in confusion, then recognition.

"Is it time for work?" she said, sitting up and yawning, then glancing at the clock. "No, it's—three o'clock?"

She turned back to Iris with a look of fear.

"What is it?" she asked.

"More bad news, I'm afraid," said Iris. "There's no other way to tell you. Oliver Parson was murdered."

Gwen stared at her uncomprehendingly at first. Then horror and resignation came into her eyes.

"So dreams do come true," she said softly.

"Don't say that," said Iris. "No matter how much—"

"How much I hated him?" Gwen finished. "No matter how much I wished him dead? I didn't want this, certainly, but—no, he didn't deserve death."

"I'm glad to hear you say that," said Iris.

"He deserved far worse," said Gwen. "He deserved to be strapped into a gurney for months, injected with God knows what until he couldn't tell the waking nightmares from the sleeping ones, and force-fed through a tube. He was let off too easily."

"Gwen, there are detectives downstairs, waiting to talk to you," said Iris.

"Are there?" said Gwen. "Well. I shouldn't keep them waiting."

"Maybe you should," said Iris. "We could call Stronach."

"No need," said Gwen, getting to her feet. "I have nothing to hide. Is that my robe you're wearing?"

"Sorry, didn't bring mine," said Iris, hastily untying it and handing it over. "I think we should dress before we go back down."

"What does one wear for an interrogation?" wondered Gwen as she walked unsteadily to her closet.

"Usually whatever one has on when they slap on the handcuffs," said Iris. "I don't think there is any recommended outfit."

Gwen turned on the light by the mirror over her dressing table and recoiled at the sight of her face and hair.

"Are they going to arrest me?" she asked, picking up a brush and going at the tangles automatically.

"I don't know," said Iris.

"How was he killed?"

"They said he was beaten to death."

"When? Where?"

"Somewhere in Soho. I don't know when."

"I have no alibi," said Gwen. "Not until I got home."

"They have to prove you did it," said Iris. "They can't if you don't tell them anything."

"I am going to tell them the truth," said Gwen. "That I didn't do it."

"But you might accidentally tell them something that they can twist and use against you."

Gwen looked at the ghost in her mirror, then slowly put the hairbrush back on the dressing table, leaving most of the tangles intact.

"I am going to wash my face," she decided. "I fell asleep with my makeup on."

Iris changed while Gwen was gone, brushing her own hair quickly before coiling it into the semblance of a bun. She turned as Gwen came back, her face scrubbed clean.

"I've never seen you without makeup before," commented Iris.

"What's the verdict?" asked Gwen.

"A tad bleak, but still gorgeous. You need to brush your hair, though."

Gwen looked in the mirror again, then ran her fingers through her blond tresses, teasing them out. She grabbed a hair clip and put it on, leaving several strands out and floating loosely about her head. Then she went into her closet, emerging a minute later wearing a plain, white linen dress over which she had draped a light blue woolen shawl.

"What do you think?" she asked. "Am I sufficiently Crazy Jane in appearance?"

"You look like you could turn men into stone with a glance," said Iris. "Maybe some makeup would counter that."

"Which is why I am not going to wear any," said Gwen. "Shall we go down and meet the gentlemen?"

"Lead the way, Madam Medusa."

The Mrs. Bainbridge who appeared in the parlour doorway was not the one the detectives were expecting. The inherent aristocratic grace was missing, while the immaculate appearance they remembered from their previous encounters had been replaced by an apparition that looked like it had swept in from the moors.

"Detectives, I apologise for keeping you waiting," she said, her timid manner matching her simple and somewhat dishevelled attire. "And for my appearance. I was not expecting callers at this hour. I understand that you wish to speak with me."

"That's right, Mrs. Bainbridge," said Cavendish. "Please take a seat."

"You're the ones who came to The Right Sort in September," she noted as she sat on an armchair across from them.

"That's right," said Cavendish.

"After torturing my partner in a dungeon all night."

"It's not a dungeon, Mrs. Bainbridge, it's an interrogation room," said Cavendish. "And I wouldn't call what I did torture."

"I would," said Sparks.

"But you're not here about Miss Sparks," said Mrs. Bainbridge. "So let's get to the point so we can all get back to sleep, shall we?"

"All right," said Cavendish. "Now—"

"I should advise you from the outset that I am a lunatic," said Mrs. Bainbridge, giving him a fixed, unblinking stare. "I was so adjudged on the seventeenth of March 1944, by the Master of the Court of Lunacy, and my status remains unchanged in the eyes of God, the King, and their servants in the Courts of Justice. Which means that nothing I say will be of any evidentiary value. Of course, you already know this."

"Was that the date Oliver Parson was appointed as your committee?" he asked.

"I suppose it was," she said. "I wasn't much aware of any of it at that point."

"How well do you know him?"

"Not that well, oddly enough. He made his monthly visits to the sanatorium, shared the absolute minimum amount of information about my finances in the shortest possible time, then left. Many of these conversations were done by telephone once I was released."

"And he represented you on the board of Bainbridge, Limited."

"Yes," she said. "I didn't pay much attention to what was going on at the company at first. He went to the meetings, and did whatever my father-in-law told him to do. I chafed under the need for him, naturally, but in time I came to understand the reasons for it."

"But something happened recently, didn't it?"

"I suppose you are referring to this past Monday's board meeting," she said.

"I heard the two of you went at each other something fierce," said Cavendish.

"There was a difference of opinion," she said. "Strong language was used."

"Tell me about it," he said, his notebook out and ready.

She gave a brief recounting of the meeting. Sparks, who hadn't heard the story in detail, listened as intently as did the detectives, her chagrin growing on behalf of her partner.

"So the partners who opposed him were Morrison—"

"Lord Morrison," she corrected him.

"Birch, and Burleigh," he said.

"Yes."

"Why do you think Parson made this motion?" he asked. "What would he hope to gain, especially with the end of his tenure as your committee in sight?"

"He may have been in league with one of the others," said Mrs. Bainbridge. "To throw control of the company to one of the limited partners in exchange for whatever payment he had negotiated. Or maybe he thought he might end up running the show himself."

"Interesting ideas," said Cavendish. "So the three in opposition could have killed him to forestall further attempts to overthrow the current regime, and the other two could have killed him to cover up the plot. What about Bainbridge himself?"

"Lord Bainbridge," she said, drawing a smirk from him.

"What was His Lordship's reaction when he heard about the mutiny in the ranks?"

"Outrage," she said. "I may be understating it."

"So he also may have had it in for Parson."

"Lord Bainbridge is an invalid recovering from a heart attack," she said.

"He's a millionaire with access to a telephone," said Cavendish. "We'll have to speak with him. Given his health, we won't wake him right now."

"You woke me," she pointed out.

"You're only a lunatic," he said. "You're otherwise healthy as a horse, as far as I can tell."

He stepped forward and leaned down until his face was close to hers. She recoiled at the sudden encroachment.

"I've dealt with lunatics before," he said. "And I've dealt with you before, Mrs. Bainbridge. Nice try steering us towards everyone else in the boardroom, but you're still our number one suspect, and I don't think you're any crazier than the rest of us right now. You can muss your hair up all you like, but you were in court yesterday to get your status restored, which means you and a couple of doctors think your sanity's normal enough to pass, so how about you drop the act and send Jeeves here to get the outfit you were wearing when you came home so we can get a good look at it?"

"His name is Percival Verger, he is one of the best men I've ever known, and you will address him with respect," she returned hotly. "Percival, please fetch my clothes from yesterday. They are in the hamper."

"At once, Mrs. Bainbridge," said Percival, disappearing back into the hallway.

"What happened in Lunacy Court yesterday, Mrs. Bainbridge?" asked Cavendish, sitting again. "Why aren't you a free woman yet?"

"Because Mr. Parson opposed my petition," she said.

"For the first time?"

"Yes."

"That must have been—maddening," said Cavendish.

He was rewarded with a quick flush of anger.

"There she is," he said, smiling. "The real Gwendolyn Brewster Bainbridge. It must have been infuriating to be so close to getting everything your heart desired, and to have it snatched away at the last second. How do you feel about him being dead, Mrs. Bainbridge?"

"I regret the untimely death of anyone, Detective Inspector," she said.

"But him less than others, I suspect."

She shrugged.

"You went to see him after the court appearance," said Cavendish. "Why?"

"I wanted to tell him that his days were numbered—as my committee."

"What did he say to that?"

"I didn't speak with him directly," she said. "I was told that he wasn't in his office. Then I was escorted out."

"We heard you slapped the escort."

"I did much worse than that," she said, smiling slightly. "I expect he's recovered, apart from his pride."

"What time did you leave Parson's firm?"

"Possibly one o'clock. I'm not sure of the exact time."

"And after that?"

"I don't know," she said. "I was in a daze. I just kept walking for hours, then I finally came to my senses and came home."

"So you cannot account for your whereabouts for nearly nine hours."

"No," she said. "Am I to understand that Mr. Parson's murder falls within that period of time?"

"His body was found at ten thirty," said Cavendish. "We don't think he had been dead for very long. Maybe an hour, according to the medical examiner."

"Then my arrival here puts me in the clear," she said, a small ray of hope in her eyes.

"Plenty of telephone boxes available to a woman wandering the streets of London," said Cavendish. "A word to a sympathetic ally, and you could return to your gracious living, knowing that someone else is getting his hands dirty on your behalf. Anyone come to mind?"

Prendergast, thought Gwen.

Sally, thought Iris.

"Sorry, can't think of anyone," said Mrs. Bainbridge.

"How about Sparks's boyfriend?" he asked. "Archie Spelling. I thought of him right away, to be honest. Didn't you, Miss Sparks? Archie's not a man squeamish about killing someone with his bare hands."

"There is nothing connecting Archie Spelling to any of this," said Sparks.

"Not yet," said Cavendish, getting to his feet. "But we've only started looking, haven't we? Never know what we'll turn up. Unfortunately, we have to waste some time talking to the board members of Bainbridge, Limited, now."

"May I point something out?" asked Mrs. Bainbridge.

"Certainly."

"My goal is to regain my status as soon as possible. Even with Mr. Parson's opposition, my best opportunity for doing that was with the current petition. His untimely death may cause the process to be postponed, or thrown out entirely. As much as I disliked the man and what he was doing, I was better off with him alive."

"Sounds reasonable," said Cavendish. "And you've had plenty of time to think about that answer after the fact. It doesn't mean you didn't go off the rails when it happened. Oh, here comes the butler. Shall we inspect the evidence, Ian?"

Percival stood in the doorway, holding the suit and blouse Mrs. Bainbridge had worn the previous day. The two detectives took each piece and went over them thoroughly.

"Immaculate," said Cavendish when they were through. "Lovely suit, by the way. Just the thing to wear to a courtroom."

He put on his hat, then turned to Mrs. Bainbridge.

"You may need to wear that in a different courtroom soon," he said. "You'll be the classiest dame in the Old Bailey. Good night, Mrs. Bainbridge. Good night, Miss Sparks. We'll be speaking with you again, I should think."

"I will show you out, detectives," said Percival.

"That way, right?" said Myrick, pointing to the front door with a smirk.

Percival stepped around them and opened it. The two detectives walked out into the night. The butler watched them until their car was gone, then closed the door and locked it.

"I will clear the coffee service, Mrs. Bainbridge," he said as he came back in. "I would advise you to get some rest. Both of you."

"Thank you, Percival," said Mrs. Bainbridge, resting her hand on his shoulder for a moment. "For everything."

She walked out of the room, then stopped at the foot of the staircase, gazing up.

"I don't suppose I could wake Millie and ask for my Veronal back," she said longingly.

"I'm here to stop you from doing that," said Iris. "Let's get you back to bed."

"I feel an absolute wreck," said Gwen. "And I don't think I convinced them I didn't have him killed."

"They didn't take you away in shackles," said Iris. "There's still hope. Maybe you were right about one of the board members being behind it."

"Honestly, I doubt that any of them could have got up the nerve," said Gwen as she started climbing the stairs. "Except Tom, possibly. He's more of a man than the rest of them combined. But he already beat Parson in the board meeting, so why would he bother?"

"What about Harold?" asked Iris, glancing down the guest wing where Lord Bainbridge was currently residing.

"Maybe," said Gwen. "He has a low threshold for betrayal. They are certainly taking a more deferential approach towards him than they did with me."

"He has a title. You don't."

"Is that how Cavendish was when you were arrested?"

"Yes, only for several hours more with my arm cuffed to the wall. Was his breath hideous?"

"I think he had a mint first."

"Lucky you."

They went back into Gwen's room, changed back into their pyjamas, and collapsed onto the bed.

"Do you think he did it?" asked Gwen. "Killed Parson because of me? I've been thinking about that possibility ever since Cavendish brought it up."

"Sally?"

"No, Prendergast," said Gwen. "He seemed obsessive, but would he cross that line?"

"I haven't seen him enough to judge."

"Why did you mention Sally?" asked Gwen. "Did something happen when you called him?"

"He was angry," said Iris. "I can always tell with him. You know how talkative he is normally. The angrier he gets, the less he speaks."

"How much did he have to say when you told him about Parson?"

"One word. 'Unacceptable.' Then he hung up and didn't answer when I rang him up again."

"That was around nine," said Gwen. "Parson was killed around nine thirty, assuming he died an hour before he was found. Would Sally have had enough time to track him down?"

"Sally is capable of many things," Iris reminded her. "And he lives in Soho."

"Where they found Parson's body," said Gwen, closing her eyes. "I'd scream into the night, only I don't want to frighten the children. It's all crashing down around me. I was so close, Iris. Even if Cumber doesn't think I killed him, there is no chance that he'll rule in my favour on Tuesday. I'll have to start all over, and I'm exhausted. I don't know if I can go through with this again."

"You can," said Iris. "You will. You are taking tomorrow off. Today, rather. Catch up on your sleep. If you're feeling desperate, call Dr. Milford. We're seeing him Thursday anyway. I'll mind the shop."

"You haven't had much sleep, either," said Gwen.

"I've come in on short nights before," said Iris. "I'll manage."

"All right," said Gwen, her voice fading.

Within moments, she was out.

Iris propped herself on one elbow and looked at her partner's expression, peaceful at last.

Was this the face that launched a thousand suspects? she wondered.

She hoped not. She hoped Parson was the victim of a random killing. That it had nothing to do with Gwen, or anyone Gwen loved, or who loved her.

But she knew deep down that there was nothing random about it.

She got out of bed and silently went into the hall, then down the stairs to the telephone. She picked it up, then dialled Sally's number.

No answer. She glanced at the clock in the hallway. Three thirty-seven.

Where are you, Sally? she wondered. What have you done?

CHAPTER 13

Quinton came into the precinct house early. Barry Loomis, his sergeant, came over to his desk while he was sorting through his case file.

"Look at him, all grown up," said Loomis. "Do you really have a case, or are you playing detective to impress Peel? You never struck me as the ambitious sort."

"I am the sort who thinks murderers should be brought to justice, sir," said Quinton. "I was under the impression that was part of our job description."

"Don't get snippy with me, lad," said Loomis. "I'm the one who has to shuffle assignments to cover your little picnic. You don't make this one stick, you'll be owing more than your share of rounds."

"As long as you all get me properly pissed when I do make the case, that's fair," said Quinton with a grin. "Tell the boys thanks."

"Speaking of Peel, he wants you to report in. At eleven. In person. Will you have a murderer in tow by then?"

"Not likely."

"Then I am taking the liberty to put you back into the regular schedule for tomorrow," said Loomis.

"Put it in pencil, Sergeant," said Quinton.

"Delusional hope is an essential part of being a detective," said Loomis. "Oh, and you got a call from your girlfriend. Here's the number."

"I don't have a girlfriend," said Quinton, taking the scrap of paper in puzzlement. He recognised the number from The Right Sort. "She's a source."

"Oh, a source. Well, lah-dee-dah," said Loomis. "I'll leave you to it, Sherlock."

Quinton waited until Loomis was out of earshot, then dialled the number.

"The Right Sort Marriage Bureau, Miss Iris Sparks speaking," came her voice, and he found himself smiling at the sound of it.

"It's PC Quinton, Miss Sparks," he said. "I'm returning your call."

"Good morning, Constable," said Sparks. "I wanted to pass on a couple of thoughts from my insightful partner, Mrs. Bainbridge."

"I'm ready," he said, grabbing a pencil.

"She pointed out that Mrs. Remagen had a strong aversion to jungles despite being married to a zoologist, so it was unlikely that she would go into a forest, even one as benign as Epping, much less choose it for her final resting place. Second, Mrs. Remagen was a careful, methodical planner. She wouldn't have left our flyer in her bag where her husband could have seen it. Our part in her posthumous scheme was not supposed to be revealed until much later."

"Brilliant," said Quinton. "Is Mrs. Bainbridge available for me to speak with directly?"

"Unfortunately, she isn't coming in today," said Sparks. "She had a difficult night. But I'd be happy to have her call you tomorrow."

"I don't know if there will still be an investigation tomorrow," said Quinton. "My forty-eight-hour pass may be coming to an end. I'm going over to speak to the chief soon."

"Well, tell him that Mrs. Bainbridge is also on your team in this," said Sparks. "Which means you have the full powers of The Right Sort backing you."

"I doubt that will sway him, but thanks," said Quinton.

"Mention the five murders we've solved this year," said Sparks. "Maybe that will help."

"Right," said Quinton, laughing. "I don't think anyone would take that seriously."

"You shouldn't make fun of your new partners, Constable. Oh, and I'm looking into Professor Remagen's unit to see if any of them are in London."

"I appreciate that. Thank you again, Miss Sparks, and thank Mrs. Bainbridge for me. Goodbye."

"Goodbye," said Sparks, hanging up with a touch of chagrin.

Why won't anyone believe we've done that? she thought.

She rang Sally's flat again, but there was still no answer. She flipped through her address book and found the number for BBC Television, where he worked part-time. The switchboard operator didn't know if he was on the schedule, but promised to have him call her.

Sparks rubbed her temples wearily, then made one more call.

"Yeah?" came a man's voice.

"Archie, it's me," she said.

"Sparks. Are you RSVP'ing about Bernie's wedding?"

"Ah, sorry, still weighing my options. No, I'm calling because your name came up last night."

"'Ow so?"

"Detective Cavendish paid us a call."

"And the other part of the 'us' is 'oo?"

"Gwen. A lot has happened since we last spoke."

She filled him in.

"Gwen would never ask anyone to do that," he said when she was done. "Much less me."

"I agree."

"But Cavendish 'as been itchin' to come after me ever since 'e was deprived of the pleasure of working me over," said Archie. "All right, thanks for the advance notice. Good to know you're on my side when the coppers come calling."

"I am Love's own peach," said Sparks.

"Are you free tonight?" he asked.

"Unfortunately not," she said, giving in to the inevitable. "An old school chum is passing through town and asked me to dinner."

"A chum of what persuasion, if you don't mind me asking?"

"Male. Oxford. Beetle enthusiast."

"Should I be jealous?"

"If I thought you'd be that insecure, I wouldn't be telling you about it," said Iris. "Do you want me to call when I get back to my flat?"

"Only an insecure man would want that," he said.

"I'll call you anyway," she said.

"Why?"

"Because I like talking to you, Mr. Spelling. So there."

"Right," he said, sounding pleased. "I'll be sitting by the phone, doing my nails."

Well, she thought as she hung up. That seems to be a decision of sorts.

Quinton got to Chelmsford at 10:45. He ducked into the gentlemen's lavatory and made sure to comb his hair thoroughly after removing his helmet. He looked at the mirror, straightened his back, and marched up the stairs to Peel's office.

Peel's secretary was there. She nodded and waved him inside directly. Peel was at his desk, reading a report. He nodded at Quinton without saying anything and directed him to the chair in front of the desk. Quinton sat and waited patiently until Peel finished the report, then looked up at him.

"You're early," he said. "Five minutes early. That's five minutes you could have been putting into your investigation."

"I didn't want to be late, sir," said Quinton.

"Still think it's a murder?"

"I do, sir," said Quinton.

"Tell me why, and tell me how you are going to prove it."

Quinton summarised his findings, including the recent observations from Mrs. Bainbridge. When he was done, Peel looked sceptical.

"What would be your next step?" he asked.

"I'm still trying to find someone who might have been a confidante of Mrs. Remagen, but she kept very much to herself, unfortunately. There was a woman who had worked as a twice-a-week maid, but she got married last year and I've been unable to track her down."

"So you need more time," said Peel.

"Yes, sir. Sorry, sir."

Peel looked at him, considering.

"I called you here because I received a telephone call this morning from Mr. Jenkin Farrow," he said.

"Remagen's solicitor?" exclaimed Quinton. "He called you? Personally?"

"As one superior would call another," said Peel. "Although in this case, I sensed he felt he was speaking to a subordinate. He was very disturbed about your prying into the life of an upstanding scholar and soldier. He spoke quite strongly about it, mentioning the place his law firm occupies in the upper echelons of London society. I am familiar with the firm, and they are indeed extremely well-connected to the citadels of power. He wants you to quash this investigation immediately before Mr. Remagen's reputation suffers even the slightest hint of tarnish. His phrasing, not mine. Apparently, you've stirred up the hornet's nest, Quinton."

"Are you telling me to shut it down, sir?" asked Quinton, his heart sinking.

"One thing you must learn if you wish to rise in this organisation, Quinton," said Peel, "is that there are vague but powerful forces that act upon us in ways we can't always foresee or control. That shouldn't be the case, I know, but even Justice cannot always withstand them."

"It shouldn't be like that," said Quinton.

"No, it shouldn't," said Peel.

Then, unexpectedly, he grinned.

"Fortunately, I don't give a damn how powerful Farrow thinks he is," he said. "The very fact that he called means you're onto something. His client must be running scared. Keep after this bug lover, lad, and get him to crack. Try and have it finished by the weekend."

"Yes, sir!" said Quinton, almost shouting it as he jumped to his feet and saluted. "Thank you, sir!"

He exited on the run. Peel watched him in amusement, then pressed his intercom button.

"Melissa," he said. "Call Loughton for me. Tell Sergeant Loomis I've given Quinton carte blanche."

Gwen slept late. She couldn't remember the last time she had slept late. It was nearly nine thirty, the sun was streaming through the window, and the boys must have been successfully packed off to school without waking her.

She stretched out in bed, then relaxed, grabbing a pillow and hugging it to her, her mind refusing to acknowledge the day's difficulties.

Glorious.

There was a breakfast tray on her dressing table. She got up to examine it. The toast was still warm and a wisp of steam rose from the teapot. Next to her teacup was a note from Iris.

Don't you dare come into the office! it said. *Millie will provide anything necessary.*

"Necessary" was underlined three times.

Do I need the necessary this morning? she thought as she poured the tea.

The cup rattled in the saucer as she picked it up, her body telling her what her mind was suppressing.

Maybe half a dose again, she thought. Enough to settle her nerves and quiet the panic gibbering away in the small dark caverns of her brain.

But she needed that brain at its peak if she was going to face the threats head-on. It was a very good brain when she turned it loose, she thought, and the Veronal, for all of its beneficial effects, would only dull it.

Accept the panic, Gwen. Embrace it. Use its energy to put the engine into a higher gear.

If energy is what makes gears work, she thought. She was uncertain as to the inner workings of automobiles. She added driving to the list of skills she should acquire once she escaped the Bainbridge house. One less employee, one more freedom.

She finished her breakfast, then sneaked down the hallway to shower. Then, refreshed, she strode back to her bedroom and pressed the button to summon Millie.

The maid knocked on the door a minute later.

"How are you feeling, madam?" she asked tentatively as she came in.

"Ready to brave the world from the safety of my bedroom," said Gwen. "Would you be a darling and do my hair?"

"Of course," said Millie, picking up the brush.

Gwen closed her eyes and let her head be rocked gently through Millie's skillful administrations. The maid braided and coiled the blond tresses, then set them with a few expertly placed Kirby grips.

"Done," she pronounced.

Gwen opened her eyes and looked at the mirror.

"Perfect," she said. "Millie, if I succeed in getting my own place, would you come with me?"

"As a maid?" asked Millie.

"As the keeper of the household, whatever it ends up being. I wouldn't be living anywhere as grand as this. It would be just me and Ronnie, and hopefully Agnes would stay on as his governess for a few more years."

"You'd be needing a cook," said Millie.

"Can you cook?"

"I can do some things," said Millie. "Mrs. Clearwater showed me a few."

"Well, we should both learn more from Prudence," said Gwen. "I don't know when I will break free of the Bainbridges, but when I do, I'd love for you to join me."

"You'll pay me the same?"

"Of course not," said Gwen. "I'll pay you more."

"I'll think about it," said Millie. Then her face broke into a happy grin. "Actually, I've already thought about it. I was hoping you'd ask me."

"Then you'll come?"

"I would be happy to, Mrs. Bainbridge," said Millie. "Now, you get your makeup on and get dressed. Ring if you need anything. I'll be here in a dash."

She left, smiling broadly. Gwen poured the rest of her tea into her cup. The rattling had subsided, she noticed.

One thing settled, she thought. Now all I have to do is avoid being arrested for murder while convincing Cumber I'm sane enough to be released to the wilds of London.

But before she could set her mind to those problems, there was a knock on the door.

"Yes?" she said.

"Mrs. Bainbridge, there is a Mr. Stronach on the telephone," said Percival. "He says it's rather urgent."

"I'll be right down," she said.

She threw on a dressing gown, then hurried down the stairs to the telephone. She picked up the handset, glanced in both directions, then answered it, cupping her hand over the mouthpiece and her mouth to prevent her voice from travelling.

"Good morning, Mr. Stronach," she said.

"I'm not so certain about that, Mrs. Bainbridge," said the lawyer. "I was at the court this morning, and the place was abuzz with some rather distressing news. Oliver Parson was murdered last night."

"Oh, dear," she said.

"It gets worse. I called in to my office, and Mrs. Merrifield told me that the detectives investigating his death wanted to speak with me. Apparently, we were the last case upon which he appeared. I wanted to warn you in case they turned up on your doorstep. I think they may suspect you of having something to do with it."

"I'm certain they do," she said. "They've already crossed the doorstep into the front parlour."

"When was this?" he exclaimed.

"Early this morning, some time past two thirty."

"Why on earth didn't you call me?"

"Because you don't give out your home telephone number to lunatics, remember?"

"Yes, yes," he said. "That is my policy. A sound one, for the most part. That's bad news, though. You must be their principal suspect. What did you tell them?"

"That I had nothing to do with it."

"Good choice," he said. "Was it the truth?"

"Do you doubt it?"

"I do not, but I had to ask," he said. "Mind you, if I were representing you on the criminal matter—"

"Aren't you representing me for all purposes?" she asked.

"My contract with the late Mr. Parson only covers the petition," he said. "I could hardly go to his firm right now and ask for authorisation to defend you for murdering one of their employees. I'd think it would be regarded as bad for company morale."

"Wouldn't this be related to your efforts to regain my status?" she asked.

"Possibly, possibly," he said. "You do have a wonderful defence in place. You're legally insane. Quite convenient. Just think, if Parson hadn't opposed your petition, you wouldn't still be a lunatic and the police could go after you full force."

"If I was found to be a lunatic murderer, I would be put in an institution for the rest of my life," she replied. "I don't find that convenient in the least."

"No, of course not," said Stronach hastily. "I was momentarily distracted by the uniqueness of your legal position. Speaking of which, your Mr. Prendergast rang me yesterday afternoon. Said he's willing to be the next friend. No romantic involvement with him, I hope?"

"I met him on a social occasion. He had some financial dealings with Bainbridge, Limited, at the time, which have since ended. He did subsequently ask me to dinner, but I turned him down, so no."

"And you don't expect any further overtures?"

"I can't predict the future, Mr. Stronach," she said. "All I can say is that there have been no promises made for this favour."

"Very well. That should suffice for the court. I'll file the paperwork. There may be another adjournment due to, shall we say, the sudden absence of counsel for the opposing side, but there's nothing we can do about that. At least there's no criminal case pending against you."

"So far," said Gwen.

"Let's hope it stays that way," said Stronach. "But ring my office if they throw you in."

"Answer the telephone when I do," she said.

"I will," he promised.

She hung up, then headed up the stairs, making the left into the guest wing.

"Come in," called Harold when she knocked.

She found him seated in his chair, wearing a dressing gown over his grey herringbone trousers, the matching jacket waiting on a hanger suspended from a hook on the closet door. Percival was hovering over him, shaving him.

"You're dressing today, I see," said Gwen. "Expecting visitors from Scotland Yard?"

"I am," he said. "My solicitor is on his way. Did you kill Parson?"

"No. Did you?"

"No."

"Good," said Gwen. "Then we both have nothing to fear."

"What did you tell them about me?"

"The truth. That you were furious when you heard about his attempt to overthrow your regime."

"I wish you hadn't," he grumbled. "Makes me sound like I turned avenging angel."

"If I hadn't told them, then someone else would have, and I would have been accused of covering for you," she said.

"Hmph," he said. "Just as well, then. Anything else I need to know?"

"Do you think anyone on the board arranged it?"

"None of them have the necessary combination of guts and lack of brains," he said.

"You don't think he presented a threat to any of them?"

"Not anymore," he said. "Not after you brought him down. If his death has something to do with the firm, though, then the most likely candidate is you. Interesting thing is while I don't think you did it, I do think that you are fully capable of doing it or having it done. And I've never thought that of you before."

"Are you saying I've risen in your estimation?" she asked, irked by the idea.

"Any businessman worth his salt is capable of murder," said Bainbridge as Percival scraped the last bit of stubble from his throat. "If you survive this investigation, you will be a worthy addition to the company."

"That's completely appalling but thanks, I suppose," she said. "I'm going back to my room. Nice to see you in a suit again, Harold. Give my regards to the detectives."

She sat by her window, her notebook resting on the sill.

Worst possibility, she thought. Someone killed Parson because of some misguided idea of helping me. Which means Sally or Prendergast.

Or Iris, come to think of it. A loyal friend with more unsavoury connections than anyone Gwen knew. Only Iris was too smart to put Gwen at risk like this.

On the other hand, Parson might have been killed for reasons completely unconnected to Gwen. He must have had other clients besides her. Other legal adversaries in high-stakes cases. Other people who despised him enough to want him dead.

Other lunatics.

Those trails would be better left to the detectives. She would only draw more attention to herself if she interfered with matters that didn't concern her, and hooray for Cavendish and Myrick if they found a better target.

So let's look at the next worst and still very bad possibility: Parson was killed because of something involving her. Which meant it was brought on by either the board meeting or the petition.

She thought back over her recent encounters with Parson. Things had never been good between them, but they had turned spectacularly sour in a very short period. He had never said anything about opposing her petition before, so why now? Why, for that matter, would he move to oust Harold now after sitting docilely at the table like a dog waiting for scraps for two and a half years?

Something must have happened to make him change his behaviour. Or maybe he thought something was going to happen. And that made him a threat to someone. Whatever it was could only be of recent vintage, and she couldn't think of anything that qualified. The granting (she hoped) of the petition, which would end his reign as her committee? Or maybe it was the return of Harold as CEO of Bainbridge.

The November board meeting was Parson's last chance to assert himself before Harold came back to reapply his boot. It was the only time she ever heard of Parson taking on someone or something bigger than himself. He was a petty man who seemingly took pleasure in bullying her while he had power over her, but quailed when faced with powers superior to his own.

Now someone with superior power had crushed him for the last time.

In the cold light of day she found herself, much to her surprise, feeling sorry for him. He was a miserable little man who led a miserable little life, a joyless creature who she had never seen smile. Not once in all the time . . .

Well, there was that moment on Monday, when she saw him in the hallway before the board meeting, but it was fleeting.

He appeared genuinely happy, though. The smile vanished the moment he saw her, so it couldn't have been the anticipation of his attempted coup that made him joyous. What was it?

She thought back to what he was doing. She had come to greet Hilary McIntyre at the door. Parson was down the hall, speaking to someone. He was facing a doorway which concealed all but a sliver of a navy blue skirt and a matching pump. Who did she see who was wearing that combination? Oh, yes. Miss St. John, who had one of the desks opposite Mrs. Stebbins. The meek little blonde, the assistant to some manager or other.

Accounting! That was it.

She reviewed her introduction to Miss St. John. She had been remarkably nervous upon meeting Gwen. Maybe that was just her manner, but Gwen was surprised that a person that nervous would be in so responsible a position. Whatever feelings Gwen had about Harold, he did run a tight ship with competent people.

So why would St. John be nervous about meeting her? Even afterwards, when Gwen was dragging Stephen Burleigh into Tom's office, she made that odd gesture of touching her throat when she saw Gwen, both when they came barging through and again when they left. And she wouldn't look Gwen in the eyes then. She looked down. Gwen remembered following her glance, but all there was to see in that direction was the wastebasket, and there was nothing remarkable about the wastebasket, just a pile of opened envelopes and discarded wrapping paper.

Pearl-coloured wrapping paper.

She had seen wrapping paper that colour somewhere else recently.

Parson's office. On the side table, next to an unwrapped jewellery box. A long one, from Fox's. The type of box one would use to hold a necklace.

Miss St. John kept touching her throat. But not when Gwen first met her. Only after she saw Parson.

Had he given her a necklace before stepping into the boardroom? Had she in turn done or said anything to warrant that gift? To bring that uncharacteristic smile to his face?

An affair between a man with complete charge over Gwen's finances and a woman who was assistant to the head of accounting at Bainbridge was a very worrisome idea.

She went over to her writing desk, picked up the pile of reports that Harold had loaned her prior to the board meeting, and began rereading them.

* * *

Mrs. Billington knocked on Iris's door around eleven thirty.

"We just got an odd sort of message," she said.

"Odd in what way?" asked Iris.

"It was a man. I didn't recognise his voice. He said tell Miss Sparks that Mr. Needly called. I tried to tell him you were here, but he hung up before I said anything."

"That is odd," said Iris. "But don't worry about it. If he wants to speak with me, he'll call back. I'm feeling a bit peckish. Would you like anything from the tea shop?"

"I would, but I'm slimming this week," said Mrs. Billington regretfully. "Enjoy it for me."

"Will do," promised Iris.

She threw on her coat and hat, then hurried down the stairs.

The telephone in the box at the corner to the right was ringing when she came up to it. She snatched it from its hook, pulling the door shut behind her.

"Where the hell have you been?" she snapped. "I've been frantic."

"I'm touched, Sparks," said Sally. "I went off on a little mission after your call last night."

"You went off during my call," she said. "After hanging up on me. Please tell me you weren't going after Parson."

"Of course I went after Parson," said Sally. "I wanted to see if he'd listen to reason about Gwen."

"Oh, Sally," she groaned. "What happened?"

"Nothing happened," he said. "I called his house, but he hadn't come home yet. So I went to the address and waited for him to show up. He never did. He must have been out on a binge, lucky sod. I finally gave up around four, came home, caught a few winks, then went over to Ally Pally to see if they had anything for me. This is the first free moment I had to return your call. Why are you frantic?"

"Parson was killed last night," said Sparks. "In Soho, no less."

There was silence at the other end.

"Well, that certainly explains why he didn't come home," he said finally. "I suppose you thought I might have done it."

"It crossed my mind, yes."

"And sitting in my car across the street from his house is not the best alibi one could present," he said. "If only cars could talk. That should be the next thing they work on."

"Sally—"

"Do the police know about me?" he asked.

"No," she said. "Gwen didn't bring up your name."

"They already spoke to her?"

"She's their main suspect."

"What can I do?"

"Do nothing, Sally," she said.

"I'm terrible at that," he said. "I have to get back. I'll call you tonight."

"I'm going out tonight."

"Ah, well, give Archie my regards."

"Not with Archie."

"Sparks! Have you found an honest man at last?"

"There are none to be found, said Diogenes. Old friend from long ago. Nothing romantic."

"There's nothing romantic about you and Archie," he pointed out. "You need to fall in love again, Sparks."

"I did fall in love, remember? It turned out poorly."

"If at first you don't succeed . . ."

"Chuck it into the river."

"That's not how the saying goes, Sparks. I'll call you tomorrow."

"Thanks for checking in, Sally."

She hung up, then headed back to the office. She found a note from Mrs. Billington. *Call Phyllis,* it said.

She rang her up.

"Phyllis, it's Sparks," she said. "Any luck?"

"I found one," said Phyllis. "A Daniel Clague. He was with your strange-named fellow in Burma until he lost part of a leg in combat. He's got an address in Hackney. Will that suit?"

"Perfectly," said Sparks. "Thanks a million."

She took down Clague's number, which turned out to be his landlady's. He wasn't in.

"But I can tell you where to find him," she said. "He holds court at the Amhurst Arms from open to close. It's on Shacklewell Lane. Do you know it?"

"I'll find it," said Sparks. "Thanks much."

She hung up, then looked at the clock. Quinton had his meeting with his chief, so he was unreachable. She pressed the lever for the intercom.

"Saundra, I'm going out for a while," she said. "I should be back by four at the latest."

"I'll manage," said Mrs. Billington. "I'm sure it must be something important if you're leaving me all alone. Where are you going?"

"To a pub in Hackney."

"I stand corrected. I'll tell anyone who asks you're out investigating a candidate."

"You're a treasure, Saundra."

Sparks had been planning to rush home during her lunch break to change for her date with Trevor. She was still wearing her suit from the previous day, which promised business and no pleasure, and needed cleaning.

Sorry, Trevor, she thought as she locked the office door behind her. You'll have to see me as I am instead of how I want to appear.

CHAPTER 14

Shacklewell Lane had been a main route for ages, and the Amhurst Arms must have been a traveller's inn when it was built the previous century. It was a two-storey affair, the stuccoed upper floor ornamented with false columns separating the tall windows.

It was one o'clock when Sparks walked in, causing first a stir, then silence as the regulars stared at her. She walked over to the bar and tapped the barmaid on the shoulder.

"I'm looking for Daniel Clague," she said. "Is he about?"

"What's he to you?" asked the barmaid.

"I'm having his baby," said Sparks.

There was a snort of laughter from behind her, and she turned to see a short, wiry black-haired gent with a thin moustache sitting at a table, wiping foam off his tie.

"Now look what you made me do," he said. "What kind of example will I be for our little one when I'm making messes like this?"

"You're Daniel Clague," she asked, going over to him.

"Danny," said Clague, rising to shake her hand, stumbling slightly as he did. "And who are you to be spoiling what little is left of my reputation?"

"My name is Iris Sparks," she said. "A friend of a friend gave me your name."

"What friends would they be?"

"One of them is Potiphar Remagen."

"Ah, the professor," he said. "He send you to me?"

"I'm here on his behalf," she said.

"Well, then, what are you drinking? More importantly, what are you buying me?"

"Two more of these," Sparks said to the barmaid, pointing to Clague's glass.

"You don't know what you're getting into," said Clague.

"At the moment, I'd say it's beer," said Sparks.

The barmaid returned with two pints of a dark brown beer.

"You bought, you toast," said Clague.

"To the Army," said Sparks, holding up her glass.

"May they get along without me until the end of time," he said, clinking his against it. "'Eyes right! Buttons bright! Bayonets to the rear!'"

"'We're the boys who make no noise, we're always full of beer,'" added Sparks.

"We won't finish the verse because there're ladies present," said Clague, winking at the barmaid. She winked back. "Although I'm not sure present company should be included. A proper lady shouldn't know that toast."

"I know lots of things I shouldn't know," said Sparks.

She took a swig from her glass, then looked at its contents quizzically.

"This is peculiar," she pronounced. "It's stout, but I'm getting something—fishy?"

"That would be the oysters," said Clague. "Encountered it first when I was laid up in New Zealand, then found out Hammerton's been making it locally when I got demobbed. It's an acquired taste."

"Thanks for expanding my horizons," said Sparks. She took another sip. "Nope, still haven't acquired it."

"So what's up with the professor?" asked Clague.

"His wife died on Sunday."

"No!" exclaimed Clague. "After all he went through. That's a crying shame, that is. He must be heartbroken."

"Hard to tell," said Sparks.

"Yeah, it would be if you don't know him," said Clague. "But why are you asking about it?"

"It wasn't from natural causes," said Sparks. "She died out in Essex County, so the police out there are looking into it. But they don't know London like I do."

"You're not a copper," he said.

"No," she replied. "But I've done some investigating for them. I've got some helpful connections, especially when it comes to the military. I looked up the professor's squad, and found you."

"How unnatural were the causes?" asked Clague.

"Enough for the police to be investigating," said Sparks.

"And who do they think killed her?"

"Prime suspect's always the husband in these cases."

"Let me set you straight on something right off," said Clague angrily. "There is absolutely no way on God's earth that that man would do anything to harm his wife."

"Convince me," said Sparks. "Convince me, and I promise you I'll convince them."

Clague stared down into his beer.

"We were a suicide squad," he said quietly. "No one told us that, but we pretty much knew. If the Japs didn't get us, the jungle would. Hell, the jungle would probably get us first, we thought. And to top it off, there was this professorial chap, twenty years older than the rest of us, saying, 'Follow me, boys,' like it was a field trip to catch butterflies."

"Did you catch any?"

"We caught plenty," said Clague. "And we lost a few. The commander was named Weir. Decent man, and smart enough to realise the professor was the one who should be telling us what to do. He taught us how to disappear, how to set traps that didn't look like traps, how to find plants we could eat and avoid the ones that would kill us. And every now and then, he would stop short, holding up a hand for absolute silence, staring ahead. And just when we were ready to start shooting at shadows in the brush, he'd step forward and grab some beetle crawling along a tree trunk and stare at it for a while. 'Look at that,' he'd say. 'Have you ever seen anything more beautiful?'"

He took a sip of his drink.

"Now, that usually would prompt some story about some gorgeous piece someone had encountered back near base," he continued. "For those of us who didn't have wives or steadies, anyway. Hell, for some who did, let's be honest. And over time, he'd tell us about the lovely Adela, and how she had saved him from being a lonely hermit in the jungle. You never saw a man more in love than him. I asked him once why he signed up for Burma when he could have put his big brain to work for something more large-scale that would have kept him nearer to her."

"What did he say?" asked Sparks.

"He said he signed up for Burma because Adela's home was there, and he was going to wipe out every Jap he could find so she could come back to it when it was all over. But she didn't. And now she never will."

"Have you stayed in touch since the war ended?"

"My war ended earlier than his," said Clague, rapping on his left shin.

There was a dull thump under the pants leg that didn't sound like flesh and bone.

"I could tell you the story about how they carried me through after I was hit," said Clague. "How he fashioned a stretcher and a tourniquet out of what was available, and how he and the others took turns humping me back fifty miles, shoving a handkerchief in my mouth when the pain and the fever got me screaming. No one would have said a word if they had simply put me out of my misery and weighted me down with stones in the swamp. They didn't do that. And when they got me back to base, they dropped me at hospital, had a shower, a hot meal, and one night in a real bed, then they turned around and went right back in."

He drained his glass.

"Have you heard from him since then?" asked Sparks.

"Letters. I wanted to get together with him in London, but he said something vague about taking care of matters with his wife. And now she's dead?"

"She is," said Sparks.

"How did she die?"

"Drug overdose," said Sparks.

"Was she ill?"

"She had cancer," said Sparks. "Do you think Remagen could have put her out of her misery?"

"I think he would have gone to Hell and back to find any possible chance of saving her," said Clague. "Like he did for me. I want to go to the funeral. Do you know when it is?"

"Saturday. Here's his number," said Sparks, scribbling down the information on a napkin and giving it to him.

"If someone killed her, you'd better find the bastard before he does," said Clague.

"We're working on it," said Sparks.

She signalled to the barmaid.

"One more for my friend," she said, giving her enough to cover the pints.

"You haven't finished yours," Clague pointed out.

"I've had all I want of it," said Sparks. "Thanks."

She left the pub and rushed back to The Right Sort, hoping she could get the taste of oysters out of her mouth before Trevor showed up for their date.

* * *

Gwen looked through her address book, then dialled a number. After several rings, someone picked up.

"Hello?" said a groggy-sounding voice.

"I would like to speak to Stephen Burleigh, please," she said.

"I'm Burleigh."

"Stephen, it's Gwen Bainbridge."

There was a brief pause.

"This isn't a social call, I take it," he said.

"No," she said. "Are you feeling able to talk?"

"Am I sober, do you mean?" he asked.

"Yes."

"Hungover," he said. "I went on a bender last night. Only got up ten minutes ago."

"I wish I had known," she said.

"You would have come to stop me?"

"I would have come to join you," she said. "Yesterday was a terrible day, and I could have used some cheering up."

"I don't get called upon for my cheery disposition much nowadays," he said.

"Was this a solitary bender, or were there friends involved?"

"Some mates from my unit," he said. "They just got demobbed and called me up."

"Sounds like a happy occasion," she said. "Where did you go?"

"Why do you care?" he asked suspiciously. "It wasn't a place for ladies of good breeding to get sloshed, if that's what you're looking for."

"This is important, Stephen. Where did you go and when did you get there?"

"Ye Olde Mitre in Holborn. Got there around seven, and we closed it down. What's this all about?"

"Oliver Parson was killed last night."

"What?"

"You heard me. The worse news is you're on a list of potential suspects."

"That's insane!"

"The better news is I'm much higher up on the list," she said. "Stephen, when we were at the board meeting, you said something about a better offer than you already had. What were you talking about?"

"I don't remember," said Stephen. "I was already several drinks in by that point."

"Nonsense. You showed up at a board meeting for the first time since assuming your father's mantle. You clearly hated being there. Someone put you up to it. If it was Parson acting on his own, that's one thing. But if someone else was pulling the strings, he might have other board members in his sights. You could be in danger, Stephen."

"I—I—" he stammered. "Is he really dead?"

"The detectives who grilled me at three this morning certainly seemed to think so."

"This isn't happening." He groaned. "He told me all I had to do was show up and follow his lead."

"Who said that?"

"Parson. He tracked me down over the weekend. Said there was a golden opportunity there, but we had to move fast."

"An opportunity to do what?"

"To take over Bainbridge, Limited," said Burleigh. "He had to make his move before Lord Bainbridge came back, and he needed one more board member."

"Who did he say was going to run the place if he succeeded?"

"He was," said Burleigh. "There's nothing in the bylaws that says the CEO has to be on the board, and he sounded like he was keen for the job. Honestly, he knew the place inside out. Knew things I never knew, details about financing, projected earnings, expansion of the African holdings, contracts with foreign defence forces. That railroad Tom was talking about—that was going to make a huge impact. You saw the October report? The jump from September was amazing, and he said the November report was going to be even more so."

"I only get the quarterlies," said Gwen. "I saw Harold's copy of the October report, but none of the monthlies."

"That's a pity," he said. "The monthlies are very exciting reading if you like money."

"I do, in theory," she said. "Did Parson say what he had planned after becoming king of Bainbridge?"

"He was going to sell off the plantations and all the holdings that weren't either munitions or copper."

"Harold would have thrown an absolute fit at that," said Gwen. "And what did he promise you in exchange for your support?"

"Money," said Burleigh. "Which I could use, frankly. But along came you to appeal to my better nature. It was nice to know I still had one. Down went Parson, and now—well, it doesn't matter much what he wanted, does it?"

"It does," said Gwen. "We'll have to explore some of those ideas ourselves when things settle."

"Really? You'd consider them, after all this?"

"Once I've looked at them carefully," said Gwen. "You should do the same. But not while you're sloshed."

"Right," said Burleigh. "And when the coppers come calling, what should I say?"

"The truth," said Gwen. "Goodbye, Stephen. Treat yourself better, won't you?"

"I'll try, Mrs. Bainbridge," he said.

She hung up.

Parson knew Bainbridge, Limited, as only an insider could, she thought. And that pointed once again to Miss St. John as a source of his knowledge.

She went back to her room and pulled out the October report from Harold's papers.

When men talk about monthlies, they mean money, she thought as she went through it.

She found what Stephen was talking about. The monthly profits had indeed jumped considerably from September, due in part to payments from the British government coming in after the American loans. She looked at the September report by way of comparison. The profits were roughly the same as in August, despite Harold's heart attack and Tom taking over. Bainbridge, Limited, was a well-oiled machine, the money coming in regular as clockwork since the war had ended.

Something about the numbers bothered her.

She looked again at the September profits. If they were regularly the same as the prior months, then the quarterly profits would have been three times the monthly amount.

She went into her closet and retrieved the large box containing her set of quarterlies. She pulled out the most recent one and opened it to the page detailing the quarterly profits. She looked back and forth between the two reports, jabbing at the numbers with her nail.

She stood up and practically ran down the stairs to find Percival in the dining room, setting the table.

"Yes, Mrs. Bainbridge?" he said when he saw her.

"Percival, would you open Lord Bainbridge's office for me?"

"Of course," he said, putting down the cloth and polish.

Harold had a private office on the ground floor, large enough for a rolltop desk, a red leather chair, a telephone stand with his personal line, and a set of walnut bookcases taking up one wall. It was these that drew Gwen's attention. There was a full set of monthly reports from Bainbridge, Limited, going back for decades. She pulled out the ones for August and July and skimmed through them, fury rising within her.

"Right," she said. "Percival, I need you to gather the last three years of reports and bring them to my room. Immediately."

"Yes, Mrs. Bainbridge," he said. "I'll see if we have any cartons suitable for the task."

An hour later, Gwen knocked—no, pounded on Harold's door. He opened it moments later, peeved at the intrusion, but whatever remonstration he had formed died before escaping his throat as he saw the look on her face.

"We need to talk," she said in a tone that brooked no dissent.

"Very well. Come in."

He held open the door as she strode in, a stack of papers in her arms. She pulled out his chair and pointed to it.

"Sit," she said.

Wondering what awaited him, he sat. She put the papers down on his dressing table, then pulled a report from the top.

"June 1944," she said. "My first quarterly report after Parson was appointed as my committee. The profits were distributed. You and I each get forty percent as general partners. Correct?"

"Of course," said Harold. "And it shows that."

"It does," she agreed. "Now, look at my most recent quarterly. Same thing, forty percent each."

"I don't see any difference," said Bainbridge.

"No, because there isn't one," said Gwen. "Only look at your last three monthlies. Add up the profits in your reports."

He took the three reports she handed him and reviewed them carefully.

"They add up differently," he said, puzzled.

"They do," she said. "In fact, they add up to ten percent more than they do in my quarterlies. The reports I have been receiving have reflected overall profits that are less than what are shown in your monthly reports."

"I don't understand," said Harold, flipping through each of the reports. "These are official reports. They're printed on company stationery."

"With the company letterhead," said Gwen. "And, while I'm no expert, using the same brand of typewriter. But throughout, there's a slight nick in the lowercase 'u' on the ones I get that's not on yours. Does the same secretary type up all of the reports for all the partners?"

"Yes," said Harold. "Miss FitzGibbons."

"And then they are sent out to the partners," said Gwen. "Only mine are sent—were sent to Parson, not directly to me. As were my payments."

"I wonder how long this discrepancy has gone on."

"I took the liberty of bringing up your monthly reports since 1944," she said, pointing to the rest of the stack.

"Those were in my private office," he said indignantly. "I don't like you going in there."

"I really don't care at this point," she retorted. "I've been going in there ever since your little Mopani adventure jeopardised our lives. The discrepancy began in the second quarter of 1944, and it's been increasing ever since."

He went through the stack, Gwen stabbing at each total so hard that she nearly pierced the paper. When they were done, Harold looked up at her bleakly.

"He's been stealing from you," he said. "All this time."

"Yes," said Gwen. "Yes, he has."

CHAPTER 15

Harold paced the room with an energy Gwen hadn't seen since before his heart attack.

"Melanie St. John has been with us since 1937," he said. "Hard to believe she'd betray us like this. Why do you think she did?"

"Love, money, some combination of the two," said Gwen.

"Do we take this information to the police?" he asked.

The "we" both surprised and pleased her.

"Not yet," she said. "All that would accomplish is to provide them with a stronger motive for me. They like to go for the simplest explanation."

"What else would you need?"

"If only I could prove he had the original reports," she said. "They're probably in his office."

"Or at his house, or in a safety-deposit box, kept in reserve," said Harold. "Or destroyed."

"It would be nice to get a sample from her typewriter at the office," said Gwen. "Something to use for comparison."

"I can arrange that," he said. "I'll have Carlotta type one up. Right after I fire Melanie."

"Don't do that yet," said Gwen.

"Why not?"

"If I'm correct about her, she'll be in a panic not knowing what's going on," said Gwen. "She doesn't know why Parson was killed, whether or not it has anything to do with her, or who knows about them. The uncertainty will be what makes her most vulnerable right now."

"And if I fire her, that will be a tip-off," said Harold.

"Exactly," said Gwen. "She might bolt."

"What do you want to do?"

"Confront her directly," said Gwen. "While I still have the element of surprise."

He looked at the clock. It was three thirty.

"She'll be at the office," he said. "Do you want to do it there?"

"No," said Gwen. "I want to pay a call on her at her home. Maybe she has the original reports."

"I'll call Carlotta and get her address," said Harold. "I'm coming with you."

"I appreciate the thought, Harold, but you aren't up to this expedition," said Gwen.

"You can't do this alone."

"I wasn't planning to," she said.

Mrs. Billington waved a piece of paper as Iris got back to The Right Sort.

"Your constable called," she said.

"Good," said Iris.

She dialled the Loughton station the moment she reached her desk.

"What's the latest, Constable?" asked Sparks when she was put through.

"I spoke to Jenkin Farrow, her lawyer, yesterday," he said.

"Find out anything?"

"Mrs. Remagen was rich," he said. "Which means Professor

Remagen is now rich. I was wondering who would inherit if he became ineligible because he killed her to get the estate. The lawyer wouldn't tell me. I don't think he liked me much."

"Strange. You're a very likable chap for a copper."

"Thank you. I think."

"That's a good thought about the alternate beneficiary, though," she said. "I wonder who it is."

"I already know," he said.

"You do? How?"

"I went and talked to Remagen directly," he said.

"My goodness! How did it go?"

"He was stunned at the idea of it being murder," said Quinton. "He hadn't heard I was investigating that angle. But he told me who the alternate beneficiary was."

"And?"

"There aren't any other close family members on either side, so both his and her estates would have gone to various charities. The bulk portion was to have established the Adela and Potiphar Remagen Chair of Entomology at Oxford. Her idea, of course."

"So no individual would have benefited?"

"No."

"Well, I have something to add to this. I tracked down a member of his unit."

"Did you? Let me get the contact so I can—"

"I already spoke to him," said Sparks.

"Ah. That actually is my job, you know."

"And I saved you an afternoon. Danny Clague struck me as an honest sort despite a peculiar taste in beers. Ever try oyster stout?"

"If I wanted brine in my beer, I would have joined the navy," he said.

"Well, I took that particular bullet for you. Clague practically worships Remagen as a friend, as a soldier, and most importantly as a husband. He said Remagen would have done everything in his power to keep her alive and happy. It's looking more and more as if Remagen isn't a murderer."

"So I'm back to square one," said Quinton. "Do you suppose Oxford University could be behind it? They're next in line for the money if they could get Professor Remagen blamed for the murder."

"As a Cambridge girl, I am honour bound to believe Oxford capable of everything that is evil," said Sparks. "But it sounds like a stretch. I suppose The Right Sort has moved up on your list of suspects now."

"It's not much of a list," said Quinton. "Remagen was first because he gets sole possession of the estate and he's not tied down anymore. He could sell it all off and grab the next boat to Burma or wherever there are pretty bugs to be found."

"What are you going to do next?"

"Go home, make myself dinner, and sit in my chair thinking about it," he said.

"Is it a two- or three-pipe problem?"

"What's that about?"

"Sherlock Holmes smoked a pipe while he sat in his study solving mysteries," she said. "The harder the case, the more he'd smoke."

"I don't smoke a pipe," he said. "I also don't have a study. Maybe that's what's holding me back."

"Tell you what, give me your home telephone number," said Sparks. "I'll ring if I have any inspirations."

"Will you be giving me yours in exchange?" he asked hopefully.

"Good try, Constable, but no," she said.

"Fine," he said. "It's Loughton three . . ."

The hallway telephone rang just as Gwen came up to it, startling her. She thought for a second about letting Percival come answer it, but she was standing right there. She picked it up.

"Mrs. Bainbridge, please," said a familiar voice. "It's Mr. Danielli calling."

"Sally!" she exclaimed. "Just the man I want to speak to."

"I'm flattered that you've been waiting by the phone all this while for my call," he said. "I heard about Parson. Sparks was worried I might have been the culprit. Were you?"

"You weren't my first choice."

"I'm almost hurt by that," said Sally. "Am I in the top three, at least?"

"Don't be silly."

"I'm not, for a change," he said. "That's one of the reasons I'm calling. I did something stupid last night."

"Maybe you shouldn't be telling me anything more."

"No, you need to know this," he said, all the lightness gone from his tone. "I went out looking for Parson."

"Sally! Why, for God's sake?"

"I was going to threaten him," he said. "I was going to release the murderous monster I've been trying to squash down ever since I came back from the war and scare the silks off that snivelling little shyster."

"Did you?"

"I never saw him," said Sally. "I watched his house, and he never came home. Then I called Sparks earlier today and found out why."

"Sally, I know you care for me, but that was an incredibly risky thing to do," said Gwen.

"I wasn't thinking straight," he said.

"Clearly."

"It was foolish."

"Yes, it was."

"It won't ever happen again."

"I need you to come with me and threaten someone else."

"I'll be there in ten minutes."

* * *

Iris heard steps in the stairwell. Not the clomping boots of Quinton, nor the measured but lighter tread of Archie in his black market Italian shoes. And it wasn't Sally, of course, because he made a point of stealth each time he came to visit, never giving away his approach until his magical jack-in-the-box appearance in their doorway. These footsteps were new to her, at least as far as the stairwell was concerned, but it was almost five thirty and they were expected. She heard them soon enough to allow herself to look lost in her work when he arrived.

"The native habitat of the mature Iris Sparks," intoned Trevor from the doorway. "Camouflaged as an ordinary office worker, surrounded by the moulted skins of her previous incarnations as well as the decaying, decapitated memories of her past lovers. I stood at the entrance to her lair, wondering if it was a trap, but ultimately decided to enter."

"Foolish mortal," said Iris, looking up with an evil grin. "For who goes up my winding stair can ne'er come down again."

"That's too bad," said Trevor. "For there's dinner to be had if you come down."

"In that case, I'll get my coat and hat," said Iris.

He helped her on with the coat, then raised an eyebrow as she picked up her train case.

"Now that gives me hope for a more interesting evening," he said. "Prepared for an overnight stay?"

"No thanks, I just had one," she said. "And I'm not wearing this suit three days in a row, so don't get your hopes up."

She caught a glimpse of the top of a black bow tie peeking out from his overcoat.

"Are you wearing a dinner jacket?" she asked in dismay.

"I am," he said.

"I'm not dressed for anywhere fancy," she said as she stepped into the hallway and locked the door behind her. "We aren't going anywhere where there're showgirls on display, are we?"

"Of course not," he said. "I want to catch up with you, not ogle bare midriffs. Although . . ."

"Do not finish that sentence if you want to live," she warned him. "All right, so where are you taking me?"

"The Gargoyle Club," he said. "We have a reservation for six o'clock. It doesn't usually get loud until later. And there's dancing, if you feel up to it. I haven't had a proper dance in ages."

"We're not going to close down the joint," she said. "I'm a working girl with regular hours nowadays, so I can't dance the night away."

"It doesn't look like your hours were regular last night," he said, tapping the train case.

"My partner had a crisis, so I stayed the night to help her through it," she said. "Sorry if it's not as lurid as what you imagined."

"You've become an angel of mercy," he said as they walked outside to where a cab was waiting.

"Don't tell anyone," said Iris. "I have a reputation to maintain."

The Gargoyle Club occupied the upper storeys of a white Georgian town house at the corner of Dean and Meard Streets in Soho. A lift took them to the fifth storey where the restaurant was located. It was decorated in a vaguely Moorish style, with motifs inspired by the Alhambra and mirrors everywhere. Framed drawings of ballerinas hung from the walls.

The cloakroom girl glanced at Iris's train case, then at Trevor, and gave Iris a conspiratorial nod of approval as she handed over their tickets. The maître d' escorted them to their table. The dining room could hold a hundred and forty, but there were relatively few patrons at the moment.

"I haven't been here since before the war," commented Iris. "We used to come down from Cambridge on the weekends occasionally to catch glimpses of the Bright Young Things. I couldn't get in during the war because it was restricted to officers. I didn't know you were a member."

"I kept current even when I was overseas," said Trevor. "Didn't want the place to go under without me, although it's not as in as it used to be. All the Bright Young Things are middle-aged now, and their lustre is fading. Brian Howard tried to pick me up once at the bar upstairs a few years back. Quite obnoxious."

"They had a Matisse hanging behind the bar," remembered Iris.

"And there was another one in the stairwell. Both gone, I'm afraid. Sold for debts. But there's still a decent menu under five shillings. I recommend the duck, and we could split a dozen oysters if you like."

"Sounds lovely," said Iris. "And if the house cocktail is still a Pimm's with curaçao, I'll have one of those."

A waiter took their orders, and returned shortly with their drinks.

"To our reunion," said Trevor, holding up his glass.

Iris clinked hers against it.

"We didn't get a chance to chat much the last time we met," said Trevor.

"You were on your way to the Amazon," said Iris. "You were very excited about it at the time."

"Which is a nice way of saying I dominated what little conversation there was."

"It was the most interesting topic available," said Iris.

"Well, now I'm back, and there is ample time to talk about you," he said. "So, how did you spend your war?"

"Secretary and file clerk," she said, using her automatic response to that question. "Nothing to write home about."

"Seems a waste of your talents," he said. "I would have thought Special Ops would have snatched you right up."

"They were going to drop me into Berlin by parachute to kill Hitler," she said. "But it turned out I have a fear of flying, so off to the secretarial pool I went."

"Pity," he said. "You would have got the job done, I'm sure. And now you're running a lonely hearts club."

"A marriage bureau, if you please," she corrected him. "Yes, since March."

"That also seems a waste of your talents," he said.

"Except it turns out that I do have a talent for matching people," she said. "And there are no airplanes involved, so it's quite the perfect job."

"Never would have guessed that in a million years," he said. "You were such a brilliant girl."

"I still am," she said.

"I know, I didn't mean it like that," he said hastily. "I just think you could be doing more than you're doing."

"How many women are on the faculty at Oxford?" she asked.

"Um."

"It's an easy question," she said. "There aren't any. Cambridge is ahead of you on that point, at least, even if they still aren't letting us have degrees. So, what do you think I should do with my life, Trevor?"

"Aren't you doing it now?"

"Clever boy," she said. "I think right now I am doing what I should be doing. As to what the future holds, who knows?"

"Any plans?"

"If I don't know the future, how can I plan for it?"

"Is your gangster part of it?" he asked.

"I thought that might be where this was headed," she said. "He is part of the present."

"Is it true love, or something else to dig at your mother?"

"I am seeing my psychotherapist tomorrow," said Iris. "I'll ask him. This is more of an interrogation than I expected, Trevor."

"I'm sorry," he said. "When I bumped into you last January, I came away thinking, 'Damn. Why did this happen right before I had to leave?' I spent a lot of nights thinking about you since then."

"You could have written," Iris pointed out.

"I didn't know where to write," he said. "And the mail delivery where I was was sporadic, to say the least. I was lucky the Oxford offer found me. Then when I saw you again at the lecture on Sunday, I thought maybe the Fates were being kind."

"Kindness hasn't been one of their more noticeable qualities over the past several years," Iris said wryly.

"Yet there we were, surrounded by aging entomophiles. It would have made for a terrific dance number if it had been a musical."

"You and the night and the beetles," Iris sang.

"The next line is 'Fill me with flaming desire,'" he said.

"Back to that again, are we?"

The oysters arrived, and he divided them into two plates.

"Suppose your future changes again," he said, digging in. "Say things don't work out with your gangster. Might a visit to Oxford entice you? It's only half an hour by train, you know."

"They have single women in Oxford," said Iris. "You don't need to waste time on me. You're a handsome, up-and-coming young don with a background of exotic adventure. They'll be queued up."

"They'll all be like Moth Girl," he grumbled.

"What have you got against Miss Seagrim?" asked Iris. "She seems a perfectly acceptable woman to me."

"Acceptable for what?" asked Trevor. "Dear God, you don't mean to tell me she's a client of yours, do you?"

"As a matter of fact, she is, although I generally don't discuss our clientele outside the office."

"Heaven help the poor chap who ends up with her," said Trevor.

"Why on earth would you say that? She has her eccentricities, certainly, but no more than any other enthusiast. Look at you and me."

"Enthusiast," scoffed Trevor. "Obsessive is more like it. I've never seen a more narrow-minded focus in anyone."

"Certainly that's not unusual for someone in the sciences."

"If you're going into the sciences, you have to be scientific," said Trevor. "Seagrim never was. She never broadened her base of knowledge to take in other branches, and you have to do that if you're going to go on. She was absolute rubbish at anything outside the department, and her lab work for anything larger than an insect was terrible. You have to get messy in the natural sciences, but that girl wouldn't go anywhere near a dissection or a dig. Yet she'd disappear into the woods with a butterfly net and a chloroform bottle at the drop of a hat. She turned every conversation back to moths. People avoided her like the plague. No one wanted to take her on postgrad, not for research, not for expeditions, nothing."

"I'm saddened to hear it," said Iris. "I found it refreshing to speak to a woman who had an interest in the natural world like that."

"The first conversation, yes," agreed Trevor. "The second, maybe. By the time you get to the third, you're thinking, 'God, does she know anything about anything else?' and the fourth will make you want to leave the country and run away into a jungle somewhere."

"Is that why you went to the Amazon?" asked Iris. "To flee Effie Seagrim?"

"We went out on a couple of dates," he admitted. "It ended after the third. Badly. However, my expedition was not driven by fear of Moth Girl, although my joy at returning to Oxford is enhanced by knowing that she is no longer there."

"I'm surprised she didn't say something to you Sunday," said Iris. "Out of courtesy, if nothing else."

"She was too busy trying to corner Remagen," said Trevor. "Ah, here's the duck. And I hear the strains of the band floating down from above. Let's waste no more time on conversation."

They ate, then Trevor stood and offered his hand.

"Milady, will you dance with a poor adventurer before he takes his next step towards obsolescence?" he asked.

"I do so much for England," she said with a sigh.

The dance floor was one storey up. A four-piece band played from a small stage at one end, the drummer in front. A few early evening couples were dancing.

"Alec Alexander's band is still here," observed Trevor. "I think he and his drum set have been bolted to the stage for the last fifteen years. There won't be any hope of hearing anything new, I'm afraid."

"You can't dance to bebop," said Iris, placing her hand on his shoulder.

The band kicked into "You Stepped Out of a Dream" at a sedate foxtrot tempo, and Trevor swept Iris onto the floor.

"When did you learn to dance?" she asked. "We never did this when we were teenagers."

"One must learn what one must if one is to conquer on the fields of love," said Trevor as he spun them expertly through a corner turn, drawing a quick rim shot from the drummer. "Does your gangster dance as well as I do?"

"He's a lovely dancer," said Iris. "With access to a few clubs that are not generally open to the hoi polloi. He may own some of them. I've never been quite sure, and I know better than to ask."

"I am going to ask no more questions about him," said Trevor. "I will accept my sorry lot, and be thankful I have you in my arms at all, even if just for a brief while."

"Take heart," said Iris, moving in closer. "A world of frustrated faculty wives awaits you."

"There's that, at least," he said.

"How do you want me to play this part?" asked Sally as he parked on the corner of Charlotte Street by Tottenham. "Verbally threatening? Physically threatening? Downright unhinged?"

"Silent but menacing," said Gwen. "A glowering from under the trilby sort of thing. I'll do the talking."

They glanced around the buildings on the street.

"That one," said Gwen, pointing to a four-storey brick building with a short set of steps opposite Scala Street.

"Not a bad location," observed Sally. "I'm surprised she can afford it on a secretary's salary."

"First, she's no mere secretary," said Gwen. "She's assistant to the head of accounting."

"Forgive me," said Sally. "I'm surprised she can afford it on an assistant's salary."

"Second, she still can't afford it," said Gwen. "Let's go pay her a visit."

Whoever Miss St. John might have been expecting when she answered the door, the appearance of Gwen with Sally looming behind her startled her to the point of trying to slam it shut. Sally leaned in and caught it effortlessly, pushing it inexorably back.

"Good evening, Miss St. John," said Gwen. "I've come to pay my respects."

"Wha—what?" stammered St. John.

"This is where you say, 'Won't you come in, Mrs. Bainbridge?'" said Gwen.

"Wha—?"

"Thank you, I'd love to," said Gwen, pushing by her. "What a lovely sitting room! Did you decorate it yourself?"

"What are you doing here?" Miss St. John finally managed to force out.

"Do you mind if I sit?" asked Gwen, settling into a large, lavender armchair by the bay window. "You should sit, too. I've come to pay my respects, as I've said. I know all too well what it's like to lose the man you love. Normally, one would visit his family, but I thought, 'Oh, dear, no one ever thinks about the mistress at these times,' so here I am. My condolences, Miss St. John. I never thought much of Oliver Parson personally, but each to her own, I say."

Sally came in and closed the door, making a point of locking it. Then he took up most of a pink-and-white-striped chintz-covered settee from where he surveyed the room like a cheetah waiting for its moment.

"Get out!" snapped St. John. "You have no right to come here like this. Get out, or I'll, I'll—"

"Call the police?" Gwen finished, nodding towards a phone on a credenza. "Go right ahead. We'll all wait for them together. How jolly!"

"Who is that brute?" asked St. John, pointing to Sally. "Why is he here?"

"He's my debt collector," said Gwen.

Miss St. John's hand went involuntarily to her throat.

"You shouldn't hide it, you know," said Gwen. "A hidden jewel might as well be paste, just as a hidden love is only a counterfeit."

"He wasn't—" she began, then she stopped. "How did you know about him?"

"About Parson and you, you mean?" asked Gwen. "It took me a while. I could have credited my disregard for my finances to my disordered mind, or the drugs they put me on, but for the last year, I have only my own complacency to blame. I've had a long history of letting people take care of me, but I've been stepping up for myself more and more lately. It was only a matter of time before I found out what was going on, and before he knew I would. And here we are at last."

"I don't know what you want from me," she said.

"As you know, I operate a small business in Mayfair," said Gwen. "Occasionally our clients neglect to pay our fee when we have successfully rendered our services. Now, we could institute some civil action, but the courts are inefficient, expensive, and time-consuming, as I'm sure your late lover told you. So instead, on those thankfully rare instances, we reluctantly, very reluctantly, call upon this gentleman to, shall we say, persuade them. And he has never failed."

St. John glanced over at Sally, who smiled. The smile provided her no comfort.

"These debts fall in the range of twenty to forty pounds," continued Gwen. "Now, Miss St. John, if I am willing to bring this gentleman in on such paltry amounts, consider what I'd be willing to do to someone who has been stealing thousands from me."

"I don't know what you're talking about," said Miss St. John.

Sally drew himself to his full height and took a step towards her, eliciting a slight shriek from the woman.

"We've examined the reports I've been receiving," said Gwen. "Reports containing financial discrepancies not in the ones received by the other board members. Reports prepared on your typewriter, Miss St. John, which we had seized the moment you left the office today. Tell me, was it love or money with Mr. Parson? My bet is the money. I match people for a living, and I don't see him fancying the likes of you."

"He loved me," she said hotly. "He was lonely and miserable with that cold fish of a wife. He loved me like no one ever has. We saw an opportunity. You had so much. You didn't need it. You could have gone on living your pampered, lunatic life and never miss what we siphoned off. But you had to go and try to get the bit back between your teeth."

"So what was the plan?" asked Gwen. "Take over the company before I came into my own?"

"The company," she said contemptuously. "A handful of old men raking in profits from the war while our boys died fighting it for them. My Oliver wanted no part of that."

"Then what was that motion at the board meeting all about?" asked Gwen.

"It gave him a reason to go to the Master in Lunacy and show him you were still the pathetic, incompetent madwoman that you are," she said. "It would have worked, too. Still will, I expect, now that you've done him in."

"I had nothing to do with his death," said Gwen.

"Then why are you here?"

"Where is my money, Miss St. John?"

"Some of it's here," she said, flinging her arms out to point at the furnishings. "He had the rest stashed away. We upped the amounts we were taking from you when he thought you might actually get restored. We were going to run away together if that happened. Go live as man and wife some place where we wouldn't be asked questions."

"And where are the original reports?"

"At his office, I suppose," she said. "I handed them back after using them to make the fake ones."

Gwen stood up.

"Get your coat," she said. "You're coming with us."

"Just kill me here and be done with it," said Miss St. John, starting to weep.

"We're not going to kill you," said Gwen. "You're going to tell everything you've told us to the police. It's over, Miss St. John."

"It was over when I lost him," she said. "I'll never find anyone like him again."

She went over to the closet. Sally quickly stepped in front of her and opened it, frisking her coat for weapons.

"Allow me," he said, holding it for her.

She slipped her arms in, looking back at him with trepidation. He picked up her bag, opened it and looked briefly inside, then handed it to her.

They walked down the stairs together and exited, Gwen and Sally leading the way. As they turned towards Tottenham Street, there was a single, loud report. The next thing Gwen knew, Sally was hurling himself into her, bringing them both down to the sidewalk.

"Stay down!" he said, his massive body shielding her. "Don't look."

But she had to look, raising her head to peer over his shoulder.

Miss St. John sat on her front steps, her hand again at her throat, staring out into the street. Then the hand slipped down, revealing the blood gushing from the bullet wound, and she sagged slowly against the front door.

CHAPTER 16

Gwen lay there, her heart beating furiously, or was it Sally's heart she felt, pounding through his chest into hers like the reverberations of a tympani?

"Stay down," he whispered. "I'm not sure where it came from. He may still be out there."

An engine revved into life from across the street. She peeked through the narrow space under the parked car next to them to see a pair of tyres spinning into action. Then the vehicle roared away.

Sally cautiously peered through the windows of the car, then held out his hand to help her up.

"Panel truck," he said. "Couldn't get the number. What are you doing?"

This last was as she pulled a whistle from her bag.

"I'm calling for help," she said.

"Put it away," he said, placing his hand on hers. "We have to leave. Now."

"But she's—"

"She's dead, Gwen. We can't help her. And when the police arrive, the prime suspect for Parson's recent murder, meaning you, is on the scene next to his freshly murdered mistress, along with the prime suspect's boyfriend, meaning me, who also lacks a valid alibi for Parson's death. We might as well tie ourselves up with ribbons and wait for the hangman. Let's go. Now."

They walked quickly towards his car. A man came out of a doorway opposite.

"Oi, what was that?" he called.

"Someone was shooting off a gun," Sally yelled back, keeping Gwen shielded from the other's view. "Didn't want to stick around and find out why."

"Right, I'm calling it in," said the man.

He disappeared back into his building.

"And now we walk faster," said Sally.

They quick-marched to the Hornet. Sally held the door for her, then jumped in and pulled away, forcing himself not to speed. He pulled a flask out of his inside coat pocket and handed it to her. She didn't realise how much she was shaking until she opened it. She took a sip, then another, then handed it back to him. He glanced around to make sure no police were in sight, then took a long swallow.

"Put the cap on," he said.

"What are we going to do?" she asked as she capped it and handed it back.

"We are going to have dinner," he said.

"What?"

"We're on a date. We're going to a restaurant where they will recognise us. We'll have a pleasant meal, maybe dance. We will be publicly visible."

"After what we just saw, you expect me to behave like that?"

"Yes, and to tell the police that's what we did when they come around asking."

"It won't be an alibi."

"Not a perfect one," he said. "But it will be a plausible explanation for why we were out tonight. Fix your makeup, and brush off your clothes. You look like someone who's been lying on a sidewalk with a brute on top of her. I hope I didn't hurt you."

"You saved me, Sally."

"I don't think I did," he said, turning north. "We came out ahead of her. Whoever was in that truck had a clear shot at both of us, and I'm not exactly a hard target to miss. He waited for us to turn, then picked her off cleanly from across the street with one shot from a pistol. He knew exactly what he was doing."

"The way you moved, though," she said, still trembling. "I didn't even begin to react."

"You're not impervious to bullets," he said.

"Neither are you. Yet your first instinct was to shield me."

"And I still am," he said. "Dinner. Dancing. Let's pretend to have fun."

It was nine o'clock when Iris got back to her flat. She poured herself some sherry, kicked off her shoes, then pulled a chair next to the telephone and dialled Archie's number. She rubbed her left foot as the phone rang three times before he answered.

"Yeah?"

"Did you let it ring three times so I wouldn't get the impression you were sitting by the phone waiting for me to call?" she asked.

"You caught me," he said, laughing. "'Ow did you know?"

"I was a teenaged girl once," she said. "We invented that tactic the day after Bell invented the telephone."

"Is that what I am now? A teenaged girl?"

"You, Mr. Spelling, are the voice I want to hear most at the moment."

"I'm glad to 'ear it. And you. Nice evening out with your old friend?"

"It was, and yet it wasn't," she said. "This is a man who occupies a special place in my heart, Archie. He was my first crush, my first kiss, and a few other firsts besides. It ended when Mum and Dad's divorce was finally settled, and I was sent off to boarding school."

"I take it 'e wasn't at Cambridge."

"No, he went to the other place, and I was off on new adventures. So it was interesting to see him again, and even more interesting to see my reactions to him."

"What were they?"

"I thought how curious it was that he showed up at this point in my life, when I'm thinking about settling down. If I had someone like me come into The Right Sort and boiled her down to her essence as we do, and then did the same thing with Trevor, I would have put them together. It was as if the Fates had summoned a man who could check most of the boxes I have. And my brain started running through all the useless but intriguing what-if scenarios. As in, 'What if I wasn't involved with you? Could he be the one?'"

"Sorry if I got in the way."

"Archie, the answer was 'No, he couldn't be.'"

"Was it?" asked Archie. "Why not?"

"Because I'm not a woman who checks boxes," said Iris. "Not for love, not for life. Trevor, as interesting a man as he is, would not bring the unexpected into my existence. And I need that."

"Funny, because most of what you and Gwen do at The Right Sort is checking boxes."

"Yes, it is. And that works for most people."

"But not for you."

"But not for me."

"Just for giggles, 'ow many do I check?"

"The one nonnegotiable, absolutely essential one," said Iris. "You're a wonderful dancer."

"And other than that?"

"You are a completely unpredictable anomaly in my life."

"I'll 'ave to look that word up later. Is it a good thing?"

"I think so," she said. "And to prove I mean it, my answer is yes."

"To which question?"

"Yes, Archie, I would love to go to Bernie's wedding with you as your date."

"'Allelujah!"

"But I have a condition," she said.

"Name it."

"It's a terrifying one, Archie. So terrifying, I'm almost too frightened to say it out loud."

"I'm beginning to get an inkling," he said.

"Archie, I want you to meet my mother."

"That is terrifying," he said. "I accept."

Gwen barely remembered eating afterwards. She did remember the dancing, pressed up against Sally, holding him tight so others wouldn't see her shaking. She even danced with a few other men, one a fresh-faced boy of twenty still in uniform who had been urged towards her by a quartet of his comrades.

"Would you dance with me, miss?" he had asked her. "They said you wouldn't, and they said I'd get a shilling each if I could get you to."

"Of course," said Gwen, forcing a smile. "Only next time, ask the girl for yourself, not for a wager."

He was nervous, shaking more than she was, which calmed her nerves slightly. His friends cheered raucously each time they passed their table. She made sure to blow them a kiss the last time through to make sure she was memorable.

"Thanks," he said when the song ended, clinging to her a second too long. "I'm Jack."

"I'm Gwen," she said, gently extricating herself from his hold. "And I must get back to my date. Thank you, Jack."

She returned to Sally who stood to greet her, making sure his height was observed by Jack and his friends.

"I believe the baby duck has imprinted on you," said Sally.

"Have we fixed ourselves firmly enough in people's minds?" asked Gwen. "I'm not sure how much longer I can keep this up without starting to scream."

"Well, we certainly don't want that," said Sally. "Let me take you home."

They didn't speak during the drive back to Kensington. When they pulled into the driveway, he cut the engine, then turned to her.

"Gwen, we should—" he began, then she was kissing him, her hands pulling his head down to hers, kissing him harder than she had done with anyone since, since . . .

He broke it off, pulling her hands away.

Don't say it, don't say it, don't say it, she prayed as he released her.

"Is anything wrong?" she asked.

He laughed, a short, bitter bark that was half amusement, half despair.

"I have been trying to hold everything together for you tonight," he said.

"I thought you were magnificent."

"I was an automaton," he said. "All reaction, calculation of escape, strategizing. That gunshot made me—everything I've been trying to forget has been forcing its way up like bile."

"Tell me," she said.

"I was underground in Italy for nearly two years," he said, staring out the windscreen. "Spying, sabotage . . . killing, you have no idea how many. I never thought I would come out of it alive, but I did; and what kept me going throughout was the idea that when the horrors finally were over, I would make it my quest to find the most beautiful thing I could and let that be my, I don't know, my oasis, my sanctuary. And then I met you, and I thought, I've found it. If I can be with her, then all shall be well. All shall be normal. All shall be calm."

"There is no calm in my life," said Gwen. "Even when I thought there was, it was only that I didn't understand what was going on."

"I don't know if I understand what's going on with you, either," said Sally. "The most fervent kiss I've had from you, and don't pretend it was for the benefit of our fake date, was after a woman was killed right next to us because of an investigation—an investigation!—that you undertook."

"Not because I wanted to," said Gwen.

"But the danger draws you in, doesn't it?" said Sally. "You crave it. You seek it out. And you drag me into it, knowing that I will refuse you nothing, but there's a cost to all this, Gwen. There's a cost to you, and there's a cost to me, and I don't want it. I don't want to lose control and lash out, or get smashed and wake up in jail not knowing who I've hurt. And I feel like events are hurtling in that direction. Can't you let them alone for once?"

"I want to," she said. "But they won't let me alone. I'm sorry I've put you through it tonight, but I am fighting for my life, Sally. And I am not some abstract beautiful thing. I am flesh and blood, riddled with flaws and needs and imperfections. I don't want to be worshipped—not by you, not by anyone. I want to be needed. I want to be wanted. For myself. I want to need and want someone for himself. And if you won't allow yourself to be who you are with me, with your flaws and your inner terrors, how can you expect me to want you?"

"Because you won't love that man," said Sally. "No one can. That's why I keep him shut away."

"You may be underestimating him," said Gwen.

"I don't think so."

"Well, if I don't meet him now, perhaps it's better that I don't encounter him later," said Gwen. "If there's one thing I've learned from being a lunatic, it's that sooner or later these things have a way of coming to the surface."

She kissed him again, more gently this time, and he didn't resist. Then she let him go.

"I want normality, too, Sally," she said, regarding him sadly. "But I may never get it. Maybe this is how my life is going to be from now on. I don't want to drag you into it if it's not what you want from me."

"I was ready to take a bullet for you tonight," he said.

"I know," she said, squeezing his hand. "But I don't want you to die for me, Sally. I don't want anyone to die for me. I've had enough death. I want someone who will live for me."

"I don't know how to do that," he said.

"Let me know when you figure it out," she said.

He got out of the car, then came around to open her door.

"Good night, Sally," she said as she got out. "Thank you for getting me through a terrible evening."

"If you need anything," he started, then he shook his head. "No, Sally. Listen to what you're saying. Listen to what she said. I hope you solve all of this, Gwen."

"I know much more than I did," she said. "The problem is how do I tell it to the police without getting arrested?"

"Or getting me arrested," he reminded her.

"Or getting you arrested," she said. "Don't worry. If they arrest me, I'll keep you out of it."

She turned and went inside without looking back. He stared at the door after it closed, then sat behind the wheel and looked up at the house, wondering which window was hers. Finally, he gave up and drove away.

I've made a decision, thought Iris. An actual decision about an actual man in my life. Won't Dr. Milford be impressed?

Two decisions, come to think of it. Trevor no longer stood atop his pedestal in the Pantheon of Past Regrets. She was almost surprised at how easy it was for her to reject him as a possibility now. His belittling her current occupation certainly greased those wheels.

And she meant it about his checking most of the boxes, so there must have been something wanting in that list. Was she finally growing up?

It may have been the fairy-tale aspect of him showing up in her life again. Her childhood prince grown up, replete with thrilling tales and specimen cases. He was too good to be true, even if he was true.

He was a gift from the gods, only she was an atheist.

I don't believe in miracles, she thought.

Wait.

She grabbed her address book, then dialled a number.

"Hello?" Quinton answered.

"It's Sparks," she said. "Are you busy?"

"As a matter of fact, I am," he said. "I bought a pipe on the way home, and I am now trying to get the hang of it. Apparently, there is a particular technique to tamping the tobacco so it draws properly. Are you sure this worked for Sherlock Holmes?"

"That's what Watson wrote, and Watson never lied," said Sparks. "Anyhow, I wanted to know what your plan was for tomorrow."

"I'm going to re-canvass the street where the Remagens live, see if there are any witnesses I missed the first go-round. Why?"

"I had a thought that I am going to pursue," she said. "If it amounts to anything, where can I reach you?"

"Leave word at the precinct," he said. "I'll keep calling in. Any hints as to what this thought may be?"

"It wants solidifying," said Sparks. "Probably a ghost of a wild goose, but it's nagging at me."

"I appreciate it, Miss Sparks."

"Good night, Constable Quinton. Don't set yourself on fire."

"Have you been talking to my mum?"

She laughed and hung up.

Gwen watched out her window until Sally finally left, the lights off in her room so he wouldn't know. Then she walked down the hall to the guest wing. Harold's light was on, visible through the crack at the bottom of the door. She knocked softly. She heard the creak of his bed, then the shuffling of his feet until he reached the door.

"It's me," she said.

He opened it.

"How did things go tonight?" he asked.

"I had a lovely date with Sally," she said. "He took me to a restaurant he knew in Clapham Junction, and we danced after."

"Did you?"

"Yes," said Gwen.

"Why are you telling me this?"

"In case anyone asks," she replied.

"Will someone be asking?"

"I hope not," she said.

She turned and walked away.

"Gwendolyn," he said.

She stopped and looked back at him over her shoulder.

"Should I fire Miss St. John?" he asked.

"I wouldn't bother about it," she replied. "Good night, Harold."

She pressed the button for Millie when she got back to her room. The maid knocked on her door a minute later.

"Yes, Mrs. Bainbridge?"

"I think I may need some help sleeping tonight, Millie," said Gwen. "Would you be so kind as to measure me a full dose of my powder?"

"A full dose, Mrs. Bainbridge?"

"Yes, Millie," said Gwen. "It's been a long day."

Cavendish arrived at New Scotland Yard at eight thirty the next morning. Josie, the receptionist, waved him over the moment he walked in.

"Parham wants to see you," she said.

"What about?"

"Something to do with the case you picked up. The Soho bloke."

Another secretary motioned him through when he got to the office. Detective Superintendent Parham was at his desk, perusing the morning reports. He looked up when Cavendish knocked.

"Ah, Nyle," said Parham. "Florey picked up a shooting last night that I thought might be of interest to you."

"Where?"

"Fitzrovia. A woman named Melanie St. John was killed on Charlotte Street. Weren't you looking into the Bainbridge company on the Parson case?"

"The company, the family, yeah. What's the connection to Florey's case?"

"She worked for Bainbridge, Limited."

"Interesting. Did she have any connection to Parson?"

"I don't know, but talk to Florey. He's still here."

"On my way. Thanks."

Florey was leaning back with his feet up on his desk, precariously balanced on the rear legs of his chair. He hastily pulled himself into a proper sitting position as Cavendish knocked on his door.

"Only me," said Cavendish.

"Sorry, thought the boss might be checking up on me," said Florey with a yawn. "I was catnapping. Up most of the night, and more to do. You're here about the St. John woman?"

"Yeah, might have a connection. What can you tell me?"

"Lived in a nice flat in Fitzrovia. Paid her rent on time, according to the landlord. Only visitor was an older gentleman, late forties or early fifties, medium height, brown hair with some bald spots."

"That could be a match for my victim," said Cavendish.

"If it is, that rules out my first suspect," said Florey.

"How often would he visit?"

"Frequently. Always around five thirty or six. He'd stay for half an hour or so, then leave by himself."

"Sounds like a married man looking for a little happiness on the commute home."

"Yeah," said Florey. "So maybe there's an unhappy wife at the end of this. How do you want to divvy up the work?"

"I'm going to take a photo of my victim to her landlord, see if he is the gentleman in question. What about you?"

"I have to track down her next of kin, get a formal identification, then sit them down and find out what they know about her friends and lovers. After that, I'll go over to her job. What was your man's connection to Bainbridge, Limited?"

"He sat on the board as the representative of a lunatic who owns forty percent of the company."

"A lunatic?"

"Mrs. Gwendolyn Bainbridge. Court-certified. She lost her marbles when she lost her husband, but inherited his fortune at the same time."

"Sounds like she came out ahead on that one," commented Florey.

"Unless I bring her in for this," said Cavendish. "Any witnesses on your shooting?"

"Not directly," said Florey. "The one who called it in heard the shot and poked his head out. Said there was a man and a woman walking away. The man said something about someone firing a gun down the street."

"Think he's the shooter?"

"Could be, or could be someone trying not to get shot," said Florey with a yawn.

"Get a description?"

"'Tall' was the word that kept coming up. Excessively tall. Late twenties, well-dressed. The woman was on his far side, so he couldn't see her."

"They didn't stick around to assist the police in their enquiries."

"They did not," said Florey. "Sad, that. Maybe they would have confessed on the spot and saved me from having to do actual work."

A messenger came up to the door with a large manila envelope.

"The doc's report and the photos, sir," he said, handing them to Florey.

He pulled out the report and glanced at it.

"Cause of death: one thirty-eight-calibre bullet in the throat," he read. "Sounds like a homicide to me."

"It's inspiring watching you work," said Cavendish. "I'll catch you up at lunch. Good hunting."

"Same to you."

Cavendish went back to Parham's office.

"Thanks for the alert," he said when he entered. "Quick question. If I say 'tall man,' does it ring any bells as to Mrs. Bainbridge?"

"As a matter of fact, it does," said Parham. "There was a case back in July. I can't tell you all the details."

"Why not?"

"It had its hush-hush side, but a man was stabbed to death over on Poplar Dock. Mrs. Bainbridge and Miss Sparks managed to solve it for us."

"And the tall man?"

"They had quite the retinue of helpers on that case. One was an almost freakishly tall fellow with a pronounced theatrical bent."

"Do you remember his name?"

"He called himself Sally."

Mrs. Billington was at her desk when Iris arrived at The Right Sort.

"There's one of you, at least," she said when she saw her. "Mrs. Bainbridge phoned. She won't be coming in today."

"I thought that might be the case," said Iris. "We don't have any appointments for today. If anyone calls for one, make it for next week."

"What about walk-ins?"

"Get their basics, then same thing. I need today completely clear."

She went to the file cabinet and pulled out a file.

"Now, just what do you think you're doing?" asked Mrs. Billington indignantly.

"I'm getting a file," said Iris, puzzled.

"And why am I here? Have you forgot that file fetching is among my duties?"

"I am so sorry, Mrs. Billington," said Iris. "I have overstepped. Forgive me."

She went into her office, sat down at her desk, and studied the application form from the file. Legal secretary, thought Iris. Legal secretary where?

There it was, under employment. A law firm called Mulgrew, Enys, Delwyn, and Reese at Number 77, Chancery Lane.

Nothing suspicious about that, she thought. Lots of people work for law firms. On Chancery Lane alone, there must be dozens. She had seen some other firm with an address near there recently. Practically next door. What was it?

Ah, yes, she thought. The firm representing—

The firm representing Adela Remagen.

She stood and dashed back into the other office, startling Mrs. Billington. Iris pulled up to a halt.

"Yes, Miss Sparks?"

"Mrs. Billington, would you be so kind as to hand me the Remagen file?"

"Of course," said Mrs. Billington, rising and going over to the file cabinet. "You could have used the intercom for that."

"I think I just ran faster than the intercom," said Iris.

"Found a match for her?"

"Maybe."

She took the proffered file and dashed back.

There was the letter from Turner, Woodbridge, and Farrow, confirming the escrow account for Mrs. Remagen. The firm's address was Number 78, Chancery Lane, right next door to where Effie Seagrim toiled away, wasting her Oxford education and dreaming of fleeing her parents and the powerful vacuum pull of the Hoover factory.

"I don't believe in miracles," Iris said to Gwen's empty chair. "I don't believe in coincidences. There are no benevolent gods."

The telephone rang. She heard Mrs. Billington answer through the wall, the professionalism of her tone coming through even though the words were indistinct. Then the intercom buzzed.

"Yes?" answered Iris.

"It's that Detective Cavendish calling," said Mrs. Billington. "He wants to speak with Mrs. Bainbridge. I told him she isn't in. Now he wants to talk to you."

"Got it, thanks," said Iris.

She connected the call.

"Good morning, Detective Inspector," she said.

"Where is Mrs. Bainbridge?" he asked.

"Not here," she said. "Still at home recuperating from encountering you, I expect."

"That would make sense, only she isn't."

"She isn't?"

"No. Jeeves said she left the house at her normal time. Any idea where she went?"

"None," said Sparks. "But I will give her a stern talking-to for leaving me in the lurch like this."

"Yeah, I'm sure you will," he said.

She could practically hear the smirk.

"Anything else I can do for you, Detective Inspector?" she asked. "Or may I get back to work?"

"One more question, come to think of it," he said. "Know anyone named Sally?"

"I've known several women by that name," she said smoothly.

"This is no woman," he said. "Tall fellow. Very tall, from all accounts. Seen in your company by my boss, so don't play dumb, Sparks."

"Oh, that Sally," she said. "Haven't seen him in a while. Why are you looking for him?"

"Why do I look for anyone, Sparks? Because I'm investigating a murder case."

"You think he killed someone?"

"I think he knows something I would like to know," said Cavendish. "Got a full name and address on him?"

"Let me check my address book," she said.

She shuffled some papers on her desk near the mouthpiece.

"Nothing in there, I'm afraid," she said. "But I believe he lives in Soho somewhere."

"Full name, Sparks."

"Danielli," she said reluctantly. "Salvatore Danielli."

"Italian, eh?"

"British, Detective."

"Think he's capable of killing anyone?"

"He's been decorated for it," she said. "Who was the victim?"

"Thanks for the help."

He hung up.

Sally's number wasn't in her book. It was in her head. She dialled it immediately.

"Hello?" he answered, sounding the worse for wear.

"The police want to talk to you," she said. "Why is that?"

"No idea," he replied.

"Sally—"

"No idea, Sparks," he repeated firmly.

"Does this have anything to do with Gwen and why she's gone missing?"

"She's gone missing?"

"As of this morning. She's not at home, she's not here."

"Which leaves the entire rest of the world, Sparks," he said. "Not my concern at the moment."

"Oh," she said. "Right then. Call me if you need bail."

"Will do."

He hung up.

What the hell happened? she thought.

Gwen must have broken it off last night. Iris was surprised there was no call to her from either or both of them to conduct the postmortem of—

Postmortem.

Cavendish was investigating a murder and wanted to speak to both of them. Was this about Parson? Or had something else happened?

All right, Sparks, Sally has been warned. But what about Gwen? Where could she have gone?

She didn't know enough to find out, especially if Sally was clamming up.

She needed to get back to Mrs. Remagen. To Effie Seagrim. She glanced at her watch. It was midmorning. Maybe she could intercept her on her lunch break.

She felt too agitated to sit at her desk waiting. She got up, put on her coat and hat, then turned off the light and walked out, locking the door behind her.

"I'm going out, Saundra," she informed Mrs. Billington. "If Mrs. Bainbridge calls, tell her that the detectives wish to speak to her."

"When should I expect you back?" asked Mrs. Billington.

"Unclear," said Iris. "If I haven't reported in by three thirty, assume tomorrow. If I haven't reported in by tomorrow, assume jail."

"Very well, Miss Sparks."

Cavendish and Myrick knew that Danielli was supposed to be tall, but his actual presence was startling nonetheless when he opened his door to their knock.

"Gentlemen," he said, looking down at their proffered idents. "To what do I owe the pleasure?"

"Are you Salvatore Danielli?" asked Cavendish.

"I am."

"We're looking into a shooting," said Cavendish. "Would you mind telling us where you were last night?"

"On a date," said Sally.

"Where?"

"Clapham Junction. Dinner and dancing at Pete's Place."

"What time were you there?"

"Not sure, exactly," said Sally. "Dinnertime. One doesn't constantly refer to one's watch when out with a lady."

"And who was the lady?"

"As a gentleman, I must decline to answer that," said Sally archly. "Nor will I expand on the other details of the evening regarding her, though they will live in my memory forever."

"How did you get to Clapham Junction?"

"We caught the trolleybus from Hammersmith," said Sally. "Which was it? The six twenty-eight, perhaps? I'm wretched with route numbers, but I think that was it."

"Was the lady Mrs. Gwendolyn Bainbridge?"

"As I said, a gentleman does not discuss such matters."

"In that case, the gentleman is going to accompany us to Scotland Yard," said Cavendish. "Get your coat."

It was a two-mile walk from Mayfair to Chancery Lane. Iris left their building at a quick pace, but soon settled down into an easier stride, decelerating to a contemplative stroll by the time she reached it.

Sure enough, Mulgrew, Enys, Delwyn, and Reese was in the building adjacent to where Turner, Woodbridge, and Farrow held sway. Quite cozy, she thought. If they sued each other, they could serve papers with boomerangs thrown from the windows.

She looked up at the two buildings from across the street, wondering how she could separate Miss Seagrim from the secretarial herd and bring her down. Various methods of tackling opponents ran through her mind, some more violent than others. She was sorting through them when a voice cut through her reverie.

"Iris," said Gwen from behind her. "What in God's name are you doing here?"

CHAPTER 17

I should ask you the same question," said Iris. "And a few dozen more to go with it. Why is Cavendish looking for you again? More importantly, why does he want to find Sally?"

"He knows about Sally?" exclaimed Gwen, turning pale. "Already?"

"What does 'already' mean?" demanded Iris. "What happened since I left your house yesterday?"

"So much," said Gwen. "And I can't tell you."

"No, no, no, that's my defence mechanism," said Iris. "You can't use it."

"I don't want you involved in this."

"Yet here I am, and I don't even know why. I mean, I know why I came here, but—"

"Tell me."

"I am following a lead on Mrs. Remagen's murder. A small one, based on a probably incorrect idea that I had, but I didn't want to waste Constable Quinton's time with it until it became something more substantial."

"What is it?"

"I've been trying to come up with a decent motive for someone to murder her," said Iris. "She was wealthy."

"And she was dying," said Gwen. "Isn't her husband the beneficiary?"

"Yes," said Iris. "But Constable Quinton ruled him out. I thought maybe whoever was next in line in the will could have set up Professor Remagen as a murderer so he couldn't inherit, but the estate was to go to various charities after him. And the same thing would happen if he dies under the current terms of his will."

"So it wasn't done for money," said Gwen.

"I think it was," said Iris. "Who else would benefit from Professor Remagen inheriting a fortune?"

"They had no children," mused Gwen. "So no one could benefit until—"

She stopped and looked at Iris.

"Until the next Mrs. Remagen comes along and marries him," said Iris. "The next Mrs. Remagen, who we were contracted to supply. A daunting task, we thought. Yet who shows up only a few days later? A new client with a passion for insects."

"Miss Seagrim," said Gwen.

"Right."

"But for her to have the professor in her sights, she would have had to have known about Mrs. Remagen's arrangement with us."

"Correct."

"How could she possibly know about that?"

"Who else knew about it besides us and Mrs. Remagen?"

"Mrs. Remagen's solicitor," said Gwen. "Whichever one set up the escrow account for our marriage bounty."

"Exactly," said Iris. "And that solicitor would also know the terms of her will, as well as her husband's. Effie Seagrim is working as a legal secretary in that building across from us. The letter we received came from the law firm in the building next door."

"Mrs. Remagen's lawyer is with Turner, Woodbridge, and Farrow?" exclaimed Gwen.

It was Iris's turn to stare.

"How did you know their name?" she asked slowly.

"That's where Oliver Parson worked," said Gwen.

"What?" exclaimed Iris.

She turned and looked at the two buildings.

"Did Mrs. Remagen know about The Right Sort because of Parson?" she wondered. "Could he have planted the idea in her head? Suggested us as a means to what she thought would be providing for her husband after her death?"

"And then perverted a beautiful, romantic idea by recruiting his own candidate," said Gwen. "Who we would have presented to Professor Remagen on a silver platter. And Remagen would have felt honour bound to accept her because he would have been given a letter written by Mrs. Remagen indicating that this was her last loving wish for him. So you are here to do what? Confront Miss Seagrim?"

"Yes," said Iris. "But we still haven't addressed why you are here."

"Mr. Parson had something that I need," said Gwen. "It may be in his office. So right now I am—what's the expression in those gangster movies? I am casing the joint."

"You're planning to burglarise a law office on Chancery Lane?"

"Something like that."

"Without me?"

"I told you I didn't want to get you involved."

"You are incapable of pulling something like this off without my help. And you still haven't told me why the police are now after you and Sally."

"I would be getting you into trouble if I told you."

"Considering I'm about to help you burglarise a law office, it seems only right for you to tell me why I'm doing it."

"I wasn't asking for your help."

"Fine. What's your plan?"

"My plan?"

"For breaking in. Climb the fire escape to the roof and rappel down to an unlatched window?"

"You know, that's not half bad," said Gwen, looking up at the rooftop. "I should wear something black."

"Not the Schiaparelli, darling," said Iris. "It's too last season for second-storey work. Seriously, Gwen, what was your plan before I showed up?"

"I was thinking of disguising myself as a charwoman and going in with the cleanup crew at closing time."

Iris burst into laughter.

"What's wrong with that idea?" asked Gwen indignantly.

"Do you have the uniform?" asked Iris.

"No, but—"

"Do you have cleaning supplies?"

"I could buy some."

"Do you know how to use them convincingly enough to fool the rest of the charwomen?"

"Is it really all that difficult?"

"Do you even know which end of a mop to use?"

"The one with the stringy things attached," said Gwen.

"That is correct," said Iris. "And once you get to Parson's office, which is presumably locked, how do you plan to get in?"

"With a jimmy."

"Do you own a jimmy?"

"No, but I'm sure there are places that sell them."

"Ah, yes, the burglary supply store at Grosvenor Square carries a decent selection. Black masks and rappelling equipment, too, in case you want to go that route."

"I have no time for ridicule right now," said Gwen. "If the police are looking for Sally, I have to move fast."

"Come with me," said Iris.

"Where to?"

"Someplace where we can sit and talk," said Iris. "If we keep standing here, someone may notice us. And you are going to tell me everything, because I cannot strategize properly on insufficient information."

"We should eat something," said Gwen. "Before the lunch rush."

"Damn, I was hoping to intercept Miss Seagrim when she came out for lunch," said Iris.

"And that was your plan? I can't say I think very much of it. She'd suspect you immediately."

"You're probably right," said Iris. "One should never make plans on an empty stomach. Lunch, then strategy."

They bought sandwiches and a couple of bottles of fizzy lemonade, then found a bench to share in a nearby park.

"We'll start with yesterday morning," said Iris. "What happened after I left?"

"I discovered that my so-called guardian has been stealing from me, almost from the beginning."

"How did you figure that out?"

"I was going through Harold's reports," Gwen began.

By the time she was through her account of Miss St. John's death, Iris was transfixed, her sandwich only half finished. She chewed rapidly and swallowed, then washed it down with her lemonade.

"You poor thing," she said, patting Gwen's hand in sympathy. "That must have been a nightmare."

"I don't know how the police could possibly have got onto Sally so quickly," said Gwen.

"He tends to stand out," said Iris. "And he is one of our known confederates."

"That sounds so illicit," said Gwen. "I thought we were on the side of the angels. I wonder if they've found him by now."

"If they have, he won't say anything," said Iris. "He can't be broken by the likes of them."

"I may have broken him last night," said Gwen sadly. "We didn't part on the best of terms. I'm sorry. I promised you I would let him down gently, and instead it happened at the worst possible time."

"He won't give you up," said Iris firmly. "He was ready to die for you. He will continue to be stalwart on your behalf. It will make him feel heroic."

"I don't want any more heroism from him," said Gwen. "I should never have brought him into this. It seemed like such a good idea when I came up with it. I should have known better."

"Well, your charlady plan doesn't sound like the best one, either," said Iris. "Even if you could find the original reports, you wouldn't be able to convince Cavendish how you got them. And they might not even be in Parson's office."

"You're right," said Gwen with a sigh. "I've been so absorbed in this, I've been unable to look at it from the outside."

"I know the feeling," said Iris.

"Which is why I am now going to tell you how we are going to deal with Miss Seagrim," said Gwen.

"You've come up with a suitable stratagem?"

"She's our client, Iris."

"Are you saying after all this that we have some ethical obligation to her?"

"No, I'm saying that she's our client. We don't need any stratagems. All we need is the right sort of car and the right sort of man. And I've got the car, and I think you may have the man."

"Intriguing."

"But we're going to have to take one more drastic step," said Gwen with a look of determination. "It's Thursday. We're supposed to be seeing Dr. Milford this afternoon. We'll have to cancel."

"Since what we are about to do sounds insane, I think that's a very good idea," said Iris. "What shall we tell him?"

"The truth," said Gwen. "That we got wrapped up in a murder investigation."

"He should be used to that with us by now," said Iris.

* * *

Effie Seagrim glanced at the clock, pulled the last page of the brief she was working on from the typewriter and placed it on the stack in her box, then put the cover on her typewriter and locked up her desk. Around her, other young women were doing the same, the happy babble of farewells and exchanges of evening plans filling the room. Effie, who had no such plans, merely smiled and muttered the compulsory inanities.

She rode the crowded lift down to the lobby, her thoughts jostling about, wondering what to shop for with her dwindling supply of coupons. She was fantasising about steaks thick as telephone directories as she walked out of the building when a voice pierced through her reveries, calling her name.

She looked up to see the woman from the marriage bureau, waving at her.

"Miss Sparks?" she exclaimed in surprise.

"You're late," said Miss Sparks. "Please, we've got the car by the kerb, but we're not supposed to park there, and I don't want to get a ticket."

"Car? What car? Why are you here?"

"For your date, of course," said Sparks impatiently. "Please hurry. He's waiting."

"My date?" said Miss Seagrim in bewilderment. "What date?"

"Your first date!" crowed Sparks triumphantly. "You got our message, didn't you?"

"What message?"

Sparks's expression turned to one of dismay.

"Oh, no," she said. "You don't mean to say you didn't get it?"

Miss Seagrim shook her head.

"Oh, dear God in Heaven, this is a disaster," said Sparks, shaking her head furiously. "I'm going to sack that woman. She told me everything was ready. My dear Miss Seagrim, as a special promotional consideration for the one hundredth date arranged by The Right Sort Marriage Bureau, we are treating the soon-to-be happy couple to a night out on the town, complete with hired car and dinner and dancing, and we are going to be photographing and recording the experience for future publicity."

"But I never agreed to that!" protested Miss Seagrim.

"Yes, you did," said Sparks. "Paragraph eleven in your contract says that we may do things like this for promotional purposes. Oh, Miss Seagrim, you must come! He's in the car waiting. And look at this car, for goodness' sake!"

Miss Seagrim gasped as she saw where Sparks was pointing. Parked by the kerb, a uniformed chauffeur standing by the rear door, was a dark blue car of almost unimaginable opulence.

"Is—is that a Rolls-Royce?" she breathed in wonder.

"Not just a Rolls-Royce!" said Sparks. "A Wraith! It's ours for the evening. Miss Seagrim, I know this is sudden, but it's all set up, and how could you possibly turn down a ride in that? And the young man—"

"But I wasn't planning on a date tonight," said Miss Seagrim. "I'm not dressed for it."

"It won't matter," insisted Sparks. "Please, come meet him; he's perfect for you. Even if it doesn't work out, imagine having a night like this even once. You'll be looking back on it for the rest of your life, I promise you."

"Oh, Lord, this is so overwhelming," said Miss Seagrim. "But just for one date—all right, yes. I can't say no to that car."

"That's the spirit," said Sparks, taking her by the arm and leading her to the Wraith as her co-workers gawked from behind her. "This is Nigel. He's our chauffeur tonight."

"Good evening, Miss Seagrim," said the chauffeur, opening the door for her. "Please get in."

"And here's my partner, Mrs. Bainbridge," continued Sparks, following Miss Seagrim into the car.

"How do you do, Miss Seagrim?" said Mrs. Bainbridge, turning around in the front passenger seat. "I'm so very glad to meet you at last. Miss Sparks has told me so much about you."

"She didn't know it was tonight," said Sparks grimly.

"No!" gasped Mrs. Bainbridge. "She didn't? Appalling. That's the last straw. We sack that woman on Monday. Miss Seagrim, please forgive our strange intrusion into your life, but you did sign up for this, didn't you? In any case, let me introduce you to the gentleman who we have selected for you. Miss Effie Seagrim, may I present Mr. Hugh Quinton?"

"How do you do, Miss Seagrim?" said a young man in the rear seat.

He was handsome enough, thought Miss Seagrim, with brown hair that was not as well-combed as she would have liked.

"Gosh, you're as pretty as they said you'd be," he said, smiling bashfully. "These are for you."

He handed her a small bouquet of flowers.

"Thank you," said Miss Seagrim, stammering slightly as she took them. "I apologise if I seem awkward, Mr. Quinton. I've never been on anything like this."

"Picture!" cried Mrs. Bainbridge, holding up a camera.

The flashbulb went off, temporarily blinding Miss Seagrim. Nigel stepped on the gas and the Wraith roared away from the kerb, hurling her back into the rich leather covering the back of the seat.

"Now, you two go ahead and enjoy the evening," said Mrs. Bainbridge reassuringly. "We won't say another word, will we, Miss Sparks?"

"That's right," said Sparks. "I'll just be a *Musca domestica* on the wall."

"Oh, that's a good one!" said Quinton with a hearty laugh. "We should try and work insect puns into everything tonight."

"Please don't," said Miss Seagrim.

"But I thought you liked insects," said Quinton. "Why, that

was the first thing the ladies told me about you. It's how they matched us."

"Well, I am a bit mad about moths," admitted Miss Seagrim.

"You see, we already have that in common," said Quinton. "Not moths, necessarily, but I have my own peculiar fascinations with insects."

"Really?" asked Miss Seagrim. "How did you find yourself drawn to them? Was it from childhood, or at university?"

"Oh, I never went to university," said Quinton.

"You didn't?"

"No, Miss Seagrim. My entry into their tiny world came through my job."

"How interesting," said Miss Seagrim. "What do you do, Mister—I'm sorry, I've lost your name."

"Nothing to fear, Miss Seagrim," he said. "It's Quinton. Hugh Quinton. Hugh to my friends, Constable Quinton to everyone else."

"Constable?" she said in surprise. "You're with the city police?"

"Oh, no, miss," he said. "I'm with Essex County. But that's where I started learning about insects. Part of the training with crime scenes."

"I'm afraid I'm not familiar with that aspect of entomology."

"Well, it's very specialised," he said. "Sometimes you find a body, and determining the time of death is important, you know?"

"I suppose," she said, desperately trying to be polite. "I'm not sure that this is an appropriate—"

"But that's where the insects come in, you see," he continued, riding roughshod over her attempt to change the topic. "We humans think we're at the top of the food chain, having dominion over every living thing that moveth, as the Good Book says, but once we go, and we all go sooner or later, don't we?"

"Yes, but—"

"Then we become food for worms and insects, and they lay

their eggs, and the eggs hatch and the larvae or grubs come out, and entire life cycles take place. And if you know which type of insect did all that, and you know how long it takes to get to that point in its development, then you can count backwards and, hey, presto, you've got the time of death!"

"I see," said Miss Seagrim faintly.

"So that's how I got started in the field," said Quinton. "I'm hoping to put all of that knowledge to use."

"And have you had any such opportunity?" asked Miss Seagrim.

"Unfortunately, no," said Quinton wistfully. "I'm still relatively new to the force. I'm working on my first murder case, but the poor woman was killed the same day, so our little friends didn't have enough time to get at her."

"Well, maybe that was for the best."

"Funny thing was she turned out to be married to someone who knows all about insects," said Quinton. "I had quite the conversation with him. A Professor Remagen."

"Professor Remagen?" she asked, her voice choking slightly on the words. "You don't mean Potiphar Remagen?"

"I do," said Quinton. "You've heard of him?"

"She was murdered?" she asked, the beginnings of panic creeping into her voice. "His wife was murdered?"

"Horrible, isn't it?" commented Sparks. "There we were, sitting and listening to him give that wonderful lecture last Sunday, and all the while someone was killing his wife and dumping her body in Epping Forest. Makes you think about the grand scheme of things, doesn't it?"

"But she can't have been!" cried Miss Seagrim. "You've got it wrong."

"I'm afraid not," said Quinton. "Someone murdered her."

"But I thought—he told me—"

She stopped. The others were looking at her intently. Even Nigel, watching her in the rearview mirror.

"Told you what, Miss Seagrim?" asked Quinton quietly.

"He told me she was dying," she whispered. "That she was thinking of ending things. Nobody said anything about murder. I thought she—she was going to die, anyway, and he said she couldn't take the pain, but—"

"Who told you this?" asked Quinton.

"A lawyer," she said. "From the office next door. His name's Parson. Oliver Parson."

"How was it all supposed to happen?"

"She was going to The Right Sort to—"

She stopped, looking around wildly at them.

"You're all in on this!" she shrieked.

"It takes a conspiracy to fight one," said Mrs. Bainbridge. "So Mr. Parson persuaded Mrs. Remagen to avail herself of our services. When did you come into it?"

"Three weeks ago. Am I going to be arrested?"

"Yes," said Quinton. "But tell me what you know, Miss Seagrim, and things will go much easier for you."

"I was at a pub after work," she said. "Drinking and feeling sorry for myself as usual. I said something about wasting my university years studying insects, and this man nearby overheard me. It was Parson. He bought me a drink and started asking me questions."

"Did he bring up the Remagens that night?" asked Quinton.

"No," she said. "But he said, 'How would you like to make some real money? Something that will give you what you want from the world, but only if you're bold enough to seize it.' I thought he was trying me on, of course, the old goat, but he wasn't. He told me to come by the office after work the next day."

"What did you think it would be about?" asked Quinton.

"I didn't know," she said. "But I figured it couldn't be much worse than dying a long, slow death as a secretary."

"How did he know about the Remagens?"

"They were clients of the firm," she said. "His boss farmed out their estate work to him. And Oliver told me what she wanted most was to make sure her husband wouldn't be alone after she died, and that I would be a good candidate for him. I said I had no way of coming into his life, especially with him still married to her, but he said she wouldn't last much longer, and he had thought of a way. He's a clever man, Mr. Parson."

"And what was supposed to happen when you landed the prize?" asked Quinton.

"I would take control of the finances. Professor Remagen was wretched with them. He let his wife handle everything. It wouldn't have been hard to funnel a good amount to Oliver. I'd get my share, and I'd get to explore the world like I was always meant to do. It seemed like—"

She swallowed hard.

"Like my destiny," she said, starting to cry.

Quinton pulled a pair of handcuffs from his coat.

"Miss Effie Seagrim, I am arresting you for conspiracy to commit fraud," he said.

He placed them on her wrists. She offered no resistance, the bouquet still in her hand.

"This really is a lovely car," she said softly.

She was still clutching the flowers when the police van arrived from Chelmsford to collect her.

Quinton had left his motorcycle at the Bainbridge house by the garage. Nigel pulled the Wraith up next to it, then opened the doors for his passengers. It was nearly eight thirty.

"Thank you, Nigel," said Mrs. Bainbridge. "This was above and beyond your normal duties."

"It was an interesting experience, Mrs. Bainbridge, and it was good to get this beauty out on the road for some exercise," said

Nigel, patting the Wraith affectionately. "We haven't had much of a chance with His Lordship being incapacitated. I'm going to put her away now. I'll be taking Miss Sparks home in the Daimler."

"Alas, I've been relegated to the second-best car," said Sparks.

Nigel opened the garage door and pulled the Wraith inside.

"Constable Quinton, would you care for a drink before you go?" asked Mrs. Bainbridge.

"I can't," he said reluctantly. "I have to take Miss Seagrim's formal statement and write up the arrest. Then I'll have to get cracking and find this Parson fellow."

"That will be easier than you think," said Sparks. "Getting him to talk will be a problem. He's in the city morgue."

"What?"

"He was murdered Tuesday night," said Mrs. Bainbridge.

"You might have mentioned that before," he said.

"We didn't want you to give it away," said Sparks. "We didn't know for certain that he was the one Miss Seagrim worked with."

"I should talk to whoever picked up the case," said Quinton. "I can't raid Parson's office without jurisdiction."

"We'd rather you didn't do that right away," said Mrs. Bainbridge. "You see, I'm their main suspect. I'm trying to clear myself."

"How?"

"We're working on that," said Sparks. "But if Miss Seagrim turns out to know anything about his murder, let us know."

"I will, Miss Sparks," he said.

He held out his hand. She shook it.

"I couldn't have done this without you," he said. "Both of you, I mean. Thank you."

"It was our pleasure, Constable Quinton," she said. "We'll talk again."

"Good night, ladies," he said, putting on his helmet.

He climbed onto the motorcycle, kicked it into life, and rode off.

"Rather dashing exit, don't you think?" observed Iris.

"He fancies you," said Gwen.

"Too young," said Iris.

"He can't be more than three years behind you."

"And I've got Archie."

"Ah. That's still intact, then."

"I'm taking him to meet Mum when this is over."

"Good heavens! Well, let's go inside and discuss things. We've missed dinner. We'll have to raid the larder."

"I'm glad Miss Seagrim wasn't involved in the murder itself," said Iris as they entered the kitchen.

"Is that what you think?" asked Gwen as she poked through the refrigerator to find the remains of the dinner.

"Don't you?"

"I think the moment Professor Remagen executed a new will, he would have signed his death warrant," said Gwen, placing a covered dish on the table. "I think she and Parson didn't stop with just a drink at a pub. Parson had compromised her enough to make her do whatever he wanted, but I doubt she would have needed much prodding once things were set in motion. I think she would have eventually slipped something into the professor's food with no more compunction than she would chloroforming a moth."

"Well, she won't have that chance now," said Iris. "And now we know Parson was behind it."

"Which doesn't get me out of the woods, unfortunately," said Gwen. "All roads lead to the dead man. I feel like we're back to the beginning again."

"Ah, Mrs. Bainbridge, I thought that might be you," said Percival, appearing in the doorway. "Good evening, Miss Sparks. I trust Nigel performed adequately?"

"He was perfection, Percival," said Gwen. "And I would appreciate it if you keep his involvement between us."

"I shall add it to the ever-growing list," said Percival.

"Have the boys gone to bed?"

"Yes, Mrs. Bainbridge. They were quite excited to see the police motorcycle. Agnes took them out back for an extended look at it."

"That will be the next topic of conversation for an age," said Gwen.

"Oh, and a letter arrived for you by messenger earlier, Mrs. Bainbridge. From your lawyer."

"Mr. Stronach? I wonder what that's about."

"Not Mr. Stronach," said Percival. "Your new committee, according to the messenger."

"What?"

"Yes, from the late Mr. Parson's firm. I will bring it to you."

He left, then returned a minute later with the envelope and a letter opener on a silver platter. Gwen slit open the envelope, then returned the opener to the tray.

"Thank you, Percival," she said. "That will be all for now."

"Very good, Mrs. Bainbridge."

Gwen waited until he left, then pulled the letter from the envelope.

"'Dear Mrs. Bainbridge,'" she read. "'In light of the untimely death of your committee, Oliver Parson, and your impending hearing at the Court of Lunacy on Tuesday, I will be assuming his duties as your committee. As time is short, I must require you—'"

"'Require'!" said Iris indignantly. "The unmitigated gall."

"Given my status, he can do that, unfortunately," said Gwen. "He wants me there at two o'clock tomorrow. Jenkin Farrow himself. I'm moving up in the world, Iris. I've landed a senior partner."

"On top of everything else, you still have to deal with this," said Iris.

"It might be an opportunity," mused Gwen. "It would give me a chance to case the joint from the inside. Get a better idea of where Parson's files on me are located."

"That's an idea," said Iris.

"And having Farrow take over my case could be helpful," said Gwen. "Maybe I could persuade him I'm sane."

"Darling, given your behaviour today you'd have trouble convincing me of that," said Iris.

CHAPTER 18

Mrs. Bainbridge emerged from the lift on the sixth floor ten minutes before her appointed hour. There was no cheery receptionist waiting for her this time. Instead, Mr. Anderson stood in the center of the reception area, his hands folded in front of him. He made no pretence of civility, choosing instead to jerk his head to the left.

"How are you feeling, Mr. Anderson?" she asked solicitously. "I trust you made a full recovery."

"You mind yourself, Mrs. Bainbridge," he said. "I'm onto your games now. Try that stunt with me again, I'll break your arm."

"I promise not to do it again," she said. "And you should be a little less hasty in using force on helpless lunatics."

"You were behaving very badly, Mrs. Bainbridge," he said. "I was doing what I'm paid to do. This way, if you don't mind."

They walked down a corridor towards the rear of the building. There was an anteroom with a secretary's desk, unoccupied at the moment. Farrow's door listed no specialties, merely the title: JENKIN FARROW, SENIOR PARTNER. Anderson knocked twice on the door, then opened it.

"Mrs. Bainbridge is here, Mr. Farrow," he said.

"Show her in, Mr. Anderson," said a man inside.

Anderson held the door and motioned for her to enter. She passed him without giving him the satisfaction of a glance.

"Ah, Mrs. Bainbridge," said Farrow, rising from his desk and coming around to greet her. "Thank you for coming in on such short notice."

"I really hadn't any choice in the matter, had I?" she replied, shaking his hand.

Behind her, she sensed Anderson shift as he saw the contact.

"Would you like me to remain, Mr. Farrow?" he asked. "She's—excitable."

"I think she and I could have a simple, pleasant conversation without you," said Farrow, holding a chair for her. "Wouldn't you agree, Mrs. Bainbridge?"

"Of course," she replied as she sat. "Thank you for guiding me here, Mr. Anderson."

"Mind that you keep it pleasant," he warned her. "I'll be just outside if you need me, sir."

"Thank you, Anderson," said Farrow. "That will be all."

Anderson left.

"I apologise for his lack of courtesy," said Farrow as he sat behind his desk. "He's been put off ever since his last encounter with you. I understand you got the better of him that day."

"I would prefer not to speak about that, if you don't mind," she said. "It was extremely upsetting."

"And we certainly don't want anyone upset here, do we?" he replied.

A pair of large cardboard file boxes marked "G. Bainbridge" sat on the side of his desk. He noticed her looking at them.

"A voluminous collection," he observed. "You've been quite the complicated client for such a short period of time. How are you feeling today, Mrs. Bainbridge?"

"In my right mind," she said. "Apprehensive over meeting you, but I understand the need for haste. I offer my condolences over the loss of Mr. Parson."

"Thank you," he said, his expression sombre. "This is where I say he was a good man and a valuable colleague. But, but, but . . ."

He tapped the boxes of files.

"I've been going through his recent filings before Assistant Master Cumber," he said. "I find myself, and I hesitate to say this, having concerns about some aspects of your representation by Mr. Parson. I realise that you are still legally considered a lunatic, and you had no prior experience with corporate matters before inheriting your stake in Bainbridge, Limited, but I must ask: Do you have any suspicions of any irregularities in the handling of your situation by Mr. Parson?"

"He was stealing from me," she said.

Farrow leaned back in his chair with a look of anguish, clasping his hands.

"Why do you believe that?" he asked.

"I had a chance to see Lord Bainbridge's financial reports and compare them with the ones Mr. Parson had been sending me," she said. "There were discrepancies. Substantial ones."

"Parson of course would have been subtracting our firm's expenses," said Farrow. "Perhaps that would account for it."

"No, Mr. Farrow," said Mrs. Bainbridge. "I considered that, but those expenses were billed after the quarterly reports came in, and were done legitimately. The skimming took place before the reports were sent to me, and the reports were altered to conceal it."

"I was afraid this might be the case," said Farrow sorrowfully. "Mrs. Bainbridge, I promise you that we will get to the bottom of this. If it turns out to be true, then we will make matters right, of course."

"When?" asked Mrs. Bainbridge.

"As soon as we can," he promised. "We will have to review all of his clients' files, now that you've confirmed our suspicions."

"But you will be giving mine priority, I hope," said Mrs. Bainbridge. "Given that you already know there are problems."

"We will," he promised. "Of course, we are going to have to request a postponement of your hearing on Tuesday under the circumstances. I will contact your lawyer."

"Oh, no!" she said. "Please, Mr. Farrow. It's taken so long for me to reach this point, and to keep me in legal limbo further would be a cruelty."

"Mrs. Bainbridge, we need to become thoroughly versed on a complex legal matter virtually from scratch," he said apologetically. "It would be to your advantage for there to be another delay. It may be upon further review of Mr. Parson's files that we will reassess your situation and withdraw our opposition to the termination of your guardianship."

"But it may not?" she asked.

"I couldn't possibly give you an advisory opinion at this point," he said. "Although having finally spoken to you in person, I am already inclined in your favour."

"Thank you," she said. "But I want this over with, Mr. Farrow. On Tuesday."

"Then I shall personally spend the weekend going over your files and have a decision by Monday," he said. "You have my word."

"Thank you."

"In fact, we should drink on it," he said, beaming at her avuncularly. "Anyone who knows law knows that a drink with me is more binding than any contract."

"I'm not sure I—"

"Sherry? Whisky?" he asked, moving to a sideboard. "Please, Mrs. Bainbridge. I normally take a glass of Lagavulin at the end of the week. Join me."

"Well, as it's Lagavulin, perhaps one."

He poured amber liquid from a bottle into two tumblers.

"I'm sure you'll think more kindly of me after a drink," he said, a twinkle in his eye as he handed one to her.

"Since you insist," she said, taking it.

She rose and wandered over to the sideboard to peruse the label on the bottle.

"A sixteen-year-old single malt from before the war," she said approvingly. "How did you resist it all this time?"

"I didn't," he replied with a laugh. "I laid in a few cases in thirty-nine when things were looking ominous. This is one of the last bottles."

The potted plants on the windowsill caught her eye.

"Aren't these lovely?" she exclaimed, turning to them. "Do you grow them yourself?"

"I do," he said. "We have a hothouse at home."

"The winter jasmine is particularly beautiful," she said, bending down to smell them. "Such a delicate odour, too."

She straightened, looking out the window at the park, then tilted back the tumbler. He saw her swallow, then she turned back to him, smiling.

"This is good," she said, holding up the empty tumbler. "I think better of you already."

"Excellent," he said, smiling back as she sat again.

"Will you be bringing Mr. Parson's conduct to the attention of the police?" she asked.

"We already have spoken with the detective investigating his death," said Farrow. "Your name came up, by the way. You're a suspect."

"So I've heard. Would you be able to provide any help if they pursue me any further?"

"I told Mr. Cavendish that I doubted you would resort to measures that drastic."

"I appreciate that, Mr. Farrow," said Mrs. Bainbridge. "It was good of you to leap to my defence without even knowing me."

"Oh, but I do know you, Mrs. Bainbridge," he said, patting the files. "I know you better than you know yourself. Lengthy progress reports from the psychiatrists at the sanatorium, Mr. Parson's notes from his interviews, the affidavits attached to Mr. Stronach's petitions."

"So you have had a chance to read them," she said, puzzled.

"Oh, yes," he said. "First thing I did after Parson's death. Everything's in there. All of your hopes and fears, your love for your husband and child, your despair over losing them. Your resentments of your family, particularly your brother."

"This—this is getting rather personal," said Mrs. Bainbridge. "Why are you bringing them up? And why did you tell me you were going to spend the weekend reading them when you've already read them? Have you already decided what you're going to do at the hearing?"

"No need to, Mrs. Bainbridge," he said, his smile gone. "There won't be any hearing on Tuesday."

"Why not?"

"Because a lunatic's status becomes moot when the lunatic is dead," he said.

She looked down at the empty tumbler in her hand, horror dawning on her face.

"Veronal is your drug of choice," he said, opening his hand to reveal a small vial. "That's also in your files, along with your fondness for single malt Scotch whisky. I imagine you're feeling the effects already."

"But why?" she whispered as the tumbler slipped from her hand to land on the carpet by her feet.

"You figured out about Parson," he said. "We can't have that get out. A close look at our operations would turn up other situations like yours. It's a pity. You were a very profitable client for us, but Parson got greedy. He doubled what he was taking from you and kept the extra without telling us. Then he panicked when you put in the petition. A greedy, panicky lawyer is a liability, wouldn't you agree?"

"You were the one who had him killed," she said.

"He brought it upon himself," said Farrow, pressing a button on his desk. "We could have kept things status quo in Lunacy Court if he had just stayed the course, but he was putting us all at risk here."

Anderson came back in.

"It's done," said Farrow. "Take her away. Goodbye, Mrs. Bainbridge. It will be a painless death, if that's of any comfort to you."

"I hope you die a painful one," she said, gasping.

"Come on, you," said Anderson, hauling her to her feet.

She staggered by his side as he walked her to a private lift in the back, which he opened with a key.

"Not so feisty now, are you?" he said as the doors closed.

"Tired," she murmured as she sagged into him. "So tired."

"You're going to have a nice long sleep soon," he said.

The doors opened to a rear exit onto a small courtyard. A delivery van was parked by the exit, a man wearing dustman's clothes standing by it.

"Is that the van you drove when you shot Miss St. John?" she asked when she saw it.

"He drove, I shot," said Anderson.

"Good shot," she said.

"Didn't want her to suffer," he said. "You, on the other hand, I'd like to see suffer, but my orders are to leave you untouched."

"Where are you taking me?" she asked as the other man opened the rear doors of the truck.

"Overdose in a doss-house, that's how they'll find you," he said. "Nice ending for a fancy lady."

"So no trip to Epping Forest like Mrs. Remagen?" she asked.

Anderson and the other man looked at each other, then back at her.

"How do you know about that?" demanded Anderson.

"Sleepy," she muttered, her head nodding towards her chest.

"How do you know about Mrs. Remagen?" shouted Anderson, shaking her.

She looked back up at him, her eyes open and clear.

"How do you know about Mrs. Remagen?" she asked.

"She knows," said the driver. "She knows we did that lady from Hampstead. How could she know that?"

"I know many things," said Mrs. Bainbridge with a smile. "Would you like to hear more?"

"Change of plans," said Anderson, reaching into his waistband. "Now, you're going to suffer."

"I don't think so," said a man from behind them.

Anderson and the driver spun in that direction to see a police constable coming towards them, four other men in plain clothes flanking him with guns drawn.

"I think they've said enough for you, Detective Inspector," said Constable Quinton to Florey, who was on his right.

"They have," said Florey. "You two are under arrest for the murders of Melanie St. John and Adela Remagen. We'll figure out the rest of the charges later."

They quickly handcuffed and patted down the two men. Florey pulled a Webley revolver from Anderson's waistband.

"We'll check this against the bullet from Miss St. John," he said to his partner.

"What about Parson?" asked Cavendish, who was there with Myrick.

"Come with me," said Mrs. Bainbridge. "We should hurry. Get his keys."

Cavendish grabbed Anderson's key fob. He, Myrick, and Quinton followed Mrs. Bainbridge to the private lift.

"Where are we going?" asked Cavendish.

"Top storey," she said. "Jenkin Farrow's office."

"So you were right about him," said Quinton as they rode up.

"So were you."

"What tipped you off?" Cavendish asked Quinton.

"Farrow tried to quash my investigation," he replied. "I thought he was doing it on behalf of Professor Remagen, but Remagen didn't even know I was investigating anything. I started to wonder if Farrow might have had his own reasons for keeping the police away."

"When we're done with this, come back with me to the Yard," said Cavendish. "I'll introduce you to a few people. And what clued you in, Mrs. Bainbridge?"

"They didn't have me arrested when I assaulted Mr. Anderson," she said. "That made no sense, in retrospect. It would have been something they could have used against me in the lunacy proceedings, but they must have already been planning Mr. Parson's murder at that point. Drawing attention to their resident killer wouldn't have been helpful, so they let my little peccadillo drop. When we learned that Parson was involved with the plot to kill Mrs. Remagen, I saw a pattern of rich vulnerable clients being bilked. Parson's murder meant someone else was also involved and considered him a threat to the operation. And Parson was assigned Mrs. Remagen's affairs by Farrow."

"Sixth storey," announced Cavendish as the lift slowed to a halt. "Children's toys, novelty items, and criminal conspiracies. All out."

She led them to Farrow's office, then tapped lightly on his door.

"Come in," he called.

"Hello, I'm back," she said as she opened it. "I've brought some company. I hope you don't mind."

He stared at her, stupefied, then his gaze took in Quinton as well as the two detectives.

"What is all this?" he asked.

"The tumbler he used to try to kill me is down there," she said, pointing to where it still lay at the foot of the desk. "There should be traces of the Veronal in it. The rest I poured into the winter jasmine over there before I pretended to drink it."

"Which would be which one exactly?" asked Myrick, going over to the windowsill.

"The one with the bright yellow flowers. So pretty, aren't they? Someone should be able to analyse the potting soil for it, I should think."

"Oh, yeah," said Myrick. "We can do that."

"And I'm willing to bet he still has the empty vial in here somewhere," continued Mrs. Bainbridge. "Don't you, Mr. Farrow?"

He looked at them with resignation, then pulled it from his waistcoat and placed it on the desk.

"How did you know?" he asked her.

"I've been taking Veronal for over two years," she said. "I know its scent, even when you try to drown it with Lagavulin. I also know Lagavulin's scent, for that matter. I rather like it. Pity I couldn't have it for real. Detectives, he confessed to me that he had Oliver Parson killed to cover up a continuing scheme to steal from me while under their guardianship. The evidence for that should be contained in those two boxes."

"Mr. Farrow, I'm going to ask you to come with me," said Cavendish.

"You can't believe her!" shouted Farrow as the detective cuffed him. "She can't testify! She's a lunatic!"

"Only until Tuesday, Mr. Farrow," said Mrs. Bainbridge. "After that, I'm very much available."

"Matter of Mrs. Gwendolyn Bainbridge, petitioner," called the clerk.

Iris, sitting next to her, gave her hand a quick squeeze. Gwen returned it, then walked into the well of the court to stand by Stronach.

The courtroom was more crowded than it had been on her previous appearance. The press had got wind of the matter when the news of the arrests broke, and the involvement of such a well-known firm drew the curiosity of the Bar, whose presence overflowed their designated seats, forcing many of them to sit in the gallery, their silks and wigs more jarring juxtaposed with the ordinary clothes of the ordinary people, lunatics and sane alike.

A barrister she didn't recognise stood at the other desk. Cumber looked at him with an expression just short of a sneer.

"Call the parties into the record," he said in a volume meant to reach the back row.

"Mrs. Gwendolyn Bainbridge, petitioner?" said the clerk.

"Present," she said, her voice strong.

"Counsel for the petitioner?"

"Rawlins Stronach for the petitioner," said Stronach.

"Committee for the petitioner?"

"Amos Maltravers, of the law firm of Turner, Woodbridge, and Farrow," said the new barrister. "Milord, I regret to inform the court of the passing of Oliver Parson, the committee in this matter. With the court's permission, I would move to adjourn this case so that we may assign Mrs. Bainbridge's case to a new committee."

"The committee is the firm, not the man," said Cumber. "You are here as a member of that firm. And as you are one of the dwindling number of the firm's lawyers who hasn't been arrested yet, I am going to deny your application for an adjournment. This matter should be heard while there is still someone left to contest it."

"Yes, milord," said Maltravers unhappily.

"Now, Mr. Stronach," said Cumber. "As I recall, where we left matters was with your request to proceed with a next friend standing in for the petitioner. I see by your filings that you have found one."

"Yes, milord," said Stronach. "May I have the court's permission to have him enter the well and be sworn in?"

"Granted," said Cumber.

"Calling Walter Prendergast," said the clerk.

Prendergast strode into the well, his chest puffed up with pride. The clerk swore him in.

"May I enquire, milord?" asked Stronach.

"Proceed, counsellor."

"Mr. Prendergast, what do you do for a living?"

"I am the chief executive officer of Prendergast and Company, an investment firm located on Birchin Lane," he said, pronouncing it carefully so that the press would get it right.

"Are you acquainted with Mrs. Gwendolyn Bainbridge, the petitioner?"

"I am."

"How did you make her acquaintance?"

"I had financial dealings with Bainbridge, Limited, a corporation run by Lord Harold Bainbridge, of which Mrs. Bainbridge is also a general partner," said Prendergast. "Lord Bainbridge invited me and the other members of the board to dinner at their home this past August. It was on that occasion that I first met Mrs. Bainbridge."

"And subsequently?"

"I met her twice more in August, then again last week when she asked if I would appear for her in this court."

"What is the current status of your dealings with Bainbridge, Limited?"

"They concluded in August," said Prendergast. "I currently have no financial relationship with the business or any of its partners."

"Apart from your business connections to Mrs. Bainbridge, and forgive the indelicacy of my question, have you been romantically involved with Mrs. Bainbridge?"

"I have not," said Prendergast firmly. "We have not had any meeting that could in any way be described as romantic in nature."

Gwen, as well as Iris sitting in the gallery, were the only ones to sense the unspoken addendum of *More's the pity.*

"I have no further questions, milord," said Stronach.

"Mr. Maltravers?"

"No questions, milord."

"Milord, I move to have this petition continue with Mr. Prendergast representing Mrs. Bainbridge as her next friend," said Stronach.

"Any objection, Mr. Maltravers?"

"No, milord," said Maltravers.

"Very well, the motion is granted," said Cumber with an authoritative rap of his gavel. "Mr. Prendergast, you may step down."

"May I remain in the courtroom to observe, milord?" asked Prendergast eagerly.

"Of course," said Cumber.

Prendergast walked past the desks. Gwen mouthed "Thank you" as he did.

"Now, the late Mr. Parson filed motions in which he brought to the court's attention certain past behaviours of the petitioner," said Cumber. "The areas which caused me the greatest concerns in terms of assessing the petitioner's sanity were her delusion that she is a detective; that she has actively interfered with investigations by Scotland Yard; and perhaps most tellingly her claim that she worked as an agent for Her Majesty, Queen Elizabeth. Mr. Stronach, are you prepared to address these issues? You have not filed any written response to her committee's motions."

"Milord, I am prepared to respond by means of a witness," replied Stronach.

"Have you previously supplied the name of the witness to the acting committee?"

"I have, milord."

"Then you may proceed," said Cumber, leaning back in his chair with anticipation.

"Milord, I wish to call Detective Superintendent Philip Parham to the stand," said Stronach.

The gallery buzzed as Parham walked into the courtroom. He nodded amiably to Mrs. Bainbridge as he walked up to the witness stand.

The clerk swore him in, then Stronach stood to question him.

"Detective Superintendent, by whom are you employed?"

"I work for the Metropolitan Police."

"In what capacity?"

"I am a detective superintendent with the Homicide and Serious Crime Command."

"And are you currently an investigator or a supervisor?"

"My duties are primarily supervisory at this point, but I like to jump in and get my feet wet every now and then."

"Have you had occasion to meet the petitioner, Mrs. Bainbridge, during the course of your duties?"

"A surprising number of times," said Parham.

"And how have you had occasion to meet her?"

"She has, in conjunction with her business partner, Miss Sparks, had significant participation in several homicide investigations that have occurred in London going back to last June."

"And what has been the nature of this participation?" asked Stronach.

"She solved them," Parham said simply.

"When you say 'solved,' could you elaborate?"

"She and Miss Sparks have investigated and identified the perpetrators of homicides in several cases where we were unable to do so," said Parham. "In one matter in particular, they were able to show that we had erred in arresting one suspect, ultimately saving him from the gallows."

"How many of these cases has she solved?"

"Not counting the most recent one, because we are still sorting everything out, a total of five cases involving, let me think, six homicides, along with assorted related crimes."

The level of the reaction from the gallery went beyond murmuring this time. Cumber rapped his gavel sharply, and the noise subsided.

"Five cases," repeated Stronach with an air of immense significance. "How would you assess the intellect of Mrs. Bainbridge, based upon these encounters?"

"I would say it's first-rate," said Parham.

"And her courage?"

Parham looked directly at her for the first time since he took the stand.

"I think she's an extraordinary woman," he said. "One of the bravest I have ever had the privilege of meeting."

Stronach turned to look at Gwen, then pulled a handkerchief from somewhere inside his robe and handed it to her.

She wasn't even aware of the tears running down her face.

"Thank you, Detective Superintendent," said Stronach. "Your witness, sir."

"Thank you, Mr. Stronach," said Maltravers. "Good morning, Detective Superintendent."

"Good morning."

"Would you agree, sir, that high intellect is itself not necessarily an indicator of sanity?"

"I would," said Parham.

"In fact, one of your most notorious cases involved the arrest of Randolph Angler, popularly known as the Butcher of East Ham. Is that correct?"

"It is."

"Mr. Angler was determined to be insane, and is now institutionalised in a facility for the criminally insane, is he not?"

"He is."

"He was considered to be a brilliant man before the revelation of his crimes, was he not?"

"He was."

"And I am given to understand that you still are in contact with him. Is that true?"

"It is," said Parham. "We still don't know all of his victims' names or whereabouts. Every year, I visit him. We play a game of chess. If he wins, he tells me another one, and we clear that case."

"How's his game?"

"For the purposes of learning everything I can while he still lives, his game is better than mine."

"Now, Detective Superintendent, in some of these cases where Mrs. Bainbridge has inserted herself, she has actually put herself in physical danger, hasn't she?"

"That is correct."

Maltravers swelled up for what he clearly anticipated to be a knockout punch.

"Would you describe someone who places herself in physical danger while attempting to solve matters better left to the police as the acts of a sane woman?" he asked triumphantly.

Parham looked at him contemptuously.

"Every man under my command puts his life on the line when he goes after the most dangerous members of our society," he said coolly. "They are the finest and bravest men I know. If Mrs. Bainbridge's actions are to be considered insane, then so are those of every detective on the force. Yes, I consider her to be sane, counsellor."

"Hear, hear!" came Iris's voice from the gallery.

Cumber rapped his gavel.

"Detective Superintendent, she made a claim that in one of these matters, she represented the Queen," said Maltravers, starting to sound desperate. "Do you know anything about that?"

"I believe it to be the truth," said Parham.

"But do you have any personal knowledge of it?"

"A representative of the royal family gave credence to that claim," said Parham.

"Do you know this person's name?"

"I am not at liberty to disclose it," said Parham.

"My word!" exclaimed Maltravers. "Did you at least verify this person's credentials at the time?"

"I did not."

"So you cannot testify from any personal knowledge of Mrs. Bainbridge's extravagant claim to have worked for them?"

"I cannot," said Parham.

There was a small disturbance at the rail. Gwen glanced back to see a gentleman speak urgently to a bailiff, then hand him a sealed envelope. The bailiff took one look at it, then immediately went up to the bench and showed it to Cumber, who leaned down to allow a whispered communication. His eyes widened with surprise.

"Counsellors, I require your presence in chambers," said Cumber. "Mrs. Bainbridge as well. The court shall reconvene in ten minutes."

The assemblage rose as he left the courtroom through a door to the left of the bench.

"What's going on?" whispered Gwen.

"I haven't the foggiest," returned Stronach. "It must be serious if he wants us off the record."

Along with Maltravers, they followed the bailiff through the rear door. Gwen noticed that the gentleman who had handed up the sealed envelope was behind them.

This is a trap, thought Gwen nervously. The door will open, and I will find myself being dragged off to the sanatorium again.

But when the next door opened, it revealed an office. Assistant Master Cumber sat behind his desk, bookshelves containing bound volumes of legal cases behind him. He had taken off his wig and was scratching his head.

"Damned thing is making my scalp crawl today," he grumbled. "Do you ever get that?"

"Occasionally, milord," said Stronach. "I can recommend a powder, if you like."

"Call my secretary later," said Cumber. "Sit, everyone. This is highly irregular, but everything about this has been irregular. You, sir. Introduce yourself."

"My name is William Bannister," said the gentleman. "I am assistant private secretary to Her Majesty, Queen Elizabeth. Here are my credentials."

He opened his wallet and showed a card to Cumber.

"They are in order," pronounced Cumber. "Counsels and Mrs. Bainbridge, Mr. Bannister has presented to the court a sealed letter."

He held it up.

"As you may see, the seal is unbroken, and appears to be from Her Majesty herself. I am now going to open it in your presence."

He broke the seal, opened the envelope, and removed a single sheet of stationery. He held it up, his hand shaking slightly.

"'To the Court of Lunacy,'" he read. "'Mrs. Gwendolyn Bainbridge acted as my agent in a confidential matter this past July. While I choose not to reveal the details, I will state that she had and continues to have my complete confidence in this and all matters. I would hope that this court will honour my wish to keep this out of the public eye.'"

He held it up so they could all see the signature at the bottom.

"How was this arranged?" Maltravers asked Stronach.

"I knew nothing about it," said Stronach.

"Mr. Maltravers, your cross-examination is over," said Cumber.

"I will brook no protest from you. In fact, I will not hear another word from you. If you choose to speak in my courtroom, I will hold you in contempt and personally seek your disbarment. Nod if you understand me."

Maltravers looked at him, then slowly nodded.

"This letter will go into the court file as a sealed exhibit," said Cumber. "There will be no record made about it. Let us resume proceedings."

They returned to the courtroom, Cumber making his entrance a minute later.

"Pursuant to our conference in chambers, there will be no further testimony from this witness," he said. "You may step down with the thanks of the court, Detective Superintendent."

"My pleasure, milord," said Parham as he left the stand.

"I am informed by counsels that there will be no further witnesses," said Cumber. "Having reviewed the filings, the exhibits submitted, and the testimony of the witness, the court rules that the petitioner's motion for change in status is granted, that she shall no longer be a ward of the Crown, and that the committeeship of Turner, Woodbridge, and Farrow shall hereby be terminated. Mrs. Bainbridge, I wish you a less turbulent life."

"Thank you, milord," said Gwen.

"Right, let's get out of here before anyone changes their mind," muttered Stronach.

They hurried out of the courtroom into the hallway, pursued by reporters. Maltravers tried to push past them, but Stronach whirled and grabbed him by the arm, then shoved him into the wall. He reached into his robe and pulled out an envelope, which he held in front of his adversary's face.

"Inside, you will find three numbers," said Stronach. "The first is the money your colleagues stole from my client, plus accumulated interest. The second is our proposed settlement for damages for two and a half years of malpractice and misrepresentation, and the third is for her attempted murder by one of your senior partners. I expect an answer by the end of the business day, and a cheque on my desk in the morning. Am I understood?"

Maltravers reached up and took the envelope. Stronach released his hold, and the barrister slunk away.

"Wouldn't we get more if we sued them?" asked Gwen.

"We should get what we can while they still have anything," said Stronach. "They'll be in receivership in a matter of months once everything gets out."

"In that case, would you accept the thanks of a grateful client?" she asked.

"I would be honoured, Mrs. Bainbridge," he said.

She threw her arms around him as flashbulbs went off. His wig was knocked askew, and she straightened it carefully after she let him go.

"Next step is the custody case," he said. "I'll get to work on that second thing."

"Second? What's the first?"

"You have to come sign a contract with me," he said. "You are your own person again."

"I will be there at nine o'clock sharp," she promised.

There were cries of "Mrs. Bainbridge!" from the reporters. Stronach stepped in front of them.

"I will be answering all questions for my client," he said. "She is going to have a well-deserved celebration."

"Come, I'll walk you out," said Parham, who was standing with Iris a few feet away.

"Mrs. Bainbridge," called Prendergast breathlessly as he finally succeeded in breaking through the wall of press. He scurried to her and shook her hand enthusiastically. "Congratulations at last!"

"Thank you, Mr. Prendergast," she said, clasping his hand. "Thank you for stepping up as my friend."

"Legally, I am no longer your friend," he said. "I hope to become one in actuality."

"You will always be my friend, Mr. Prendergast," she said.

"Then when a decent interval has elapsed, I shall resume my quest," he said.

"I look forward to it," she said.

He smiled broadly, then trotted off.

"Aha!" said Iris.

"We'll see," said Gwen. "Shall we go?"

Parham guided them to a lift not available to the general public and showed his identification to the operator. Once they arrived safely at the street, he waved and walked to his car.

"So was that mysterious letter from the Queen?" asked Iris.

"Yes," replied Gwen.

"I thought it might be."

"How did you— Iris, what have you been up to?" asked Gwen suspiciously.

"What makes you think I've been up to anything?" Iris returned with an innocent expression.

"You do know one of the best forgers in England."

"Do you honestly think I would have Jimmy the Scribe forge a letter from the Queen?" Iris asked indignantly. "Not to mention official-looking credentials from the Palace for a fake messenger, just so I could help you?"

"Yes," said Gwen. "I think you entirely capable of doing just that."

"Well, I am, in fact, but I didn't need to go to all that trouble," said Iris. "I made a quick call to Lady Matheson. She owed us from that mess we cleaned up for the Royals."

"You blackmailed her?"

"It wasn't blackmail," protested Iris. "I merely mentioned that you could use some help, and wouldn't it be awful if they started questioning you under oath? Who knows what topics might be brought out?"

"And that's not blackmail?"

"Of course, it isn't," said Iris. "At least, I hope it isn't. We should start celebrating, shouldn't we?"

"We should," said Gwen. "I'm buying."

CODA

"We heard you were offered a job," said Iris a few nights later.

They were sitting in a pub in Loughton around the corner from the precinct where Quinton was stationed. His entrance with the two women from The Right Sort caused a stir among the locals.

"I was," said Quinton. "Homicide and Serious Crime Command. Your Mr. Parham was most complimentary."

"He should be," said Gwen. "After all, you were the one who saw poor Mrs. Remagen and realised the truth."

"Did you find out why they brought her to Epping Forest?" asked Iris.

"I asked Anderson that when we interrogated him," he said. "He said they thought Scotland Yard might look into it more closely if they left her nearby, but we poor, unsophisticated Essex lads wouldn't see anything other than a poetic suicide."

"They were wrong," said Gwen.

"It would have been nice to have kept the case," he said ruefully. "But she was murdered in London, and jurisdiction is jurisdiction. 'Police Constable Hugh Quinton of Essex County rendered invaluable assistance.' That's how it came out in the reports."

"We know what you did," said Iris, patting his hand.

"How did he get her to take the overdose?" asked Gwen.

"He told her that if she didn't, he would kill her right there and make it look like her husband murdered her," said Quinton. "She didn't hesitate for a second once he said that."

"Poor woman," said Iris.

"Brave woman," said Gwen.

"I turned down the job, by the way," said Quinton.

"Really? Why?" asked Iris.

"I don't care for London much," he said. "I'm Essex born, Essex bred. Chief Peel offered to make me a detective in Essex. I'll be the youngest one they've had in years, he said. There's plenty of crimes that need solving here, and I know the territory."

"Then our loss is Essex's gain," said Gwen, holding up her glass. "To you, Detective Quinton."

"Haven't got the promotion yet," he said, laughing. "And my friends call me Hugh, remember?"

"Now, Hugh, the next thing you need to do is find yourself a nice girl," said Iris.

"I found one I liked, but she was otherwise engaged," he said, grinning at her.

"Well, if you need any help, we do run an agency along those lines," said Gwen.

"I think I want to put some effort into finding one on my own," he said. "No offence, but the people who come to your place—they're all a little bit lost, aren't they?"

"We're all a little bit lost," said Gwen. "We help people find each other again."

The telephone rang at the office the next morning. A moment later, Mrs. Billington buzzed Gwen to take the call.

"The Right Sort, Mrs. Bainbridge speaking," she said.

She listened for a minute, then smiled.

"That's wonderful, Mr. Culpepper," she said. "I'm so pleased.

I'm sure Miss Sparks will be pleased as well. Thank you so much for informing us. Yes, keep us up to date. Goodbye."

She hung up, then grinned at Iris.

"I'm going to win that bet," she said.

"Culpepper and Forsberg? I don't believe it," said Iris. "I still think—"

A clattering of footsteps ascending the stairs interrupted her thought. Seconds later, Collette Forsberg burst through the door, a wild look in her eyes.

"How did you know?" she demanded, pointing her finger accusingly at them.

"Know what?" Mrs. Bainbridge asked innocently.

"Yes, know what?" Sparks asked her partner.

"You knew I wasn't telling the truth when you met me," said Miss Forsberg.

"I did," said Mrs. Bainbridge.

"You knew that Mr. Macaulay and Mr. Merriman were as far from what I wanted as you could possibly get."

"I figured that out," said Mrs. Bainbridge.

"You're some kind of witch, aren't you?"

"Maybe I am," said Mrs. Bainbridge, smiling. "How did your date go with Mr. Culpepper?"

"Oh, God, I think I love him," she said, practically sobbing. "Damn you, damn you, damn you."

The overhead light flickered again. They all looked up at it.

"I'm going to fix that," said Miss Forsberg, holding up a toolbox she had brought with her. "I don't want this place to burn down. I'm going to look for your Mr. MacPherson and get the key to the fuse box. I'll be back."

She stomped out of the office.

Iris opened her bag, searched for two pennies, and handed them over.

"You really are a witch," she said. "How did you manage that one?"

"Her entire interview was an attempt to deceive us," said Gwen. "She didn't want us to find her a husband. She didn't want to leave home at all. But I couldn't figure out why, when her father was clearly so horrid. Then I saw the look on her face the first time our light flickered. Our light flickered, and her face lit up."

"What did that tell you?"

"It wasn't her father she was afraid to leave," said Gwen, looking up at the light. "It was the shop. It was her entire world, and she loves it. She knows how to repair things. She understands electrics, and Lord knows I don't. Do you?"

Memories of mastering booby traps and detonators flashed through Iris's mind.

"Not in the slightest," she said. "So what was it about Mr. Culpepper that caused you to select him?"

"He's an ironmonger, Iris," said Gwen. "He has a shop in Gospel Oak. He said that in addition to a wife, he was looking for a partner because the work was too much for him to handle. I think we've just found him both."

"And we're getting our light fixed for free," said Iris. "You're amazing."

"I am," said Gwen. "I wonder if those are her footsteps returning."

"Couldn't be," said Iris. "I've made a game lately of guessing what the person will look like based upon their sound. These aren't hers."

"Whose, then?"

"A man, certainly. Not young, not elderly. Uncertain—there! He's stopped. He's considering whether or not to go through with this."

"A new customer?"

"I hope so," said Iris. "I've not got any closer to affording a new flat."

The footsteps resumed. The two women went back to their work, trying not to stare out the door.

Then a man appeared at the threshold.

"Oh!" said Sparks in surprise. "Professor Remagen!"

"You know me," he said.

"I was at your lecture at the Royal Entomological Society," she said. "I'm Iris Sparks. This is my partner, Mrs. Gwendolyn Bainbridge."

"How do you do, Professor?" said Mrs. Bainbridge, coming around to greet him. "I am so sorry for your loss."

"As am I," added Sparks.

"So you do know about her," he said wearily. "I thought it might have been some obscene prank when I found out about it."

"Please sit," said Mrs. Bainbridge. "We'll ring for tea."

"I won't be staying long," he said, taking one of the guest chairs. "Is it true? Did my wife come here?"

"She did," said Sparks. "We only met her the one time, but we both thought she was a courageous and wonderful woman. How did you know she came here?"

"I was transferring our legal matters to a different firm after I learned—after Constable Quinton informed me of the circumstances of her death. He didn't specify your business, but among the papers was a record of an escrow account and—"

He stopped, covering his eyes with his hands for a moment, then pulled out a handkerchief and wiped his eyes.

"There was a letter in the file from her to me," he continued. "Along with a contract she signed with the two of you. Quinton said that she was persuaded to come to you by her solicitor."

"Professor, we would never have taken her on had we known what was behind it," said Sparks. "All we knew is that she came here to see to your happiness after she no longer could."

"Constable Quinton told me that her death was without pain," he said. "I can be grateful for that much, at least. But what those animals took from me—I can't begin to describe it."

"They took away your chance to say goodbye," said Mrs. Bainbridge gently. "I know what that's like. I lost my husband in the war."

"Yes," he said, looking at her. "That's it. The last thing she should have seen and heard was me telling her I loved her."

"Professor Remagen, we cannot possibly hold you to this arrangement," said Sparks. "We will be more than happy to cancel it and refund the money."

"No," he said. "It's what she wanted for me. But it's too soon to think about it."

"And she took that into consideration," said Mrs. Bainbridge, trying desperately to hold back her tears. "However long it takes, when you are ready, please come back to us. We'll be here."

He stood, looking at something only he was seeing.

He's one of the lost, thought Sparks. He can find his way through a Burmese jungle, but he's lost everywhere else.

"Constable Quinton also told me you were instrumental in bringing her murderers to justice," he said. "Thank you. You are honourable people. When I'm ready—I will follow her wishes."

He turned and left, his footsteps heavy on the stairs.

"I'm going to keep Mrs. Billington company for a while," said Iris, getting up and walking to the door. "You have yourself a good cry. Buzz when you're done."

She closed the door behind her and walked over to the reception room, then curled up on the sofa reading the real estate ads while Mrs. Billington typed letters of hope for future romances.

Twenty minutes later, the intercom buzzed. Iris waved off Mrs. Billington's move to answer it, then walked back to her office where Gwen sat behind her desk, staring at the index cards containing the essentials of their clients, looking like nothing sad had ever happened.

"You promised him you'll be here when he comes back," said Iris.

"Yes," said Gwen.

"No matter how long that takes?"

"No matter how long it takes."

"Good," said Iris, sitting behind her desk and pulling her own boxes of index cards towards her.

"What we do here is important, Iris," said Gwen. "Each time we ease someone's loneliness is an accomplishment on par with any miraculous discovery. I feel blessed every time it happens."

"What about your loneliness?" asked Iris.

"I'm not lonely," said Gwen.

"Where did you go that afternoon?" asked Iris. "After you left Parson's office last Tuesday and didn't come home until evening? And don't tell me you wandered in a daze that entire time. I want the truth."

"I went to the East End," said Gwen, staring at the cards in her hands. "I went to Benson Quay."

"What's in Benson Quay?"

"Des's carpentry shop."

Iris swivelled in her chair so she was facing Gwen.

"Look at me," she said.

Gwen turned to face her.

"Did you speak to him?" asked Iris.

"No," said Gwen. "I watched from a distance. I saw him go out back and haul some lumber into the shop. I even went up to peer in the window to watch him. I watched him, Iris, and he was just like he was in my dream, only I couldn't summon up the courage to go inside."

"Do you want him?" asked Iris. "I'm not talking about love now, or marriage, or anything more complicated than a primal, carnal desire."

"And that's not complicated?" asked Gwen.

"Do you want him?" repeated Iris.

"No," said Gwen. "Not him. I want Ronnie. I want him, but he's dead, and I will never have him again. So I want to let him go, but I don't know how."

Iris stood, walked over to the coat-tree, grabbed Gwen's coat and hat, and tossed them to her.

"Come with me," she said.

They turned right on Oxford Street, heading towards Oxford Circus.

"Where are we going?" asked Gwen.

"Not far," said Iris.

She turned right on Regent Street, coming to a halt at a store entrance in a six-storey white building.

"No," said Gwen when she saw it.

"Yes," said Iris, taking her hand. "It's time."

Jay's of Regent Street sold mostly high fashion items now, but their roots lay in the previous century's craze for fashionable mourning attire, their principal and greatest client being Queen Victoria, who wore their finest, blackest gowns for the last forty years of her life. The showroom for their current collection was on an upper storey, safely removed from the displays of fancy gloves, furs, lingerie, and other items of a livelier, more forward-looking character.

A saleswoman of middle years and a professionally sombre mien approached them quietly as they entered.

"May I help you, ladies?" she enquired in soft, soothing tones.

Gwen hesitated until Iris nudged her forward.

"How do you do?" she began. "I'm here for—"

She stopped. The saleswoman waited patiently.

"I lost my husband, you see," Gwen continued.

"I am so sorry, madam," said the saleswoman. "When was this?"

"The third of March 1944," said Gwen. "At Monte Cassino."

"Over two years ago," said the woman. "I must say the traditional mourning period—"

"Is over, yes, I know," said Gwen. "But things were very much in a state of—of—of confusion when it happened, and I've never had the chance to, you know, mourn him properly."

"I understand entirely," said the woman. "Are you looking for full mourning? A traditional gown? Or some of the less obtrusive accoutrements?"

"What do people do nowadays?"

"There hasn't been as much call for the full mourning outfits lately, sad to say. There has been too much death and too little time. And cloth rationing has not been our friend."

"No, of course not," said Gwen, looking around at the varieties of black garments. "I also run into the height problem. It tends to limit my options."

"I'm sure we can find you something," said the woman. "And our tailoring department is second to none. May I show you what we have?"

They walked through racks of gowns and suits, shelves of hats, gloves, and veils. Suddenly, Gwen pulled up short, transfixed by a two-piece ensemble worn by a gleaming white mannequin mounted on a pedestal. The bodice was a black mesh with embroidered lace trim, the buttons down the front surrounded by soft black cloth shaped into rose petals. The skirt was joined to it by a wide satin waistband, with fine bugle beading formed into two interlocking hands meeting at the center. Similar bands encircled the skirt at the knees and the hem.

"Whose was this?" whispered Gwen, her hand involuntarily reaching out to feel the fabric.

"It has never been worn," said the woman. "It was made for a young widow fifty years ago, but she herself died before she ever wore it."

"What was her name?" asked Gwen.

"Montmorency," said the woman. "Lucy Montmorency."

"She was tall," said Gwen, walking around the mannequin.

"She must have been," agreed the woman.

"May I—may I try this on?" asked Gwen.

"It's not for sale," said the woman. "And it's completely out of date."

"I won't buy it," said Gwen. "But could I wear it? Just for a minute? No one has to know."

The woman looked around. The room was otherwise deserted.

"Come with me," she said, unhooking the dress from the mannequin. "You'll need help."

Iris waited, watching the door for other customers, but none came. She heard a rustle of antique silk behind her. She turned and gasped.

It fit as if it had been made for her. Gwen walked into the place of mourning as its rightful queen. Her feet were bare. She glided through the racks with silent grace, stopping to pluck a hat from the rack and gently place it on her head, letting the veil flutter slowly down over her face.

She came to the triple mirror and turned to face it from the center, her reflection looking back from three directions, her face concealed by the thickness of the veil, doubled by the ones worn by the three women watching from the other side.

The saleswoman came to stand next to Iris.

"Stunning," she breathed, mesmerised.

Mourn me to the hilt. Out-Niobe Niobe with your tears, thought Gwen.

"Goodbye," she whispered.

Then without warning she collapsed in front of the mirror, huge, shuddering sobs racking her body. The saleswoman started to rush towards her, but Iris grabbed her by the sleeve and shook her head.

The sudden squall ended. Gwen slowly pushed herself up from the floor, then turned to them unsteadily.

"Thank you," she said to the saleswoman. "And I will take the hat."

"Of course, madam. Let me help you change."

They disappeared into the dressing room. When they emerged, the woman placed the hat in a box, tied it with a black ribbon, then rang up the sale.

"I apologise for my display," said Gwen, handing over her payment. She added a shilling to the total. "For your trouble."

"That's all right, madam," said the saleswoman. "It's happened here before."

Gwen picked up the hatbox, then joined Iris at the entryway.

"Ready?" asked Iris.

"Yes," said Gwen. "I think I am."

ACKNOWLEDGMENTS

In addition to sources previously cited, the author would like to thank the following:

For a general and quite harrowing overview, *The Female Malady: Women, Madness, and English Culture, 1830–1980,* by Elaine Showalter.

For the Court of Lunacy, works by Janet Weston and Akinobu Takabayashi.

For the history of the Gargoyle Club, Maurice Bottomley and whoever writes under "The Drinker" in the blog *A Drinker's History of London.*

For entomological sources, works by David L. Pearson, Fabio Cassola, T. Shivashankar, A. R. V. Kumar, G. K. Veeresh, J. G. Wood, and Radomir Jaskuła. The author agrees that she spent too much time reading about tiger beetles, but notes that she wrote a poem in the third grade about the life cycle of the caddisfly that was read over the school's public address system, perhaps launching her career as a writer. Perhaps not.

Questions on various topics were answered by Annice Collett of the Vintage Motor Cycle Club library; and especially David Howdon, Chair of the Selborne Society Limited, who was kind enough to share the most recent moth list for Perivale Wood, now exceeding 544.

The author takes full responsibility for any errors made. Fortunately, she caught all of them but one. See if you can figure out which one it is!